Pr

How to Love a Duke in Ten Days

"Tantalizes readers with the couple's teasing and building passion."
—*Publishers Weekly*

"An un-put-down-able story that combines sensuality, tenderness . . . and memorable characters."
—*Kirkus Reviews*

"In this brilliantly conceived start to her captivating new series, Byrne once again delivers the beautifully nuanced characters and seductive storytelling her readers have come to expect, while at the same time deftly conjuring up the spirit of Victoria Holt's classic gothic romances."
—*Booklist*

"An amazing story of how two broken people find a way to heal each other . . . A beautifully written historical romance that was impossible to put down."
—*Affaire de Coeur*

. . . and Kerrigan Byrne's other captivating novels

"Byrne's writing comes to vivid life on the page."
—*Entertainment Weekly* on
The Duke with the Dragon Tattoo

"Another winner in a stellar series."
—*Library Journal* (starred review) on
The Duke with the Dragon Tattoo

Also by
Kerrigan Byrne

All Scot and Bothered

KERRIGAN BYRNE

St. Martin's Paperbacks

This is a work of fiction. All of the characters, organizations, and events portrayed in this novel are either products of the author's imagination or are used fictitiously.

First published in the United States by St. Martin's Paperbacks, an imprint of St. Martin's Publishing Group.

ALL SCOT AND BOTHERED

Copyright © 2020 by Kerrigan Byrne.
Excerpt from *The Devil in Her Bed* copyright © 2021 by Kerrigan Byrne.

All rights reserved.

For information, address St. Martin's Publishing Group, 120 Broadway, New York, NY 10271.

www.stmartins.com

ISBN: 978-1-250-31886-2

Our books may be purchased in bulk for promotional, educational, or business use. Please contact your local bookseller or the Macmillan Corporate and Premium Sales Department at 1-800-221-7945, ext. 5442, or by email at MacmillanSpecialMarkets@macmillan.com.

Printed in the United States of America

St. Martin's Paperbacks edition 2020

10 9 8 7 6 5 4 3 2 1

To all the girls who were told they couldn't . . .
And did it anyway.

PROLOGUE

According to Cecelia Teague's calculations, she approached the close of her second day in captivity.

She couldn't remember the last time her father had locked her in the cellar's green room for so long.

Perhaps he'd finally gone mad.

Would he ever unlock that door again?

Would the world forget she ever existed?

The questions pecked at her in the gathering dark like carrion birds at a fresh corpse.

She'd done nothing wicked or wanton. Nothing to merit her schoolmates' violent cruelty nor her father's pious fury.

She'd merely been the first girl, at thirteen, to best everyone at the village school at calculus. Even the final-year students. When Mr. Rolland, the teacher, had accused her of cheating because of her age and sex, she'd reminded them that Maria Gaetana Agnesi had written the modern-day textbook on differential and integral calculus.

Mr. Rolland then banished her to the corner to stand until her feet ached and her skin burned with humiliation.

Thomas Wingate, the butcher's son, had seized her at lunch, shoved his thin, ruddy face in hers, and called her nine kinds of foul names as he ripped her spectacles from her face and crushed them into the mud. He spat on her before shoving her on stomach over a felled tree and exposing her drawers to his entourage of lads, who all howled their mirth.

Fraught and humiliated as she was, Cecelia hadn't shed a single tear until Mr. Rolland had threatened to go straight to her father, the Vicar Josiah Teague.

The threat had been directed at the boys.

But as Cecelia had predicted, she was the one who paid the price for their sins.

For in the eyes of her father, the sin was *hers*.

The original sin.

She'd been born a girl.

As the Reverend Teague marched her to the green room, he hissed at her the usual litany of condemnations, ignoring her vehement protestations.

"Just like your mother, allowing any gobshite to lift your skirts. I'll see you in the grave before you become a jezebel." He'd thrust her roughly through the cellar door, causing her to stumble down the stairs and land in a heavy heap on the packed-dirt floor. His lips had pulled away from his tea-stained teeth in a grimace of unmitigated disgust. "I thought you too fat to draw the carnal notice of man."

"I didn't *do* anything," she cried, ignoring the grit of the earth beneath her knees as she rose to press her hands together as though in prayer. "Please believe me. I would never—"

"You are a *woman* now." He wiped the word away

from his mouth with the back of his hand. "And there is no such creature as an innocent woman. You tempted those boys to sin, and for that, you must atone."

Her remonstrations were lost when he'd slammed the heavy door, ensconcing her in shadow.

Cecelia settled into a corner, growing accustomed to the increasingly frequent punishment. She'd her primer to keep her occupied at the very least, as she'd thrust it into her bodice before her father had stormed into the schoolyard.

The panic hadn't encroached until a day, a night, and the next day had slipped by.

When her bucket of water ran dry, she'd succumbed to a fit of histrionics.

Cecelia banged on the door until the meat of her fists throbbed. She pitted her substantial weight against it, bruising her shoulders.

She pleaded at the keyhole like a convicted man might do on the last night of his life. She vowed to be good. To behave. Promised anything she could think of to soften her father's heart, or God's. She even confessed to sins she'd not committed, hoping her perceived candor and penitence would buy her freedom.

"Please, Papa, *please* let me out," she sobbed at the shadows of his feet, two pillars of condemnation against the thin strip of light beneath the door. "Don't leave me alone in the dark."

"You were conceived in darkness, child, and to eternal darkness you'll likely return." His voice was as loud and stern in their small parish home as it was from the pulpit. "Pray and ponder upon that."

The shadows of his feet disappeared, and Cecelia dropped to her knees, her fingertips reaching for the last of the light of his lantern as it faded away.

She curled up next to the door like a dog awaiting its master's return, her trembling cheek pressed to the dank floor as she searched beneath for the return of the light.

Conceived in darkness. What did that mean? And how was it her fault?

Cecelia called her prison the green room because the moss clinging to damp stone was the only color to be found in the cellar of the modest cottage. Some long-ago vicar with a family too large for the two-room house to adequately contain had partitioned a section of the subterranean space into an extra bedroom. Which was to say, a cot and trunk had been shoved into the corner.

In the summer, she would open the window and curl up in the anemic shafts of sun or moonlight, drinking in what she could. One day, the Reverend Teague's boots had appeared at the window and kicked dirt inside, showering her with soil.

She'd begged him not to lock the window from the outside. Not to take away the only light she knew.

"I won't escape," she vowed.

"I'm not afraid you'll escape," he blustered around a rare and colorless laugh. "It isn't as though you could fit through a window this small."

It was the first time Cecelia had hated her body. The size and shape of it. If only she were wraithlike and delicate, perhaps she could slither through the window and slip away into the night.

Not that she would . . . she was too afraid of the dark.

And she'd nowhere to go.

Over the years, she'd faced the green room with more courage. The fiends and monsters her fanciful fears conjured never once attacked her. Spiders and other very real denizens of the dark scuffled and shuffled and spun their webs but had yet to hurt her.

The sounds of the mice and such eventually became a serenade, preferable to the awful silence.

It amazed her what she could adapt to. The gnawing of thirst and hunger. The putrid scent of a neglected chamber pot and her unwashed body in a poorly ventilated room.

She snuck a blanket from her own bed into a cupboard one day when her father had been out proselytizing. This, she wrapped around her in the night, pretending the feeble warmth she found within belonged to something—someone—else.

She'd lean against the wall, hugging the blanket to herself, and fancy that her arms clinging to her middle were the arms of another, holding her as no one had ever done. That the planes and curves of the cold stones at her back were really the carved strength of a man. Of a protector. Of someone who didn't leave her alone in the night.

To face the dark by herself.

Because even as her imagined childhood torments fell away with the advancement of each year, one never did.

In the absolute darkness beneath the earth, something more insidious than a ghost lurked in the green room. More unrelenting than hunger. More rotten than filth. More venomous than any spider.

Loneliness.

An all-encompassing word, as correct as it was inadequate.

What began as boredom and isolation slowly became a void of silence inside of her, a yawning chasm of emptiness that no meal or interaction seemed to sate.

Because even when she was free, the room was always there, waiting for her next perceived slight, her next accidental sin.

The anticipation of being tossed into hell was almost as torturous as the endless hours she spent in her prison.

Cecelia prayed as her father bade her, but not the prayers she'd been forced to memorize. She would drop to her knees every night, prostrating herself before a cold and condemning God and imploring with the fervency of a pilgrim for one thing.

Someone to save her from this gray-and-green hell in which she lived.

This time, she prayed until her dry tongue stuck to the roof of her mouth and her tears would no longer come. Her stomach, too empty to churn, seized with the acid flavor of terror. After two days, she barely had the strength to sit up, so she lay against the stone wall, her blanket wrapped around her.

I don't think he means to let me out this time.

The realization opened up the void within her. The one where the light used to be, where God used to live.

The hinges on the cellar window protested as the vicar yanked them open, and a bucket of water sloshed as her father lowered it to the ground with uncharacteristic haste.

Cecelia pushed herself to sit on trembling arms.

"You drink and wash, just in case," her father barked. "But if you make a sound whilst they're here, you'll never again see the outside of this room, do you mark me, girl?"

He didn't wait for her reply. The window banged shut and he walked away without bothering to lock it.

Cecelia sat in frozen astonishment for a few breaths before scrambling toward the bucket. She didn't heed the filth of her hands as she cupped them into the vessel and greedily slurped the contents. Unable to slake her thirst thus, she lifted the entire bucket to her lips and all but drowned herself in the process of tipping it back to wet her greedy throat.

Footsteps marched overhead, a short, staccato sound very different than that of her father's heavy-soled boots.

They were upstairs. Who were they, that could alarm her father so?

Setting the bucket down quietly, she climbed the stairs and crept to the door, crouching to listen beneath the crack.

"Where y'all keeping her, Preacher?" a foreign feminine voice demanded in an accent Cecelia couldn't have conceived of even if her mind hadn't been muddled by hunger.

She pressed her hand to the cool wood of the door. Were *they* looking for her? Had her prayers been answered after all these tearful years?

"The whereabouts of my daughter is of no concern to a whore."

This was no great clue to the identity of the woman. To Josiah Teague, every daughter of Eve was likely also a secret prostitute.

"Not a whore, just a businesswoman," the lady had the audacity to correct her father as she moved closer. "I was warned you were a sanctimonious charlatan. You look down on us, pray for and pity us. You condemn and humiliate us, all the while unaware that we do nothing but sit around and laugh about that limp, useless little appendage swinging between your legs."

"You *dare* to—" The rest of the words cut off in a whoosh, as though they'd been stolen from him by a blow to the gut.

"Oh, Hortense told us all about your impotence," continued the woman. "We are all aware you're *not* that child's daddy."

Hortense. Her mother.

At this revelation, Cecelia must have fainted because the next thing she knew she was being scooped off the floor and clutched against the plump, pillowy bosoms of a stranger. "Why, you poor darlin'," a syrupy voice cooed.

"Bless your sweet, little heart. How long has that mean old preacher kept you cooped up down here?"

"I . . ." Frightened, uncertain, Cecelia glanced up the stairs to see her forbidding father being held at bay by a man significantly shorter than he, but wide enough to fill the entire door.

Her questions were answered the moment the reverend's eyes met hers. Black eyes, the same color as his hair.

As his soul.

No . . . not her father. He was lean, tall, and sharp, his nose long and his chin severe.

When Cecelia had studied her soft round features in the mirror, she'd never noted the slightest hint of him, and now she knew why.

She didn't belong to him.

Thank God.

A tear slid out the side of her eye as she looked up at her savior, the most beautiful human being Cecelia had ever glimpsed.

Her dress, a deep shade of gold, shone impossibly vibrant in the dismal underground gloom. Her skin and hair glowed as golden as brilliant bullion, though her eyes were curiously dark. She'd painted her full lips the same shade as hothouse calla lilies.

The woman was round and soft, like herself, and an astounding luminescence shone from her as though her entire being was suffused with light.

"Cecelia, darlin', my name's Genevieve Leveaux, but my friends call me Genny. You have any particular objection to being my friend?"

Another tear fell. She'd never had a friend before.

Entranced, Cecelia lifted her fingers to brush at the woman's face. She caught herself in time, distressed at the dirt on her hands. She would no sooner mar her savior with her filth than she would finger paint over the *Mona Lisa*.

"Don't leave me here." The first words she'd spoken in days felt like rusting metal in her throat, but the plea had to be made.

"Oh sugar, you won't spend another minute beneath this foul roof. Can you stand up?"

Cecelia nodded, and let the angel pull her to her feet. She swayed and found herself once again face-to-breast with the woman.

"Come on, now." Tucking her arm firmly around Cecelia, Genny helped her up the stairs as her stout and extraordinarily well-dressed companion shouldered the reverend out of the doorframe and into the hall.

"Whew, sakes alive!" Genny exclaimed none-too-delicately. "No offense, honey, but like my grandmama back in Louisiana used to say, your stink could singe a polecat's nose hair."

Dazed and dizzy, Cecelia followed without replying, mostly because she didn't understand a word of that beyond the general gist. She'd not washed in almost three days, and the shame struck her dumb.

To distract herself from her humiliation, she cataloged the life she was leaving behind. The wobbly table at which they ate their silent meager meals, her every portion rationed, and her every bite berated. The dilapidated parlor, eternally empty of company. The sitting room with the perpetually cold hearth, even though a rainy October was upon them, where she'd read nothing but the Bible and other canonical texts by firelight until her eyes crossed.

"It is my duty to save her from the sins of her mother!"

Josiah Teague finally found his voice, though Cecelia couldn't make out his features from across the room. "Most men wouldn't have brought up a girl begot in sin against his own marriage. Remember that, Cecelia, when you're tempted to commit immoral acts by these fallen, *forsaken* women! I would have saved your soul. I can save you still!"

"Oh, quit your bleating, you limp-peckered billy goat." Genny shifted Cecelia behind her as the guard strong-armed Josiah into a chair at the table. "There's more singin' God's praises and hollering hallelujahs in *my* house than yours, believe you me." With a saucy wink, Genny turned to Cecelia and bent down to bring their faces level. "Now, aren't you just a perfect porcelain baby doll," she crooned, touching the tip of her finger to Cecelia's pert nose. "I knew you'd be a pretty child, but you just beat all."

"Thank you, Miss Leveaux." Cecelia's cheeks were so warm, she feared she'd contracted a fever.

"Miss Leveaux! You hear that, Wexler?" Genny straightened to give her mirth room to shake out of her in the most cheerful laugh.

Wexler didn't laugh. Didn't move. He stayed where he was, looming over Josiah Teague in a threatening manner.

Wiping an invisible tear of hilarity from the corner of her eye, Genny leaned back down to Cecelia. "You call me Genny. We're friends now, remember?"

Cecelia nodded, flicking a glance to the man who'd been her father, thinking that her last memory of him would be of his blurry face, as her spectacles were still crushed somewhere in the schoolyard dirt.

It was all right. She knew what expression he wore.

"You have any other frock than this, baby? You must

have grown out of this—well, we'll call it a dress if we have to—a year past."

"She doesn't need to succumb to the sin of vanity," the reverend hissed, his features mottled with such contained rage and fear, his skin had darkened from crimson to violet. "She's a weak-willed, gluttonous girl. Look at her! I've done my best by her, but she sneaks food in the middle of the night, and no amount of discipline, correction, or isolation will break her of the habit. It's not my responsibility to buy her new clothing when she's bursting out of a perfectly reasonably sized garment."

"You excuse me a minute, honey." Genny pulled herself to her full height, stomped past Wexler, and struck Josiah Teague across the face. Hard. Hard enough to rock him back in his chair.

Gaining his balance, the reverend surged to his feet, but was again wrestled back down by the block of muscle that was the silent and enigmatic Wexler.

Genny didn't even flinch. She caught Cecelia and swept her outside to a sumptuous coach, tucking her into a fur-lined cloak.

The abiding Wexler remained inside for a moment, and despite everything, Cecelia opened the curtain and anxiously watched the door.

"Don't you worry that pretty red head of yours." Genny settled across from her and spread her skirts before patting Cecelia's hand. "He's just signing some papers."

"What papers?"

"Tell me about you, darlin'," Genny encouraged with a gentle smile. "What do you do to keep occupied? What have you been taught other than prayin'?"

Shyly, Cecelia she pulled her notebook away from her middle where she'd kept it, extending it to the woman.

Genny looked down at the book for a pregnant moment, opening it with two careful fingers as though she expected a monster to be flattened between the pages.

Cecelia held her breath as the woman began to turn the pages with increasing speed until she met her gaze with shining eyes.

"No one told me you were an artist, little doll."

Cecelia crinkled her forehead in bemusement.

She was no artist. No poet or otherwise. She'd attempted those pastimes with painstaking effort when she was isolated, to disastrous effect.

She snatched the notebook that was extended back to her and looked down at what she found there. Just exponents and theorems, limits and derivatives, formulae, functions, and corresponding graphs.

She glanced up to see a satisfied smile reveal Genny's brilliant white teeth. "You'll take to where we're goin', honey, of that I have no doubt."

Cecelia nodded, afraid to ask. She sank into the cloak, trying to pluck an emotion from the bevy of them swirling through her like a storm. Was she relieved? Apprehensive? Sad? Elated?

Some perplexing concoction of all these things, she decided as she watched Wexler leave the parish cottage.

Mostly, she was hungry.

"I'm famished." Genny once again seemed to read her mind. "Let's stop at the Crossland Inn for the night and get you fed and washed. I hear they have these splendid little cakes sprinkled with—"

"Oh, I'm not allowed cakes," Cecelia informed her with no little distress. "To indulge is to sin."

Genny reached forward and grasped her hands, imprisoning both of them in her firm, strong grip. Her eyes glowed like bronze heated in the forge of her temper as she tossed her tight blond curls away from her cheeks.

"You listen to me. You push all notions of sin and abstinence out of your head, hear? Your life is your own. From now on, you want cakes? You eat cakes. You drape yourself in color and you eat and wear and enjoy whatever you desire whenever you fancy. From this day forward, you deny yourself nothing. You feel no shame. You are who you are, and what you are is beautiful."

The kindness stung Cecelia's eyes with tears. "I'm not beautiful. I'm fat."

Genny contemplated that for a moment, her lips twisting pensively before she said, "Honey, some people are going to tell you that, but when they do, you remember my words and you mark them because this is my area of expertise. When you grow, you are going to *devastate* men. With those eyes and lips, that hair and skin, with what you have beginning to show beneath that dowdy old frock . . ." Genny rocked back, fanning herself as though the temperature in the carriage had suddenly spiked.

"You'll be a force to be reckoned with and make no mistake. 'Course, there will be those who prefer little waifs with little waists. And you'll find that most men are too delicate to abide a woman whose brain can do what yours can. It'll intimidate the tarnation right out of them. But honey, you'll wield a power you don't yet understand. You'll capture, control, and *destroy* any number of men."

Cecelia bit the inside of her cheek, suddenly feeling very overwhelmed and light-headed again. "I don't want to destroy anyone." And she'd never imagine holding a captive, not after what she'd been subjected to.

Genny's face softened, and she tucked back a renegade

curl from Cecelia's cheek. "I was told you'd be sweet, like your mama."

"You knew my mother?" Cecelia grasped onto that with both hands, brimming with questions.

"I met her once, when she visited," she said vaguely.

"Visited wher—"

"Let's go see about those cakes!" Genny rapped on the ceiling of the coach, and the horses lurched forward with a slap of the reins. "After a huge supper, a hot bath, and a good night's rest, we're gonna go fit you with some proper gowns in any color you want. You never have to worry about money again, and isn't that a blessing? You've a fortune at your disposal now, as you're the heir to one of the most important, most influential people in London society."

It took several tries for Cecelia to regain her breath to ask, "Is it . . . is it my real father?"

Genny's lips pressed together. "I'm sorry, sugar, but I can't say. Just know that it's someone who cares for you very much. Someone who loved your mother."

Cecelia allowed that answer to assuage her for a couple of weeks as she was whisked into a cocoon of expensive hotels, ships, and villas. Of seamstresses, chefs, haberdasheries, and lady's maids. She visited Paris on her way to their destination, awestruck by the glamorous city and even more dazzling inhabitants.

The Ecole de Chardonne institute for girls might have been the most romantic Gothic castle she could possibly conceive of. The staff there fell over themselves to accommodate her as she was escorted to the enchanting tower with a collection of windows overlooking the sparkling Lake Geneva. This was to be her new home.

She was humbled. Grateful. Sufficiently awestruck.

And yet when she sat upon her bed in the tower at the

end of the day, the same emptiness tormented her. Because even though her windows were large and grand instead of small and grimy and she had all the food, warmth, and care she could conceive of . . .

She was still alone in the dark.

CHAPTER ONE

Castle Redmayne, Devonshire, 1891

Seven years was too bloody long for any Scotsman to go without tupping a woman. Or was it closer to eight?

Cassius Gerard Ramsay, Lord Chief Justice of the High Court, convinced himself the extended abstinence had to be why he was currently plagued with a physical malady he hadn't suffered since his adolescence.

An unwelcome, *agonizing* public erection.

He'd be forty before too long. Surely he was immune to such afflictions at this age. Indeed, he'd trained such weaknesses out of himself years ago.

Life had taught him a man must rein in his appetites with an iron fist and unshakable self-mastery lest he be controlled or irreparably damaged by them.

And yet here he was, a captive to his cock, posturing to hide his body's instant—nay, violent—reaction to the sight of the buxom and mystifying Miss Cecelia Teague licking truffle chocolate from her ungloved fingers.

In the middle of a soiree at Castle Redmayne, no less.

Despite his stern inner admonishments to keep his

notice elsewhere, his gaze was tugged back to her by an invisible rope over and again to linger at her heart-shaped features.

He needn't waste time wondering why. She was exactly the sort of women he'd always found himself drawn to. One with more curves than straight lines. Lush. Luxurious, even. Her skin the color of rich cream, her lips the hue of his favorite cordial.

All wrapped in a silky violet confection that contrasted with her extraordinary copper ringlets shining in the luster of the chandeliers.

Her azure gaze was a paradox. Wide and candid . . . but mercurial.

Damned if he didn't find that the most intriguing combination.

A living sin, was Cecelia Teague. A wicked brew of both innocence and indulgence. The female equivalent of a truffle.

The tip of her finger disappeared into her mouth as she sucked the last bit of flavor from her skin.

Ramsay swallowed a tortured groan, biting the inside of his cheek hard enough to taste blood as he crossed his legs. Uncrossed them. Shifted positions and crossed them in the opposite direction.

Seven. Fucking. Years.

Or is it longer? The entirety of his thirties seemed to be one long endless span of labor and loneliness, bereft of the splendid visual feast that was the naked female form.

And what a delectable morsel Miss Teague would make, after all the laces, ruffles, and ridiculous contraptions were peeled away, leaving only honest curves, intriguing dimples, fine hair, and supple, pillow-soft skin.

How had he gone so long devoid of the warm weight of

a woman's thighs testing the strength of his shoulders as he brought her to shuddering completion?

Long enough to nearly forget the feel of a woman's sex. The secret moisture, the yielding, intimate flesh, the unholy pleasure.

Cecelia Teague bent to select another truffle from the crystal dish, affording him a view of her more than generous décolletage. Every wicked thing he'd done, every act he'd fantasized about or even conceived of flashed through his mind in a heart-pounding storm of lust.

Sweet Christ, those breasts would tempt a saint. They'd spill over his hands like fresh cream.

A trickle of sweat slid from his nape into his collar as he inhaled sharply, imagining the warm, inviting scent of the downy skin in the cove between them. The salt of it under his tongue, the unbearable softness—

"May I offer you a taste, my lord Ramsay?"

It took him an eternity to process Miss Teague's casual suggestion. Finally, he blinked and eloquently inquired, "Er—pardon?"

"You were staring as though you desired them." Her spectacles magnified her curiously dark eyelashes as they lowered shyly across her cheek. "And I grant you, they taste every bit as good as you're imagining they would. Creamy and rich, with a hint of salt. You've never had better, I'd wager my life on it."

All the moisture abandoned Ramsay's mouth. His gaze flicked down to her breasts and he swallowed, dragging them back up to her earnest expression.

Surely she wasn't offering a taste of her flesh. Not . . . *here*. He was no stranger to the propositions of society maidens and matrons, alike, but never so explicitly.

His turgid arousal twitched and strained, making no

mistake about what his unruly libido hoped he would do with her offer.

He glanced helplessly around at the soiree's other guests, milling like over-bright hummingbirds at a lilac bush, never staying in one place for too long.

Had anyone else marked her shocking proposition?

"Alexandra and I share a weakness for decadent chocolate, you see." She selected one from the dish with the discretion a jeweler would show a selection of diamonds. "These are imported from Belgium. The texture is indescribably above par, and just wait until you find out what's at the core."

Confounded, Ramsay stared at the chocolate, cursing himself for nine kinds of fool.

She'd been offering him a truffle. Of course she had. What on earth had led him to think she'd proposed a taste of her flesh? Perhaps he'd been so mesmerized by her husky voice, like smoke swirling over the finest brandy, the words hadn't registered properly.

He cleared his throat and glared daggers at his half brother, Piers Gedrick Atherton, the Duke of Redmayne, who was too absorbed in the animated story of his wife, Alexandra, to notice.

Ramsay hoped if he simply glowered hard enough, the reprobate duke would come save him.

No such luck; Redmayne and the duchess busied themselves with their peers, doing their utmost to ingratiate the prodigal Countess of Mont Claire, Lady Francesca Cavendish, into select society.

Christ, Miss Teague was only invited to this blasted castle because she was longtime school chums with Lady Francesca and Lady Alexandra. The three women had been inseparable for decades, as he understood it, and his brother had married Alexandra knowing that Francesca and Cecelia were part and parcel of the bargain.

So why wasn't the beguiling Miss Teague mingling with *them* rather than tormenting *him*?

The lady in question smiled a little ruefully and sank her teeth into the truffle, savoring it as a condemned man might his last meal. "I'm still sated from our sumptuous dinner, all told," she said from behind the hand she held in front of her lips to protect her chocolate-filled mouth from view. "But I find my appetite for dessert forever unquenchable."

Ramsay almost swallowed his tongue. *Unquenchable.* Like his ravenous, devious desire. His skin was sensitive, hot, and stretched very thin over his frame. Everything felt more sumptuous. Decadent. The velvet of the couch beneath him. The fragrance in the air.

This was dangerous. This moment. This lust.

This woman.

It was in instants such as this a man lost everything by making the wrong choice. Like asking her to dance, or to walk with him in the gardens so he could ruin her in the rosebushes.

He was not that man. He never would be that man.

Grinding his teeth together, Ramsay hoped that if he was taciturn enough, she'd merely wander away.

Ignorant of his lustful thoughts, the woman bent over again to select him a truffle. "You should take one. Alex won't mind, if that's why you hesitate. She's endlessly generous."

Ramsay flinched. Miss Teague blithely called the Duchess of Redmayne, lady of perhaps the longest-standing title in the empire, "Alex." As if nothing had changed since their childhood. As if she were utterly secure in a room full of ancient aristocracy, impervious to the fact that people went out of their way *not* to talk to Cecelia because they considered her beneath their notice. She was neither titled nor rich, as far as anyone knew or cared. If anything distinguished her in this company, it was her lambent hair and uncommon height.

Was she truly as nonchalant over their rebuffs as she appeared? She must be, to eat three truffles in a room full of cruel opinions.

"Go on, have a try," she prompted, extending the chocolate toward him.

"Thank ye, but nay," he clipped, unable to school a husky rasp from his reply. "I doona indulge."

"In chocolate?" She pulled back, regarding the truffle as though offended on its behalf.

"In anything."

She gaped at him as though he'd committed treason, or a blasphemy. "Come now, my lord, one taste can't hurt. Besides, I've already taken it from the dish and would be thought very rude to put it back." A mischievous smile deepened the dimple on her cheek as she wriggled the sweet between her thumb and forefinger in a dainty dance of enticement.

"I canna imagine why ye want me to partake so avidly."

"It's obvious you're ravenous," she answered. "You won't stop staring."

Was it possible she was being coy? "I give ye leave to enjoy it on my behalf. I'll not be tempted," he said through clenched teeth.

Her mouth twisted as though she was deciding whether or not to frown. In the end, she shrugged and popped the delicacy past her lips, letting out a contented little moan of appreciation.

Christ, he was a bloody liar. He'd bloody well be tempted. He'd been *tempted* by Cecelia Teague since he'd first laid eyes on her at Redmayne's engagement soiree several months prior. Then again at the wedding.

They'd been introduced formally, and he'd bowed over her extended hand. Kissing it had felt wrong, somehow, because of the swell of lust even that innocuous gesture provoked.

Since then, he'd avoided her at all costs, not that it was difficult. They certainly didn't share any social or professional spheres, but for the attachment to his half brother Piers and her friend Alexandra.

However, it seemed the duke and duchess were unnaturally attached to each other since their hasty wedding, so the tempting Miss Teague would be impossible to evade.

Ramsay let out an impatient breath and tried to focus on someone—anyone—else.

He *should* be pressing hands with visiting diplomats like the Count Armediano, an Italian businessman and shipping magnate with mysterious origins. Or perhaps discussing tomorrow's address to the House of Lords with Sir Hubert, the Lord Chancellor, or probate taxation with the Prime Minister.

Aye, he should be working, exerting his will upon those he required to attain his various political and legal objectives.

And yet . . . he couldn't stand until he'd brought his unruly cock under control, which would be easier to do were he not in Miss Teague's voluptuous vicinity.

"How very lamentable." The true pity in her voice returned his gaze to her vibrant beauty.

"I'm sorry?" Unnerved at her propensity to address his innermost thoughts, he shifted once more and considered the merits of agricultural property law, just to see if that would cool his physical distress.

"We were discussing your lack of indulgences." She slid him a mischievous half smile that produced the most diverting dimple in her cheek. "My lord Chief Justice, if you're half as distracted when hearing cases, I fear for those presenting evidence to you."

To his utter surprise, amusement spiked rather than his ire. It was a rare individual who ever dared tease him.

Rarer still that he enjoyed it.

"Ye'll have to pardon me, Miss Teague, it's been a trying day. My manners were peeled away by interactions with the odious dregs of our society, leaving my thoughts unduly burdensome."

"I'm sorry to hear that." She seemed to smother a curious anxiety with an over-bright but sympathetic smile as she spread her hands over her skirts. "Would you care to discuss it? Often, I find if I unburden myself, I go away feeling much lighter."

"I would *not*." He hadn't meant for the words to escape in such a terse manner, but the subject of his current worries was not fit for the fairer sex. Indeed, it concerned the disappearances of young ladies. Young girls, rather. Which was not a rare thing in such a metropolis as London, but the investigators of the case had found evidence of an insidious ring of smugglers, traffickers, and profiteers. Ones who might be trading in the flesh market, turning the poor and immigrants into slaves, pricing them per pound of flesh.

A few of the captured criminals pointed their fingers in astonishing directions when interrogated regarding their suppliers and customers. The aristocracy, the government, the military, and even the church.

He was surrounded by corrupt and debased men, and

these smugglers often mentioned one word out of fear: *rubricata*. One of the many Latin words for "red."

Troubled and absorbed by these affairs of state, Ramsay had little to offer a soiree, but couldn't send his condolences with such illustrious guests so near to election. And so, after making his obligatory compliments to the guests at dinner, he'd found a quiet corner near the fireplace unoccupied by those who needed to see and be seen at one of the Duke of Redmayne's marvelously celebrated fetes. He'd ruminated for a moment, working his way toward a perfectly splendid brood before Miss Teague had plopped down in a pile of skirts to pick at a dish of chocolates and stir him into a pique.

She scooted forward in her seat, making as though to stand. "If you do not wish to speak, I'll leave you to your contemplations, my lord," she said, seeming not only unoffended, but unaffected.

"Nay," he snapped without thought.

Her eyes widened at his visceral objection, but it shocked none more than himself. Perplexed, Ramsay watched her intently. What was it about this woman that evoked such a powerful response? No one ever caught him so thoroughly off his guard.

As much as he wanted to be free of her, he apparently desired her close, and the force of that desire discomfited him.

Which meant he should encourage her to flee his vicinity immediately.

"Doona abandon yer chocolates on my account," he found himself saying before he ground his teeth even harder, lest he do something untenably ridiculous, such as ask her to sit in his lap. Hadn't he just been hoping she'd leave?

Her eyes glimmered with pleasure, and then softened

with understanding. "May I fetch you a drink to help soften the woes of the day?"

He shook his head, acutely aware of how important it was to keep his wits about him in her presence. "I generally abstain from drink. I've consumed the one glass of wine I allow myself at dinner."

"A life without chocolate and wine." She cocked her head, pity once again dimming the sparkle in her eyes. "How dreary. What do you do for pleasure, my lord?"

Pleasure. When was the last time he'd allowed himself any?

"I work."

Ramsay's hand fisted at his side so he wouldn't slide it over the expensive aubergine chair beneath him. He still did that sometimes, tested a texture as if he couldn't believe it was real.

Even after all these years.

As a boy, he'd never have imagined something so soft existed. The bed he'd slept on had been hard. His home cold and empty in every imaginable way, along with his belly, and eventually his heart.

All of this because his family was prone to indulging in selfish pleasures, and it had brought them nothing but shame, misery, and devastation.

His mother had preyed upon the weak and base natures of men until she ruined them. His father, once thusly ruined, had become a slave to every form of pleasure, and it had eventually killed him.

Redmayne's father, their mother's second husband, had made her a duchess. She'd repaid his affection and devotion by cuckolding him so often, he'd finally hanged himself in a fit of drunken despair.

Even Redmayne had indulged in adventure to the point

of obsession, until the swipe of a jaguar's claws had cost him his handsome features, and nearly his life.

And look at him now, equally under the thrall of his formerly impoverished bluestocking wife, who'd also nearly gotten him killed on more than one occasion. They seemed impervious to the fact that the ton whispered about them even as they gorged upon Redmayne's wealth and influence. But how long would that last?

Nay. Nay, indulgence was a curse and pleasure a peril. Something that controlled a man until he was no longer himself. Until he'd surrendered power, dignity, or both.

He'd given over to temptation in his younger days, temptation that had very much looked like love.

And it had very nearly been his undoing.

His eyes rested on Miss Teague, once again, his notice snagged by the intriguing way her pale skin disappeared as she pulled her gloves back on. *Rested*. How long since he'd done that? Just sat quietly and allowed himself to enjoy a lovely view. Lord, but she was so pleasant to look at, and just as wondrous to listen to. She'd an air of softness he'd never before witnessed, and it boggled the mind how he could be both aroused and comforted by her all at once.

How could she so thoroughly inflame him by covering up more skin? There was nothing intrinsically seductive about the gesture, and yet he found it more provoking than a dozen dancehall girls undoing their corsets.

"Forgive me if I'm prying," she said, forgetting, or merely giving up on, her previous question. "But I'm curious as to the reasons for your . . . abstinence."

He studied her, searching for a double meaning in the word. For a lascivious undertone. Did she ken that he was without a woman? That he so acutely desired her now?

He found only genuine interest in her open expression, and so he gave her a genuine answer.

"It's a tactic, more than anything."

"A tactical war against chocolate and wine?" That half smile again, the one that put the *Mona Lisa* to shame. Both shy and impish without a hint of coyness or guile.

"In my line of work, one must be above reproach. Therefore, I avoid all excess that could lead to addictive partiality or a weakness in moral character. Such as alcohol, idle pursuits, rich food, gambling—"

"Women?" Count Adrian Armediano slithered into the conversation, an expression of charm and challenge carefully arranged upon his dusky, too-handsome features.

"That should go without saying," Ramsay reproached. "Especially in front of one."

"On the contrary. A woman is not a weakness, but a strength." Armediano turned to Cecelia, his lips curling with a feline appreciation Ramsay instantly disliked. The Italian slid a white-gloved hand along the back of her settee in a gesture that managed to be both seductive and unthreatening. "A life without women is not one worth living."

Cecelia's cheeks flushed a fetching peach beneath the count's frank, appreciative regard.

Ramsay scowled, his fingers curling into fists.

One could not appreciate a woman if one's eyes were plucked out.

Armediano moved with a practiced elegance, flicking open a jacket button as he sank intolerably close to Miss Teague. He swiped two glasses of champagne from a footman and flashed a smile that never reached his calculating golden gaze.

She accepted the proffered wine with a gracious, appreciative noise, glancing wryly at Ramsay as she took a delicate sip.

The count had the eyes of a raptor, Ramsay noted. Sharp and hard. He missed nothing as he glided through the ton with unobtainable ease. No one felt much threatened by someone so foreign and far above.

Until he dove for his prey.

Poor Miss Teague was a soft rabbit about to be clutched in his talons.

Bristling with masculine heat, Ramsay crushed the predator rising within himself. He'd no reason to lock horns with this man. Cecelia Teague was nothing to him but a passing family acquaintance. What did he care if she fell prey to a rake?

"Can you think of anything better to end an evening with than champagne?" she asked dreamily.

"Just the one thing." The count left his meaning unmistakable as he drew his knuckles over what little skin of her arm was visible above her gloves and below her sleeves. A rise of gooseflesh appeared where the man had trailed his touch.

Ramsay could have cheerfully broken Armediano's fingers. One by one.

Her nipples would be hard. And another man made them so.

"Forgive my intrusion upon your conversation," the count offered without one iota of sincerity. "But I couldn't help but overhear the subject and it both intrigued and distressed me. Are you not miserable, my lord Chief Justice, denying yourself the pleasures life has to offer?"

He'd be less miserable if it were still a practice to display severed heads on the London Bridge. What an appropriate ornament Armediano would make.

"Not at all." Ramsay uncrossed his legs, the new arrival

to their conversation beginning to redirect the blood from his nethers. "I have constructed a comfortable and successful life through will, focus, labor, and discipline. One need not seek sin and scandal to find contentment."

"No man is without sin," Armediano chuckled, flicking his gaze toward Cecelia. "Nor woman."

Cecelia made a soft noise in the back of her throat, examining Ramsay as if he were an equation she couldn't solve. "One must wonder if contentment is enough. Are you not lonely, my lord Ramsay? Or bored?"

Ramsay wanted to explain to her that most people didn't understand loneliness—not until they'd experienced true isolation. One could be lonely in a room full of people. Or in the arms of a lover. There were many forms of loneliness. He wondered if she'd experienced them at all.

Instead he hedged. "I'm a busy man. I havena time for boredom or loneliness."

"How fortunate for you," she murmured. Blinking away the wrinkle that had worked its way into her troubled expression, she drank deeply before announcing, "I confess I sometimes overindulge in chocolate and champagne, as there are few other pleasures afforded a spinster bluestocking."

"Bravo." The count lifted his glass.

She and Armediano tapped rims with a grating chime. Ramsay felt his very veins tightening around his blood as he struggled to maintain his composure.

"I am told you studied at the Sorbonne, Miss Teague." The count's eyes gleamed from beneath his dark brows.

"You are well informed," she replied.

"With your charming friends, the Countess of Mont Claire and the Duchess of Redmayne?"

Ramsay noted that the Italian's expression was entirely

too keen for such a casual question, and his eyes narrowed. A man unused to criminals and liars might not have noticed.

"Alex was not a duchess at the time, but yes, we attended the Sorbonne together, and the Ecole de Chardonne institute for girls on Lake Geneva before that."

"Where you formed a society, I understand, Rastrello Rosso."

"Not rakes, dear Count," she corrected with a pleased smile that rivaled that of the flames. "Rogues, we were the Red Rogues."

"She speaks Italian!" the count marveled.

"Only terribly," she demurred. "And where did you learn of the Red Rogues, sir? We were a trio of little renown."

"On the contrary." The count slid closer, until his knee touched hers. "University-educated women are still a rarity, even in France. And a trio of such *belle donne* as you do not go unnoticed, especially ones with a penchant for pastimes only allowed to men."

To her credit, Miss Teague gracefully tugged her knee away and tucked a forelock of hair back from her brow in a self-conscious gesture. "We are determined to live extraordinary lives, my lord."

Ramsay couldn't help himself. "And make extraordinary marriages?" He nodded toward the duchess.

Her expression dimmed, a crease appearing between her brows. "We actually vowed never to marry, though Alexandra's circumstances changed."

"You're saying your friend the Countess of Mont Claire does not plan to wed?" the count inquired. "Does she not need an heir to her fortune and title?"

"That is not her primary concern at the moment," she answered vaguely.

"And what about you?"

Cecelia adjusted her spectacles, nearly squirming with discomfort. "What about me?"

"Forgive my crass foreign manners, are you not in need of an advantageous marriage? It is not common for a mathematician to make a fortune."

Cecelia shook her head, her skin whitening from cream to a ghostly shade. "I—I don't . . ."

Ramsay found a man of his size rarely needed to raise his voice. When he offered a rebuke, he spoke low and even, but he leaned forward to emphasize the breadth of his shoulders. "If ye ken it isna appropriate to discuss finances in our society, Count, then it is not an ignorance of manners that prompts ye to ask, but a breach of them."

To his credit, the count didn't retreat, but he certainly changed tactics. "You must forgive me, of course. No offense was meant."

What an arse. Not to beg for forgiveness, but demand it.

"None was taken," Cecelia said with a solicitous hand on his cuff, though she did cast a grateful look in Ramsay's direction.

His own arm twitched with absurd jealousy.

"So chivalrous, Lord Ramsay." An undercurrent of malice lurked beneath the pleasant, silken tones of the count's Continental accent as he turned his gaze to Ramsay. "Tell me, Miss Teague, as you are so fond of numbers. What are the odds that the Lord Chief Justice here is as morally unimpeachable as he claims?"

Cecelia let out a nervous laugh, her color deepening slightly as she slid her gloved finger against her cheek in an oddly shy gesture. "That is an easy equation. Odds are divisible by the number of outcomes, and in this problem, there are only two outcomes possible. That a man is good, or that he is wicked. Thereby there is a fifty percent probability that any man is one or the other."

"And what would be your assessment?" the count pressed. "What are people but a collection of choices? Would you say Lord Ramsay is good? Or wicked?"

Ramsay shook his head, grappling with his temper. "She's known me all of five minutes—"

"Forgive me, but you are mistaken, Count Armediano." Cecelia surprised both of them by interrupting. By daring to correct a member of the aristocracy. By talking over a man.

"I've always believed people are more than just a collection of choices. It is why their worth—their worthiness—cannot be calculated mathematically. A person is a complicated amalgamation of their experiences, education, environs, illnesses, and desires. And one cannot ignore more physical variables such as nutrition, traditions, ethnicities, nationalities . . . and, yes, actions. But that is why we may not quantify them so easily." She cast Ramsay a meaningful look he couldn't begin to define, one brimming with a haunted sadness that tugged at a primitive protective instinct.

"It is also why I would find your position so daunting, Lord Ramsay. I could not condemn another human being, even as a High Court justice. I feel as though I would never truly know what punishment or mercy a person would deserve."

The Count Armediano took a contemplative sip. "Is it your experience, Miss Teague, that people get what they deserve, one way or another? Do not good people suffer, and evil people achieve success?"

"That is unfortunately so."

Ramsay watched her throat work around a dainty

swallow as she slid a sidelong look toward Lady Francesca and Lady Alexandra.

She continued, "I still try to believe that good ultimately
triumphs in the end. Especially when there are those who
work so diligently to keep evil at bay, such as Lord Ramsay, the duke and duchess, and Lady Mont Claire."

"Not you?" the count drawled.

This elicited a laugh from her. "Of course I desire to
be good, to do good works, but Alexandra is a doctor of
archeology, and so she preserves the lessons of history
and the legacies of those who have gone before us. The
duke has his tenants and employees, and he sees to the live-
lihoods of many. Francesca—"

Miss Teague cut off sharply, and Ramsay watched the
count's spine straighten as if he'd been skewered.

"Well, Francesca has her life's mission, and it's a worthy cause," she finished vaguely. "But I'm afraid I have
not found what it is I'm going to give to this world to
make it better."

"Miss Teague, you are an unpredictable, exquisite
creature." Armediano spoke to her, but also affixed his
eyes upon the collection of nobles in the middle of which
Francesca Cavendish sparkled like a rare ruby, her crimson hair shining brilliant in the light of the chandeliers.

"Thank you, my lord."

"And you, Lord Ramsay, disabuse me of the notion
that the Scots are nothing but hedonistic barbarians."

Ramsay's blood froze and his muscles iced over, hardening into shards of tension.

Barbarians?

The count had no idea what barbaric was. For certainly this pampered princeling would have been crushed
by the conditions in which Ramsay had been whelped
and forged. He had the swarthy complexion of a man

raised beneath a forgiving sun. Had he ever known cold? Or hunger? Abandonment? Cruelty?

Had he ever killed to eat, or to live?

Ramsay would have staked his fortune against it. Aye, his bleak upbringing, or lack thereof, would have crushed the elegant man.

But as he opened his mouth to flay his skin with his cutting tongue, Cecelia beat him to it.

"I think such a notion was disproved centuries past by any number of Scottish people such as John Galt, Robert Burns, and Joanna Baillie, and the tradition continues with Robert Louis Stevenson," she stated. "That is, if the notion ever held merit at all."

Ramsay wished he knew what to say. Never in his life had anyone come to his defense.

He'd fought his own battles.

"I must beg your pardon a third time, Miss Teague." The count put a hand over his heart and bowed his head in contrition. "Might I entice you to walk with me in the gardens?"

"Surely ye're aware that for her to do so is not appropriate in our society, Count Armediano," Ramsay explained. "To ask her is crude and unseemly."

The count's dark eyes flashed, but his manner remained pleasant as he blithely answered, "I was not aware."

What horseshit. Ramsay's eyes narrowed. "She is unchaperoned and therefore not allowed to share the private company of one man."

Especially that of a handsome, unmarried Continental aristocrat with a gaze only meant for the boudoir.

Cecelia stood, obliging them to do the same. Her eyes flashed with the whisper of a distant sapphire storm that never truly surfaced. "As a sovereign entity, I am *allowed* to do what I wish," she said stiffly.

Count Armediano sent him a glance of masculine victory. "Does that mean your wish is to walk with me in the garden? I vow to keep your reputation intact."

Ramsay's blood went very still, his lungs constricted as he waited for an answer that should mean nothing to him.

As if summoned by an invisible distress signal, a dapper older gentleman in dinner dress appeared at Cecelia's elbow and murmured what sounded like rapid French into her ear.

Her features instantly melted into an expression of keen relief as she took his proffered arm, reaching across her body to rest her free hand on his in a gesture of easy fondness.

"Some other time, perhaps." Her features became still, carefully placid. "Thank you for the . . . stimulating conversation, gentlemen, but I must bid you a good evening."

Cecelia didn't bother with a curtsy, and Ramsay couldn't bring himself to blame her as he watched her bustle sway with the enticing movement of her wide hips as she glided away from them both. Her head tilted toward her shorter, stocky companion's in rapt conversation as the Frenchman gestured expansively.

"Bad luck for you, Count," Ramsay said wryly. "It seems the lovely Miss Teague's affections are spoken for." The Frenchman must be wealthy, indeed, as he was nearly old enough to be Cecelia's grandfather, and was as weathered as an old leather boot.

"Not so. That is Jean-Yves Renault. He's something of a mascot to these Red Rogues. Miss Teague hired him away from their finishing school at Lake Geneva, and they famously go nowhere without him. He's essentially Miss Teague's valet, if a woman can have such a thing."

The count's black brows drew together. "I am surprised you did not know that."

Ramsay turned to contemplate the man. "I'm surprised you do."

The count gave a Gallic shrug. "It does one good to know with whom he is getting into business, and into bed with. The duke and I have many shared pursuits."

"Indeed." Ramsay found himself expelling a breath he hadn't been aware of holding. He'd heard of Jean-Yves Renault but had never met the man. He knew his brother Piers was grateful to him for a service to Alexandra and her friends in their younger years, but was also disinclined to speak of it.

He'd never been more than passing curious until tonight.

"These Red Rogues, they are like three rosebuds, conspiring to bloom with such brilliance, they'll never be challenged by any other in the garden." Armediano's voice was touched with awe as he watched Cecelia gather with Lady Francesca and Lady Alexandra to press their heads together in a strictly feminine collaboration. "They are fascinating women, are they not?"

"They're frightening," Ramsay said darkly. "I'd avoid them, lest catastrophes befall ye."

He, too, walked away from the distasteful count, but not before he caught the flash of understanding on the man's features. To anyone nearby, his words might have sounded like a flippant warning.

But they both knew the intent.

A threat.

CHAPTER TWO

Miss Henrietta's School for Cultured Young Ladies,
London, 1891—Three Months Later

It took Cecelia entirely too long to arrive at the realization she'd inherited a gambling hell.

In her defense, Miss Henrietta's School for Cultured Young Ladies seemed perfectly innocuous from the outside.

Number Three Mounting Lane was located in West London, tucked several streets away from the fashionable side of Hyde Park.

The rectangular white mansion reminded her of a Greek pantheon complete with imposing pillars and resplendent arborvitae leading up the circular drive.

A solicitous white-wigged butler met her at the massive front door and ushered her into a lavish parlor done in varying shades of red and gold. Cecelia marveled at his uniform of a century past and did her best not to giggle at his high-heeled shoes and the falls of lace at his wrists.

Even as the reign of Queen Victoria gave rise to Gothic

glamour and intriguing innovations, everything about Number Three Mounting Street boasted the overdone opulence of Versailles in the days of King Louis XIV.

And all of it now belonged to her, passed on by her mysterious benefactor, who'd turned out not to be her father but, in fact, her mother's sister. Henrietta Thistledown.

The reading of the will had been short and terse, whereupon Cecelia was granted everything in Henrietta's name, including her School for Cultured Young Ladies, a selection of other properties, and a staggering fortune.

Henrietta's solicitor had handed a sealed letter to Cecelia after their appointment with strict instructions not to read it until she was secured in Henrietta's office at Number Three Mounting Lane. So she'd taken a carriage straightaway.

Cecelia couldn't bring herself to sit on the receiving room furniture that appeared too delicate to support her weight, so she paced, comforted by the clack of her boots against the marble floor.

She studied the missive, turned it over in her hands, stroked the fine striations in the expensive paper. An ache bloomed in her heart and a stone lodged in her throat as she battled an emotion akin to loss.

All this time, she'd assumed her father had been the silence on the other end of her letters.

For years, she'd been expected to write a monthly correspondence before her allowance was released to her accounts. Updates regarding her education, travels, and health. She'd dutifully penned this paternal shade who'd begun to take shape over the years. Some man in a mansion much like this one, lonely and bound by the strictures of society. Loving her from afar. Pining for her company.

The revelation of her maternal aunt would have been less disappointing, she supposed, if she'd not gleaned the knowledge of her relation only after the woman's sudden death.

As such, she mourned two people.

Two people she'd never had the chance to love properly.

Emitting a melancholy sigh, Cecelia drifted to the window overlooking the square garden in the throes of its vibrant late-summer bloom. It was situated in the middle of the manse, surrounded on all sides by tall white stone walls boasting long windows from which to enjoy the view of—

Cecelia clamped both hands over her mouth, the sight before her pinning her feet to the ground.

On a stretch of perfectly clipped grass not seven paces from the window, a dark-skinned woman in a butter-yellow ball gown bounced astride the hips of a half-naked man. The prone figure held her hips as though to keep her from flying away as he thrust upward with such vigor, it appeared as though he were trying to dislodge her from his lap.

On the heels of Cecelia's shock rode an absurd and intense anxiety for the young lovers. It was only half noon on a summer's day. If *she'd* spied their brazen liaison in the gardens, surely someone else would.

Slowly, a few additional details began to permeate her absurd musings.

The girl's gown was also about one hundred years out of fashion, just as the butler's attire had been. Her dark hair was powdered, a practice that had died several decades hence. Her lips were almost comically rouged, as were her cheeks and . . .

Cecelia's hands moved from her mouth to press against

her heart as the man reached up and freed the girl's breasts from the low bodice.

Her nipples—enviably high, impossibly pert nipples—were rouged as well.

Cecelia should have looked away, but instead she found her breaths increasing to match the rhythm of the shameless copulation.

This was no gentle rendezvous; nor was it a romp, per se. The man's rough hands pinched at the woman, grabbed at her breasts, her throat, until his fingers found their way into her mouth.

All the while the woman rode him at a galloping pace, baring her teeth to playfully bite at him, exerting just enough pressure to send her lover into obvious fits of delight.

Without realizing it, Cecelia's hands slid from her heart, over her sedate navy-and-white-striped gown, to settle low on her stomach, where a flurry of hummingbirds might have taken residence. Some heavy sensation bloomed beneath her hand. Heavy and empty at the same time. An ache, but not a pain.

An urge, but not a hunger.

It brought to mind those languorous mornings on Lake Geneva watching the boys of le Radon Institute for Boys scull their boats across the mirror-smooth water. Their bodies surging and pulling, every muscle engaged. The rhythm of it had done something to her, even as a girl of seventeen.

"Forgive me for keeping you waiting, but—"

Cecelia gasped and whirled, her gaze colliding with that of Genevieve Leveaux, who stood in the doorway swathed in bright pink and bedecked with an inordinate number of bows on her Georgian bodice.

She rushed to the window, unable to fully block Cecelia's

view, as it seemed she'd outgrown Genny in the nearly fifteen years since they'd seen each other.

"Blast and damnation," the older woman hissed. "Today of all days." She threw the latch and leaned so far out the window, Cecelia worried she'd fall. "Lilly Belle! This is your last warning before I throw you out on your ear! You've been told to keep that sort of enterprise elsewhere. We are not *that* kind of business!"

Cecelia noted that Genny's sinuous voice and whimsical American patois hadn't changed a whit, even after so many years in England.

"But Lord Crawford came looking for table games, and since we're closed today, he offered another kind of sport. He prefers to rut out of doors, don't you, darling?" Lilly reached behind her and slapped his thigh, much as one would the flanks of a horse.

"I prefer an audience," he managed breathlessly.

To Cecelia's—well, she couldn't say horror, but she didn't quite have another word to describe the amalgamation of shock, titillation, and distress within her—Crawford and Lilly didn't pause. The discourse didn't even interrupt their rhythm. In fact, Crawford stared right at Cecelia and increased his pace, grasping Lilly by the hips and thrusting upward rather mercilessly.

Cecelia didn't know whether to laugh, cry, run, or . . .

Or continue to watch.

"I said *not today*, you insatiable slag," Genny bellowed, her drawl losing its syrupy edge to shards of ire. "Our new *headmistress* is here, and this isn't the fashion in which we planned to receive her, is it? Now finish Crawford off and send him on his way. And if I catch you at this again—"

"I thought. She wasn't. Coming. Until. This. After. Noon." Lilly's diction was interrupted by the increasing intensity of what was happening beneath her.

"I'm coming . . . right . . . now," Crawford warned, his voice thick with strain.

Cecelia could stand to watch no longer as a strange and unsettling contortion overtook Crawford's beakish features. Cheeks on fire and her bodice suddenly too tight, she whirled and launched herself toward the door.

It opened before she could reach for the handle, and the butler burst in, red-faced with panic. "Three carriages full of lawmen are turning onto Mounting Lane," he panted.

Cecelia looked to Genny, shocked beyond words. Mounting Lane. Never had there been a more apropos address. Had she inherited a brothel?

The butler cast a wary glance toward Cecelia. "I'm told the Vicar of Vice is with them."

Vicar of Vice? Cecelia mentally searched through everything she'd ever read regarding civics and politics. She arrived at the conclusion they were using a moniker no one claimed willfully.

A litany of words that would have made a sailor blush burst from Genny as she returned to the window. "You get that cull out of here now, Lilly!" she screeched. "The Vicar of Vice is blocks away, and he's bringing his army to our door."

"Again?" came Lilly's plaintive whine from the garden as she tucked her breasts away.

Genny slammed the window shut and locked it before finally turning to Cecelia, her panicked amber eyes softening with regret as she fluffed at her perfect brassy-blond coiffeur. "Well, honey." She hurried to where Cecelia stood at the door and took her hands. The all-but-forgotten letter crumpled slightly between their palms.

They both looked down to the piece of paper, then back to each other.

Genny had barely changed in fifteen years. Her skin remained smooth and unblemished but for a slight deepening in the creases next to her expressive mouth, to the right of which a painted black heart hovered. Her tight curls were threaded with a whisper of silver at the temples, but she was as exquisite as the day they'd met.

"This isn't at all how I wanted to welcome you." Genny freed the hand in which Cecelia clutched the letter but kept the other locked in a firm grip as she turned to the butler.

"Winston, you make sure Crawford has paid Lilly, dressed, and gone before those carriages have a chance to breach the gates. Then you rip through this entire place and make certain they find *nothing*."

"Yes, madam."

Genny launched herself through the door, nearly yanking Cecelia's arm out of its socket as she dragged her along. "I'd hoped we'd have time to discuss everything, but the wolves are howling at the door."

"Wolves?" Cecelia tried to keep up both mentally and physically as she allowed herself to be pulled back through the extravagant marble entry toward a small door hidden in dark-wood panels beneath the columns of the grand staircase. She pushed her spectacles up the bridge of her nose, afraid they'd come loose in their hurry.

"That letter is from your aunt Henrietta," Genny explained with forced patience. "Read what you can before the vicar busts the door down."

"Who *is* this vicar?" Cecelia paused, feeling as though she stood at a dangerous threshold, both literally and figuratively. She didn't give the other woman a chance to answer the first question before a second followed: "Where are we going?"

"To the private residence." Genny gave her another

strong, impatient tug. "Follow me. We haven't time to dil-lydally."

"To what?" Astonished, overwhelmed, and skeptical, Cecelia tugged her hand out of Genny's grip. "I've never heard the word *dilly*—"

"I know this is a lot to take in, but I need you to listen to me, doll." Genny's face darkened as she hung her hands on her broad hips, all tolerance replaced by audacity and urgency. "The man who's fixin' to kick our door in is comin' to take everything from us. From *you*. This is a casino and a school—regardless of what you just saw. The school allows women to work while they are taught a trade. But that man would sooner see every girl livin' under our protection put out on the streets to sell their bodies in the gutters to cutthroats and ironworkers. So if you don't want to spend the next several years in prison on whatever trumped-up charges he has on his warrant this time, you'll follow me, you'll read that letter, and then you'll use every wit in that pretty head of yours to fend him off, you hear?"

She shook Cecelia none-too-gently. "He's your enemy now. One of many."

Cecelia stood rooted to the ground, staring incoher-ently at the woman as information digested slowly.

Enemies? She'd never in her adult life had rivals, foes, or adversaries, let alone *enemies*.

This morning she'd taken breakfast and coffee in a Chelsea café. At the time, her greatest concern had been a bit of ennui and some existential anxiety about what to do with her recently acquired degree in mathematics.

And now she faced *prison*?

The very idea made her dizzy.

"What if we reason with this . . . this Vicar of Vice? What if I told him that I inherited the establishment no earlier than this very morning?" Cecelia cringed at the plaintive, desperate note that had crept into her voice. "Surely he can't accuse me of a crime yet, I've only just arrived."

Genny made a coarse sound. "There's no reasoning with the Vicar of Vice. He hates anything that could be considered enjoyable. Gambling, drinking, acting, dancing. He hates whores most of all."

"But if this isn't a brothel, you've done nothing illegal . . ."

Genny's eyes flicked away. "What the women who work here do to make ends meet is none of our concern, and I'll admit Lilly isn't the first girl with culls I've turned a blind eye to. But no, we don't serve sex to our customers, only the suggestion of it."

They burst into the private residence, and Genny paused a moment to lock the panel behind her before propelling an absorbed Cecelia up a flight of cobalt-carpeted stairs. Ivory damask wallpaper sped by in her periphery as she was led down a hall with white wainscoting and dark-wood floors.

Genny herded her into a tasteful, feminine study done in soft creams, white wickers, dazzling sapphire accents, and canvas paintings.

It bore no resemblance to the opulent and overdone palace of carnality occupying the floor below them.

Cecelia marveled as she took in the refined objets d'art and tranquil furnishings, cheerful sunshine slanting in through a skylight.

The gambling hell, by comparison, had been dimly lit by gas lamps and candelabras, the light flattering and golden, lending the feel of an enchanted evening, even at noon.

Genny was kind enough to allow Cecelia a moment to

twirl about like a simpleton, absorbing her surroundings before the older woman dragged her toward the only masculine piece of furniture in the room. The desk faced the door on a raised dais, backlit by floor-to-ceiling windows through which rays of sunlight created celestial pillars to anoint the occupant with a golden glow.

"Sit," Genny ordered in a voice one generally saved for hounds. "Read."

Cecelia sat and broke the seal on the letter knowing she would never be truly ready to receive the contents therein.

My darling Cecelia,
If this letter has reached you, dear niece, it means I have been murdered.

She gasped, struck with a chill even the sun-facing august room couldn't dispel. "No one said anything about a murder. Do you know—?"

"Not now. Keep reading," Genny clipped. "I'll get you ready to meet the devil."

Cecelia puzzled over Genny's slew of evocative names for their enemy. "How can one be a vicar, a devil, and a wolf all at once?" she wondered aloud.

"Lord love a goat, girl, do you ever stop askin' questions? Maybe the answers are in that letter . . ." Genny snatched a ruffled scarlet cape from a stand and swirled it around her shoulders before she turned and riffled in a cabinet, her movements jerky and frenetic.

Cecelia found her place, fighting both numbness and panicked disbelief.

I have done precious little good in this life, but I'll meet whatever comes after knowing that my girls are safe and together.

You may or may not have heard of me, but I am who they call the Scarlet Lady.

Your mother, Hortense, was my twin, younger by seven minutes. We were each of us born into a life of poverty and drudgery, which I escaped into a profession equal parts glamour and guile. Hortense, however, did not. She bound herself to the contemptible Vicar Teague, who disdained me and forbade our relationship as sisters. Your mother and I kept in touch over the years because the attachment we forged in the womb could not be severed, even by her death.

Her last missive to me, dear Cecelia, was a plea to watch over you. To give you the life neither of us had. I have been an entrepreneur in many trades, one of which was that of a courtesan in my early days. I'm not ashamed of it. However, that is not the legacy I leave to you.

Our power does not reside between our legs, you and I, but between our ears. I do not steal hearts any longer, my dear, but I do collect debts. Debts and secrets. Secrets that could bring this empire to its knees. Secrets that hypocrites and charlatans have paid dearly for me to keep. It is my intention to take on the Crimson Council, Cecelia, but this is a dangerous endeavor. Everyone else who has attempted to do so has been killed. And so if I am gone, this is the why of it, and I have chosen you to carry on my work.

Cecelia closed her eyes against a well of tears.

Genny took advantage of this, relieving her of her spectacles before she ruthlessly powdered her face.

The Crimson Council? She'd never before heard of such a thing. How strange that her life seemed hued by a certain shade. The Crimson Council. The Red Rogues. The Scarlet Lady.

A distant pounding reverberated through the building like the hammer strokes of Hephaestus.

"Christ almighty," Genny swore. "He's at the school door. He'll tear it apart before coming here to do the same. Hurry, darlin'."

Cecelia's eyes popped open and she sneezed white powder into the crook of her elbow. "Why are you making me up?" She sniffed, hiccuped, and sneezed again.

"He can't know who you really are, not yet." Genny kept her quiet by painting crimson rouge on her lips in thick, masterful strokes. "You must be the Scarlet Lady."

"Who is *he*?" she finally asked. "And why can I not meet him as I am?"

"Can you read without these?" Genny motioned to her spectacles.

"I prefer to," Cecelia said dazedly. "They're for seeing distances. I'm nearly blind without them."

Genny tucked them away, and didn't have to tell her this time to continue reading.

Cecelia, you must watch over Phoebe. She is your sister in all but blood. If the law finds her here, she's in imminent danger. You must keep her from her brutal father at all costs.

She opened her mouth to ask Genny about this *Phoebe* when a cacophony of masculine commands and feminine objections filtered through the walls of the residence from the school next door. Footfalls and doors crashing with no little violence sent her galloping heart into a sprint and caused her hands to shake.

"What do I do?" Cecelia asked, feeling suddenly very young.

"What you have to," Genny said as though the answer were obvious. "*Whatever* you have to. Even if it's offering up that generous set of tits, you hear? Whatever it takes to keep this household safe. That's your responsibility now."

Dumbfounded, Cecelia looked down at the bosoms in question, hidden by a billowing scarlet cloak that suggested she might wear something more interesting beneath it than a sensible day gown.

When she lifted her head, Genny plunked a towering pale wig upon her crown, one so blond it might have been silver. It added at least half a foot to her already impressive height and was bedecked with enough red bows and pearls to make a Christmas tree jealous.

Genny finally seemed to relax as she arranged a fall of silvery ringlets over her shoulder. "You actually look like Henrietta, give or take twenty-five years." She fetched a mirror from a sideboard and held it up to Cecelia.

The transformation stole her breath. She couldn't see her entire form, of course, nor did her reflection contain the top of her ridiculous wig, but it did, indeed, appear as though she'd stepped out of a bygone century as a glamourous ingénue in the court of eighteenth-century Versailles. Her cheekbones seemed leaner, contoured by rouge, her red lips fuller and more than a little wicked, her face a ghostly shade in comparison. Her eyes lined and colored, and her lashes thickened.

She didn't look at all like herself. She couldn't tell if she loved or hated the effect.

That same ominous knock echoed through the residence, this time coming from the door in the garden.

"Open the door. We've a warrant to search the premises."

It struck Cecelia as absurdly funny that the representative from Scotland Yard actually boasted a Scottish accent along with a voice so deep, she wondered if he could simply bellow the entire house down.

Like the wolf in the story.

And here she stood, in her red hooded cloak, waiting to be devoured.

Cecelia pressed her fingers to her mouth to hold in a whimper.

"Sit here." Genny guided her to the impressive velvet chair behind the white marble-topped desk. "Don't stand unless they force you to. *This* is your throne. Your seat of power. Besides, you're as tall as a lamppost and would be easily recognized by that feature alone." She produced a black lace masquerade mask from the desk and tied it over Cecelia's eyes and nose, securing it with a silk ribbon in the back. "Just use that brain of yours to get rid of him, honey. That's all you have to do."

Oh, was that all? Cecelia felt it was a terrible moment to mention that in times of stress her brain tended to go on holiday.

"I'm giving ye thirty seconds to open this door or I'll kick it in," the cavernous brogue threatened. "Nothing would give me greater pleasure."

That voice . . .

Cecelia's features crinkled behind the mask.

Something about the fathomless frigidity of the brogue was familiar. As were the chills it lifted on the fine hairs of her body. A voice like that belonged in a forgotten dwelling deeper than even the volcanic forge of hell.

In that place so cavernous and cold and full of shadows, only one being could hold court there.

One being whose sole reason for existence was to punish those who were wicked.

Genny hurried to the open window and leaned out of it. "Don't you touch that door, I'll be down to admit you directly."

"Thirty. Seconds," the Scotsman repeated.

Genny pivoted, running her hands down her bodice, visibly shaken. "I nearly forget how monstrous big he is," she breathed. "I declare, he could rip the iron gates from their hinges with one hand."

With that confidence-shredding observation, Genny took the space of a breath to compose herself, then swept out of the study before Cecelia could ask one of a thousand questions that sprang to her lips.

Fear twanged tight in her belly. She knew of only one deep-voiced Scotsman with monstrous proportions. However, he wasn't with Scotland Yard. He wouldn't be able to step away from his bench as Lord Chief Justice to break in the door of a common—or uncommon, as the case may be—gambling house.

Would he?

Cecelia was suddenly so frightened, she was tempted to rip off her ridiculous disguise and bolt.

She pushed herself into the desk, tugging at the cloak's tightly laced collar as sweat gathered beneath her wig in the hot and humid afternoon. Glancing down, she read more of the letter, grasping at anything to do other than sit and tremble as the law advanced on her.

I wish I could have met you, darling. Your letters have been a comfort and a balm to me all these years. I gave you as long a life as I could without secrets. But now it is up to you what you do with them. The school beneath my gambling enterprise is everything to me, and to the women who rely upon it. I know your heart. How good and soft it is, but you are of my blood, which means you've steel constructed to your spine. You'll need it, I think, and for that I am sorry.

I'm delighted we share traits, a few of which are an affinity for numbers, codes, and formulae. These secrets I protect I have confided in no one, not even Genevieve. I have, however, written them down in a book, along with where to find the evidence you'll need. You'll discover the codex in a springboard beneath the top drawer of the desk at which you sit. Open the drawer and press the bottom of it. Use the Pollux cipher to decrypt the combination, which is the name of our favorite poem.

The one that pierced your heart when you were sixteen.

"*Aeneid,*" Cecelia whispered.

The key to the codex, Cecelia, is in the color we both find very dear.

Good luck, my heart, and goodbye.

Blinking back a bevy of emotion, Cecelia turned the clever dials, replacing the letters of the epic Greek poem title for numbers. She gasped when the bottom of the hidden compartment gave way, depositing a finely crafted diary into her hand.

She ran her fingers over the innocuous binding, finding the pale flesh color of the leather a little disturbing. Opening it, she leafed through the pages. It didn't at all surprise her to see almost no words, only symbols, numbers, formulae. Dates, perhaps, if she remembered her Sumerian numerals correctly . . . or was this the Babylonian sexagesimal system? She squinted, turning the book sideways.

Voices echoed off the marble of the foyer.

Genny's.

And the devil's.

Even as her stomach turned an anxious flop, a part of her stirred. *Parts* of her. The section of her brain that came alive at the idea of solving a cipher.

And a different place, altogether.

A place she'd been attempting to ignore since she'd spied the frenetic copulation in the garden. A soft, feminine depth that hummed and clenched at the danger she instinctively sensed in the approaching man.

She was afraid, she realized. And stimulated simultaneously?

How tremendously bizarre.

Squirming in the thronelike chair, her boot connected with something soft under the desk.

Or rather, someone.

A little squeak from beneath produced a strangled sound of astonishment from Cecelia's own throat. She launched back in her chair, nearly tipping over.

Steadying herself, she leaned to the side to peek beneath the desk, using one hand to stabilize the wig atop her head.

A pair of hazel eyes gaped back at her from a cherubic face.

A girl.

Cecelia quickly estimated her identity.

"Phoebe?" she whispered. For some reason, she'd suspected the girl from Henrietta's note to be grown. It'd never occurred to her that she would harbor a child.

The girl nodded, honey-colored ringlets falling over her shoulder as she pressed her finger to her lips.

Cecelia nodded back conspiratorially, wishing she knew more about children and how to gauge their ages. She could be seven or so, though her eyes seemed older, perhaps? And it was impossible to tell for certain, what with her little body folded beneath the dark underbelly of the desk, half concealed by the ruffles of Cecelia's own skirt and cloak.

Footsteps pounded up the stairs as Genny's loud protests echoed down the hallway.

Blast it all. Just who *was* this Phoebe?

Sisters in all but blood . . . so it would seem they were not related.

Was she the secret Henrietta had been killed for? Was her life also in danger? And if so, from whom—this Vicar of Vice?

There was simply no time for answers.

"Phoebe, I need you to stay under there," Cecelia whispered. "No matter what you hear, can you remain silent until those men leave?"

The girl smiled gravely, holding her finger to her mouth.

"Very good," Cecelia praised. "I'm Cecelia. Henrietta has charged me to keep you safe and I promise to do so." she vowed, doing her best to school the panic out of her voice. She'd never broken a promise; she hoped to God she could keep this one. "Can you guard this book for me, Phoebe? It belonged to Miss Henrietta, and I don't want anyone to take it."

The girl snatched the diary and clutched it to her chest, wedging herself further beneath the desk. Cecelia straightened and shoved the letter in her bodice just as the door to the study burst open with such force, it rebounded off the wall.

The man filling the doorway caught it in his enormous hand.

Had Cecelia been a fainting woman, she might have expired on the spot. As it was, her head swam with both rejection and recognition. Her eyes widened in an endeavor to take in the full magnitude of the masculine form before her.

Blood retreated from her extremities, and she became immediately grateful her pallor was concealed beneath the face powder.

Because even though she could make out none of his features without her spectacles, the unparalleled height, breadth, and specific hues of this particular Scotsman were undeniable.

She knew him. Of course she did.

Lord Cassius Gerard Ramsay.

They were practically related now that Alex, the sister of her heart, had recently married his brother.

And yet she knew little about him. He was a man of mysterious origin, strict principles, and, if his claims should be believed, zero indulgences.

She'd spoken with him on only two prior occasions, and their interactions had been—well—rather confounding.

He'd watched her that night at Castle Redmayne with a deep scowl and hungry eyes.

She often lay awake at night revisiting the evening and the two men who'd dominated it. One, an Italian count as handsome and sleek as the devil, dark curls tamed with pomade and Phoenician features alight with masculine interest.

And the other, Lord Ramsay, a golden-haired archangel. A stalwart warrior for all things he deemed just and right and good. A paladin of sorts, who might have been knighted years past by some fortunate maiden for slaying dragons and demons alike.

And now that self-same man stared at her from the doorway, his eyes the color of a winter's moon glinting with that righteous warrior's wrath.

In those eyes, *she* was the dragon he'd come to do battle with.

To vanquish.

The temperature immediately dropped in his presence, the atmosphere around them thick and preternaturally silent. It was the ethereal kind of muffled quiet one experienced during a fresh snowfall. Not the absence of dissonance, but a void in the center of it all.

A cold and lonely place.

Just as the chill he brought with him was discordant with the warm sunlight filtering through the windows, so was the sight of a body so large and rough-hewn as his trapped in such an expensive suit.

No, she'd been mistaken before. He was no angel. His was a barbaric build. One that belonged draped in Viking skins, furs, and armor as he bled for pagan gods on a battlefield. Indeed, it was as if the fabled gods of war crafted him for the distinct purpose to crush, to conquer, and then to rule. He didn't occupy space, he filled it. Commanded it. He owned the earth upon which he stood as there surely was no man or army alive that could wrest it from him.

He advanced, clutching documents in his fist as though they were Excalibur.

Dumbstruck, Cecelia did nothing but stare as his features came into focus, sharpening with terrifying exactitude as he closed in.

She detected no recognition from him, only rage.

She groped for something to say, a witty, caustic introduction that she could use to chip away at the ice. But apparently, her shock at the sight of him had stolen not only her wits, but her breath as well.

He tossed the papers in front of her. Cecelia glanced down to find a Writ of Warrant signed by his own hand.

"Do ye ken who I am?" he rumbled in a voice meant only for them.

Genny tumbled into the room behind him, followed by a handful of constables and a detective in a smart suit.

"Everyone in the empire knows who you are." The pitch of her voice was breathy, higher, and unintentional.

As was her French accent.

Genny let out a strangled noise.

Lord, what am I doing?

She'd simply panicked. She couldn't risk him recognizing her voice. Who knew what kind of memory he possessed?

"It's important that ye know my name," the giant Scot said.

"I know your name," she replied.

He lifted a golden brow in a silent dare. "Say it, then."

Something in the command thrummed a sensual vibration deep in her body, and she had to squirm to quiet it. "Lord Ramsay."

His chin dipped once in a curt nod. "And to what name do ye answer?"

Cecelia leaned back in her chair, to give her lungs more space as they seemed to be one breath away from eminent collapse. "Why, I should think you've heard of me as well, my lord, as you're currently calling upon my establishment."

Did he recognize her at all? Could this preposterous, overdone disguise be enough to keep the secret of her identity intact, at least for the moment?

He grimaced, scanning the room with an expression one might wear if one had stepped in sewer sludge. "It's quite impossible that a man such as I would have the opportunity to suffer an introduction to a woman such as *ye*."

If only he knew.

Her lids fluttered closed in what she hoped he read as a coy gesture and not the retreat it was. "I am known to all as the Scarlet Lady. It is a thorough pleasure to make your acquaintance, my lord Chief Justice." She reached her gloved hand out to receive him.

He snorted, his lip lifting in disgust as he regarded her

hand as one would rotten rubbish. "Pleasure has nothing at all to do with my visit, as ye can well see." He gestured to his army of police.

"A shame. Such is not generally the case." Cecelia found a measure of her fear replaced by indignation.

"Tell me. Yer. *Name*." This he demanded through gritted teeth, though his voice never rose even one octave. The effect was most terrifying.

"I believe I already did."

"Yer Christian name."

"I am not a Christian."

At his silent glare of effrontery, she shrugged. "I've noticed that often a church is a structure to confine God built by those who claim to speak to or for him. I find other ways to edify my soul. Besides"—she lifted an overdramatic hand to press against her chest—"why would you want to be acquainted with someone as lowly and woebegone as I?"

"I doona want anything resembling an acquaintance with ye." He leaned over, spreading both of his enormous square hands on the desk between them. Threatening to mesmerize her with those silver-blue eyes. "But ye should ken the name of yer enemy, so ye ken what name to curse when I destroy ye."

Chapter Three

An unsettling awareness paralyzed Cecelia as she stared into the eyes of her enemy.

Awareness of the child hiding at her feet. Of the book containing possibly lethal secrets clutched in her innocent hands. Of the expectation and caution in Genny's demeanor.

Of everyone's gaze glued to her, waiting to see what she'd do next. What she'd say to the brutishly large and powerful man leaning over her desk.

His nostrils flared and a vein pulsed at his temple before disappearing into his thick, luminous hair.

She could almost feel the heat of his breath, like that of a dragon. A dragon, she noted, who'd dined on something sweet for his last meal and washed it down with coffee rather than tea.

Strange that they should both prefer coffee in the morning. What else did they have in common, she and her adversary? Must they be adversaries at all? If she revealed herself, explained her situation, might he soften?

No. No, his expression was diamond-hard and uncompromising, as was his reputation. He was the Vicar of Vice, the sworn enemy of her aunt. And just because his brother was a good man didn't mean he was.

As she well understood, so many men used piety to disguise their cruelty.

In that case, she decided, if this man insisted upon being her adversary, she'd have to kill him.

With kindness.

Drawing on every bit of her finishing school education, she did her level best to smother her panic with politeness. She pressed her hands flat on the desk and forced herself to remain still.

"You may call me Hortense Thistledown." She plucked her mother's name out of pure desperation, hating that it would become a blasphemy on this man's tongue.

What would *her* name sound like in that graveled brogue of his? *Cecelia.*

As soon as the unwanted thought filtered into her mind, she shook her head to be rid of it.

"Might I invite you to sit down, my lord, whilst I peruse your documents?" She gestured to one of three dainty chairs facing her desk, belatedly concerned for their structural integrity against his impressive bulk. "Genny, would you please fetch His Worship and associates some tea and refreshments?"

Genny looked as though she'd asked her to consume the contents of a chamber pot.

A few of the constables brightened at the mention of food and tea, immediately deflating when Ramsay put up a staying hand. "Doona be absurd. This isna a social call, madam." His eyes flickered around the room, his expression suggesting he would rather be surrounded by a Whitechapel cesspool than her aunt's tasteful décor. "I'm inclined to touch as little in this place as possible. Who kens what depravities have occurred on which surfaces?"

"Oh come now, what sort of wickedness could possibly be conducted upon such dainty furniture?" She gestured to the Louis XIV settee and chairs, genuinely stunned when a few of the constables muffled a chuckle or two.

Heat spread to Sir Ramsay's eyes as he glanced at the furniture in question and then back to her. Her question had angered him. She read something else in the heat, as well. A banked emotion beneath the anger, something leashed. Chained.

Dangerous.

"It is not in yer best interest to mock me, woman."

"I wouldn't dream of it, sir," she answered, bemused. "But I vow the only blasphemies this room is subject to are taxes and paperwork." She summoned what she hoped was a charming smile, though her mind whirred with unknowns—she couldn't have said for certain the surfaces *hadn't* been sullied.

"And whilst this visit of yours might not be social," she added, "we can still be civilized, can we not?"

His eyes narrowed. "Search everything."

The constables made quick work of the room. They pulled books from shelves, turning them upside down to leaf through pages; took drawers from sideboards, looking beneath them; and upturned the furniture.

Ramsay stood with his arms locked behind him, completely still in the midst of the chaos, his eyes never leaving her. "Civilized," he scoffed. "Nothing about ye belongs in a civilized society."

"Upon that, we must disagree." It was perhaps the most argumentative statement she'd ever made in her life, but the circumstances of the day had frayed her nerves to the snapping point. "As most of civilized society seems to spend their leisure time here."

His glare was so full of enmity, Cecelia couldn't bring herself to look at him any longer. How strange, that a man possessed of such a savage countenance could accuse *her* of being uncouth.

To cover her cowardice, she reached for the warrant, swallowed a lump of trepidation, and began to read.

"Hortense Thistledown," he said, echoing her pseudonym, thus calling her attention before she'd gotten through the first line. "Ye are related to Henrietta, then? I was unaware she had family. Hid you away in France, did she?"

Smythe had been their family name. Thistledown must have been another of Henrietta's facades, much like the wigs and masks and makeup.

Cecelia wasn't ready to answer the question, and so she didn't. She searched through the legal documents until reaching the appropriate charge.

According to the warrant, the police were searching her property for evidence in connection with the disappearance of a young girl named Katerina Milovic. A Russian immigrant who'd been taken from the streets of Lambeth just yesterday. She was the sixth in a string of missing maidens. All aged about thirteen.

"How did ye come to be in charge after Henrietta's death?" Ramsay demanded. "I've not seen ye on the premises before. I always assumed Miss Leveaux would take up the mantle of the Scarlet Lady once Henrietta—"

Cecelia held up one finger as she scanned the rest of the warrant, her eyes snagging on the distressing pertinent information. The Writ of Warrant suggested the proprietress of Miss Henrietta's School for Cultured Young Ladies was suspected of nabbing the children and selling their innocence to clients for incredible sums of money, which put her under the suspicion as an accessory to rape, kidnapping, and possibly murder.

Lord Ramsay was only silent long enough to recover from his indignation. "Ye're brave, madam, to presume to hush me."

Cecelia's hands trembled now with more outrage than fear. She tapped the paper with the extended finger she'd used to halt him. "It states here I am suspected of being a bawd. Of kidnapping young girls and selling their . . . their . . ." The word was heavy on her tongue, salacious and never uttered in mixed company, certainly not with a young girl cowering in her skirts. "Their *virginity*." She leaned in to offer an aghast whisper. "To someone who would dispose of them after."

"Doona play the innocent," he spat, the intent of his emphasis clear. "Every titled or wealthy man in the city knows what's for sale at this so-called school."

She chose her words carefully. "I wonder, my lord, what cause you have to suspect that these girls are connected to my aunt. Even if, for the sake of argument, I admitted to marketing . . . pleasure, which I categorically do not. It is a mighty leap to accuse Henrietta or I of something of this magnitude without substantial evidence."

"I have an informer," he stated.

Genny leapt forward, unable to contain herself any longer. "Like hell you do, you lying swine. We help girls who come to us, we don't prostitute them—"

A constable seized Genny, pinning her arms behind her in an effort to grapple her toward the door.

Cecelia held up a hand, chewing her lip as she puzzled. The unpleasant metallic tinge of rouge set an unbidden grimace on her face. "If what you say about an informer is true, wouldn't the witness be mentioned in the warrant?"

"I didna say witness," he clipped, his arms crossing over his impressive chest in a defensive gesture.

"So, you signed this warrant on the grounds of hearsay, then?"

"I signed that warrant because those little girls need to be found!" His fist connected with the desk, and Cecelia felt Phoebe stiffen with shock against her calf.

She assessed Ramsay, his menacing posture, his flaring nostrils, the lips he curled back to show sharp incisors.

Not a wolf, she thought. A lion. The Nemean lion, perhaps, his thick golden hide impervious to weapons and claws sharper than blades.

It would take a herculean act to vanquish him, of this Cecelia was certain.

And God help her, but she was in the lion's mouth now.

With a deep breath, she drew herself up in her chair and leaned casually against the plush velvet, hoping to diffuse the tension with her ease.

"I'll be frank with you, my lord, I did not know Henrietta well, and I cannot be certain of all her sins, but I can promise you this. Whilst I am the owner and . . . proprietor of this institution, you will never have cause to suspect me of doing something so insidious to a woman or a child. Furthermore, I will use whatever means at my disposal to assist you in finding Katerina Milovic and any other missing girl." She cast a glance at Genny, whose self-containment seemed at the end of a short tether.

Cecelia hated that she couldn't be *certain* her aunt, the woman responsible for her fortune, might also be a monster. She hoped to God it wasn't true. That Lord Ramsay's suspicions were misplaced.

Ramsay leaned in further. "And I'm supposed to take a woman like ye at her word, am I?"

"My word is all I have until time can prove that you might trust me."

"*Trust* ye?" he scoffed, pushing off the desk as if he needed distance from her odious presence. "I think ye are a wolf in sheep's clothing, Miss Thistledown."

"Better that than a sheep in wolf's clothing," she bit back. "You politicians, forever bleating and being led about by the herd, snarling as though you had teeth with which to bite."

The vein in his forehead pulsed as his skin mottled, taking on a deep-purple hue. "How dare ye—"

"How dare *I*?" she echoed. "I've enjoyed Emmental cheeses with fewer holes than the so-called evidence notated in this warrant." She folded up the document and tossed it to his side of the desk. "Furthermore, one must ask oneself what a justice of Her Majesty's High Court is doing down from his lofty bench, kicking in doors with common footpads, and terrorizing the respectable young ladies of my school in the middle of the afternoon. This stinks to me of a political move by a man with hopes of being the next Lord Chancellor. And I refuse to be fodder for your aspirations."

He stalked around the desk, and Cecilia fought a flush of panic.

"The nonexistent respectability of yer employees notwithstanding"—he stabbed a finger at the wall separating the residence from the school—"I am going to make ye the same promise I made yer gutter-harpy of a predecessor." He towered over her, and it took every fiber of self-containment Cecilia possessed not to jump away and flee.

She remained seated, staring straight ahead, not looking up for fear that was ceding some kind of power.

And also, that her wig might slip off.

His next words pierced through her with all the strength of a Spartan's lance.

"When a child goes missing in this city, I'll kick in every door of every establishment like this one until I find the culprit, starting with yers." Ramsay placed one hand on her desk and the other on the back of her chair. He leaned down, bringing his lips terrifyingly close to her ear.

"And know this, I'll hang anyone who was responsible for captivity. For degradation. And for possible murder." His breath was hot against her ear and neck, sending little thrills of exquisite terror down her spine. The sweet scent of it mixed with the starch of his jacket, the cedar-fresh aroma of linen, and something darker, muskier, plied her senses and muddled her wits until his next sentence.

"I care *not* if rope is wrapped around a bearded throat or one that's . . . elegant and lily white. It all stretches the same."

Cecelia fought the urge to bring her hand to her throat, fearing any reaction might make her appear guilty.

He straightened. "Surrender the ledgers and accounts with the names of yer clients."

"I do not know the whereabouts of such ledgers," Cecelia claimed honestly before crying, "Just what do you think you are doing?"

He wrenched open the drawers of her desk and began to rifle through the contents. "I have the authority to search everywhere. So ye stay right where ye are and keep yer hands on the desk."

Cecelia complied as beads of sweat trickled between

her breasts and from her hairline. There were too many factors—the heat of the stifling cape, the relentless summer sun, the child at her feet she'd been tasked to protect, and the fear that he might find what he was looking for. She didn't truly know Henrietta, after all. Not enough.

And yet she wanted to hope.

"There is a compartment hidden here." He groped beneath the drawer to her left, and his features tightened victoriously as he found the dial. "What is the combination?"

"*Aeneid*," she whispered.

He stared at her, unblinking, his features carefully blank before he moved the dials and discovered the now-empty secret compartment.

"What was here?" he demanded.

"Something Henrietta hid before I arrived," she answered honestly.

Cecelia was a breath away from a conniption when Sir Ramsay slid her chair back to open the thin desk drawer directly in front of her.

She didn't know which shocked her the most—that he could move her occupied chair with the strength of one arm, or her fleeting, absurd urge to test the texture of his gold locks as he bent to investigate the contents of the drawer.

When he found only a collection of writing implements, stationery, and a magnifying glass in the thin drawer, Cecelia deflated her lungs in relief.

"Nothing of note here, my lord," reported a constable. "Nor in the private bedrooms, either. Unless you want to confiscate items such as this." He brandished a book.

Cecelia squinted but could not make out the title from across the room without her spectacles.

"Bring it here." Ramsay reached for it, and the constable

deposited it readily. Upon opening it, he made a disgusted sound and dropped it as though it had burned him.

Cecelia suppressed a giggle, lodging it firmly in her throat. The book landed open to an erotic depiction. A man stood erect in all possible ways, and a woman knelt before him, his shaft disappearing into her willing, open mouth. Beneath the photo, a lewd and detailed list gave instructions for fornicating thusly.

Despite everything, Cecelia scanned the directives with great interest.

"What is the meaning of this?" Ramsay roared at the constable. "Do ye think now is the time for juvenile antics?"

"N-no, my lord!" the constable sputtered as a few of his cohorts did their best to hide their own mirth. "I thought . . . I just . . . What would books like that be doing here if Miss Thistledown is running a school as she claimed? Seems like a book a bawd would own."

The question seemed to mollify Ramsay, though he cast a suspicious look at the pale constable before addressing Cecelia. "He raises a pertinent question. Does filth like this belong in a school for *cultured* young ladies?"

Cecelia fought the urge to slam the book shut. Instead, she leafed the page to the side, uncovering picture after picture of erotic acts, not all of them only including two people. She could barely bring herself to look.

She couldn't bring herself to look away.

"This premises is not technically the school, sir." She cleared a sudden husky note from her voice. "This is my private study. And these books are for my own . . . personal use."

A collection of shuffling feet and throat clearing suggested her ploy had the desired effect.

"Now." She carefully closed the book, splaying her hands on the intricate cover. "Are you quite finished with your search?"

He glared down at her. "Nay, my men are still combing every inch of yer business. The search might take all day. Or all night. After that, we'll post guards at yer door just to make certain Katerina Milovic doesna show. Ye'll lose a great deal of income then, will ye not?"

At the moment, lost revenue was the least of her concerns. "Do what you must, sir. You'll find no one by that name here."

"Because ye've sold her already, perhaps?" Ramsay baited. "Or she's being held somewhere else?"

Cecelia lifted her chin two haughty notches. "I won't dignify that ridiculous notion with a response."

Mostly because she had no idea. However, if she discovered evidence of any such goings-on, she'd turn herself in and face the consequences owed her aunt. It was the least she could do.

"Tell me, Miss Thistledown . . ." He stepped from behind her, seemingly unable to stand her proximity a moment longer. "Where were ye off to?"

"Off to?" she echoed, confused.

His gazed dipped below her neck, increasing in intensity until she actually feared he could see through the layers of her clothing. "Ye've a cloak on. Either ye were leaving, or yer hiding something. Is it yer person that needs searching?"

A note in his voice produced an extra thump from her heart.

"Your warrant does not suggest that you may put your hands upon my person." She could not help but stare at his hands, now fisted at his sides. They resembled hammers, square and large and inelegant. The skin stretched over knuckles interrupted by old scars. Evidence of past violence, perhaps? "B-besides," she managed. "It is ungentlemanly to remark upon a lady's attire."

He snorted. "Ye are no lady."

"Granted, but what, pray, would happen to me were I to burst into *your* courtroom and demand to know what you're hiding beneath your robes and white wig? I'd probably be hanged or publicly flogged or some such hideous thing."

He swiped at the air, drawing an invisible line between them. "Don't ye dare compare your vocation to mine."

"I wouldn't dream of comparing our vocations, my lord. Mine is much more honest, more ancient, and historically the most vital to any empire."

"Outrageous!"

"How so?"

He paused, a victorious gleam creeping into his vitriolic glare. "Are ye admitting, Hortense, that ye are a bawd?"

"My dear Justice, I was referring to the education of young ladies, obviously. Every great empire thrived considerably better when they began educating their females." She injected a matching victory into her smile. "Now kindly take your leave so I may continue my work. And I'd request that the next time you take it into your mind to call, you do so on more friendly terms." She gestured to the door as if the room didn't appear as though Typhoon, himself, had visited, leaving nothing but disarray.

He whirled, stepping over the carcasses of her upended furniture as he stormed to the door. He held it open as constables filed from the room, some of them with rather sheepish looks on their faces. Others with disappointed expressions.

Cecelia didn't give in to the urge to celebrate that

victory. She'd made no friends today. Not by making fools of the police and one of the most powerful men in the realm.

Ramsay paused before he took his leave, his chin touching his shoulder. "The next time I come back, it will be with shackles and chains."

He slammed the door behind him hard enough to shake the entire house.

"I'll be goddamned," Genny marveled, her eyes sparkling. "You were magnificent!"

"I was?" A trembling overtook her, threatening to shake the wig loose from her head.

"Lord, I took you for a bluestocking, but I never knew you had that kind of poise and sass in you. And the accent? Where'd that come from?"

Cecelia could only shrug. "My butler is French." She pushed back from the desk, moving to the window to watch Sir Ramsay stalk to an imposing, somber carriage, tucking himself inside with grace rarely observed in a man of such heft.

"Genny." She said the woman's name with unmistakable gravitas. "Genny, *please* tell me they won't find anything. If you're honest, I vow to keep you safe, to absolve you of any punitive actions. I'll pay you most handsomely, but I *must* know if Henrietta was a bawd, or if anyone has ever been kept here against their will. I must make reparations if Henrietta's committed such heinous crimes—"

"Hush, honey." Genny was at her side in an instant, taking Cecelia's hands in hers to turn them face-to-face. "Look into my eyes so you know the truth. The women who work here dress provocatively and, like Lilly, they occasionally take lovers and we look the other way. That's the whole of it. We—*you*—do not sell sex, and certainly not children."

Cecelia searched Genny's earnest features for a lie, but

was only reminded of the woman's kindness and unabashed affection. Her savior. Her friend.

When she nodded, Genny squeezed her hands, bringing them to her mouth to press a fond kiss to her knuckles, like she was a beloved sister.

Genny released her to reach for the wig, removing it.

Cecelia expressed a sigh of relief to be rid of the heavy thing, and she divested herself of the cloak as Genny poured a pitcher of water into a bowl and wet a cloth.

Bending down, Cecelia peeked under the desk where little Phoebe still huddled.

"You can come out now, darling," she soothed. "The men are gone."

The girl peered out at her from the shadow under the desk, her features a bit blurry as Genny hadn't yet returned Cecelia's spectacles. Phoebe tugged on a crisp white pinafore tied over a somber black mourning dress. "If it's all the same to you, miss, I'd prefer to stay, but here is your book. We didn't let him find it, did we?"

"Indeed, we did not." Cecelia took the book from her, puzzling over the girl. This was no sort of place for a child, what with a gambling hell next door and cruel lawmen kicking the doors in. What could Henrietta have been thinking? "Are you not lonely under there? Would you not like to come out so we may be properly introduced?"

The girl shook her head. "I have my dearest friends, Frances Bacon and Fanny de Beaufort." She held up two plush dolls, one with golden curls, and another with red. "They are excellent company, but they only like to talk to me, Miss Henrietta said so. I might like to come out, but *they're* not ready to meet you yet."

Cecelia understood. "How fortunate you all are to have found each other," she said, unwittingly adopting the over-bright cheer she'd always despised people for addressing children with.

Phoebe peeked at her shyly. "Do you have anyone like Frances and Fanny?"

"I do, indeed," Cecelia explained with the requisite warmth that accompanied thoughts of the Red Rogues. "My two dearest friends are Francesca Cavendish, the Countess of Mont Claire, and Alexandra Atherton, the Duchess of Redmayne. We met at school and formed a club for girls with red hair called the Red Rogues. They are also most excellent company, and often wary of strangers like Fanny and Frances are. But they'll love you instantly, and I think you shall like them a great deal."

A sharp pang of agony pierced the softness she intrinsically felt for the girl. To alleviate the boredom and isolation of her childhood, the same imagination that had conjured monsters in her nightmares could also summon friends from the motes of dust in the cellar she'd been locked in or from shadows on a moonlit night.

She'd willed them into existence like a God, creating full and vivid characters with which to laugh and dream and converse.

They'd provided most excellent company. They'd kept her safe from the ghosts she heard in the wind, or the demons the Vicar Teague had convinced her were encircling her endlessly, awaiting the right moment of weakness in which to drag her soul to hell.

Or worse, possess her body.

She might have gone mad without these imaginary friends. She might have given over to the dark.

Still, there was nothing like true human companionship.

Phoebe studied her silently for a moment, and then scooted her friends deeper into the recesses of the desk.

"If you'd like to get Francesca and Alexandra, I can keep them safe under here."

Cecelia's heart became a puddle of tenderness. The sweet child thought her friends were dolls.

It struck Cecelia with dizzying gravity that she was this girl's custodian now. The closest thing she had to a mother. The responsibility weighed heavier on her shoulders than did the entire ordeal with Ramsay.

She'd never had real parents of any kind, the closest paternal relationship being that of Jean-Yves. And if she really inspected it, the Frenchman had no real duty to her beyond that of a beloved employee. She loved him like a father, truly, but she also paid his wages and sent him on errands. He was both confidant and occasional adviser, but he'd never exhibited any kind of authoritarian tendencies.

Mostly he just went along with whatever new schemes she and her Red Rogues hatched with a very Gallic sort of bemused acceptance. So long as he had his wine, his pipe, and his papers, he was a generally easygoing sort of fellow. His affection was gruff but his disposition always warm and open. He'd befriended her when she was little older than Phoebe, and without his guidance, she'd have been completely alone.

Fervently wishing for that guidance now, Cecelia tried one last time to cajole the girl out. "Francesca and Alexandra wouldn't fit under there, I'm afraid. They're rea—" She caught herself, understanding that Phoebe's dolls were as real to her as Alexandra and Frank actually were. "They're grown, like me, and have homes of their own. I'm going to a party tonight at a duke's manor to see them. Would you like to put on a pretty dress and come along?"

"But *he's* coming back." Phoebe shook her head, shrinking away. "He's bringing chains and shackles, he said so."

"Lord Ramsay won't be back today, darling," she soothed.

"How do you know?"

At that, she paused. She really didn't.

A tide of uncharacteristic anger rose in Cecelia against Lord Ramsay. She realized he'd some history with Henrietta, but as far as he was concerned, he'd never been introduced to Hortense, and he still treated her as if she were rubbish he desired to discard into the Thames.

And to think, her best friend was married to his half brother. Lord Ramsay and the Duke of Redmayne were as different from each other as inverse numbers on a grid. Ramsay, of course, being the negative integer.

Lesser than.

Except in stature, because by her estimation Ramsay outweighed the duke by a half stone and was slightly taller. And also in appearance, but only because Redmayne had been disfigured by a jaguar. *Not* because she found the rather brutal planes of his face arresting.

She supposed Ramsay might have the upper hand auditorily, as well. Where Redmayne's voice was as smooth as silk sliding over velvet, Ramsay's had a sonorous commanding depth, graveled and grisly. Much like the stones shaped to make a cathedral. Rough to the touch but contained. Orderly.

Echoing with no small bit of judgment.

Genny bent to hand Cecelia the wet cloth and pointed to a door to the adjoining room before offering Phoebe an indulgent smile.

Cecelia took the cloth gratefully. "You stay there for a while longer, Phoebe, and look after your friends," she said. "I'll come check on you in a moment."

Phoebe nodded.

Rising, she accompanied Genny through an upturned

bedchamber to a washroom, where she grimaced at her reflection in the gilded mirror.

She wouldn't have come out from under the desk, either. The wig had ruined her hair, and without it and the mask, Cecelia's makeup appeared clownish and overblown. Applying the washcloth to her face, she scrubbed away at it, revealing her familiar features with relief.

"You'll have to excuse Phoebe, honey, she's a shy little thing," Genny explained. "Henrietta cared for her like she was her own, spoiled her like nothing I've seen, but rarely let her out of this house."

"Do you know who Phoebe's father is?" Cecelia queried, plucking the pins from her hair to shake it down.

"Another secret Henrietta took to her grave. Maybe it's in that book there." She motioned to the coded diary Cecelia had set on the counter.

"Perhaps." Cecelia accepted the brush Genny handed over and tamed her mane as best she could, expertly knotting it and stabbing with pins to keep it in place. It would have to do for now. "Do you think he has anything to do with why Henrietta was killed?"

"Ramsay? Or the father?"

"Either." Cecelia huffed out an anxious breath. "Both?"

"He might, at that," Genny frowned, rubbing her forehead, her eyes glimmering with grief. "This establishment has long been a playground for the rich and the powerful. There are more transactions made here than poker and roulette. Business, trade, politics, and sometimes a criminal enterprise or two are struck at our tables. Fortunes won and lost. And perhaps lives bought and sold. None of us are safe until this puzzle Henrietta left for you is solved. If we can't figure out who our enemy is, we won't see them coming."

"Well . . ." Cecelia stuck the final pin in her hair and

accepted her spectacles from Genny, grateful for the world to be in focus once more. "We certainly know one of our enemies, and next time he comes at us, we won't be caught unaware."

"We most certainly will not," Genny said vehemently.

"I want to find these missing girls." Cecelia worried at her lip. "We need to help."

"Oh honey," Genny took her arm firmly. "You have to forget Katerina Milovic. It's a tragedy, terrible to be sure, but that little girl is long gone. Young ones like her disappear all the time, taken by men with unthinkable desires. If they're found, it's usually their corpses, or worse, the shells of what is left of them after these men steal their souls. There isn't anything we can do but protect our own."

Helpless tears pricked Cecelia's eyes. "That can't be. There must be something that can be done." She plucked up the book of codes and slipped it into the pocket of her skirts. First she'd hire more staff to put the residence and the business to rights, then she'd coax Phoebe out from beneath the desk by promising to take her to her flat in Chelsea, where men with chains would never find her.

Once the girl was safely in the care of Jean-Yves, Cecelia would be about her business.

In order to succeed in her endeavors, she would need to acquire a great deal more information about Sir Cassius Gerard Ramsay, as he seemed determined to bar her at every turn.

Luckily, she was invited to dinner at his sister-in-law's house this very evening.

Which would be the perfect time to learn his weakness.

CHAPTER FOUR

Ramsay cursed his traitorous body to the outer reaches of hell and back as he let his head fall back against the carriage cushion.

That damnable book, the one with the depictions of every imaginable form of intercourse, had brought his cock to attention. *Not* the woman to whom it belonged. She had nothing to do with it.

He *did not* desire the Scarlet Lady.

He was a man. A Scotsman, no less. And the renderings of fornication woke within his body pulsating temptations to which he'd vowed never again to succumb. Memories of positions he'd preferred, longings for depravities he'd not yet tasted, and also for those he'd denied himself for so long.

Hortense Thistledown had casually turned the pages of said text, running her silk gloves over the pictures as though discovering them for the first time. Her manner had been cavalier, but her rouged lips parted as though the depictions of iniquity astonished her.

Or perhaps they'd a similar effect upon her as himself. Perhaps she'd experienced a rush of desire.

He wished he could see what she hid under the mask, the wig, and the frippery. Was her skin truly pale under the white powder? What color was her hair? Was her figure as voluptuous as he'd imagined beneath the shapeless crimson cloak, or had she padded it for effect?

Even though Ramsay detested her ilk, the photos in the book had elicited unbidden thoughts. Had invaded his mind, threatening to rob him of his moral high ground.

Did the Scarlet Lady take famous, wealthy lovers as her predecessor had?

His fingers gripped the cushions of the carriage bench as he rejected the question slithering through his thoughts like a serpent in Eden.

He shouldn't wonder such things. He shouldn't want. Crave. Ache.

He must forget those lips. He must not imagine them wrapped around his cock, leaving rings of rouge and silken moisture behind.

His breath hitched as his body hardened further.

Nay, her mouth was, no doubt, too practiced to tempt him. A woman in her profession learned well and early the yearning of a man for such an act. In fact, she was arranged with artifice to fuck a man's wits right out of his head.

Her scent, for example, not a French floral or an expensive musk, only a sweet vanilla with a tinge of something spiced. One meant to rouse several physical hungers at once.

Her makeup, the crimson color of sin, applied to articulate that talented mouth.

Her wit had made her all the more desirable. A sense of enjoyment hummed beneath his rage, plucked by their

repartee. Her challenge had made him feel . . . awake.
Alive.

She's a viper, he reminded himself. A woman who'd
possibly sold her soul to the devil, along with the innocence of young girls.

The prompt was enough to douse his desire.

He could not allow himself to become beguiled. Not
like so many of the men with whom he operated.

Titled lords and wealthy judges, magistrates, and politicians were so often led about by their cocks just as easily as their purse strings.

Crafty old Henrietta Thistledown had held many of
those purse strings in her own hand.

She'd chosen her successor wisely; he'd give her that.
Hortense was a force to be reckoned with in her own
right.

The death of Henrietta had seemed the perfect time to
strike against the gambling hell. The old woman had always been so deucedly careful. Every time he thought
he'd had her dead to rights, she seemed to reach out and
pluck the strings of one of her powerful puppets, and yet
again she'd be pulled out of the mire. It was as though the
entire *haute ton* owed her favors.

For Christ's sake, he'd taken down Afghani warlords
and Barbary pirates in Algiers more easily than Henrietta, and he had to admit to some relief upon the news of
her death.

The head of the snake had been severed, which he'd
hoped meant fewer girls would disappear from his city.

When he'd garnered news of poor Katerina Milovic
after Henrietta's death, though, he knew he had to act.
Because the kidnappings did not stop once she was in the
ground.

He'd swarmed the establishment today, a Friday

afternoon, when the working wealthy in the emerging merchant class struck out early in search of a good time at the sides of the idle rich.

They must have known he was coming, because there wasn't a card sharp in sight and the place had been devoid of customers.

And then there had been belowstairs, which oddly enough resembled an actual school.

A stern butler named Winston had followed Ramsay and his constables around the bottom floor, insisting he leave the belowstairs tenants alone. These women had not all been glittering butterflies who ran the tables and the dice. Many of them had the hollowed eyes of refugees; some of them didn't even speak English.

But he'd no grounds upon which to exert his authority, because no one had been involved in illegal activity at the time of his arrival.

They'd been in class. Their papers in order.

But who did they think they were fooling?

When the carriage halted, Ramsay hesitated to disembark. He buttoned his long jacket over his chest and hips, waiting for his arousal to cool.

Why her? he wondered. Why now? After so many years of keeping his appetites leashed in chains of iron, why did his body seem to strain against them? For a soulless she-devil, no less?

Her and one other. Cecelia Teague.

It'd been three months since he'd last seen her, and the comely woman still often permeated his thoughts.

When he was on the bench, he'd remember her mouth sucking softly on her finger, dragging her teeth across the pad to scrape the last vestiges of chocolate. Once at a debate in the House of Lords, when men bandied insults and screamed over one another, he'd longed for someone with her gentle wisdom. If only these angry, volatile men could make a study of her respectful reprobation.

Aye, he summoned Miss Teague to his mind entirely too often. Christ, he hardly knew the woman. And she was certainly no fit companion for a Lord Chief Justice. University-educated? Opinionated and independent. While she was agreeable, she was by no means demure. And she made no qualms about her indulgences. For all he knew she could be an alcoholic or a fiend for any number of vices.

Her cherubic features could hide a deviant.

His mother had certainly carried an air of innocence about her, and she'd lived her life in such a way that she'd given the whore of Babylon a run for her money.

Or perhaps the Scarlet Lady.

Hell, they might have been friends, Gwendolyn Atherton and Henrietta Thistledown.

And then there had been Matilda. The last woman he'd been tempted to trust. Ramsay pinched the bridge of his nose as a headache bloomed behind his eyelids. What a disaster that had been.

Still . . . Cecelia had none of the mischief or deviousness that had sparkled in the eyes of his mother. Nor had she any of the courtly manners and skill at artifice Matilda had displayed.

She was so unabashedly charming. So smooth and soft and lovely.

Perhaps . . .

"My lord Ramsay?"

He started and looked to his left at the footman waiting uneasily holding the carriage door ajar.

"We're here, my lord. And the Lord Chancellor is awaiting you in his study."

"Aye," he said curtly, pushing all thoughts of the

troubling Miss Teague out of his mind as he disembarked the coach. Ramsay mounted the steps two at a time, eager to establish a plan of action against their new adversary.

The Scarlet Lady could not be a hydra, sprouting two heads for every one that was severed. Eventually she would be vanquished, and he needed to be the man to do it if he wanted to secure the appointment to the next chancellorship.

Christ, perhaps the current Lord Chancellor had been right to suggest Ramsay should seriously consider getting a wife. Some respectable duty-bound woman with whom to beget a brood and to further shore up his respectability.

His gut twisted at the idea, rejecting it as violently as he would a toxin.

He'd never meant to marry. And yet he couldn't bring himself to have another mistress, not after last time.

And so he'd do what he'd always done. Work his mind to exhaustion, and then when that work was finished, he'd punish his body with exertion until he was too fatigued to stand.

As he mounted the stairs to the very top, something told Ramsay that even when he collapsed into his bed after this punishing day, a pair of crimson lips would haunt his dreams.

CHAPTER FIVE

"I cannot believe you invited *him* to dinner!" Cecelia's whisper would have been a scream were her throat less constricted by panic.

She'd been in the middle of catching up the Red Rogues on the harrowing events of the day when the butler announced Lord Ramsay's arrival. She'd yanked both the Rogues into Alexandra's private parlor at the Redmayne Belgravia terrace just in time to slam the door as Ramsay's wide shoulders rounded the corner.

Even the soft sages and calming earth tones of the sophisticated solarium had little effect on her as she held Alexandra in her clutches. Her fingers curled like talons on her friend's puffed sleeves as her trembles shook them both.

"Cecil, what's gotten into you? I've never seen you like this!" Alexandra regarded her with a horrified astonishment one would save for someone who'd suddenly begun to leak blood from her eyes.

Francesca stood vigil by the door, cracking it open

slightly to spy upon the men gathering in the great hall. "Have you forgotten the part where your brutish brother-in-law is endeavoring to hang poor Cecil in the public square? I imagine that has something to do with her current overwrought state."

Alexandra gently attempted to pry Cecelia's fingers from the meat of her arms. "Well . . . in my defense, I posted this dinner invitation weeks ago."

"You could have warned me he would be here!" Cecelia released the Duchess of Redmayne, putting her hand to her own forehead, then to her cheeks, not finding the fever she was certain to fall plague to at any moment.

"Until five minutes ago, I wasn't aware of the need," Alexandra reasoned. "As you said, he *is* my brother-in-law. Besides, it might have raised his suspicions were I to retract the invitation . . . don't you think?"

"I'm too distraught to think." Cecelia wrapped her arms around her own middle as she whirled to pace the room. She realized she was being hysterical, but the day's events had rattled her composure so greatly, she'd been aching for the safety of the Rogues' company. She'd used up her allotment of composure for the day, and she'd been relying on their collective wisdom and encouragement, expecting to take the evening to discuss her rather pressing problem and to make some decisions.

Now, it seemed, the wolf was at the door once again, and if he discovered her real identity, there was no telling what he would do.

"What are they doing out there?" Cecelia asked Francesca anxiously.

"Oh, the usual sort of masculine greeting rituals," Francesca scoffed, her scarlet skirts nearly catching in the door as she closed it behind her. "Shaking hands, slapping backs, and comparing the standards and pedigrees of their horseflesh, no doubt." She tossed her carefully arranged crimson ringlets in the fashion of one more used to a stable than a salon. "I've a mind to join them."

"We should, I suppose," Alexandra urged. She straightened the cameo on her high-necked gown of shimmering peach silk, which contrasted most strikingly with her neat auburn hair and warm chocolate eyes.

"I cannot face him," Cecelia squeaked, her knees giving out. She collapsed onto a velvet chair in a puddle of overwrought curves and shimmering sky-blue skirts. "If he recognizes me, you might as well start weaving my noose."

Alexandra placed a hand on her shoulder. "Perhaps it's better that you see him first here at Redmayne Place. If he does recognize you, you'll have all of us to protect you." She stepped to the cabinet, removing a crystal decanter, three glasses, and a bottle of their most potent Ravencroft scotch. Once it was poured, Alexandra took a seat at Cecelia's side and offered a glass.

"I don't even think Redmayne *can* protect me from his elder brother," she said glumly.

"He would if I asked him." Alexandra's lips twisted wryly. "But perhaps we should think of how else we might extract you from your predicament."

"Let's," Francesca agreed, pushing the chocolates toward Cecelia. "First have a few of these. They go splendidly with scotch and will help you think."

Cecelia plucked one from the dish and sank her teeth into the decadent truffle, allowing it to melt into her mouth and spill a blissful velvet sweetness over her tongue. "I love you," she sighed, trying not to think of the night she'd consumed the same truffles in front of Ramsay.

"I love you, too, darling."

"I was speaking to the chocolate."

Francesca's balled-up glove hit her in the shoulder, evoking a much-needed laugh.

Gratitude suffused her as she observed her friends. The fiercest and most fantastic relationships she'd cultivated over the years. They were her family, and she did, indeed, love them dearly.

Francesca had become Frank, the vibrant-hued, fearless outdoorswoman with a lithe, boyish figure set apart by pert, elven features and emerald-green eyes.

Alexandra was Alexander or Alex, the studious idealist with a rebellious streak and more excellent ideas than she had freckles, which were numerous. With a bounty of mahogany hair and a perfect formula of physical proportions, she was the beauty of their roguish threesome.

Cecelia, or Cecil, was their treasurer, their confidante, and their mediator, good with . . . good with numbers and hopeless at just about everything else.

This was the company in which she felt the most secure.

Alexandra refilled Cecelia's drink before she'd even realized she'd emptied the first glass. "I'd very much like to meet your new ward—Phoebe, is it?"

"And I'd like to see this School for Cultured Young Ladies," Francesca added. "I wonder, what do you plan to do with it?"

"Therein lies the question." Cecelia stared into her glass as though the answers could be etched into the crystal beneath the whiskey. "I'll look after the child, of course. She deserves a safe home, and stability, and all the affection and education I can provide. I need to find out who her father is, if only to protect her from him." She took another sip. "The . . . business, though. I haven't a clue what to do with it yet."

"You could sell for a tidy sum, I imagine," Alexandra suggested.

"I could, but there's Henrietta's murder to consider. I know I wasn't acquainted with her, but she was family, and she did so much for me whilst asking nothing more than a letter in return. I feel a responsibility to at least make certain her memory is done some justice, and her killer found."

"Her secrets could get you killed, as well, Cecil," Francesca said ominously. "I'm not certain it's all worth it, are you?"

Cecelia pondered that for long enough to realize there was no simple conclusion.

"Could the secret have something to do with Phoebe?" the Duchess of Redmayne finally inquired. "Or perhaps these missing young girls Lord Ramsay has accused Henrietta and you—er, the Scarlet Lady—of procuring?"

"Could be both," Cecelia sighed. "Or one of the other. I know she was afraid of an organization called the Crimson Council. Have you heard of it?"

Francesca stiffened but said nothing.

Her interest piqued, Cecelia asked, "Do you know something about them, Frank?"

"The Crimson Council strikes a chord in my memory . . ." Francesca trailed off, a dark mask of unease settling across her features. ". . . from long ago."

"Long ago as in . . . when your family was massacred?" Alexandra sank down next to Francesca and propped her chin into her palm, resting her elbow on her knee. It was the posture of a student, not a duchess. She'd certainly been one longer than the other. "Frank, is it possible that if the Crimson Council has something to do with organized crime in London, it could be connected to the deaths of the entire Cavendish household, your household, *and* also Cecelia's infamous aunt?"

Francesca shook her head, but Cecelia had seen just that gesture enough times to realize it was not in denial, but in distress. "It's entirely possible. Which means, Cecil, that you could be in greater danger from them than Lord Ramsay could ever pose."

Cecelia downed the rest of her drink, trying to reason through her panic.

"Perhaps it *is* best Piers talk to his brother," Alexandra suggested. "Convince Ramsay you're both on the same side before the truth comes out."

Cecelia shook her head, a frigid chill sliding down her spine at the memory of their interaction. "You didn't see him today, Alex. He so much as said he'd like to see my neck stretched on the gallows. And that was before I . . . I antagonized him."

"You?" Alexandra gaped. "Antagonize?"

"*You?*" Francesca echoed. "The same Cecelia Teague who drafted a peace treaty the one time Alex and I quarreled in school?"

"I don't know what got into me today." Cecelia marveled at her own actions. "He was so disdainful and condescending. Even cruel in his self-righteousness, and I couldn't help but rise to the occasion. Though I suppose I don't blame him of being ill mannered if he suspected me of hurting children."

Alexandra's lips twisted into a grimace of regret. "Those are traits of Ramsay's that do not always ingratiate him to Redmayne. They've a complicated relationship as brothers, though it seems to have improved since our marriage. My husband has mentioned that Lord Ramsay's upbringing was even more . . . difficult than his own. In fact, I gather that Piers rather pities his brother, though I've never inquired as to why." She chewed on her lip as she thought.

"I don't know that Ramsay should discover you just now, Cecelia, until I'm able to discuss the matter with my husband. I can't say how the Lord Chief Justice would react if he recognized you. He is quite . . . stalwart in his principles."

"Stubborn and inflexible, you mean," Francesca supplied.

"Also that."

"What we need is more time and more information," Francesca declared. "I say we go to Miss Henrietta's School for Cultured Young Ladies tomorrow and do a bit of snooping around. Perhaps interrogate your new employees."

"*You* just want to see a gentleman's gambling hell." Alexandra nudged Francesca with a playful elbow.

"I'll not deny it," Francesca admitted with a sideways smirk. "But we can use the opportunity to figure out a little bit more about what might have happened to Henrietta and what sort of dangerous liaisons she'd made. It's most important, I think, that you do what you can to decipher that codex right away. If there's anything about the Crimson Council, it's likely in there."

"I was thinking the self-same thing," Cecelia agreed, picturing the disconcerting book she'd locked in her safe.

"I'll make your excuses to the dinner party," Alexandra offered. "We'll say you're beset by a headache and had to retire, and then we'll all go out to the school tomorrow morning and see what we can learn."

"A capital plan." Cecelia drained the last of her scotch, feeling immediately better now that she didn't have to face her situation alone. "I can't thank you two enough."

"What ho, wife?" Piers Gedrick Atherton, the Duke of Redmayne, strode through the parlor door, his scarred features made less disconcerting by a close-cropped raven beard and the tender smile softening his hard mouth.

Alexandra beamed at her husband as though the three vicious slashes across the left side of his face didn't exist.

Cecelia thought it a miracle that the duchess, who'd once been tortured by the mere touch of a man, now found herself happily married to the Terror of Torcliff. A duke as large, menacing, and dark as the devil.

It was likewise as strange to see such a primal beast as Redmayne treat his wife with a gentility bordering on worship.

"Forgive the early intrusion," Redmayne said, addressing them all. "We are dowdy old men who are much too serious and yearn to be part of your jollity." He moved with the loose-limbed grace of the exotic predators he famously hunted before his life-altering encounter with a jaguar had lent him a new respect for the wild.

"You are the opposite of a dowdy old man and well you know it." Alexandra rolled her eyes at her husband. He was a man in his prime, barely past five and thirty. Strong and fit and much too feral for a duke.

Upon reaching the arm of Alexandra's chaise, Redmayne bent his dark head to place a kiss on her temple. His lips lingered there longer than was strictly proper in mixed company, as if he couldn't help himself from savoring the scent of her hair.

Cecelia watched them with a certain melancholy longing twisting inside of her, until Redmayne's words registered with a spike of panic.

We.

He'd not intruded alone.

A tall shadow in the doorway drew her attention.

Lord Ramsay had followed his brother, and now blocked Cecelia's only route of escape.

Blast and damn!

Unable to look at him, Cecelia's panicked gaze collided with Alexandra's, and her friend stood nervously, giving her one surreptitious shake of her head. A warning not to do or say anything to draw attention to herself.

Ramsay melted from the shadows of the door as Francesca and Cecelia stood to perform a curtsy.

"My lady," he said, addressing Francesca. "Miss Teague." Eyes the color of an Antarctic glacier found Cecelia and lingered, locking her feet in place as he bent at the waist in the stiff echo of a bow.

"How do you do?" As she executed a second curtsy, the pace of Cecelia's breath doubled even as her corset seemed to shrink several inches, restricting her lungs to an impossible degree.

Was this why women fainted? Was it possible to be so cold as to shiver while standing so close to the fire?

The cold, she realized, emanated not from the air, but from Ramsay. From some hollow place behind his frigid eyes.

Eyes that had still not left her.

Did he recognize her? Would the next words from his lips condemn her?

Time seemed to bend around Cecelia as she looked over at him, or rather *up* at him. Of course, it couldn't have been for longer than a fleeting moment. But that moment had all the impact and hues of the fireworks on Guy Fawkes Day.

Not because he was handsome. Nothing about the fierce and brutal planes of his face was meant to please the eye. His chin and jaw were much too square and thrust forward with unyielding menace. His tall forehead, crimped with an eternal scowl, shadowed his impossibly light, unforgiving eyes.

His nose was more patrician than barbaric, she noted. A great Caesarean nose from which to look down upon the rest of the people he considered beneath him.

But his lips.

Cecelia's gaze snagged there with a desperate fascination. A man would have to be chiseled with ferocity to own such a luscious mouth without seeming feminine.

They were lips made for sin, for wickedness.

Hadn't the devil once been an angel? Perhaps she'd been wrong to attach that moniker to Redmayne. It didn't stretch the imagination to picture Ramsay as the Star of the Morning. A favored son of golden hair and skin.

God's own heir.

Ramsay's evening suit and white tie were impeccable. Expensive. His hair, cut to fashion, gleamed like precious metal in the light from the sconces.

But as always, his features betrayed his lack of nobility.

His Scots accent wasn't that of an aristocrat. His brogue brought to mind a rather savage, sky-clad people with the same pagan brute strength and superfluous muscle he hid beneath his impeccably tailored jacket.

In fact, Cecelia could find nothing gentle about him. Not the shards of ice that passed for pupils. Even the way he stood projected unaffected arrogance. As though he'd learned well and early that life was naught but a contest for dominance, and he expected everyone in his vicinity to play by the rules. His rules. Because he wrote the laws and enforced them with an iron fist.

How terrible it must be to stand beneath his bench in shackles searching his face for traces of mercy.

This man quite obviously didn't know the meaning of the word.

As Francesca would sometimes say . . . she was buggered.

Cecelia looked down at the cream carpets, praying for the first time in years.

Dear Lord, or . . . the other one. If either of you could simply open up a hole in the floor large enough to swallow me entirely, I'd be much obliged. I care not at this moment where it takes me. I'd rather burn in eternal hellfire than spend another minute pinned beneath the gaze of—

Francesca's sharp elbow interrupted her prayer, such as it was, and she looked up to notice that all the eyes in the room, not just Ramsay's, were directed at her.

Apparently, she'd been addressed. But by whom? And what did they say?

"P-pardon?" she asked, pushing her spectacles back onto the bridge of her nose where they belonged.

"Poor thing," Alexandra crooned with a meaningful look. "She's been complaining of an awful headache," she explained to the room at large. "Perhaps you might go home and get some rest."

Cecelia nodded woodenly. "Thank you. I believe I shall."

Redmayne's forehead crimped with a filial concern. "I'll have Cheever call for the coach, Miss Teague."

"No thank you, Your Grace, I'll take a hansom back to—"

"Ye'll take my carriage." Ramsay's words were less an offer than an order. "It's waiting down a side street through the back garden. I'll accompany ye to my footman."

"I'm quite capable of finding my own way through a garden." Cecelia glanced at him more sharply than she'd intended. "I'll see myself out."

Ramsay's eyes dropped from her features with something

that might have looked like indignation on a less brutal face. He knew she wanted nothing to do with his company.

"I'll take her home." Francesca stepped forward. "We can dine another evening."

"But we've made your favorite, Lady Francesca," Redmayne interjected. "And besides, it's a rare night my brother offers his company, let alone his chivalry." The duke turned to Cecelia with a disconcerting smile. "You'd be sorry to miss such an infrequent occurrence."

Cecelia felt the blood drain from her face as her gaze collided with Ramsay's. Her limbs went cold, numb, then flushed with tingling heat. The room spun slightly, bending as if she were on a ship rather than in one of the grandest homes in the West End.

"Ye are pale, lass, and a bit unsteady." His low Scots brogue rumbled like distant thunder over the Hebrides. "The least I can do is make certain ye're conducted safely."

Conducted where? Prison?

She put a hand out, whether to steady herself or to stop him from coming closer, she hadn't decided yet. "Really, I'm—"

He enfolded the hand in his and nudged her closer, tucking her arm against his biceps. "Besides, I'd have a private word with ye. It willna take long."

A private word, with the Vicar of Vice . . .

Could she do this? Could she possibly avoid his scrutiny long enough to make it through the back gardens unexposed? If he should look too closely, might he see that *she* was the woman behind the mask, the makeup, the wig, the accent, and the cloak?

Surely her disguise hadn't been that impenetrable.

Somehow, her feet were moving. She cast a desperate glance to her friends in time to see Alexandra and Redmayne holding some silent conversation with their eyes.

Francesca looked about to say something when Cecelia shook her head.

If he'd already guessed her identity, it was too late. And if he hadn't guessed now, he was unlikely to in the dark.

But to refuse would be suspiciously rude.

Ramsay held open the door for her. She barely heard her friend's worried well wishes, for all she noted was his gaze like a branding iron as he followed her into the night.

CHAPTER SIX

Ramsay awaited a verbal assault as he led the apprehensive Miss Teague into the ducal gardens of Redmayne Place. To his surprise, he was met with none.

She walked beside him, her arm tense within his, her back straight as a mooring post as she stared at the flowers with undue resolution.

She didn't want him to look at her, which was deucedly irritating, because he yearned to do exactly that, survey every inch of her in the moonlight.

He should have used the quiet to contemplate just what exactly he'd done by inviting her out here.

And why the devil he'd done it.

Instead, he couldn't help but appreciate that he didn't have to work so hard to adjust his stride to fit hers. She was uncommonly, almost indecently, tall for a woman.

Her legs must go on for eternity.

He firmly squelched the thought, doing his best to appreciate the lobelia, hollyhocks, and calendulas as they passed.

London's relentless lights reflected off lazy, intermittent clouds. The gold of gas lamps competed with the silver of the full moon, and the uncommonly warm evening had coaxed the blossoms to bare themselves with shameless abandon.

In Scotland, a night such as this one, laden with heady perfume and spiced with enchanting expectancy, would belong to the Fae.

Ramsay told himself he didn't miss home, that this hollow longing was for something else. For justice. For redemption.

For serenity.

A serenity that hovered over the evening, threatening to spill over them if they'd only let it.

A silent breeze toyed with one of Miss Teague's copper ringlets, tossing it against her cheek. His hand itched to brush it away as she lifted her head toward the kiss of air, her face a mask of appreciation.

The world was so cold, and that chill had become a part of his own body's fabric. Like eternal winter. Or a lonely Highland moor in January.

Except where their arms linked, her warmth lingered and threatened to spread.

Her scent, a mixture like spun sugar and summer berries mingled with the fragrance of the gardens, inundated his olfactory senses with a gluttony of delicious aromas. The rhythmic clip and crunch of their steps on the stones hypnotized him, draining some of his tension with a percussive sort of magic.

"You're rather silent." Her gentle remark conveyed no censure, only uncertainty. "For a man who wanted a private word."

Silence, Ramsay had discovered, could be as loud as a brass section in a symphony. He'd learned to conduct silence like a maestro. It made people uncomfortable, often driving them to reveal too much about themselves to fill the void.

But not Cecelia Teague. She'd remarked upon the quietude, drawing both their focuses to his weapon of choice.

A weapon he hadn't meant to deploy against her.

It was merely that her nearness effectively emptied his mind of the weight of his responsibilities and the frustrations of the day. And the lift of that burden was rather miraculous.

"Forgive me," he started.

"Not at all," she said carefully, still not looking away from the flowers at her side. "There's no need for conversation between us."

"Nay." He paused, turning to face her, their arms sliding away from each other's. He missed the warmth immediately. "Nay, Miss Teague, I'm addressing my behavior toward ye and the Count Armediano during our last interaction at Castle Redmayne. I'm not usually so . . ." He groped for a word.

"Domineering?" she supplied, her dimple deepening as she threw him a cheeky glance before it darted away. "Overbearing, impolite, officious—"

"Aye." He held up his hand in a gesture of surrender. "Aye, take yer pick. I was all of that and more."

His admission seemed to startle her. "No harm done," she finally said. After lifting a shoulder, she turned back toward the path, drifting away in a graceful glide, her skirts flowing as though her feet never touched the ground.

He fell into step with her easily, wondering if she'd truly forgiven him.

If now was a good time to offer his arm again.

If she'd take it.

He locked his hands behind him to stop himself from reaching for her. "In my defense, combat was my initial civil service. I learned to be a warrior and then a commander before I was a lawyer. Domineering is in the job description, ye ken. No matter how much discipline I cultivate as a gentleman, it's not always easy for a man to temper edges sharpened by violence."

"That I believe," she said with a wryness he couldn't decipher. "Tell me, did I stumble into the middle of a war with the count I was unaware of?"

Only over her attentions.

"Sometimes it feels as though I'm at war with the entire world." The unintended admission was met by her hesitant pause. "A regrettable by-product of my profession, I'm afraid. I'm forever at odds. Harmony is a luxury I'm rarely afforded."

She looked over her shoulder at him, her gaze less reproachful than curious. "I imagine you'd find more harmony if you practiced a bit more leniency."

A strange word, *leniency*. One he was certain had never been used in a sentence containing himself. In fact, his ruthlessness had made his career. His life. It'd often been his only weapon. When one had nothing to one's name but sheer determination, one tended to rely on it with astounding frequency.

And yet the fact that Miss Teague found him so unyielding rankled.

Perhaps because he could not find one *un*attractive quality about her, but she so obviously considered his ruthlessness a flaw.

"I suspected the count's intentions toward ye were reprehensible, and I'll admit that my first instinct was that of a soldier, not a gentleman." Never in his life had Ramsay explained himself as he did now. He'd never so yearned to be understood. The longing unsettled and distressed him, and yet he couldn't seem to stop himself from admitting, "I'm rather famously unpossessed of the skill and charm so easily wielded by men such as Count Armediano and my brother."

That produced another of her mysterious smiles. "An inconvenient character trait for a man in your position."

"Character flaw, ye mean."

"Not necessarily." She regarded him like he was a problem she'd eventually have to solve, neither agreeing with his estimation, nor rushing to assure him of the severity of his self-assessment.

With no forthcoming placations or condemnations, Ramsay couldn't be certain what she thought of him. As a man who'd made his fortune examining people under a microscope, tearing apart their lies, and meting out their sentences, he found her peculiar inscrutability disconcerting.

Why did he even care if she held him in her esteem?

The answer was simple. Because he wanted her. He . . . *liked* her.

"Are ye ill, Miss Teague?" Her ghostly pallor concerned him, and her fingers trembled slightly on his arm.

"Why do you ask?"

"Yer headache."

"Oh." Her mouth thinned into a frown as if she'd forgotten her headache existed. "I've had a trying day, my lord," was all she gave by way of explanation. "I'm sure some rest will put me to rights."

She walked for a moment in silence, turning his own weapon upon himself.

Which could be the only fathomable reason why he blurted, "Why are ye not married, Miss Teague?"

She hesitated. "A woman may not marry if she is not asked."

"Ye've never been asked?"

"What about you, my lord?" she quickly volleyed. "I can imagine only few women in this city who wouldn't leap at the chance to be your wife."

"I've spent too much of my life dodging the shrapnel of my family's rather famously disastrous marriages to have any desire to embark on my own."

She nodded, though his statement seemed to trouble her. "But don't you believe there's someone for everyone?"

"Quite the contrary," he scoffed. "I believe there's no one for anyone. I'm not one to believe in soul mates and kismet, Miss Teague. Marriage is just like anything else of its nature. A legal binding contract between two people."

She paused beneath a bower of lilacs, replacing the sky with blooming violet flowers that complemented her gown. "What about love?" she asked.

"What about it?"

"Do you *not* believe in love?"

"I suppose I do," he replied, though he interrupted her relieved sigh by continuing, "I believe love is a construct of people to explain away their biological urges and unreasonable attachments to each other. It's a word that can explain away otherwise unexplainable behavior."

She regarded him ruefully. "Unreasonable attachments? Surely you don't feel that way about the duke and Alexandra? They're undeniably in love."

"They're besotted, I won't deny that, but their attachment is young. Life hasn't yet had a chance to rip them away from themselves. From each other."

She shook her head slowly as though she couldn't believe him. "I just—don't understand how you can be so . . . so . . . cynical."

Ramsay shrugged. "Years of practice, I suppose."

To his utter surprise, she laughed.

And even in the dark, her laughter felt like sunlight on his skin.

He was disconcerted enough by the sensation not to commit to the threatening smile twitching at the corner of his lips.

"I've found it's better to be cynical than to be naive," he asserted. "Safer."

Her regard turned wary. "Are you implying I'm naive simply for believing in love? Because I'll have you know, I've seen some of the worst humanity has to offer."

"Is that so?" He highly doubted she'd suffered more trials than a broken bootlace. Her smile was much too genuine. Her eyes sparkled with curiosity and mirth, un-haunted and dauntless. Her clothes were expensive, and she ate well enough to keep her body delectably round. He searched her gaze for grief. For shadows. For the pain that makes one cold. Or hard.

Or in his case, both.

All he found were sapphires sparkling in moonlight refracted by glass and silver wire. Suddenly, his fingers itched to take off her spectacles. To see if her eyes were truly so deep an azure, and her lashes a fan of such a distracting hue.

"I've seen the worst," she repeated with absolute conviction. "And I wouldn't at all consider myself credulous. I'm merely . . ."

"Romantic?"

"Optimistic," she offered.

"Idealistic, you mean."

She shook her head. "More . . . hopeful."

He grunted. "Hope. The currency of dreamers."

A little frown pinched her brow. "And what's wrong with that?"

He fought to maintain his mask of impassivity as a familiar hollow, wintry feeling rose within him. "Dreams die."

"Everything dies." She shrugged her insouciance over that fact, threading her fingers around some lilac blossoms. "But dreams are full of hope, and without hope, my lord, you might as well hang us all on your gallows, for we've no reason to be human anymore."

It took him longer than he liked to absorb her meaning, and he didn't have time to process the effect her words had upon him. So he deflected.

"What is it ye hope for?" he wondered. "A husband?"

"Lord, no!" This time she laughed long enough to be slightly insulting.

"But ye believe in love? Someone for everyone and so on, but doona wish it for yerself?"

"Love and marriage have little to do with each other, I've noticed," she replied. "And I don't think I shall ever be shackled with a husband, thank Jove. But I fully intend to fall in love."

When he didn't reply, she examined him intently, as though she attempted to read the answers in his bones. "I'm interested to learn the reason you inquired about my marital status at all, my lord," she challenged. "It's either a cruel inquiry or a meaningful one."

He both admired and was irritated at her direct assertion because . . . it was both cruel and meaningful.

"It's a question ye still havena answered," he prompted.

She crossed defensive arms over her breasts, deepening the cleft between them. "My answer might offend."

"I promise to remain unoffended," he vowed, valiantly keeping his gaze from drifting beneath her chin.

She made a sound of disbelief in the back of her throat before conceding. "For a woman of my means, marriage is inexorably less beneficial in all ways than my life as a spinster."

"How so?"

"My property and my money remain my own. My will and reputation, as well. I am not a part of the aristocracy and so I am able to move more freely about the world. I ask permission from no one, and take nobody's opinions, emotions, or"—she lifted meaningful eyebrows at him—"*judgments* into account when I make decisions. I am free, my lord, and have not yet met a man to whom I am inclined to give up that freedom."

"Freedom." Ramsay's satisfied nod seemed to baffle her. "How incredibly odd, Miss Teague, that our reasons for remaining unattached so closely resemble each other's." Stranger still, that he'd never felt freer to be himself than in her presence.

She blinked several times. "Very odd, indeed. I shouldn't have thought we had anything in common."

"I think if we looked deep enough within ourselves, we'd find glimpses of each other. I see a reflection in yer eyes, I think. A part of myself. One that might be kinder than the truth." Christ. When had he become a bloody poet?

"Your reflection would only be in my spectacles, my lord." She looked away, her hand toying restlessly in her hair.

What had gotten into him? Something about their conversation flirted with danger.

She assessed him as if he were composed of formulae

she was intent upon unraveling. "It's because of your mother, then, if I had to guess."

Ramsay stiffened. "What in God's name are ye referring to?"

Her words were measured, careful. "Alexandra shared with me what happened to the previous duke, Redmayne's father, how he hung himself from the grand balustrade at Castle Redmayne when your mother abandoned him for a lover. That's what you meant when you referred to your family's disastrous marriages."

He searched her features for pity, for judgment, and again only found her gentle curiosity. Something about it, about the way she picked him apart. Softly. Meticulously. With no apparent need for supremacy or seduction. No need to use information against him.

He found himself powerless against it, words spilling from lips famously locked. From a vault that hadn't been opened since before he'd become a man. "The previous Lady Redmayne knew how to pick weak men. And she knew how to break them." Or rather, they allowed themselves to be broken by her.

"Ah," she murmured. "Did she do something similar to your real father?"

The wintry feeling bloomed into a frozen void, the one contained within him for so many years.

Decades. One opened by a length of time so dastardly, neither rage nor passion nor acquisition could heat it.

"My father died when I was a lad of nine or so." The how of it didn't matter. Neither did the why of it. He didn't want Cecelia Teague to see the void. To find the vault. To know what he kept there.

"And so you were taken in by Redmayne's father?" she asked.

"Aye. He sent me to Eaton at fifteen with Piers, then Oxford after that."

She bit her lip in contemplation. "You say he was weak, but he also sounds like he was a kind man."

He made a dismissive gesture, closing his heart to the pain. "Kindness can be its own form of weakness."

"Not in my experience."

"You are lucky then, if that is your experience."

"Do you not have to be kind at times to perform your vocation?"

"Nay. Kindness . . . it's not a virtue I'm afflicted with."

"Afflicted?" For once, disappointment touched her expression. "And here I thought one must be kind in order to be good."

"One must be fair and just." How had they come to be speaking of this? He wanted to return to their repartee of before. He wanted to stop fortifying the wall he'd built years ago around his heart, his soul, his entire self, because she was somehow chipping away at it.

Not like a battering ram, but subtly. Like time, and water, and earth. If he wasn't careful, she'd leave it in ruins, and then where would that leave him?

Exposed.

"My coach is just past this gate," he said, resting his hand on the lock of an iron gate securing the back garden from the street.

"Wait." Her hand landed on his arm and locked his feet to the ground like a shackled prisoner.

He felt her touch in every part of his body.

"I should like to see you again," she said with earnest sincerity. "We're practically family now. Don't you think it's very important we get on?"

"We arena related. Not by blood." This felt particularly significant.

"No, but perhaps we could be friendlier. I'd like to know more about you," she prodded. "And I'd like you to get to know me better. To understand certain things . . ."

Why? he wanted to ask. *To what end if not matrimony?* "Do ye have a confession to make, Miss Teague?"

"I might."

Her answer mystified and exhilarated him. If he were to make a confession in this moment, it would be to desire. Would her confession be the same?

The atmosphere between them shifted from tentative challenge and merciless discovery to something softer and warmer.

Here she stood. Looking up at him with her eyes wide and open upon his face. Her lips relaxed, threatening to part.

Close enough to touch. To taste.

"As much as I hate to agree with Count Armediano upon anything, I must say, ye are an extraordinary woman," he crooned.

Her lashes fluttered down over her cheeks, where he was glad to see her peachy blush return. "That is kind of you to say, my lord."

A muscle released at the back of his neck, allowing his head to lower toward hers. "Ye doona have to call me that. Ye're not in my court."

Eyes as deep and blue as Loch Ness beneath the sun lifted to meet his. "What if I *was* in your court? Would you condemn me?"

"Never."

"*Never* is a dangerous word." Her breath smelled sweet, like chocolate and scotch.

"So is *always.*"

"If not *my lord*, what should I call you, then? Cassius?"

"Ramsay will do just fine."

Her eyes darted away, but not before he caught a flash of something. Shyness? Or a secret? The night whispered a warning, but it was too late. The moon-drenched darkness had become his undoing, the gardens his prison. He couldn't have escaped even if he'd wanted to.

"I like your names," she whispered, swaying forward. "Ramsay. And Cassius."

He hated his name. He hated it every day. "I like yers."

She blinked. "Would you say it?"

"Miss Teague?"

"No, might you call me Cecelia?"

"Cecelia." He drew out the syllables, letting his tongue linger over them. Learn them.

She closed her eyes, seeming to savor the word with the same vigor as the truffles. "Again?"

An invisible restraint shackled his bones, this one not of cold hard iron, but of velvet. It tugged him toward her. Drew her name out of his chest like a poem, and then a prayer.

"Cecelia."

Her lips parted.

And he was lost.

Lost to the thundering of his heart. To the pull of her body, as powerful and unavoidable as the influence of the moon on the tides.

Their breath mingled. Her scent tangled with that of the lilacs, unbearably lovely.

His lips hovered. Met hers. Stilled.

For a heartbeat, or maybe an eternity, he stood like that. Paralyzed. Not from fear. Not exactly.

A hunger crawled through him like a beast with many claws. A beast locked away for a time longer than infinity. Raw, uncontained sexuality that had no place in such orderly, sedate gardens roared to life and threatened to rip his self-control to shreds.

As though she sensed the beast, Cecelia made a small, intimate sound.

One dangerously close to surrender.

Don't, he silently begged. *Don't make me want you this much. Don't give me something else to fight. To crush. To contain.*

But contain it, he did. Just as he always had. As he always would.

He locked it away in a trunk of iron. Chained it. And threw it into the dark void where his heart should be.

She didn't reach for him, nor did she do anything else wanton or wicked. She just accepted his mouth with a sweet sigh, tilting her head to receive more of him.

He lifted his hands to her face, intent upon gently holding her still so he could extricate himself from a kiss that shouldn't be.

His thumbs drew up the line of her jaw and over her cheek, finding no angles, no hard lines. Somehow, he was cupping her face. Tilting it back. Drawing her in rather than pushing her away.

The roaring of his blood in his ears became a growl and then a purr.

He satisfied his hunger by licking his tongue through the seam of her lips as though trying to get at the cream in a pastry.

She opened for him with a sigh. Never had he found something so sweet. So decadent.

Had he expected any different from her?

She was soft beneath his kiss, but not passive. Her lips melted against his, her face tilted into his palm, giving over to his strength. Giving over to the experience.

She was an innocent. She kissed like a woman unused to kissing. Her little motions instinctive rather than practiced. Her tongue ventured forward, then darted away. Her breaths hitched and trembled.

His restless tongue enjoyed her. Coaxed her. Stroked and slid inside her mouth in a velvety dance of desire.

He closed his eyes as he supped on her lower lip, then her upper before delving to taste her once more. He explored her features with his fingertips, employing the butterfly-light strokes of a blind man, memorizing her topography. Absorbing the details of her—the divot in her chin, the supple skin over her cheekbones, the distracting shell of her ear, and the silken trails of her brows—before returning to cup her face.

Warm. She was so warm. Her mouth, her skin, her soul. It chased the constant chill from his bones, replacing it with a distressing, delectable heat.

That heat built within him. Called the beast once again to the surface. It prowled beneath his skin, rippled along his nerves, lancing an intense lust through his loins.

She's yours for the taking, it growled.

Ramsay tore his lips from hers, his hands unable to release her. Not just yet.

She stared at him, her eyes wide, glistening behind spectacles partially fogged with the moisture of their combined breath.

"Christ, ye're lovely," he said in a voice raspy and dark. One he didn't recognize as his own.

"So are you," she replied dreamily, evoking a chuckle.

"Lass, I'd best return ye home." If he didn't, he'd ruin not just her reputation, but her coiffure, her dress, her composure.

Her innocence.

His soul.

She nodded languidly, her eyes unfocused. Inebriated, but not with drink. With desire. Possibly with the inevitability of what came next for them both. Her gaze locked on his lips with an almost puzzled consternation. As if to ask if his mouth had stolen her ability for speech.

She's yours, the beast whispered. *Claim what you want.*

Nay. He reluctantly let her go, turning from her while he still could, to open the gate and call to his coachman down the lane.

He'd promised never to have another woman in sin.

And Cecelia Teague was a woman with no desire to be claimed.

What would it take to change her mind?

Because without knowing it, or probably even meaning to, she'd begun to change his.

CHAPTER SEVEN

For the entire next morning, Cecelia had to bite her own tongue to keep from screaming the truth.

I kissed Ramsay.

She was adept at keeping secrets, wasn't she? She'd helped to bury the body of Alexandra's rapist in a poppy garden behind their school on Lake Geneva. She was one of the few people in the world who knew that Francesca, the Countess of Mont Claire's real name was Pippa Hargrave. That she was an imposter bent on revenge against those who'd murdered her family and the real Francesca Cavendish.

She'd never revealed to anyone that Vicar Teague wasn't her father. That she was a bastard and a fraud. Unwanted. Unloved.

Unclaimed.

She knew she'd made a mistake last night by being alone with Ramsay. She didn't *exactly* want to hear the Rogues' opinions on it, because certainly they'd be unfavorable considering she was lying to the man.

And because he was intent upon her utter obliteration.

So why did a confession regarding last night's tipsy indiscretion burn her tongue, demanding to be spat out?

For the most part, she'd been able to contain herself. But during the rare moments her friends were silent, as they were now, standing in the foyer of a gambling hell that had recently become hers, the confession bubbled in her throat like expensive champagne. Threatening to burp forth, condemning her for an absolute fool.

I kissed Ramsay. I can still feel him on my lips. Taste him on my tongue. Sense the scrape of his callused fingertips across my cheek.

I kissed Ramsay, and I never wanted to stop.

"Oh my." Alexandra's breathy exclamation paralyzed her.

Cecelia swallowed. Twice, curling her lips between her teeth.

Had she spoken out loud?

Alexandra and Francesca drifted further onto the floor empty of people but full of every sort of gambling implement. Tables for dice were stacked next to a gilded roulette wheel. Next to that, card tables for baccarat, faro, and keno sheets were neatly stacked in rows of three, leaving plenty of room for men to make their way to the long oak bar behind which any drink could be served.

The place somehow endeavored to be elegant and garish at the same time, and Cecelia couldn't wait to get her hands on some of the games. They were mostly about odds and numbers, after all.

Winston, the butler, gathered Francesca's emerald gloves and parasol, Alexandra's cream lace cape, and Jean-Yves's hat, cane, and jacket from limbs gone rather slack with awe.

Thus loaded, he gestured for Cecelia's own lavender

parasol and matching lace gloves, but she didn't want to add to the burden, so she declined.

"Thank you, Winston."

His reply was stiff and diffident, though respectful.

"My, my." Francesca craned her elegant neck, gawking at the lurid murals on the domed ceiling that would have made even Michelangelo blush. "Well, I never."

Cecelia tilted her own head back, squinting through her lenses. She hadn't noted the scandalous fresco during her prior visit. But then, she'd spent most of her time wanting to stare at the marble floor, not the ceiling.

Gasping, she clamped her hand over Phoebe's wide blue eyes.

Jean-Yves gave the depictions of frolicking and fornicating nudes above him a scarce glance. His attention was arrested by the women of Henrietta's School for Cultured Young Ladies as they glided down the grand staircase like proper Georgian butterflies.

Cecelia shared an astonished glance with the Rogues.

Did Jean-Yves frequent such places in his free time? He was so dapper, almost respectable in his afternoon suit, despite the craggy, sun-browned features of a man used to hard labor out of doors. His silver hair, now too thin for much pomade, stood out in little tufts without his hat. He smoothed at it self-consciously as a blush spread all the way to his scalp.

The Rogues each looked as though they might giggle . . . or gag.

The young ladies on the stairs were dressed both congruently and dissimilarly. Their gowns as varying in size and color as the women themselves.

A waifish nymph with straight, shining raven hair wore a pink gown with the front tied above the tops of her stockings and garters secured by two bows, allowing a peek of her smooth, bronze thighs. She could have been an Egyptian princess.

Behind her, a lady twice as large as Cecelia boasted a sleek, floor-length seafoam gown with a bodice that lifted her enormous breasts close to brushing her double chin. The tan crescents of her areolas rose above expensive lace, her nipples threatening to escape with every shiver of her abundant flesh. She gave a come-hither toss of her tumble of gold hair, and flashed a smile that promised boundless generosity.

Cecelia gawked at the women now in her employ.

One even boasted curls as coppery as hers, and . . . She adjusted her spectacles. Was that an Adam's apple?

"Miss Cecelia," Phoebe protested, her little fingers pulling at the hand over her eyes. "I've already seen the ceiling."

Cecelia cringed. What else had the poor girl been exposed to so early? Lord, what kind of guardian was she to bring her back here? What sort of guardian had Henrietta been?

She thought of the missing girls. Girls not much older than Phoebe.

What if this place had something to do with them?

The Lord Chief Justice certainly seemed to think so.

I kissed Ramsay.

She shoved the thought violently aside.

"*Bienvenue*, honey!" Genny descended from the landing above, gliding down the stairs behind the carnal display, passing each brazen caricature of fantasy.

She rushed to embrace Cecelia and tweak a shy Phoebe under the chin.

Genny slid her dark eyes over Jean-Yves, rendering his pink blush a solid scarlet. "Well, hi there, handsome. I'm Genevieve Leveaux, but you can call me Genny."

Jean-Yves sputtered for a moment, and Cecelia came to his rescue by making introductions.

Genny greeted them with a delighted kiss on each cheek. "The infamous Red Rogues. Henrietta used to read me your letters about these two." She bowed to each of them before gesturing to the grand staircase. "Allow me to present the ladies behind the tables. You won't meet sharper dealers, card sharps, dice throwers, or bookies in all of Blighty."

A few chuckles echoed in the vast marble entry.

"I'm so eager to make each of your acquaintances." Cecelia curtsied and petted Phoebe's hair as she addressed Genny. "But first, I'm here to gather a few of Phoebe's things. Do you mind if we take her to the residence and *then* have a look around and make proper introductions?"

Genny laughed long and loud. "Why you askin' me, darlin'? The place is yours."

Somehow it didn't *feel* like hers. It might have belonged to Genny for all her knowledge and know-how. Her history.

But in truth, it belonged to a ghost. To Henrietta.

"Mademoiselle," Jean-Yves said close to Cecelia's ear. "Allow *me* to take Miss Phoebe to the residence to collect her things. Then you inspect your new . . . holdings without a care."

"You don't want to stay?" Genny winked at him, flashing brilliant white teeth. "A man as handsome and well turned out as you could make some money here, along with a few new friends."

"A man as old and simple as I can only appreciate so much beauty at a time, madame, before it becomes a danger to my health." He bowed over Genny's hand before gathering up Phoebe's. "Come along, *ma petite bonbon*. We can select your favorite things for your new room."

Cecelia watched them go. She'd long since outgrown the name Jean-Yves christened her with the afternoon they'd met. Cecelia had been a chubby, bespectacled girl drowning her sorrows in bonbons. How lovely that another lost little girl got to enjoy the moniker, the sweets, and all the gentle masculine guidance that came with it.

Between her efforts and those of Jean-Yves, maybe Phoebe wouldn't so much miss having parents. The idea cheered her exponentially.

"What about you, Duchess, Countess?" Genny offered. "Can I interest you in a little game of chance?"

"I think I'd like that, after our tour." Alexandra primly tucked a stray curl the color of burnished teak beneath her wide-brimmed hat.

Francesca ignored them all, studying the place and the employees with forthright but indifferent assessment.

A rather resplendent man with a grand mustache toddled down the stairs, begging the pardon of the line of ladies. He was red-faced and sloe-eyed and nearly glowed with a besotted grin at them all as he accepted his hat and coat from a footman and whistled his merry way out the door.

"Was that . . . ?" Alexandra stared after him as a coach trundled up the circular drive.

"It couldn't be . . ." Francesca gaped.

Cecelia took her spectacles from her nose to shine on her sleeve, replacing them to search for a royal seal on the carriage.

Genny placed a finger under Cecelia's chin, urging her mouth shut. "He's not *first* in line to the throne or anything . . . and at the rate he's goin', his mother will outlive him."

When none of the Red Rogues seemed inclined to recover from a royal sighting, Genny said, "We keep a few bedrooms upstairs in case people are disinclined to go home in a state of inebriation." She linked her arm through Cecelia's and tugged her past the staircase, where a lady she recognized as Lilly drifted down, lacing a white bodice with pink ribbons.

Cecelia found it difficult to meet the girl's earnest, smiling gaze as the last time they'd met she'd been bouncing atop an earl. And she was certain the lovely girl had just serviced a prince upstairs.

Both dazed and amazed, she followed Genny past an intricate railing and toward a staircase leading to the lower level, this just as well appointed as the one to the second floor.

Before she stepped out of sight of the main floor, she caught a glimpse of a lithe masculine figure slithering toward the door, more shadow than man.

Count Adrian Armediano donned his hat over a shine of ebony hair and punched his fists into a dark jacket.

He glanced back toward their procession, and Cecelia nearly tripped down the stairs in her haste not to be seen.

"Is that the count from your do last month?" Francesca whispered from behind her. Never one for subtlety, she lifted on her tiptoes to watch him leave. "Where did you find him, Alexander? There's something so off-putting about him, and yet familiar. As though I've hated him before, but I can't remember why."

"He's done business with Redmayne," the duchess replied pensively. "Supposedly he wields an immense amount of influence both here and internationally. I confess I was barely listening when the duke told me about him, because I was sifting through a trunk of samples sent to me from Syria at the time."

"Redmayne should know better than to expect to distract you with conversation," Francesca teased.

"Redmayne knows *exactly* what to do to distract me," Alexandra said with a sly wink. "Cecil, you spent some time at the soiree talking with the count. What was he like?"

"Charming," she answered. *And a bit frightening*, she didn't say. Something about him bespoke a darkness— no, a deviousness—that had both intrigued her and set her on edge.

"Truly charming?" Alexandra challenged, "Or simply in comparison with your *other* conversation companion? My inscrutable brother-in-law."

Cecelia wheezed out a nervous giggle, leaving the question unanswered. "Speaking of him, Genny, I'll say the extra cleaning staff did a smashing job. One could never tell that only yesterday this entire place was crawling with police."

With *him*.

She could feel his presence here. A sword over her head. A threat in her ear. A liquid weight low in her belly.

A thrilling, perplexing clench between her thighs.

I kissed Ramsay.

"The police did less damage than I feared," Genny said with a relieved sigh. "More clutter than anything. We were even able to open for the evening. Now, let me take you on the tour."

Belowstairs at Miss Henrietta's School for Cultured Young Ladies was a revelation.

Because it was, in fact, a school for cultured young ladies. And uncultured ones. Older mothers. Immigrants. And people who might otherwise be sent to the workhouse.

Cecelia was barely aware of the enthusiastic Lilly joining their tour group as Genny led her and the Rogues past classrooms packed to the gills with women and, yes, even little girls, describing each class with aplomb and pride.

The ingenious arrangement both dazzled and humbled Cecelia. Some ladies sewed elaborate costumes, presumably for the employees abovestairs, training to be seamstresses and modistes. Others toiled in the kitchen with the chef, feeding the students, employees, and customers lavish meals while learning about a career in service to a grand house.

There were ongoing lessons in deportment, speech, civics, penmanship, and basic mathematics.

Genny led her past rooms of foreign ladies learning English, and beyond that, women operating a mock switchboard that resembled the one for the new telephone service the government had begun installing in the city.

Cecelia paused there, hoping to catch her breath as she took it all in. How brilliant. How utterly—

"One wonders"—Francesca's sharp tone cut through her thoughts as her friend regarded Genny with narrow-eyed suspicion—"how these women, the young girls especially, afford their tuition."

"The house pays it," Lilly rushed to answer. "And men aren't allowed belowstairs. Not ever. Even all the instructors are women." She glanced over the line of ladies pulling large plugs from the switchboards and reconnecting them. Some worked with confidence, and others struggled, squinted, and became flustered beneath the regard of visitors.

To ease them, Cecelia moved down the hall away from the classrooms, toward a large arched door at the back of the manse. "How extraordinary," she marveled, strange and unwanted tears threatening to brim in her eyes as the enormity of her new position impressed itself upon her. She turned to Lilly.

"You pay for their educations by—by entertaining the wealthy with vice? How do you feel about the arrangement?"

"It's our choice and we make it." Lilly's answer rang with resolution.

Cecelia paused, searching the girl's kohl-lined hazel eyes for fear or deception.

"Why?" Alexandra whispered.

"Why give any of those hard-won earnings to people you don't care about?" Francesca pressed further. "Are you quite certain Henrietta doesn't—*didn't* force you to?"

Lilly's eyes darkened, and her wig trembled with her outrage as she stepped from beneath the duchess's touch. "I have the most honest profession in the world, Your Grace," she answered with a dignified calm, though it was obvious she'd been offended. "I'd rather dress in pretty clothes than sew them. And I'd much rather fleece wealthy men for money than serve their food or clean out their chamber pots. I like what I do. Most days I love it. Show me many people who are so lucky."

"Truly?" Cecelia asked, a bit heartened by the emphatic declaration. "Do many of the other employees feel the same?"

Lilly patted her on the arm. "Here at Miss Henrietta's, we're lavished with handmade clothing tailored just to us. We get to sleep late and play all night. We're served meals that any toff would be proud to eat. We're provided rotating days off and medical care when we need it. This is far better than what's out there on the streets or in factories. All that's required of us is to keep our mouths closed, our ears and eyes open, and we each give an equal percentage of our earnings to the running of the school."

"Well . . ." Francesca breathed in disbelief. "I'll be buggered."

Genny stepped forward, smoothing her hands over the lavender bodice that accentuated the pink hues in her ivory skin. "Many of the girls here are the daughters, mothers, sisters, or other kin of the women who work or have worked upstairs. The customers often lavish the lucky girls with jewelry, money, and gifts that they're allowed to keep or send to their families."

"But . . . what about the other day, Lilly? You're not expected to . . . service the clientele?"

Her brown shoulders shook with laughter as she met Genny's eyes. "That was my own business, ma'am. Some women find a full-time keeper, and a few rare ones get themselves husbands."

"Husbands?" Alexandra gasped.

Lilly let out a guffaw, the only slip in her articulate and cultured manner thus far that whispered of a life once lived in a very different part of London. "I receive more marriage proposals monthly than London's most sought-after debutantes, I'd wager. But I have too many men I enjoy in my bed to tie myself to just one."

Cecelia found herself filling with a strange well of emotion. Relief, she initially thought. Then pride. And after that . . . joy. Her legacy wasn't simply a den of vice, it was an entire philanthropic endeavor. How brilliant. She could think of no other word but that. Brilliant.

Marvelous, perhaps.

And terrifying. That a man could take this all from her. A man of single-minded resolve and fathomless fortitude. A man on a relentless quest for justice. Bedeviled with an almost pathological aversion to what he considered sin.

And also, an unspeakably wicked tongue.

I kissed Ramsay.

"Would you care to see upstairs now?" Genny offered, gesturing to the arched doors at the end of the corridor.

"Lead on," Cecelia murmured, clustering close to Alexandra and Francesca as they followed Genny out into the garden square in the center of the building protected on all sides by the manse.

The cool of the gardens caressed her face, the high walls of the edifice creating shade even in the summer. The lush evergreen grass and vibrant blossoms reminded Cecelia of another garden.

Cecelia's gaze locked to the hedgerow where she'd first spied Lilly with Lord Crawford. She stared at the spot, fixated by a sight transposing itself over the memory. A man with gold in his hair and ice in his eyes. And the woman—the woman had a familiar form and features.

The ones she looked at in the mirror every morning.

A copulation that had never taken place. And never would. Because Sir Cassius Gerard Ramsay wasn't the type of man to dally out of doors.

He wasn't the type to dally at all.

Except . . .

"I kissed Ramsay!"

The gardens fell silent. Not just silent. But still. Too still.

Until all three women turned in tandem to gape at her.

"Tell me you're jokin'," Genny demanded, advancing forward.

"I'm joking." Cecelia said obediently. "I didn't kiss Ramsay."

"Thank heavens," Alexandra breathed.

"He kissed me."

Genny shooed them all up several flights of stairs and into the private residence, where she pulled them into Henrietta's old bedroom, closed the door, and leaned against it. "Tell us everything. Where did he kiss you?"

"Nowhere but the lips, upon my word." Cecelia's cheeks heated.

It was only when Alexandra put a hand on her forearms that she realized she'd crossed them in a defensive gesture. "I think Miss Leveaux is asking where, geographically. Was it in the gardens last night?"

Cecelia nodded, feeling like a child about to be chided.

"I *knew* we should have saved you from going out there with him." Francesca paced the room. Even the swish of her emerald train managed to sound angry.

Cecelia shook her head. "That really wasn't neces—"

"Was he cruel to you?" Alexandra asked.

"Why didn't you tell us?" Francesca demanded.

"Well, I—"

"Does it seem he suspects you of being the Scarlet Lady?" Francesca drew up to Cecelia's other side, creating a familiar buffer the trio made whenever one of them was in distress. "Did he do this to ruin you? Seduce you, maybe, to lower your guard?"

Cecelia shook her head. "That didn't seem to be what he—"

"We'll murder him first," Francesca vowed. "You *know* we will."

Alexandra scratched at her temple and tucked a stray hair into her cap. "It just doesn't make any sense that Ramsay would use such deplorable physical cruelty. Redmayne insists his brother has lived like a monk for almost a decade. He doesn't even keep a mistress."

"And the mighty shall fall." Genny's quiet murmur sliced through the room like a claymore, silencing them all. "This," she laughed, her eyes sparkling with victorious mischief at Cecelia. "This is too good. *Too* delicious. I couldn't have planned this more perfectly, honey."

"What are *you* on about?" Francesca directed an indignant scowl at Genny, as though she didn't appreciate an interloper into what should be a Rogue-exclusive discussion.

"Don't you see?" Genny navigated the crimson furniture of the boudoir toward them, her finger toying at the ringlet brushing her clavicle. "The Lord Chief Justice does want to ruin Hortense Thistledown, the Scarlet Lady. *However*"—she took Cecelia by the shoulders and turned her to face her friends—"he desires to woo Miss Cecelia Teague, the shy, bespectacled spinster bluestocking and daughter of a simple country vicar."

Cecelia squirmed as her fellow Rogues gawked at her.

Genny continued, "Your Cassius Ramsay is a Scotsman with Scots appetites buried deep beneath British repression. Cecelia couldn't be more suited to him. A soft body built for sin, but sturdy enough to take a rough Scottish pounding." She slapped Cecelia on the rear.

"Genny!" Cecelia gasped and hopped forward, pressing her hands to her face and then her rear. "I never!"

"Tell me I'm wrong, then," the woman challenged.

She wanted to . . . but then she remembered the latent hunger she'd sensed beneath his kiss. The urgency that bordered upon danger.

Alexandra, the only married Red Rogue, assessed Cecelia with new eyes, the eyes of a woman well used to the desire of a man who shared Ramsay's blood. The British half, granted, though her husband's paternal ancestry was Viking nobility dating all the way back to before William the Conqueror. One look at him and it was impossible to doubt he'd been spawned by marauders and battle-hungry savages.

"Cecil," Alexander prodded. "Is it possible there's truth to what Miss Leveaux says?"

Cecelia reached for the delicate little leaves carved

into the dark-wood bedpost, tracing them intently as she answered without meeting anyone's gaze. "I do not believe the Lord Chief Justice recognized me as Hortense Thistledown."

"He wants *you*?" Francesca screwed her face in disbelief.

"Is that so difficult to fathom?" Cecelia's retort escaped more peevishly than she'd intended. "That someone like him could want me?"

"*No*," Francesca rushed, reaching for both her hands. "God no, Cecelia. That isn't at all what I meant. Genny's right, you've the illicit appeal of the most buxom of courtesans and the respectability of a church mouse. It's not that we don't believe *anyone* would want you, it's that it's difficult to process that someone like Ramsay would do such a cruel and calculated thing as kiss you in the gardens after pretending to be a paragon of respectability. Not to mention threatening you."

"He—he didn't seem cruel. Nor was he impertinent or disrespectful." Cecelia didn't want to defend him, but neither did she want him condemned for something she'd fully consented to.

Even enthusiastically participated in.

"In fact, he was . . . well, he didn't kiss like someone who'd lived as a monk for a decade. Or he must have an excellent memory. His kiss was . . ." She hesitated. Warm and wet and demanding. It had hinted at a dormant beast, something violent, volcanic, and eminently masculine. But also soft, deferential, and rather lovely. What word encompassed all of that, and still held her privacy intact?

"We're not to believe you *enjoyed* it, are we?" Genny recoiled. "He's your enemy, Cecelia, or have you forgotten? He'd have you strung from the closest lamppost if he could."

"I *haven't* forgotten." Cecelia insisted. "It's only that, we connected in a rather constructive way. He's—different from my initial estimation. Better, perhaps. Kinder. He said he and I were similar souls. It was as though he could see parts of himself in me."

"I can guess which parts," Genny muttered.

Alexandra smothered a laugh with her dainty hand but composed herself quickly. "What do you think he's after, Cecil?" she queried. "Did he speak to you of intentions? Courtship?"

Cecelia shook her head, feeling oddly bereft. "He seemed worried about my reputation. We *did* speak of marriage at length, but more in the hypothetical sense, not in a way that would make one assume he was about to declare intentions. Rather the opposite. Indeed, we shared our reservations about the institution as a whole. Though, he seemed amenable to the idea of us seeing each other again."

"Well, I'll be damned," Genny exclaimed, slapping her hands together. "We have him right where we want him!"

"We do?"

"You're in a very auspicious position."

"I am?"

Genny clapped her hands in delight. "Oh, would that Henrietta were alive. She'd be thrilled to her toes. You have one thing Henrietta could never even dream of having, and now you can use the Vicar of Vice's desire for you to bring about his demise."

Cecelia chewed the inside of her lip. For someone so good with formulae and figures, Cecelia felt woefully lost in a labyrinth of shadows, sex, and deception. "I'm not comfortable with causing anyone's demise, especially a man who's only trying to do his job."

"Did you forget he threatened to see you hanged for something for which you are not guilty?" Francesca surprisingly threw her lot in with Genny.

"Of course not, but surely there's another way."

"Are you all willing to resort to violence?" Genny asked.

"No," Cecelia stated firmly.

At the same time Francesca answered with a vehement, "Yes."

And Alexandra chimed in, "Only if strictly necessary."

Genny addressed Cecelia, as it was her unfortunate decision to make. "If we can't dump his body in the Thames, then we must consider other options."

Cecelia had a feeling the woman was only half joking. "What about proving my innocence in the disappearances of these girls? He'd have no reason to bother me, then."

"Perhaps, eventually." Genny made a dismissive gesture and checked her reflection in the mirror on the wall. "But his indictment of you is immediate, Cecelia. There's no time to conduct your own inquest. I'm tellin' you. You must find that part of Ramsay that he would show no one. That secret that would destroy him. You dangle it in front of him, then you lock it away. If you keep him at an impasse, you're safe."

"Like Henrietta was safe?" Cecelia locked her fists into her skirts, clutching them in frustration. "Isn't doing precisely that sort of thing what got her killed?"

Genny sighed, slumping into a straight-backed chair. "I know Henrietta left you that letter, honey, but the truth of the matter is she was found dead in this very bed and I was the one who found her. She looked peaceful . . ." Genny released a troubled sigh and pressed her fingertips to her forehead, massaging at what appeared to be a gathering headache. "The old bird was a bit paranoid these past few years, and I'm startin' to wonder if her death wasn't exactly what it appeared to be. A woman succumbing to nothing more insidious than time."

"What are you saying? Henrietta couldn't have been much older than fifty." Cecelia was stymied by Genny's change of tune. Just yesterday they'd discussed the probability of murder. That perhaps Ramsay or his ilk had had something to do with the demise of her infamous predecessor.

"I'm saying that your immediate problem is Ramsay. He's a powerful man in all ways, physical, financial, and legal. But *you* are a woman. And a woman's power is in her sex and her secrets. And here at Henrietta's School for Cultured Young Ladies, we collect secrets like jewels."

Cecelia puffed out her cheeks, feeling very overwhelmed. "I wouldn't even know how to go about discovering his secrets. We've only interacted yesterday, and I can't say I behaved in a manner that would instill anyone's confidence in my intellectual prowess in that regard."

But then, he had been open with her. Well, perhaps *open* was the wrong word. Forthcoming, if not confidence sharing. They'd had a more intimate conversation than she'd ever imagined they would.

"Luckily, you have an entire stable of women who make a living of manipulating men." Genny smiled deviously. "Every man is a puzzle of need, little doll. Find the missing piece and snap it into place, and he will do whatever you want. He'll tell you whatever you ask. He'll be yours to command."

Cecelia's first inclination was to laugh, but in the woeful manner that staved off threating sadness and the accompanying tears. She couldn't imagine even wanting the power Genny alluded to, let alone wielding it.

The men in her life had made her feel nothing but helpless, worthless, or some strange amalgamation of both. The Vicar Teague, classmates at university, scholars, bankers, and solicitors. They either condescended to her or over her or ignored her outright. Most men made her feel more deficient than desirable. More fatuous than formidable. She was ever too much or not enough.

Too plump, tall, educated, shy, or independent. Or not pious, respectable, noble, or young enough.

Her only power had been in her wealth, and even that came with its social limitations, especially now because of the origin of said moneys and the secrets willed to her along with it. Secrets she never asked for. Secrets she might be forced to use as weapons in a fight for survival.

"Ramsay's part of your extended family, Alex," she pleaded. "Is there anything you can think of that could help? Any way we could get him to leave this, leave *me*, alone without taking such drastic measures?"

Alexandra's freckled nose wrinkled. "I confess Ramsay has always been such a mystery to both Redmayne and me. A rather grumpy, obdurate mystery."

"Henrietta had some of us perform a bit of reconnaissance on him in the past," Genny supplied. "Not that it will be of any help to us now."

Cecelia tried to picture a company of reconnaissance-gathering revelers and had to fight a giggle. "Why not?"

"He's just so tremendously *boring*." Genny slumped down and rolled her eyes. "He wakes at dawn, goes to work behind his lofty bench. Ruins people's lives. Goes home at the end of the day, or to his club where he often leaves red-faced and sweating. Then he eats alone and retires at a disgustingly early hour." She made a noise of antipathy. "I'd pity him if I didn't hate him."

"Then what makes you so certain that Ramsay has any secrets?" Cecelia fretted. "He could be as virtuous and steadfast as he claims."

"I *know* he does," Genny said. "We just have to find the evidence."

"*How* do you know?"

Genny's lovely eyes darkened to a char black, her features pinching with distaste and loathing, finally etching her forty years into her skin. "Because men like him *always* have secrets. Before he was a barrister or a justice, he was a Scotsman and a soldier. He has blood on his hands and shameful marks on his soul, I'd wager my life on it." She leaned forward, her features hard with purpose. "We just have to get you closer to find out what they are."

Did Ramsay have blood on his hands? Square and rough and mercilessly strong as they were, it didn't stretch the imagination.

And yet they'd been incomprehensibly gentle as they'd stroked her jaw, cupped her face, grazed her lips.

Could it be that his piety was really penitence? Perhaps he'd done something so wrong once that he'd devoted his life to fixing it.

Or to cultivating a persona to hide sins he still committed under the cover of darkness.

Was she brave enough to find out the truth? Maybe, but not through dishonest means.

She opened her mouth to say so when a ripple of electric power vibrated through the air. Every hair on Cecelia's body stood on end as a strange silence engulfed her. Then a curious rumble threw her off balance as a white light blinded her. A force as powerful as a kick from a horse's hindquarters knocked her into the other Rogues with a thunderous sound no less than apocalyptic.

They clung together, dropping to the ground as glass bulbs shattered from the sconces on the walls, emitting electric-blue sparks. The chandelier swung violently on its chain above them, and for a terrifying second Cecelia was certain it would fall, fragmenting over them all.

Just as suddenly as the quake began, it passed.

A gentle ringing settled into the darkness for the space of three breaths before noises permeated the muffled void.

Screams. Running footsteps. Cries and chaos.

Not a quake, Cecelia realized with alarm.

An explosion.

"Is everyone all right?" Francesca asked, even her un-flappable demeanor pale and shaken as she gripped their hands almost painfully.

An acrid scent clung to the air, like char and smoke but more bitter.

Cecelia did a swift self-assessment, checking to make certain her limbs all worked. They, too, trembled but were otherwise unharmed.

"I think so." Alexandra struggled to her feet, dusting some of the plaster from the ceiling off her skirt. "Cecil?"

"I'm not hurt." She and Francesca helped each other up and turned to Genny, who'd taken shelter behind the chair. "Genny?" Her voice seemed over-loud in ears that refused to unplug.

Fingers curled over the chair's back before Genny used it to pull herself to a standing position. Her eyes were as round as saucers. Plaster flecked her hair, causing her to look like an angel in a snowstorm. "What . . . just . . . ?"

"I've been to enough dig sites to recognize the percus-sion of a bomb," Alexandra said unsteadily, her amber gaze fixing on Cecelia, though she addressed them all. It

was the terror and the tears in her eyes that affected Cecelia more than her words ever could. "Ready yourselves
for what we might find when we go out there, ladies."

Cecelia's limbs were jolted with energy as she surged
for the door. "Jean-Yves," she cried desperately. "Phoebe!"

CHAPTER EIGHT

Cecelia didn't give in to tears as she raced through swirls of sun-sparkled plaster dust. Distraught women poured into the hallway, creating an obstacle course of hysterical humanity.

She delegated their safe escape to Genny and sprinted down to the main floor, keeping a clawlike grip on her resolve as Francesca and Alexandra flanked her. Their boots made delicate crunching sounds when they hurried over fragments of the grand chandelier and cracks in the marble floors as the cries from belowstairs beckoned them.

They fought the tide of panicked, soiled students, some with minor injuries, racing up the stairs, and directed the crowd toward the front door, praying another detonation wasn't imminent.

A numb sense of calm engulfed Cecelia when she took in the damage to the school, protecting her from the heartrending sounds of fear, grief, and pain. Smoke and dust choked her, but she could neither feel nor see heat from any lingering fires.

That didn't mean they weren't smoldering somewhere.

The farther they moved underground, the more it became apparent that the damage centered on the west side of the manse, above which a crater had been carved into the structure where the office of the residence had once been.

Cecelia ached to run back upstairs and pick her way through the rubble of what had been her aunt's home. To scream and scream and scream until all her terror and agony conjured up the two most innocent people she knew. She *needed* Jean-Yves and Phoebe to be alive, but she simply couldn't step over other injured bodies to find them.

Her conscience wouldn't allow it.

At a time like this, she couldn't thank the stars enough that her band of Rogues were of one mind in a crisis.

That this wasn't their first brush with death or tragedy.

Alexandra was a doctor of archeology, not medicine, but a decade of fieldwork had granted her a great deal of opportunity to learn more than her share of emergency medical training. She had her gloves off and sleeves rolled up before any of them as she checked an older woman slumped in the hallway. The duchess's soft, doe-like features became grim as she found no breath or pulse. She closed the old woman's eyes and moved into the switchboard room where the wall-sized panels had toppled over, trapping a few ladies inside the room and landing on the leg of one screaming girl.

Francesca, who was strong and muscled for all her wiriness, was already directing those who stayed below-stairs to help lift the panels with the strength of their flanks rather than their backs.

Cecelia joined the effort, heaving with all her might and weight, but the panel refused to budge more than an inch, which caused the poor trapped girl to yelp with pain.

"Let it go," Francesca directed. "We'll have to use a different strategy to move it." She shook out her arms as though they could take no more.

"No!" Cecelia cried over the injured girl's plaintive sobs and the pleas of the imprisoned women in the room, begging to be let out. "No, they cannot be trapped in there. You lift! All of you. Lift!"

Alexandra nearly collapsed after a herculean effort, her features red and her shoulders trembling. "It's too heavy, Cecil, we need leverage."

"They can't be left in there," Cecelia panted, turning so the entirety of the weight was pressed against her back. "You don't know what it's like! They can't be trapped be-lowground! Help me!"

Sweat and tears burned her eyes, blurring her vision almost as much as did the steam of exertion and dust gathering on her spectacles. Something in her back twisted and seized, but she let the agony fuel her as she pushed and strained with a desperation bordering on the hysterical.

Trapped underground. Was there anything worse? To fear that you might never see the sun again. That you stood in the room where your bones would be forgotten.

She knew what it was like. The terror and despair of it.

She had to get them out of the basement.

Help me. Help them. Please. Please . . . Please! Cecelia didn't know if she prayed or screamed or both, but a beam of light appeared in her periphery and a tremendous blur of dark blue and gold flew forward and took the place at her side.

Cecelia didn't register the terse, growling words, but the women behind the panels backed away, and Alexandra and Francesca joined in the effort once more. She could only make out male thighs the size of Stonehenge boulders bunching beneath fine blue trousers as they took up the burden next to her and heaved. The weight disappeared from her shoulders a few seconds before a mighty crash shook the basement.

Cassius Gerard Ramsay scooped the injured girl from the ground as if she weighed no more than a sack of grain.

The panels lay where he'd heaved them to the side, allowing the women trapped in the room to file out one by one beneath Francesca's direction into the hall, where those who were able dashed toward the stairs.

Ramsay stepped out of the rubble and made for the exit, pausing only to lock and hold gazes with Cecelia for a breathless moment. He made a very quick assessment of her body from head to toe that left her still and trembling before returning his striking gaze back to hers.

Fire and ice. Fury and . . . distress? Relief? Vexation?

She hadn't the chance to interpret before he strode away with all the alacrity his wounded burden could tolerate.

One of the other women, a middle-aged mother with the bones of a bird, leaned heavily on the wall as she fell behind the others making their getaway.

Cecelia did what she always had in a crisis, wiped her mind of all but the task at hand. Reaching for the woman, she draped the thin arm around the back of her neck and half carried, half dragged her up the stairs and out onto the lawn.

It might have been all of ten minutes, an hour, or perhaps an eternity before they'd sifted through the carnage of the manse to make certain everyone was out.

Cecelia wiped dirt and sweat from her forehead with the back of her hand, panting with exertion as she went back in once again after depositing a dazed and only partially dressed girl from upstairs on the front terrace. A cigarette girl, Melisandre, had fallen into her own wardrobe, cracking her head on a corner when the blast had occurred. But it seemed her confusion had as much to do with shock and a general personality trait than a head wound.

Though one could never be certain.

Cecelia thought she heard Ramsay say her name on the lawn, but her spectacles were too smudged with dirt and ash and possibly blood to see much in the bright afternoon.

Despite her growing sense of panic, she couldn't leave anyone behind. So each time she deposited someone to the safety of the yard, she dove back into the manse with an increasing sense of doom.

She had to find Jean-Yves and Phoebe. Every time she searched, someone else reached for her, needed her, distracted her from her aim.

The aftermath wasn't as dire as she'd initially feared.

And yet it was worse than she'd ever imagined.

Four dead. Four poor souls lost. Because of *her*, because of enemies she didn't even know she had and had done nothing to cultivate.

The old woman Alexandra had found, then a French instructor named Veronique, her student, Jane, and a young footman who'd been in the residence.

They'd only found bits of him.

Nine others were wounded enough to need ambulances, which had been sent for and were, even now, racing up the drive in a thunder of hooves and masculine voices along with the police and the fire brigade.

Beyond that, minor cuts, abrasions, and burns seemed

to be less cause for complaint than the emotional devastation of having undergone such an ordeal.

Cecelia paid no heed to the arriving armies of men
and the gathering gawkers as she raced through the hall
toward the rear of the main level, careening for the secret
door that separated the residence from the business.

A familiar form limped out from the dust-clogged
hallway amalgamating slowly through the filth on her
spectacles.

"Winston!" she cried, running to him and letting him
lean heavily upon her. He was caked with dust, dirt, and
soot, and his wig was nowhere to be found.

He'd taken her family back to the residence. And if
he'd survived, then . . . perhaps there was hope. "Winston, are you all right? Where are Jean-Yves and Phoebe?"

"The littl'un wanted to dig up a treasure in the gardens,
madame!" The butler hollered as though the blast had
taken away his ability to hear. "I don't think they came
back inside yet!"

Cecelia frantically called for help, handing the poor
butler over to the first faceless person who could take him
before picking up her skirts and dashing down a side hall
toward the courtyard.

Her heart gave an electrified lurch as she found Phoebe
hunched over a prone Jean-Yves in the gardens, shaking
his limp shoulder.

Cecelia let out a raw sound of denial, unable to even
form a word so simple as *no* as she rushed forward and
sank to his side in a tuft of filthy skirts.

"He won't wake up." Phoebe half climbed into her lap.
"He threw me across the hedge when the wall fell, and
now he won't wake up! Is he dead?" Her tiny body trembled in time with Cecelia's as she struggled to speak

through hysterical hiccups. "He can't. Be dead. I've only. Just. Lost. Henrietta!" She gulped, her ability for speech dissolving completely.

Cecelia held Phoebe's stricken face against her, clutching her close and crooning to her so the child couldn't watch the tears stream down her own cheeks. All she wanted to do was collapse over him and dissolve into the mess of terrified sobs that had been threatening to overwhelm her since the day began.

But she simply couldn't. Not now. Not yet. Jean-Yves needed her, for once, and she'd die before she failed him.

His shoulder and upper torso were covered in debris, and a small trail of blood leaked from one ear. He was so disturbingly still. His body, built wiry and strong with years of labor, seemed small against the pile of rubble and stone and a film of white chalk.

But his chest rose and fell with steady breaths.

Rejoicing, Cecelia pulled young Phoebe away from her bosom to look her in her watery eyes. "Darling, look, he's breathing. He's alive."

"He is?" Phoebe sniffed.

"Yes, pet. But someone needs to go fetch an ambulance medic for Jean-Yves from the front lawn. Do you think you can do that whilst I try to lift these stones from his shoulder?"

Phoebe surged to her feet. "Don't let him die before I get back!"

A lump in Cecelia's throat obstructed a reply as Phoebe scampered away in her little black shoes and soiled pinafore.

It wasn't a promise she was equipped to make on his behalf.

"Jean-Yves," she whispered through a fall of tears as she reached over him, gingerly pulling bricks from his arm and shoulder. She spoke as she worked, trying to school the despair from her voice, careful not to start a fall of more stone and debris that could crush them both.

"I shouldn't be surprised if you are tired of doing your best to look after us Rogues. You've spent ten years wiping our tears, suffering our absurd hilarities, and enduring our schemes. . . . I promise we won't cause you any more trouble. . . . Just . . . don't . . ." Her throat closed. She couldn't say it. "I'm not ready to be without you." Her voice broke, and she smoothed a mat of silver hair to his head.

"I know your sweet wife and lovely daughter might be calling you from the beyond, and I won't hold it against you if you go to them." She heaved and trembled beneath a particularly heavy stone before swiping at her tears with her sleeve. "Perhaps I've kept you too long," she fretted. "Longer than I deserve. But . . . Phoebe needs a fatherly figure, and I can't think of anyone better to—"

"You must not weep, *mon bijou*." Jean-Yves's hoarse, breathless voice washed over her like a miracle. "I cannot lift my hand to wipe your tears."

Relief drove Cecelia to her knees, and she lifted his uninjured hand for him, holding it against her wet cheek. "I won't!" she promised, even as her sobs increased.

"You ridiculous rapscallion," he drawled, a grimace overtaking him as he coughed weakly. "I cannot open my eyes. The light, it is too bright, and I am so fatigued."

"Don't fall asleep," she admonished, frightened that if he did, he truly would never wake again. How she wished she could dim the sun or call the eternal gray back over the London skies, if only to comfort him. "Phoebe will want to make certain you are all right. Promise me you won't sleep before she returns."

The girl in question arrived dragging a burly ambulance

medic in her wake like a tiny blond tugboat. Another medic was followed by Francesca and Alexandra, each of them pale, filthy, and alarmed.

The medics freed Jean-Yves from the rest of the rubble, wrapped his head wound, and secured his arm to his chest with no small amount of foul language on Jean-Yves's part.

"Do not fret, *mon Rogues*," he grunted when they could finally load him onto a stretcher. "You are not ready to be unleashed upon an unsuspecting world unchaperoned."

"I'll follow you to hospital." Cecelia clutched his hand.

"No need. I've had enough bruised or broken ribs in my day to know what they feel like," he said. "They'll patch me up, set my shoulder, and send me home with the most wonderful morphine."

"We're coming to hospital, old man," Francesca declared, her stubbornness doing little to conceal the hardwon fondness softening her gaze. "You're too wounded to fight us on this."

"A herd of stampeding rhinoceroses wouldn't keep us away," Alexandra chimed in, smoothing his hair with cautious gentility.

"The three of ye are going exactly nowhere," growled a most unwelcome voice.

Cecelia's mouth turned to ash when she looked up to see Ramsay storming into the gardens like an advancing general. With his features drawn into a furious mask of wrath, she had to fight a very primal instinct to flee such a masculine, mercenary onslaught.

It was a wonder that nations didn't fall before him, with a countenance that fierce. That rivers didn't divert at his word and mountains shouldn't move to make way for his march.

Genny had been right: It was easy to forget how astonishingly large he was until one was faced with two-hundred-plus pounds of Scots muscle and icy wrath charging forward like a golden bull. Head low. Nostrils flaring. Untouched by the chaos and destruction around him.

Untouchable.

Cecelia was surprised to find that she rather disliked the idea of him trailing his disgust and self-righteousness all over her establishment.

Indeed. Whether she liked it or not, it was *hers*. She owned it.

And she would now be forced to own *up* to it.

There would be no seducing secrets from the Vicar of Vice. Not now that he was about to find out just who exactly she was.

Her tongue felt like sandpaper as Ramsay planted his boots a few feet away from them, his gaze making a trail of blue fire up and down Cecelia's filthy frame.

"First of all, is anyone wounded?" he snarled.

"Other than the Frenchman on the stretcher and nine others being hefted into ambulances?" Francesca retorted, folding her arms.

"The wounded on the lawn are being seen to. My question is directed at ye *ladies*." The word dripped from him with acerbic sarcasm as he adopted the exact same posture.

Cecelia noted how his suitcoat stretched over the bulk of his shoulders, straining at the seams. It seemed he could flex but once and the entire thing, though very well made, would be forced to give way.

What a strange thing to notice at a time like this.

She put a hand to her forehead. Perhaps she was concussed.

"We're unharmed, thank you, Ramsay." Alexandra answered her brother-in-law's query when it became apparent no one else was about to.

"Does my brother know ye're here, Yer Grace?" The last syllable slithered from between his teeth like a hiss.

"Of course he does," Alexandra replied. "Which is why I expect him to burst through the doors any moment wild and disheveled and terrified for me." Alexandra's bravado had begun to fade, her bright brunette eyes now pinching with strain. "I should like him to hurry."

Cecelia wrapped her arm around Alexandra's waist to offer what comfort she could until her husband arrived.

What would it be like to have someone care and worry for her as Redmayne did for his wife? With all of himself. The duke would have thrown his own body over his duchess in a blast such as this. He'd have carried her to safety on two broken legs. He'd have bled out before allowing harm to come to her.

Cecelia didn't want to feel sorry for herself, but with Jean-Yves so frighteningly injured and a new charge to look after, she felt heavier than she ever had both physically and otherwise. Weighted down with unknown secrets and unidentified enemies, the blood of four innocent souls, the innocence of missing girls, and the safety of everyone now in her care and employ.

Ramsay blinked at Alexandra, disbelief etched into the hard frown lines bracketing his mouth. "Ye mean for me to believe Redmayne allows ye to come to this place?" He gestured to the rubble.

"Redmayne *allows* me nothing. I am my own person and ask permission of no one." Alexandra slid her gaze to Cecelia. "However, I was touring the school to see if I wanted to add it to my more philanthropic endeavors. As it turns out, I categorically do. Especially now."

Cecelia would have expressed her undying gratitude to Alexandra had she not been interrupted by the explosive din of an enormous burning beam of wood, which chose that moment to roll down the mountain of rubble toward them.

In a manner that very much remind her of a charging bull, Ramsay lunged forward with his arms open and scooped up all three women, sweeping them back as the log landed in a volcano of sparks and dust and ash in the exact spot they'd gathered.

It was rather like being swept up by a brick wall.

He jerked away the moment they'd been deposited to safety, leaving Cecelia feeling oddly bereft. To wield such tremendous strength was unimaginable to her.

But to be buttressed by it. Shielded and supported by it.

To rely upon and be rescued by it.

How extraordinary.

Ash and dust filmed her spectacles, obstructing her vision completely. The grit of it gathered on her face and settled in a chalky-tasting skein on her teeth. A fit of wheezing coughs overtook her, and she bent forward with her hand over her mouth to regain her breath.

No one said a word, but a handkerchief was thrust into her hand.

Cecelia wiped the dust and ash from her lips, nose, and chin so she could breathe.

It smelled like him. Like clean linen, sharp soap, and . . . books.

She paused to pull the scent deep into her beleaguered lungs before swiping off her spectacles to clean them with the unsoiled side of the soft cloth.

She searched the gardens anxiously, noting that Frank and Alexander were gaining their balance and their breath behind her, but were otherwise unharmed.

Phoebe stood safely some distance away, pressed against the far wall, her features indistinguishable.

Jean-Yves had thankfully been conducted from the room by the medics before the log fell.

No harm done. Cecelia opened her mouth to thank Ramsay, but he spoke before she was able.

"Jesus kilt-lifting Christ. It's *ye*."

It was hard to discern from his voice if he was more furious or incredulous.

Cecelia glanced over at him, finding nothing but the blunt shapes of his features and the stunning size of everything else. Then she held her glasses up to bring the world—and the man—into focus.

Catching her reflection in the one window that remained intact, she saw what Ramsay did. The soot about her face was shaped very much like a masquerade mask. Covered thusly, without her spectacles on and her hair dusted with ash and debris, she unequivocally resembled the woman he'd met only yesterday in the ruined residence.

The woman he detested.

The Scarlet Lady.

"It is I," she confessed upon a wistful sigh.

She'd kissed Ramsay . . .

And never would again judging by the antipathy with which he currently regarded her.

His hair had become disheveled, and the high collar of his crisp suit was now smudged with grime, his necktie missing. But his eyes. His eyes glinted with silver storms, the blue vanishing almost completely.

If the storm wasn't about to be unleashed upon her, she'd have taken all the time she could to admire and absorb it.

To bask in the ferocious beauty of it, as she'd always been fond of storms.

Lud, she thought wryly. The blast must have blown the wits right out of her head.

He took a threatening step forward, his shoulders seeming to grow along with his wrath such that Cecelia was ashamed to notice she'd retreated a step into the safety of the Rogues.

He didn't yell. Indeed, his voice lowered several impossible octaves. But something in the depth and precise enunciation of his orders lent them more gravitas than a thunderous roar.

"Someone kindly tell me just what in the veriest *fuck* is going on here, and who the bloody hell *ye* really are." He stabbed a condemning finger in Cecelia's direction, and she put her hands up as though said finger were the end of a pistol.

"I would be happy to explain, my lord." She fought to keep her voice even. "Although . . . I'd request that you mind your language in front of—"

"This house is so entirely sullied, my language willna make one jot of a difference, madam," he sneered, raking her with a glare so sharp and loathing it might have had claws.

His disgust, while expected, still stung. No, it burned. Igniting a fire of indignation within her breast.

"I beg *your* pardon, sir," Cecelia said with just as much control as she could muster. "You obviously have a personal vendetta to discharge here. However, you are in the presence of a countess and a duchess of the realm, and as such, it is beholden upon you as a gentleman to show them, your betters, the deference due their station."

"Betters?" he snorted with derision. "Ye no more believe someone can be born yer better than I do, regardless of the company ye keep." He thrust his jaw toward the noble ladies. "But vendetta or no, I'm here because an explosion just endangered my city, and I do intend to ken how and why."

My city, Cecelia thought mulishly. As if he owned London. The sheer arrogance of the man. The abject pomposity. If she'd had the courage to engage her wit in confrontations, she'd tell him exactly what she thought of him. But it seemed her courage had begun to fail her.

"What's going on here," Francesca answered from behind her, "is that someone tried to murder our Cecelia in her own establishment. Now, just what do you plan to do about it?"

Ramsay ignored Francesca like an oak would a gnat.

"Which introduction of ours was a lie?" A severe note underscored his question, and Cecelia wondered if he, too, thought about their enchanted evening.

About their kiss.

"I didn't lie to you," Cecelia said.

"Ye told me yer name was Hortense Thistledown," he accused.

"I said you may *call* me Hortense Thistledown," she corrected. "Think of it as a . . . business moniker. A nom de plume, if you will."

"And the French accent?"

"I'll admit that was a bit of . . . improvisation on my part," she hedged.

"Call it what it bloody was. A falsehood." Though his voice remained even, Cecelia sensed she'd reached the edge of a very long rope. The edge that might have a noose attached to it.

If he wanted the truth, Cecelia decided, then the truth he would get. "Yesterday morning I found out that I had an aunt named Henrietta Thistledown in the same sentence that I was told she'd expired and willed to me her business. You rudely interrupted my initial assessment of the place by threatening to kick my door in, and I was forced to defend my inheritance by whatever means I deemed fit."

He'd begun shaking his head in the middle of her statement. "I'll pretend for a moment that doesna sound like utter horsewallop, and ask why ye would feel the need to defend yerself from the police if ye're not breaking the law?"

"Because Henrietta told me in a letter that her enemies had become my enemies, and those enemies were law-breakers *as well as* lawmakers. If you're familiar with her, then you must be aware of her clientele, half of which sit in the House of Lords and on the justice benches beneath you." Cecelia gauged his reaction, treading carefully here. How much should she reveal? How much did she trust Cassius Ramsay? She took a deep breath.

In for a penny . . . "Henrietta told me she was possessed of debts and secrets that could get her killed. That put me and the school in danger. And . . . just look what's happened." She swept her hand to encompass the disaster.

His eyes narrowed to thin shards of ice. "Ye want me to believe that Henrietta left ye one of the largest of the ill-begotten fortunes in the land and ye'd never even met her?"

That's what he focused on?

"We might have done," Cecelia corrected. "Genny said she remembered meeting me as a very small girl—"

"I'm to believe that ye, the daughter of a widowed

country vicar, were planning on taking up the mantle of the Scarlet Lady with no training, knowledge, or know-how of such an endeavor?" Condescension edged out suspicion as he spoke.

"I took plenty of classes in economics at university, I'm fairly confident in my abilities to run a successful gambling venture—"

"Ye simply sat down at a solicitor's office yesterday, learned of the death of an infamous family member, and thought to yerself, why not contribute to the depravity of an already rotting and decrepit city?"

"That's not at all what I—"

"Ye think I'm naive enough to believe that ye stumbled into this profession *yesterday*?" He advanced as he spoke, until he was almost nose-to-nose with Cecilia. For the first time maybe ever, she was grateful for her height and her heft, and drew upon every inch she could claim.

And still he loomed over her.

How did one do that? she wondered. Turn standing into looming. She'd never wished so intensely as in that moment for the knowledge of a proper loom.

As it was, she simply threw her shoulders back and lifted her chin, wishing that any kind of conflict didn't make her stomach roil and a cold sweat to bloom. "You don't have to believe a word I say, my lord. I suppose your only task would be to find out who has done this to my establishment and why."

At this, his eyes went flat. All the electricity leaching out of them as if disappointment deflated his anger.

"Ye are right, of course," he stated coldly. "Tell me, Miss Teague—or is it Miss Thistledown?—did yer aunt give ye any indication as to the nature of these dangerous secrets?"

"Well, not exactly." Cecilia swallowed, doing her best

not to be cowed by the cords in his neck and the vein pulsing at his temple. "Not . . . in so many words."

"Speak plainly," he clipped. "Aye or nay?"

"Nay—er—no. She categorically did not reveal them to me . . . as of yet."

He eyed her with great suspicion, and Cecelia knew she was being obtuse in trying to avoid a lie, but also not wanting to reveal anything that might put her in more danger. She was not so foolish as to reveal the existence of the codex before it could be deciphered.

"Ye're telling me ye have no idea who would want to do something like this?" he asked.

"Not a clue."

"A motive, perhaps?" he pressed. "A rival, a dissatisfied customer, unpaid debts, an unhappy employee, et cetera."

Cecelia shook her head. "Could be anyone, all told. I've not yet been able to find the accounts."

Alexandra bent down, swiping her finger through the white film blanketing the rubble. She lifted the finger to her nose, smelling it, and then touched the tip of her tongue to the substance before spitting delicately. "We at least know what agent was used in the explosion," she said.

"Gunpowder," Ramsay stated drolly.

"Precisely." Alexandra looked over at him as though he'd surprised her. "How did you know?"

"I was a soldier, remember? I'd recognize that scent anywhere." He eyed his sister-in-law. "How did *ye* know?"

"Refined black powder is often used in excavation," Alexandra answered. "It leaves behind this white residue and tastes of steam and sulfur with a hint of something like urine from the saltpeter." She rubbed her thumb and forefinger together, testing the substance. "I wonder, though. This was a rather small explosion, as these things go. Contained to this specific part of the house. Also, there's a taste here I can't quite decipher. Bitter . . ."

Francesca lifted her skirt and toed the rubble with the tip of her boot. "Could there have been an agent other than gunpowder involved here? Nitroglycerin, perhaps?"

"Nitroglycerin is too unstable for such calculated destruction." Cecelia slid from beneath the chill of Ramsay's impressive loom to crouch near the fall of stones that made a treacherous ramp of debris up to the ruins of the second floor of the residence. She remembered something she'd learned about in a chemistry and alchemy lecture she'd attended at Cambridge not so long ago given by a Dr. Alfred Nobel.

"The French recently manufactured a melanite that is more stable than nitroglycerin." Cecelia reached down to duplicate Alexandra, swiping at the powder with her finger and testing it with the tip of her tongue before she spit it out.

"Just as I suspected," she proclaimed. "It's likely a trinitrophenol they've named carbazotic acid. Because of Dr. Nobel's advancements in explosives, one is now able to cap and contain carbazotic acid in a bomb with a rather predictable blast radius." She looked up, her stomach flipping over with dread. "Also, he spoke of a timing device used in the railway attacks claimed by the Irish Sinn Fein a couple of years ago."

"So the culprit could have been long gone before the device even detonated?" Francesca lamented. "The devious pillock, whoever he is!" She kicked at a rock.

As if he'd come out of a trance, Ramsay made a low noise containing what she thought was a foul word, drawing their attention. "Explosive compounds. Carbazotic acid. Where in the name of the bloody devil did the three of ye come from?"

"Ecole de Chardonne for girls on Lake Geneva," Francesca answered.

"And the Sorbonne thereafter," Alexandra supplied helpfully. "Along with a few supplemental courses through various Continental and American universities."

He blinked once. Twice. Regarded them as though he would put them under a microscope.

He eyed Cecelia with a new misgiving, and it didn't take a mind reader to realize that he wondered if she was responsible for the destruction of her own home. "I thought ye were a mathematician. What does that have to do with extensive knowledge of explosives?"

Cecelia stood and opened her mouth, but Alexandra beat her to it.

"Oh come now, Ramsay, you cannot think she had anything to do with this."

"And why not?"

Alexandra scoffed. "Though her study was primarily mathematics, she would, of course, be educated in the applications thereof, which would mean a rudimentary knowledge of physics and chemistry. In fact, we attended many courses together."

"Yes." Francesca stepped in to champion her. "And as Cecelia stated, she still insists upon attending boring lectures all the time. What would she have to gain by blowing up her own place?"

Cecelia leveled a droll look at Frank just as Ramsay's mouth flattened into a thin line.

"There are cleaner ways of getting rid of evidence." A muscle ticked in his jaw. "Yer friends are awfully protective of ye, Miss Teague. Almost as if they ken ye're guilty of something."

Cecelia straightened, doing her best to meet his gaze

head-on. "It's ever been thus, my lord, we protect one another."

"Cecelia's of a generally shy and sensitive nature," Alexandra explained. "And she's only just been through something unthinkably traumatic. Perhaps we can finish this another time, Ramsay."

He grunted out a strange sound that Cecelia thought might have been a laugh if a lion had rendered it. And if one could laugh without smiling. "Shy? Sensitive? Now I ken ye take me for a fool, but no one is that gullible." He raked fingers through his thick fall of hair. "Chemistry and physics . . . My grandmother Ramsay would have burned ye three for a cadre of witches."

Until now, Phoebe had been so quiet and still, her presence was all but forgotten. She marched toward Ramsay until she stood beneath him, little fists planted on nonexistent hips.

"Anyone with eyes can tell she's *not* a witch," the girl declared, unfazed by the golden giant even as she tilted her head all the way back on her neck to look up at him.

Cecelia watched, stunned as something no less than miraculous happened.

Ramsay's face, which she'd been thus far certain was carved from the same stone and ice as his heart, softened in increments until his eyes were pools of liquid charm and his mouth no longer pressed into his ever-present frown.

With such an expression he appeared almost . . . handsome.

Almost.

"Where did ye come from, wee lass?"

"I don't know." The clear-eyed girl stood like the proverbial David against Ramsay's Goliath. "But you can't truly believe in witches, and I know you can't burn them anymore."

"Of course no one will burn," he said, almost apologetically. "Though, not to naysay ye, lass, but I know for certain this particular trio of redheaded ladies have a penchant for trouble. Multiple explosions, fires, gunfights, kidnappings, and nefarious brews that once even put my brother in an enchanted sleep for a full day and a night." He crouched down, still not bringing him eye level with the girl, but stretching his soiled clothing in the most diverting of ways over his legs, arms, and shoulders.

"Doesna that sound like the doings of witches to ye?" he asked gently.

Phoebe glanced over her shoulder at Cecelia, her expression uncertain.

Cecelia knew she should be mad enough to spit nails, but instead she found herself unable to do aught but watch the conversation unfold.

"She's too pretty to be a witch," Phoebe decided with an adorable wrinkle of her brow. "And besides, her nose isn't even a bit warty, nor are her fingers gnarled." She looked back to Ramsay, no doubt to see if she'd made a convincing enough argument.

The Scot in question was staring at Cecelia. "Och, lass, ye've the right of it, I suppose."

Cecelia fought the urge to fidget beneath his intense regard. One that carried weighty questions and even heavier accusations.

Also, she wondered if he realized that he'd agreed she was pretty . . .

"What's yer name, child?" The rumble of his voice as he spoke to the girl threatened to unstitch something deep within Cecelia's belly.

"I'm Phoebe." She curtsied.

"It's a pleasure to meet ye, Miss Phoebe." They shook hands briefly, and the ghost of a smile haunted the corners of Ramsay's mouth. "I'm—"

"I know who you are. You're the Vicar of Vice. You were yelling last time you were here. I hid under the desk so you wouldn't take me away."

Every muscle in Ramsay's features and body tensed once again, turning him into his usual statue of stone. "What is such a wee thing doing in a place like this?" he demanded with barely leashed fury. "Will I find her if I search the missing persons reports?"

"I'm not missing, I'm right here." She held her arms out and waved as though he might be blind. "I'm Phoebe Thistledown."

"She belongs to me," Cecelia rushed, reaching for the girl's hand and pulling her into the safety of her skirts.

Ramsay's frown returned, along with a deeper, bleaker look as he studied Cecelia, then the girl.

Cecelia knew she'd lost all esteem in his eyes. She'd passed the point of no return.

They were true enemies once again.

"She . . . doesna resemble ye," he finally said.

"I imagine she takes after her father."

"Ye imagine." His lip curled into a silent snarl of disgust. "Are there so many men in the running for her patrilineal line?"

"That's not what I said." Cecelia lifted her chin a notch. "And I'll thank you not to speak thusly in front of the child. You've subjected her to enough profanity already."

A bit of his high color drained from his face, and he possessed the grace to look abashed as he and the girl stared at each other with a similar sullen suspicion.

"Forgive me, Miss Phoebe," he murmured, shocking Cecelia past all comprehension.

Phoebe nodded her forgiveness, then finally asked, "You're a justice?"

"Aye. And I suppose ye are all free to go and clean up and be seen to, though ye'll not leave London until this inquest is completed." His gaze collided with Cecelia's, chilling her at least ten degrees. "Except for ye. I've questions for ye still."

Phoebe stepped in front of her. "If you're a lawman, you can't hurt anyone," she reminded him. "And you'll let her come home with me, because she hasn't done anything wrong."

He blinked down at the girl, his voice less jagged than before. "Home? Do ye not reside here, child?"

"No, we live on Cranford Street with Jean-Yves. I have a bed made from fairy wood and ivy, a robin nests in my window, and Cook made me extra cherry tarts for breakfast."

Ramsay brushed at the thighs of his trousers, releasing a bone-weary breath. "If yer ma's done nothing wrong, then she's nothing to fear from me, child."

"She's not—"

"What do you say I take little Phoebe to hospital," Francesca interrupted, collecting the girl's hand from Cecelia's. "She *was* close to the blast and I still think she should be examined along with Jean-Yves. You can meet us there, Cecil, when you're through here, and we'll all escort you home."

"Will you be accompanied by Mr. Derringer?" Cecelia queried. Someone had attacked her in the open and made it clear that they had no scruples about collateral damage. Phoebe's safety was paramount.

"No, but I have employed Mr. Colt." Francesca grinned.

"Don't fret, my dear, we're well looked after." She patted her pocket where she always kept a pistol.

"Thank you, Frank." Cecelia meant it with all her heart, as Francesca swept poor Phoebe away.

Phoebe's high, sweet voice echoed down the eerily empty marble hall. "Why does she call you Frank? That's a man's name."

"It's a secret," Francesca said indulgently. "If you're very good for the doctor, I might tell you the story of the Red Rogues."

"I like stories," Phoebe declared.

"I instinctively knew you did."

"And I'm always good."

Francesca's laugh was genuine and husky. "No one is always good, and one cannot be inducted into the Red Rogues if that is the case."

"Then . . ." Phoebe seemed to think about it for a quiet beat. "I must misbehave?"

"Regularly."

"Can you teach me how?"

"Oh, you darling girl, I thought you'd never ask. Auntie Frank will be your most enthusiastic instructor."

"Should I misbehave for the doctor, then?"

"Of course not."

"When should I?"

"That is an excellent question—Oh dear, do stand aside by the wall with me."

"Why?" Phoebe asked.

"Because you don't want to get trampled by a duke."

At the sound of heavy running footfalls, Alexandra's grip tightened on Cecelia's.

"Where is she?" The Devonshire accent echoed from the walls of the hallway, raw with equal parts anxiety and ferocity.

"In the courtyard gardens," they heard Francesca dictate. "She's unharmed, by the by."

Redmayne was a devilishly dark streak of animalistic motion as he broke from the door of the entry to see his wife standing at the bottom of explosive debris.

"You're welcome!" Francesca's amused call from the hallway went unheeded.

With a little cry, Alexandra released Cecelia's hand.

Glass from myriad broken windows intoned the duke's and duchess's desperate footsteps across the ruined gardens as their rush forward ended in a collision of bodies that would have driven a smaller man to his back.

Redmayne, however, enfolded his little wife into his chest, curling strong shoulders over her as she reached into his jacket and banded her arms around his back.

One large hand cupped the back of her head, and the other drew itself up and down her spine as he pressed his scarred cheek to her crown.

Despite his gentle handling of her, a string of foul curses that would have turned a buccaneer's cheeks red ripped through the air. "I'm never letting you out of my sight again, do you hear me?"

Alexandra burrowed deeper into his chest. "I'm all right. Not even a scratch on me. There's no need to worry."

"No need to—" He thrust her away from him, examining her well-being for himself. "This is the second explosion you've escaped without a wound in as many years. So help me, there will *not* be a third."

"I'm glad you came." Alexandra leaned heavily on her husband, and he instantly bent to scoop her into his arms as he sent his brother an unspoken message with eyes the identical shade of wintry blue.

Ramsay nodded once.

"I'm taking you home," he murmured to his wife.

"But." Alexandra looked anxiously over her husband's shoulder, her mask of soot mostly left on the duke's shirt-front. "Cecil . . ."

"Ramsay's with her." Redmayne didn't even pause.

"That's what I'm afraid of. He wants to hang her, you know."

"Yes, but not today," the duke replied, as though it was the furthest worry from his mind. "We'll deal with that after I get you home, bathed, and thoroughly examined." His tone was neither teasing nor censorious nor even overtly sexual. Just incontestable.

Inevitable.

Cecelia and Alexandra both shrugged at each other helplessly as Redmayne conducted his wife away, but not before Cecelia caught a copper gleam of relief in her cherished friend's eyes.

She stared at the empty doorway through which everyone had disappeared for a few moments, drifting toward it. Away from Ramsay's proximity. Taking the moment to indulge in a few bracing breaths as she looked up into the rare bright-blue London sky.

Bracing for the storm.

"The Scarlet Lady," Ramsay said as though he still couldn't believe it. As though the title tasted like the scum along the shores of the Thames. "The Lord Chancellor always told me that the devil's greatest trick is convincing ye he doesna exist. . . . I never truly kenned what he meant until this moment."

"You think I'm the devil?" She whirled to face him, aghast.

"Nay." His jaw set into a granite square, but the vein at his temple still pulsed beneath where a forelock of hair had come free of its pomade to hang over his surly brow.

"Ye're little more than a succubus." He raked his fingers through his mane, sculpting the forelock back into place. "How did I not see it before? Ye're built for naught but debauchery and deceit. I canna believe I allowed myself to be taken in and tempted by the likes of ye."

"It was not my aim to tempt you—"

"Horseshit." He regarded her with a careful gaze, barbed but also a little broken. As if there was a part of him that wanted to believe her.

"Truly. I desired peace between us. Perhaps more." She took a tentative step toward him. "Everything I said last night was the truth. Everything that passed between us . . . it was real."

The shadow of vulnerability vanished, replaced by such stony disgust, she wondered if she'd imagined it.

"Nothing about ye is real. Not yer name, not yer niceties. Yer kisses are currency and your sex is yer weapon. Doona imagine I will be fooled by ye again."

It was difficult to pretend his cruelty didn't sting. One would think that after so many years, she'd have perfected some sort of mask of insouciance. That a childhood spent with the Vicar Teague would have taught her to hide her emotion. That the jeers and harassment she'd suffered at university would have inured her to the pain.

She'd tried so often to be hard. To deflect and defend against the barbarism of men and the censure of other women with walls like Alexandra, or spikes like Francesca.

But to her eternal frustration, she'd remained a soft place for insults to land.

They always stung. Or burned. Hurt and humiliated her. If someone wasn't making her feel too big, clumsy, and contemptible, then they were making her feel very, very insignificant.

How was it that men could hurt women, and they forever went unpunished?

How was it that a man could stand in the middle of the chaos that had become her life and rake her with his claws of ice as though he had the right?

Was it justice? Did this man, this arrogant, dastardly, giant of a man really consider himself the epitome of the word?

Something formed in the pit of her chest. Something dark and heavy. Bleak and hollow. She'd call it fear, but not so cold. Anger but not so hot. Hurt, but not so weak. Perhaps an amalgamation of all these things.

Brewing like a storm of her own.

He made a noise full of hostility. "Ye kiss like a virgin, I'll give ye that."

"And you kiss like a man who would know the difference," she volleyed back. "A man who would turn a virgin into his whore and then blame her for the deed."

"Never." His eyes glinted with lightning. "Do *not* presume to know me. I'm not like the weak-willed men who slink like shadows through this door to pay for hollow fantasies and pretty fallacies whilst ye fleece them for money. Ye doona think I already ken that Henrietta harbored lethal secrets? That someone would want her dead? More and more often I follow the evidence of rank misdeeds right to this doorstep." He stalked closer now. Loomed impossibly larger. "Ye know more than ye're letting on, woman. Do ye expect me to believe ye have no idea who would want ye dead?"

"Besides you?"

"I've never heard anything so absurd!" He threw his hand up in frustration, and it was everything she could do not to flinch before she realized it was merely a gesture. "Doona test me."

"Or what?" she challenged, tossing his soiled handkerchief at his feet. "How am I to know you had nothing to do with this? You certainly are single-minded in your hatred of this place. You showed up here rather instantaneously after the blast. Don't tell me you were just in the neighborhood."

"I was, in fact." His expression darkened from surly to downright malevolent. Haunted by a rage too dark to be spoken. "One of the missing girls was found in a garden of an estate not far from here. Katerina Milovic, and I'll tell ye, the bodies taken from this place would haunt ye less than what was left of her."

Cecelia's hand flew to her mouth in a vague attempt to keep a threatening sob from escaping.

The poor child.

She had thought of the girls often since learning of them the day before, fearing that they'd been kept belowground somewhere. Alone. Frightened. Innocent despite what was being done to them.

"Garden?" she whispered. "What—in whose garden was she found?"

"Lord Luther Kenway, the Earl of Devlin." He watched her expression with alert eyes, no doubt to gauge her reaction. "Does that name mean anything to ye? Is he one of yer customers?"

Cecelia shook her head, more in horror than denial. "I'm telling you once more, I have no idea. It is as much a mystery to me as it is to you where Henrietta's client ledgers are. All I know is that Genny made new ones for today. There wouldn't be more than a page, but it's yours if you want it."

"Ye doona find it odd, that Katerina was found so close to yer establishment?"

"I don't know." She was starting to sound like a parrot. A desperate one. "But I had nothing to do with it."

"How do ye expect me to believe ye?" he asked. "Henrietta's fortune had to be built with more than just the revenue from this place. I still think she procured young girls for wealthy men, and I'm not convinced I can take your word regarding your ignorance. Especially since ye've proven to have such an aptitude for performance."

"I would never—"

"I doona want to hear it." He turned toward the rubble and gazed at it intently. "I'll comb through every stone, every passage. I'll continue to dismantle this house until I find what it has to do with those missing girls."

"I'm telling you, there is nothing to be found here!" She'd reached her limit of baseless accusations, and could take no more. "I'm sorry for these missing girls, more than you know. I will do what I can to help you find them. But on an unrelated note, I have a bevy of women and girls who are also in danger, do you understand? People *died* today, and so many more were injured. Not only the women who work in my gambling hell, but seamstresses and orphans and cable workers and widows. Every woman in this house is entitled to protection and justice. Every. Woman. Despite your hypocritical personal prejudices on the matter."

He made a derisive gesture. "Better a hypocrite than a liar."

"Are they not one and the same?"

He glared down at her, pulling his contemptible superiority about him like a mantle. "Principles are not prejudices, madam, and though I'm not perfect, I endeavor to be. I stand for something." He thumped his chest with one beat of his fist. "I fight on the side of justice. I am a man of integrity and purpose with an empire to look after. What are ye but the warden in a gilded prison of slags and reprobates? I hope to see the rest of this place reduced to rubble; the very existence of it offends me!"

That's it. The dam of Cecelia's long temper broke. "What am I?" This time she advanced upon him. "What am *I*? I'm a woman of both intellect and compassion. Of morals and mercy, despite what you may think. You want to see something truly offensive? Go back to your lofty manse, Lord Chief Justice, put on your robes and your wig, and then take a good, long look in a mirror. If you're even capable of doing so from where you've taken permanent residence up your own arse."

His golden skin had previously flushed red with emotion and was now tinged with a bit of purple. Cecelia was grateful that she no longer stood near him, as she might have been immolated in the blast of fury and malice that emanated from him in waves.

To his credit, he said nothing. He did nothing but seethe.

Cecelia opened the door wider, too incensed to be afraid. "In case you were confused, that was an invitation to leave."

He strode with the contained movements of a man carrying a device that might detonate at any moment. Smooth and slow until he reached her and paused beneath the arched threshold of the garden door.

He leaned into her, and his scent pervaded her senses with an intoxicating effect.

"Listen well, woman." His voice was both jagged and smooth, like hot wax dripping over shards of glass. "Ye and yer ilk are a cancer on this country, and I'm the surgeon preparing to cut it out. Ye're such a clever lass? Then ye're smart enough to fear me. To watch for me. Because I've had it with the vice and violence. If ye're even considering a misstep, know that from now on I'll be the hot breath down yer neck and the chill from the shadows. The moment I find the *whisper* of guilt about ye, I'll lock ye up and throw away the key."

Cecelia stood still beneath his onslaught, her fists clenched upon the latch of the doorway flushing alternately with fury and fear and . . . fascination.

He leaned even closer, his breath indeed hot on her ear. "Ye'll find, Miss Teague, that I'm a man without mercy."

At that, he strode away, taking his atmosphere of frost with him.

"I knew that already," Cecelia whispered, trembling as she listened to his measured footsteps fading as the rest of the chaos of the place engulfed her.

"It's nothing to be proud of."

CHAPTER NINE

Ramsay dripped with sweat. With blood. And still the insatiable animal rippling through his veins wouldn't be appeased.

He'd fought anyone in his exclusive fraternal club who would dare stand against him, making the most ridiculous concessions just to entice a man to try. He allowed contenders almost twenty years his junior to take their bare fists to his face while he still wore his gloves. He gave them canes and sticks while he fought barehanded. What did he care? Court was out of session for several weeks more, and he had no reason to heed vanity.

He ached to hit something. Someone. Yearned to feel flesh give way beneath his fists. He needed someone to knock some sense into him. To summon the extreme focus that accompanied pain.

All too soon, there was no one left to fight. He'd defeated them all.

Until someone had called upon his brother.

He should thank whoever'd had that idea. Or take him out in the alley to be shot.

The jury was still out.

Redmayne was as close to his physical equal as he could possibly get in this city. Ramsay outweighed his brother by almost a stone, but the duke had built his impressive stature by climbing the tallest mountains in the world, fording the longest rivers, and hacking his way through environs not fit for human inhabitation.

Pound for pound Redmayne was the strongest man he knew, besides himself, and that strength was compounded by the agility of a jaguar.

So, Ramsay decided, he wouldn't feel guilty for hammering him into the dirt.

He threw a right hook that might have broken a tooth—or a jaw—but Redmayne ducked, following through with an uppercut to the solar plexus that stole his breath.

Ramsay punched the light of victory right out of his brother's eyes with a lightning-fast left jab.

Redmayne spit a bit of blood onto the ground beneath them and circled to his left, wiping at his lip with the back of his knuckle. His muscles bunched and rebounded as he hopped from foot to foot.

Come to think of it. They should do this more often.

"Marriage is making ye soft, brother," Ramsay taunted, shaking his arms in front of him to keep them loose, feeling strong and raw and male.

"And age is making you slow," Redmayne charged. His first blow glanced off Ramsay's chin and the second one missed altogether as he weaved out of his way and danced to the duke's side, landing a punishing shot to his ribs.

"Ye were saying?"

Redmayne coughed a bit but recovered admirably.

"Who are you fighting, Case? A certain redheaded Rogue? Or are you simply at war with yourself?"

"Donna call me Case in public." Ramsay lunged, landing a devastating blow to the body and paying for it by taking a hit to his jaw that left a ringing in his ears.

"What public?" Redmayne gestured as he spun away, opening his arms for a brief moment to encircle the empty room.

The hour was late, and the club would likely be closed had he and Redmayne not lingered. The elderly had gone home to bed, and young dandies would have supped and moved on to chase vices and late-night delights.

They'd have to find somewhere other than Henrietta's now.

"I have no desire to discuss the Scarlet Lady," Ramsay snarled.

"I never mentioned her name," Redmayne said, smugness tugging at the corners of his mouth. The expression emphasized the scar on his upper lip, barely concealed by his close-cropped beard.

"Doona condescend to me." Ramsay lashed out. Missed. Regrouped.

"I'm not condescending, I'm condemning." Redmayne's eyes glinted the same wintry blue Ramsay saw in the mirror every day.

The one reminder of the heartless mother they shared.

"What possible reason could a hedonistic git like ye have to condemn me?" Ramsay was so astonished by the ludicrous notion, he dropped his hands and took a well-placed jab to the mouth.

His teeth cut into his lip, and the metallic tang of blood offended him. He spat it onto the ground as Redmayne delivered another scathing blow, this time with words.

"Cecelia Teague was the victim today, and you treated her like the villain."

There it was. The reason he'd punished himself in this manner. The truth that he'd wanted to pummel out of himself until he could bandage it with righteous wrath.

She haunted him. Nay, she possessed him like a demon that refused to be exorcised. The tracks her tears had made through the grime on her face lanced him every time he closed his eyes. Her words tangled inside his head, creating tornadoes of doubt that threatened to rip through everything he believed to be true.

Why?

Because he wanted her? He wanted her like he'd wanted nothing before. Like a blind man desires to see color, or a starving man craves a meal.

She was a flame dancing in the distance across the cold tundra into which he'd been born, tempting him closer. Calling him to bask in her warmth.

But he knew that if he relented, her flames could prove to be hellfire, consuming everything good about the life he'd built from nothing.

Nay. He was a man of focus and commitment, of sheer will and uncompromising discipline.

Or he was until he caught a whiff of her intoxicating aroma. Until her bright-azure eyes unstitched him and her body beckoned for him to fill his hands with control-melting allure.

He couldn't afford that. Not now. Not when the bodies of young girls were being shredded and left like so much compost in a path that led straight to her door.

Not when bombs were going off in the middle of his city.

"Ye ken as well as I do that a villain may play the victim." He circled his brother, looking for a weakness in his guard. "One devious mind can be more dangerous than an advancing brigade. It's why the Home Office employs spies."

"She's not our mother," Redmayne reminded him drolly.

"She could be a thousand times worse."

"I can't believe that. Alexandra says Cecelia Teague is less dangerous than a kitten."

"She certainly has claws," Ramsay muttered, throwing a few halfhearted test punches that glanced off his brother's blocking forearms. "Think about what could have befallen yer beloved lady wife today," he reminded.

Redmayne's swarthy visage darkened. "It's all I've been thinking about."

"The blame for that may be thrown at Miss Teague's feet."

"Not so," Redmayne argued. "The fault lies with whomever detonated that explosive. Do you have any suspects, by the by?"

"Only half of the London elite," Ramsay groused. "I'm not certain she didna have a hand in it, herself."

Redmayne glanced around his fists and lowered them carefully, wordlessly suggesting a break by gesturing toward the water pitcher. "Are you really so blinded by your hatred of her that you would suspect her of sabotaging her own livelihood and putting those she cared about in such danger?"

"Ye insult me to assume it's hatred that drives my suspicion, and not logic."

"Logic has little to do with lust."

"Fuck off." Ramsay gave his brother his back, snatching a cloth from where it hung and mopping at his brow. Was he truly so transparent? Was his lust for the Scarlet Lady so readily predicted?

"I mean no insult, brother, but these remarkable

women are not easily ignored." Redmayne set two glasses on the sideboard and filled each one from the water pitcher with the same measured calm in which he answered. "They are fiercely loyal to one another, and share a bond built of a past not many can claim. Perhaps you, as a soldier, could possibly understand it someday."

Ramsay turned to study his brother's enigmatic features. The duke's words concealed more than they revealed, and the thought made him murderous. Was everyone fucking hiding something from him?

"What are ye insinuating?" he demanded. "Speak plainly."

"Only that I don't believe a woman who would do for my wife what Cecelia Teague has done would risk Alexandra's life by putting her in the vicinity of an explosive device." Redmayne shrugged as Ramsay narrowed his eyes.

"What do ye mean? What did she do for yer wife?"

Redmayne cast him a mysterious glance over the rim of his glass. "That isn't for me to say."

Ramsay had to try extremely hard not to crush the delicate glass in his fist. "More secrets. More shadows. Christ, this woman is full of them. Is it any wonder I doona trust her?"

Redmayne carefully examined him before making a decision. "Did it ever occur to you that you don't trust women because our mother—"

"*Our mother* destroyed two weak husbands and a handful of lovers," Ramsay snarled, feeling the well of black hatred that rose at the very mention of her. "Cecelia Teague—nay, the Scarlet Lady—might alone have the power to bring our entire empire to its knees through scandal and debt. That, dear brother, is why I doona trust her."

Even at this uncharacteristic burst of temper, Redmayne kept his calm. "Perhaps that is the fault of those who perpetrate the scandals, and not the one who catalogs them."

Ramsay grimaced in disgust. "Ye sound just like her."

"Is that so bad? She's a kind soul, Case. She didn't ask for any of this."

"She *lied*, Piers," Ramsay exploded, wishing these outbursts would cease. That he could control them as he controlled everything else. "She had every opportunity to tell me who she was. There's a reason she didna, and that reason canna be a safe one."

His brother's dark brows lifted with deliberate skepticism, and Ramsay took a swig of water to escape it.

"Which opportunity should she have taken? Before or after you kissed her?"

Ramsay choked on his water.

"Women talk to each other," the duke offered by way of explanation. "And my wife talks to me."

"Then ye should be eternally terrified."

Redmayne's self-satisfied sneer made him wish they were still in the ring so he could wipe it away with his fist. "On the contrary, I know my wife is more than gratified."

One. Good. Hit . . . and he could knock Redmayne flat on his arse. "Ye bloody, bourgeois bastard," he muttered drolly.

"Call me what you want." Redmayne poked him in a bruise forming on his ribs, just as he'd done when they were tussling boys. "But I'm not the one who kissed the same woman I'm trying to indict. I imagine that won't go over well in court."

When Ramsay didn't reply, Piers ventured, "Forgive her, Case. I'd stake my life on the fact that she's done nothing wrong."

Ramsay could still bring himself to say nothing. Despite everything, he respected his brother too much to verbally accuse him of being blinded by his affection for his wife. One of them had to keep a level head. One of them had to keep their eyes open, because if Cecelia was a criminal, her entire band of Rogues could be implicated.

She'd been right about one thing: It was his duty to protect all the citizens of London and beyond. Even those he did not approve of.

It was their right to live without fear of remonstration or danger.

Unless they perpetrated the crimes.

Redmayne took his silence for acceptance. "Don't be hard on yourself, either. You didn't know who she was when you wanted her."

Wanted. The word implied past tense.

If only he knew.

The truth hadn't extinguished his hunger.

Ramsay slammed the glass down harder than was necessary, wishing that he could punch more things. That he could incite Redmayne to beat the memory of her lips, her flavor out of his mind.

"I'm not angry because I kissed her," he confessed. "I'm not even that angry at her for being who she is."

"Then what—"

Ramsay swiped at the entire table, sending glass shattering to the floor. "I left yer house that night with the word *wife* on my lips, for Christ's sake!" he roared. "A handful of minutes in the garden with her and I was ready to hand over my—" He couldn't say *heart*. He couldn't give what he didn't have. "My name. Even in the wake of her telling me why she didna want it. I should have guessed. I'd met her that morning and then allowed her to seduce me that very night and I never connected the two women. What kind of miserable imbecile does something like that?"

"Jesus." Redmayne scrubbed a hand over his already tousled ebony hair. "It's worse than I thought."

"I forgot myself for a moment." Ramsay's voice dropped so low, he could barely hear it as his shoulders sagged with shame. "I forgot what people are. I wanted to believe . . ." He let the sentence die, because it made him feel weak.

Redmayne reached for his shoulder and Ramsay shrugged him off, not knowing what to do with the affectionate gesture. "Never ye mind. My point is that any man who would take such a crafty woman at her word is a fool."

Redmayne sobered, speaking with the conviction due his station. "Then you must uncover the truth, for everyone's sake."

Ramsay stalked toward the exit, stretching the skin of his knuckles over tight fists.

"That, my brother, is exactly what I intend to do."

In the two days since the explosion at Henrietta's, Cecelia had taken every precaution to hide her identity. To her employees, the workmen she'd hired to clear the disaster area, and the students at the school, she was Hortense Thistledown, Henrietta's niece.

Only a select few people knew Cecelia Teague.

She arrived and left by way of a secret tunnel entrance and had spent most of her time at hospital with Jean-Yves. From there, she'd retrieve Phoebe at Frank's in Mayfair or Alexander's in Belgravia and never took the same route home.

Redmayne, bless him, had twice escorted her in a hackney rather than his ducal carriage, keeping one ever-vigilant eye on their back. He'd assured her they'd never been followed.

I'll be the hot breath down yer neck and the chill from the shadows.

The threat reverberated through Cecelia as she hurried through the darkness. The clack of her shoes on the cobbles echoed her loneliness back at her. The streetlamps seemed too dim and pallid, even in her posh part of town.

She clutched Phoebe's hand and drew the girl closer to her skirts, doing her best to pretend she wasn't afraid.

When they'd visited the chemist around teatime to pick up an opiate pain tonic for Jean-Yves, the man had been furious that his shipment of supplies was late. He'd begged them to return in the evening, and Cecelia felt sorry for his missing an entire day's revenue. She even bought a digestive aid she hadn't needed to assuage her guilt, and his pocketbook, with a promise to return after hours.

It seemed ludicrous to take a hackney a mere five blocks from her tidy row house in Chelsea to the market street. But now, as a bank of summer fog drifted over from the Thames and washed the cobbles with an eerie glow, the fine hairs on her body sang with electric awareness.

Her usual habit was to send Jean-Yves or an errand boy for a carriage if one didn't loiter nearby. But she hadn't the time in the two days since the incident to hire another man-of-all-work. Besides, she'd been afraid doing so would hurt his feelings. Unlike Alex and Frank, she'd not previously possessed the kind of fortune for footmen, and traveled too much to make them necessary.

Since her cookmaid had been out of town visiting an ill sister, and Jean-Yves had been stoically sweating from pain without his medicine, Cecelia could stand his suffering no longer, and had no choice but to take Phoebe along for the errand.

She scurried past a particularly dark alleyway in between two cozy buildings, peering into the gloom that seethed with malice.

If Ramsay was out there in the shadows, wouldn't his watching her make her feel safer? She certainly wasn't breaking any laws. So why did fingers of dread dance along her spine?

Because the last time they'd spoken, she'd truly feared him. That brutal visage would intimidate anyone, and combined with the cruel threats on his lips, he'd been downright terrifying.

Cecelia picked up the pace, earning her a protest from Phoebe, who had to trot just to keep up with her long stride. The child would much rather give her attentions to the candy the chemist had offered her than navigating the dark cobbles.

"I'm sorry, darling," Cecelia murmured, measuring her stride to make the girl more comfortable.

Something in the air, in the mist, whispered to instincts she'd never honed. A primal, perhaps untapped maternal intuition that told her to snatch up her young and flee.

But she was being ridiculous, surely.

It was at times like these one might wish for a man. Someone to perhaps rely upon to look after one's safety. A strong set of shoulders and heavy, scarred hands with a masculine penchant to protect his family.

She tried not to give this fantasy man thick, orderly strands of fair hair or an uncommonly square jaw. Nor did she paint his lips full or his eyes quicksilver blue. Of course she didn't, because any semblance of just such a man in her life was impossible now.

Because he detested her.

A strange sound from across the street startled her. A can or a bottle grinding against the cobbles as it rolled. Something, *someone*, had to have disturbed it.

Cecelia's breath burned in her lungs. She reached into her pocket, palming the knife Frank had given her. Both the Countess of Mont Claire and the Duchess of Redmayne had taken to carrying pistols in their purses at a young age, but Cecelia was too skeptical of the contraptions to be comfortable having one upon her person. She knew how to shoot one, because the ladies had taught her, but to carry one around at all times unsettled her in the extreme.

She was simply too clumsy for all of that. She'd be certain to shoot her own boot off or, worse, kill someone accidentally. Besides, her poor eyesight did not a good markswoman make.

Though at this very moment, she reconsidered her position most heartily.

If she'd been alone, she'd have run the two blocks home, but with Phoebe at her side she couldn't go very much faster.

She opened her mouth to suggest she carry the girl home when another sound broke through the mist from up one of the stairways leading to the landing of row houses behind her.

This one metallic. Like the click of a key in a heavy latch, or maybe the hammer of a pistol? She'd have to hear it again to be sure.

Footsteps dogged her own. Heavy footsteps.

Someone tall was behind them, taking one step to every two of hers and four of poor Phoebe's. This time, when Cecelia's walking turned to rushing, the girl made no argument, as she, too, sensed the same danger in the dark.

The footsteps behind didn't hasten, and Cecelia breathed a little easier as she gained some distance.

Until she ran headlong into a wall of solid male chest.

One quick inhale told her it was categorically not Ramsay.

This man reeked of unlaundered clothing, cigar smoke, and gin with a pungent, almost astringent, cologne.

Cecelia gasped and hopped back, looking up into a half-rotten smile covered by an ill-kempt mustache.

"I beg your pardon, sir," she breathed, shoving Phoebe behind her and stepping to the side to go around him.

He matched her movement, blocking her escape. "Ya might beg." His posture and tone remained agreeable, making his words all the more chilling. His breath smelled of refuse as a smile of relish spread over his craggy features. Evil gleamed in dark eyes much too small for such a large man. "Aye, you'll beg aw'right. But there'll be no pardon."

Panic flared, and Cecelia drew the knife from her pocket, brandishing it at the brigand. "Step aside," she commanded, in a voice she wished were stronger. "Or I'll scream for the watch."

"We timed this so's that 'e won't 'ear ya." His smile became a rancid leer. "But 'e will find what's left of ya, sure enough."

We. He wasn't alone.

Cecelia did the only thing she could think of. She tossed Phoebe around the man. "Run!" she called. "Don't look back."

Phoebe's little pumping legs were the last thing Cecelia saw before the man charged her.

His heft lifted her bodily off her feet as he dragged her into the darkened alley and slammed her against the bricks hard enough to deflate her lungs. "You'll pay for that, ya fat cow," he vowed before he jerked his head in the direction Phoebe had fled.

Another bruiser streaked by. The man with the pistol. The one whose footsteps she'd heard behind her.

Cecelia's anxiety gave way to the instinct from before. She could not allow him to get to Phoebe. She'd die first.

Or kill.

Cecelia slashed out blindly with her knife, fighting to draw breath into lungs that refused to obey. She was able to drag the blade in a short slide across the man's chest before he grasped her wrist and pressed hard against a tender spot.

Her fingers went limp of their own volition, and the knife clattered uselessly to the ground, taking her hopes of survival with it.

"I'll cut ya slow for that."

Anger gave way to rage, intense and absolute. At herself just as much as her attackers. If any harm befell Phoebe it would be her fault. She'd taken the girl from the safety of their home.

Gathering a burst of strength, she squirmed and fought like a wild creature. She clawed and scratched and pushed at her large assailant with enough effect to throw him off balance.

She might be a fat cow, but her weight lent her strength many delicate females just didn't possess.

Jacket buttons scattered. Her spectacles were dragged from her ears and her hat was wrenched painfully from her head, ripping some hair along with it. The sound of it separating from her scalp was loud and dreadful.

She finally drew in enough air for a wretched semblance of a scream. Could anyone hear? Would they come to her aid?

A fist snaked out of the darkness, striking her with enough strength to snap her neck back and bash her head against the brick.

The second man? Had he gotten to Phoebe? Or was this a third attacker?

She crumpled to the ground. Cheek throbbing. Vision swimming with darkness and strange flashes of electric light.

Her periphery dimmed and her vision tunneled, focusing on a flash of silver.

The knife.

She made a desperate, half-blind grab at it, but a boot stomped on her fingers, hard enough to draw a sob, but not to break the bones.

Not yet.

The man who'd struck her, slimmer than the first, bent to retrieve the knife. His teeth were white, his nose long enough to thrust out from beneath the shadow of his bowler cap. But she couldn't make out his features. Not in the half dark without her spectacles.

"You all was warned what would happen if one of them girls ran." His voice was young and sharp, though it sounded as though his nasal passages were blocked with a cold.

"What?" Cecelia shrank against the brick, trying to make herself small. Doing her best to understand what he was saying. This wasn't the man who'd chased Phoebe. He was too thin.

Had the girl escaped? *Please God let her get away.*

"We need one more now. Your littl'un will do nicely."

"No!" Cecelia's cry erupted as a moan. "No, take *me*. Don't touch Phoebe. She's just . . ." She fought for breath, for consciousness. "She's just a child."

"Yeah." The bigger thug grabbed her by the hair, yanking her head back and exposing her throat. "That's rather the point."

"Where's the book?" The thin man pressed the knife to her throat, its cold steel biting into the thin skin. "Give it over to the Crimson Council and we might let you live."

She knew they were lying. They had no intention of letting her live.

A raw, strangled noise filtered to them from the street. A gunshot broke against the stone.

The two men looked at each other.

"He'd better not have shot the girl," the lean one said.

Cecelia gave a desolate cry, her heart withering in her chest. *No. Not Phoebe.*

A shadow shifted, lunged, and Cecelia was roughly released.

She blinked a bit dumbly as the knife dropped to her lap.

The brutish man crashed against the brick wall opposite Cecelia and was held there by an even larger, taller form.

Cecelia squinted, struggling to see.

The thin man sprawled out on the cobbles, though how he'd gotten there was a mystery to her.

The crunch of flesh meeting flesh drew her notice back to the two shadows at the wall. One was large, the other enormous.

Ramsay.

He was the only man of her acquaintance with such a tremendous build. The only one who could move with such astonishing quietude.

The only man who even growled in a Scottish accent.

The names Genny had called him made so much sense now. He was the devil, relentless and inescapable, bringing with him all the punishing castigation the dark could devise.

He'd a pistol in his left hand, but he subdued the thrashing brute easily, shoving the gun beneath his chin. He ignored the one blow the man managed to land at his temple and drove his right fist into the thug's face again and again with single-minded acumen and unparalleled skill. Little cracking sounds might have been bones breaking, or rotten teeth falling to the cobbles.

Cecelia found that she didn't care.

The thin man gained his feet, and for a moment Cecelia thought he might save his compatriot when he surged toward the tussle.

She took up the knife, opening her mouth to warn Ramsay, but there was no need.

With one mighty roar, he grasped the brute's head and snapped it to the side. The man's spine made a sound Cecelia would never forget.

Ramsay lifted the pistol and executed the thin man with one expert shot to the forehead before the thug with the broken neck had folded to the dirt as though he had no bones left.

Cecelia clapped her hands over her ears, tucking her chin down as the deafening blast of several more shots rang out through the narrow alley.

Even when the last echo died, she didn't move. Barely dared to breathe. The clicks of the empty pistol matched the painful rhythm of her heart.

Ramsay hadn't stopped pulling the trigger.

Whatever world she found out in the darkness might be untenable. The tragedy too great to bear, the failure enough to crush her. She'd never live with herself if—

"Cecelia?"

The small, watery sound of her name tore a raw sound of pure joy from her chest.

"Phoebe!" She scrambled to her feet and lunged for the little shadow that stood backlit by the entry to the alley.

Scooping the girl against her, Cecelia cradled Phoebe's head into her neck as little arms and legs latched around her middle and clung like a burr. The child's tears slid down her throat into her collar, and her own leaked into Phoebe's silky, honey-colored ringlets.

"Are you hurt, darling?" The question dragged from her throat with a husky horror. "Did he harm you?"

Phoebe shook her head, pulling back to look over her shoulder. "The man chasing me grabbed my arm, but *he* saved me."

Cecelia whirled in the middle of the street to find Ramsay standing in the entry to the alley a mere three paces away. His heavy shoulders and chest heaved with labored breaths. His nostrils flared and his eyes flashed, locking with hers.

Not a wolf, she thought again. A lion.

He stood over his kills proud, unrepentant. His broad features etched with a ferocity she'd assumed civilization had bred out of the modern gentleman. It was why their empire espoused such rigid strictures. Because might had once taken precedence over manners. The men who were able to incite the most fear were the ones who wielded the power.

And man forever desired to separate his kingdom from that of the beasts.

But it just wasn't so, she realized. Not really. Not in times such as this when threats to one's life stripped away the layers of courtesy, civility, and superior intellect.

Leaving the soft animal exposed. Vulnerable.

It didn't matter how many tall steel buildings contained the economy and the empire, or how many layers of finely spun clothing contained the flesh. People were essentially predators. They'd forever prey on one another.

And if that was so, a woman might count herself fortunate to rely upon the protection of the king of beasts.

She might not be ashamed to succumb to the possession electrifying his unblinking stare.

Something welled within Cecelia she'd never before experienced and couldn't identify.

Was it emotion? Or sensation? Or strictly a primitive physical reaction? She hadn't the time to analyze it.

Lights were beginning to appear in the windows of the row houses, splashing gold over the mist. Some brave souls peeked out into the night, though none of the gentlefolk dared to venture where gunshots had been fired.

Ramsay shook himself from whatever thrall the recent violence had over him, and he reached her in three swift strides.

"Give me the girl," he ordered.

"No." The word escaped her before she had time to think about it. She had to fight the urge to bare her teeth at him.

They were both creatures of instinct tonight, it seemed.

His hand encircled her upper arm with his fingers, and Cecelia gaped at it, for her appendage was not slender.

The grip was surprisingly gentle, coaxing, even though the stony familiarity returned to his expression. "Ye're trembling hard enough to shake her loose."

Was she?

Cecelia suddenly noted a curious weakness in her arms. Her knees seemed to have all but disappeared, threatening to fold her legs from beneath her.

"Give her over, Cecelia." Her name in his low, cavernous

brogue vibrated through her, washing over the tremors of terror like a soothing balm.

She loosened her grip on Phoebe, allowing the child to make the decision.

To her astonishment, the girl levered away from her and turned her torso to stretch tiny arms out to Ramsay. The man had frightened her, once upon a time, but Phoebe was a canny child and recognized strength and safety when it was offered.

She looked even smaller in the arms of the burly Scot. Her legs couldn't span his ribs; nor could her arms reach the breadth of his shoulders. Instead, she hooked an elbow around his neck and rested her cheek on his shoulder, reaching her free hand for Cecelia.

Doing what she could to stave off the trembling of her fingers, she threaded them with Phoebe's and allowed Ramsay to lead them home.

They navigated around the third body sprawled on the cobbles, bleeding from a gunshot wound to the chest. His was the shot she'd heard.

Ramsay kept Phoebe's face angled away, making certain she didn't see any of the night's carnage.

"What . . . what about the police?" Cecelia hovered closer to his side when they passed the last alley before reaching her steps.

How could he be both so calm and so vigilant at once? He'd just killed three men.

"I'll deal with them once ye're safely inside," he said. "For now, I'm not letting ye out of my sight."

What had once been a threat now became the ultimate comfort.

Cecelia climbed her stairs after Lord Ramsay on legs made of quivering custard. Inside her, a maelstrom of thoughts and fears twisted and battered at her.

He would be in her home, this man who hated her.
Who'd kissed her.

Who'd killed for her.

For someone so practiced at calculating odds, Cecelia
couldn't even begin to predict what the outcome of this
interaction would be.

CHAPTER TEN

Ramsay often woke with a violent jerk before dawn licked at the black ribbon of the Thames.

This time, however, consciousness drifted over him in languid increments. He felt confused, befuddled, but didn't want to give in to that just yet.

A delectable scent enticed him into further awareness. Bread, but sweeter. And coffee. His hand rested on his chest, and a soft blanket slid back and forth over the wounded mounds of his knuckles with every measured breath.

A wooden scratching sound permeated the languor. Repetitive, but not unpleasant.

He cracked one eye open the merest slit, not ready to commit to cognizance.

An etched-glass lantern flickered not far away. When had he lit it? He generally slept in absolute dark. Drapes drawn and . . .

He yawned and scratched at his suit jacket.

And naked. He always slept naked.

Granted, he had taken three lives last night.

He dropped his lid closed with a heavy breath. Killing or tupping always had the same effect on him. A weighty fatigue. Like a blanket that wanted to smother his thoughts. To douse his deeds and deliver him into the welcoming darkness.

He must have arrived home and collapsed into bed still fully attired.

Except . . . when had he?

His memories churned behind his eyelids in a garbled array of images.

He'd paid a private investigator often used by their office to watch Miss Teague's home, but he'd arrived in the evening for reports to find the man had abandoned his post.

As he'd settled in to surveil the cozy light pouring from her windows, a fracas had distracted him. Miss Teague had sent her little girl running up the cobbles before she'd been shoved into the alleyway by a brawny bastard.

By a man who'd signed his death warrant by touching her.

Ramsay hadn't thought before reacting. His long legs chewed up an entire block by the time the man chasing Phoebe had caught her up. He'd grappled the fucker, shot him with his own gun, and leapt down the alley in time to see Cecelia go down beneath a sharp blow.

It was all so clear after that. Slow and perfectly encased in his mind's eye.

A black, icy wrath had overtaken him, threading his blood with murder. He'd dismantled the brute with his bare hands before emptying the entire pistol into his scrawny comrade.

Never had he taken lives so willingly.

He'd escorted Cecelia and Phoebe to Cecelia's surprisingly modest but tidy row house and followed her inside.

She'd turned in the entry, cluttered with scarves, umbrellas, and outdoor attire of every color, and stared at him for a long and intense moment.

Ramsay still couldn't say why he'd done it, but he'd shifted the girl further to his shoulder and extended his arm to Cecelia Teague.

She'd hesitated only for the space of a breath before collapsing against him. She didn't speak or scream or dissolve into sobs. No one said a word or made a sound for an inexplicably long time.

The two females merely clung to him and trembled. Their gratitude warm, unspoken, and absolute.

Ramsay drowsily let his palm drift to the place on his pectoral where Cecelia Teague's cheek had rested. It felt as if she'd branded him, the heat of it reaching through the flesh and the muscle and bone into the ticking center of him. Expanding along his veins. Surging emotions through him he couldn't identify if he'd had a dictionary in hand and a hundred years to study it.

The white-hot rage with which he'd dispatched those brigands had been washed away by a welling of protective tenderness. For a moment, he'd forgotten all about obligation and honor, about her past or his duty.

Once he'd had Cecelia Teague and that child safe in his arms, nothing else mattered for a precious quiet moment.

Surveying their foyer, he'd noticed that a door stood ajar to what might have once served as a comfortable parlor if not for the long bed upon which a short man reclined.

Ramsay had locked gazes with the elder, recognizing him at once as the gentleman who'd been carried away from the wreckage of Henrietta's manse. The man whose bedside Miss Teague hadn't left until he'd been released from hospital that morning.

Jean-Yves Renault.

A strange communiqué had passed between the men as Ramsay had stood there encircling the two ladies in his protective, albeit entirely improper, embrace. The old man had eyed the exchange with extreme concern, then great interest.

"*Mon bijou?* What has happened?" he'd croaked out in French.

Cecelia had stiffened and stepped out of his hold with a graceful movement and a glance that managed to be both conciliatory and grateful.

Ramsay had to force himself to let her go.

Mon bijou? He found he didn't care for that endearment at all. Or for the fact that any man had one for her. This troubled him more than a little.

The night progressed quickly after that. He remembered releasing Phoebe into her care and listening to Cecelia's explanation of events to Mr. Renault before he left to deal with the police and identify the dead.

He'd immediately returned to the Teague household to start in on the many things in need of discussion. He'd thought to find them mopping at tears and asking thousands upon thousands of questions.

Instead he was admitted by Cecelia, who had changed into a serviceable gown. She explained in a somewhat harried manner that she was without proper staff, she'd only just settled Mr. Renault down with laudanum for his injuries and was in the middle of bathing Phoebe.

Her vivacious hair had been tousled and curly with moisture, and her face glowed pink with a sheen of mist from the hot washroom.

Ramsay had noted the red mark beginning to swell beneath her cheek, and a burst of rage had struck him dumb enough to allow himself to be ushered into her study, whereupon she'd pointed at the decanter of scotch, mumbled something about putting Phoebe to bed, and promptly disappeared.

Her home was well decorated, he'd noted, but not well insulated. He could hear almost everything that went on in the rooms above. The splashes of a bath. The high-pitched sweetness of a distraught child's many questions. The low, husky tones of Cecelia's answers meant to comfort and reassure.

He'd stood in the middle of the room for what might have been an eternity, staring at the ceiling. The foreign and wondrous sounds of a home conjured a strange ache in his middle. He rubbed at the hollow wound as he listened to what a childhood might have been like. Comforting words, reassurances, encouragements, warm baths, and gentle touches: These things existed only for others.

As a child, he'd bathed in a freezing loch.

Eventually Ramsay had drifted to the scotch at the sideboard, searching for a refuge from his uncharacteristically maudlin thoughts. He didn't normally imbibe, but the night's revelations needed their edges dulled. He'd sip only one drink until she'd finished.

They had much to discuss.

Because pondering the implications of what he'd found outside had been entirely disturbing, Ramsay had busied himself with inspecting her study.

A decidedly female study if one had ever heard of such a thing. In his experience, women had parlors and solariums with which to . . . do whatever it was women did.

Cecelia Teague had books.

He'd folded into a high-backed leather chair across

from the brick fireplace and let the scotch burn down his throat, lighting a small fire in his belly.

Cecelia's lullaby drifted through the night from somewhere else in the house, and his breaths instantly deepened and slowed, becoming languid as his muscles unraveled.

What a different life she led than he'd expected. Her study was crowded by bric-a-brac, random travel souvenirs and mementos. She'd done it in dark, exotic carpets and blond wood. The desk beneath the window looked out onto a street that was little more than a tucked-away square of Chelsea one might not even realize as part of a bustling capital.

Not the lair one would attribute to the Scarlet Lady, or even her heir. The woman that until tonight he'd suspected of the foulest deeds.

Cecelia's innocence in the disappearances of the girls had been validated, and he had to stay until he could inform her of how. Until he could plan their next move, because now their fates were entwined . . .

Ramsay's last memory had been of her bookshelves.

She'd begun another lullaby at Phoebe's request, and so he'd settled in to wait even longer. Examining the titles of her literary collection in the light of the lone lantern, he'd feared its contents to be as inflammatory as the pornographic scripts in Henrietta's residence. Instead, he found titles such as *The Matrices of Spherical Astronomy.* And further texts on Boolean algebra, standard deviation, classic cryptography, ciphers of the ancient world, and—

Wait a fucking minute.

The lone lantern?

Jesus bloody Christ.

Ramsay's eyes shot open, and found what he feared the most.

The Matrices of Spherical Astronomy.

Nine kinds of curses splashed against the back of Ramsay's lips as panic flushed the last vestiges of slumber from him.

He'd fallen asleep in the Scarlet Lady's study, as soothed by her lullaby as a child of seven.

God's blood, he'd never done such a ridiculous thing in his life. He could only hope he hadn't been out long. That she hadn't noticed his blunder.

Ramsay's hand moved. The blanket snagged again on his roughened knuckles. He squeezed his eyes shut, awash with . . . shame? Mortification? Something very like it.

Cecelia Teague had happened upon him slumbering in her chair like a gigantic useless git, and—sweetheart that she was purported to be—she'd left him to his repose.

But not before covering him with a bloody blanket.

The image of it trapped his breath in his throat. Cecelia bending over him, draping the soft knit over his slack body. Had she touched him? How close had her body been—close enough to draw her into his lap?

Oh, that she'd woken him. That she'd made some sort of din, slammed a book or two and spared them both this very awkward situation.

At that troubling thought, he sat up and drew the blanket down his chest, running a hand over his hair to slick any strays back.

It took the cessation of the rhythmic scratching for him to truly identify it.

A pencil.

"You're awake."

Ramsay's heart kicked against his ribs. His head turned stiffly on his shoulders, unwilling to face what he was certain to find at the desk behind him.

Or rather, *whom*.

That husky voice. The lower harmonics of which were

laced with such sensual tones, they could barely be reconciled with the dulcet sweetness of her corresponding melody.

Mother of all that was good and holy, but her voice did things to him. Hardened his sex and softened his heart. Weakened his will and his walls and filtered through the cracks in his fortifications.

If the sound of her was dangerous, the sight of Cecelia was almost his undoing.

The lantern light gilded her with an angelic aura often depicted in the paintings of Catholic saints. She could have been a Pre-Raphaelite muse. Her eyes so wide and full of light, even without her spectacles. Her cheeks round, ivory, and peach. Her chin dimpled. And her hair—those glorious curls—escaped a loose and hasty braid that fell over her shoulder, longer than was fashionable.

She appeared a cherub but for the midnight-blue silk wrapper turning her every generous curve into a dark sin. The lace of a high-necked nightgown hid any hint of flesh, but he knew the garment was a summer one, thin and gossamer.

Were he to unbelt the robe, he'd see right through it in the lantern light.

Ramsay's mouth went dry.

Simultaneously, Cecelia made a nervous noise in her throat before gesturing to the side table with her writing instrument. "There's coffee and biscuits. Croissants, if you prefer. My cookmaid is absent, so if you require heartier fare, I could suggest a café nearby with an excellent breakf—"

"That willna be necessary." He held up a hand, cursing every god of Eros he could think of. He was almost forty-goddamned-years-of-age. Could he go at least once in this woman's presence without an unwelcome erection? He shifted uncomfortably in the chair, grateful she couldn't see his lap from her angle at the desk.

Not that she was looking. She'd returned to the book she'd been hunched over, making swift notes on a paper.

It was only then that Ramsay noted the evidence of strain tightening her features, even in the immensely flattering golden light. She was more pale than peachy. Her full mouth compressed into a line, shadows smudging the delicate skin beneath her eyes. Eyes that were both focused and a bit frenzied.

"Ye should have woken me," he admonished gently.

She didn't look up. "I apologize for keeping you waiting for so long, I had a deuced time putting Phoebe to bed."

A pang, sharp and powerful, pierced him at the thought of the wee lass. Her tiny trusting arms and her large hazel-gray eyes. "Entirely understandable," he said. "How is she?"

"Alive, thanks to you." Cecelia glanced at the closed door to her study, as though she could check on the child through the walls. "Resilient," she proffered further, her eyebrow tilting as though the fact surprised her. "She seems so delicate, but I'm learning that she and I are more alike than I realized. The more information she has, the easier it is for her to process. That being said, I don't exactly know what or how much information is proper for a child of seven."

"She's a lucky girl," Ramsay murmured before he meant to.

"Lucky how?" She sighed, digging her fingers into exhausted eyes. "In less than a week she's been witness to a fatal bombing and a shooting. It's a wonder she's not entirely traumatized. As it is, I shouldn't wonder if she will bear the scars of this night for ages."

Ramsay wanted to call the tight ball in his chest respect, but there was a great deal else jumbled up in there. Worry, admiration, wariness, protectiveness, possession?

"She's lucky ye're a good mother to her," he said lamely.

Her gaze flicked to him, and then quickly away. Her auburn lashes fluttered down over her cheeks as she pretended to study the work beneath her. "That remains to be seen," she murmured.

He'd pleased her. Ramsay was glad to see some of her color return.

"Unlike me, ye've not slept," he noted.

She shook her head, tapping her pencil on the desk. "I won't sleep. I can't. Not until I've figured out what Henrietta's done. Not until those I love are safe."

Guilt made an oily slick down Ramsay's spine. He'd been so blinded by enmity, by what he considered to be lies, that he'd missed the truth. A truth that might have cost her life.

He opened his mouth to reveal what he knew when she tossed her pencil into the spine of the book and stood, obliging him to do the same.

He buttoned his suit coat, hoping she didn't look down. "I must admit that I might have been . . . unduly brutal, earlier."

She shook her head. "I would say you were brave. Brutality was necessary against those men, I'm afraid."

"Nay." He fought the very juvenile urge to squirm. "Nay, I mean with ye. The things I said when last we met . . ."

"Oh." She blinked at him, as though he'd astonished

the wits right out of her. "I suppose, if you were not so vigilant against me, then tonight might have been my last." She took a step closer. "That man who . . . who would have . . . Well, he proved you right a bit, didn't he? Henrietta must have been involved in something unthinkable to amass such enemies." She shut her eyes for the space of a trembling breath. "If I'm honest, you were forgiven the moment I saw you in the alley. However, your apology is formally accepted, of course."

"I . . . hadn't apologized." Had he?

A soft smile tilted her soft mouth. "You seemed to be working up to it. Am I mistaken?"

"Aye. Nay." Ramsay turned around, dismayed to find nowhere to advance and no place for retreat. "Christ, I mean, I am *attempting* to apologize, I just havena . . . ever . . ." He trailed away. How did one go about doing this?

"You mean for me to believe you've never had to ask for forgiveness?" Her voice behind him wasn't mocking, exactly, but his discombobulation seemed to incite a gentle note of amusement. "You've never made a mistake?"

None he'd readily admitted to. "I didna say that," he quipped, turning back to face her. "I tend to avoid people unless I'm functioning as the Lord Chief Justice, and then it matters not if I offend. Furthermore, I doona have the luxury of making mistakes, let alone subsequent apologies."

She observed him with clinical precision for a moment before declaring with unwarranted sympathy, "You must be very lonely."

He flinched as if he'd been struck. "Must I?"

"Are you not?"

He didn't used to think so.

Loneliness was abandonment. Lonely was being forgotten. It was not hearing the voice of another human being for months. Years. Lonely was no one caring if you lived or died.

He'd been lonely before in his life.

What was he now?

One of only several men who'd ever held his position in the world. He'd be chronicled in history texts, and the laws he wrote would govern the whole of Britain. He spent days in the company of important and powerful figures. How could such a man as he possibly be lonely?

How could he feel so hollow and bleak?

"You were a soldier," Cecelia ventured, saving him from having to answer her previous question. "You didn't happen to work with cryptography, did you?"

He shook his head. "Soldiering for me was mostly tedious marches through unforgiving terrain interrupted by bouts of frenzied bloodshed."

"How awful," she murmured.

Much of it had been awful. But as a youth he'd been so angry, so impossibly fuming that he'd relished in the feral violence of it. The regimentation. The fact that he'd belonged somewhere. To something greater than himself. His name was posted on a list with a rank that told him his place and importance. Gave him goals, aspirations. Medals and honor.

"The military." She held up a finger up with an unspoken *aha*. "*That* must have been where you learned to see the worst in people."

"Decidedly not," he answered. "People are always more than ready to show ye their worst nature. They're just begging for an excuse, it seems. For a rope to hang themselves with."

"Not you." She looked up at him with something like understanding. "And not I, despite what you may think."

This time, it was Ramsay who looked away. "I fear, Miss Teague, ye've only seen the worst of me."

She gave him a reprieve from her keen observation, bending down to retrieve an expensive leather-bound diary from her desk.

Ramsay took a careful step forward, aware of how small the room had become now that they both stood in it. How close she was. How easily she would become undraped. Undressed.

Undone.

He wasn't lonely now. He felt hungry. Angry. Needy. Hot. His clothes seemed to scratch and bind. He was tired of talking. Tired of the questions she asked that revealed too much of him to her.

He was so. Fucking. Tired.

If only there was a soft place in which to lose himself.

His hand reached for her of its own volition. Suddenly she seemed like the answer to everything.

At the same time, she was one gigantic question mark.

"My aunt Henrietta left this for me upon her death." Cecelia shoved the open book into the hand that had reached for her, interrupting . . . God knew what he'd just been about to do.

"It's a codex of some kind," she continued, unaware of his mood. "All her enemies, her nefarious deeds, and I dare think her ledgers and her secrets lie herein. Thus far I haven't been able to make heads nor tails of it, though I have found this book on decryption of known ciphers. It seems she's left me clues, somehow; I just need time to figure out what they are."

Ramsay did his best to compose himself. To stem the tide of yearning and focus his garbled thoughts on the task at hand.

God but she spun him about. Her scent. Her shape. Her

sound. She was a delicacy—nay, a feast—for his senses, and the senses not currently occupied by her screamed for him to do something about that.

If only he could touch her.

Taste her.

He flipped through the book blindly. The symbols and formulae therein might as well have been written in hieroglyphs. "Ye think . . . ye can decipher this?" If so, she was a bloody genius.

She nodded. "I'm more determined than ever to understand what Henrietta was up to. I just need time."

His fingers stilled upon the pages as he prepared to reveal to her what he'd learned. "Time ye may not have," he said, welling with regret. "Yer enemies know as well as I do that ye're Cecelia Teague and not Hortense Thistledown. They ken where ye live now."

She chewed on her lip, thrusting a hip into her hand as she pondered this. "Yes, and who's to say who *they* are?"

Ramsay grimaced. Wishing like hell he didn't have to tell her this. "Those men I killed today . . . *I* knew them. *I*'ve hired them in the past."

She shrank away, clutching at her wrapper and gown. "Hired them? Surely not to—"

"The one I gunned down in the street, I employed him to watch ye during the day whilst I was engaged elsewhere. I thought he was trustworthy. He's often in the employ of other agents of the law, including my superior, the Lord Chancellor."

"No." She clapped her hand over her mouth.

"Aye," he confirmed as her brow knitted into an expression of horror and disbelief. "I heard what those men said to ye," he continued. "They intended to take yer little girl, to replace the one they'd lost. I believe they referred to Katerina Milovic." He brandished the codex at her.

"They asked for this book, and if there's something in here that incriminates yer aunt as well as the Lord Chancellor, I need to ken what it is so I can crush him."

Cecelia seemed to compose herself and drifted forward, reaching out for the diary. "My lord, you'll need to consider this carefully. What is in this book could go to the very top of the chain. Even above Redmayne's head, you understand? I saw a member of the *royal family* leave Henrietta's establishment right before the bombing. And also the Count Armediano."

"Armediano?" he growled. "That rat bastard could certainly have something to do with it." He thought darkly of the count's fingers on the soft white flesh of her arm.

"These revelations could be dangerous for the both of us." She clasped his free hand between her two palms, imploring him to listen. "If that bomb was connected to a timing device, anyone in the world could have planted it. All of Henrietta's records but this have been destroyed, and I wasn't at Henrietta's that morning to see who else might have left it."

"Why not?"

She glanced away guiltily. "I didn't sleep the night before."

"I'm sensing ye're not a grand sleeper." He let his thumb drift over her fingers.

"I am, usually," she argued. "This was your fault on both accounts."

His fault? He considered this. The morning of the bombing was right after the dinner party at Redmayne's.

A carnal memory glistened in her eyes and stained her pale cheeks a dark, guilty shade.

Suddenly he knew exactly why she hadn't slept.

Because she'd been up contemplating their kiss.

As had he.

"Ramsay."

His name on her lips stopped his heart and corded his muscles. He became like a statue, his every marble molecule waiting for the chisel of her next words.

"I need you to believe that I'm neither criminal nor bawd. I need to you trust that I'm embroiled within this catastrophic mystery against my will and better judgment, and that I am as committed to doing what is right as you are. Even if we might disagree as to what that is. I need an ally, not an enemy. I have enough of those, and I *promise* you, I've done nothing to deserve them."

The earnest intensity glowing on her heart-shaped face threatened to melt the steely cold center of him within a feminine forge.

He fought the rising molten wave of warmth. He could not afford to let her shape and mold him to her will. He could not—would not—be one of the men who undoubtedly fell to their knees before her, waiting to be anointed her knight in shining armor.

"Tell me you believe me," she pleaded, her eyes going soft, gathering little jewels of moisture at her lashes. "That you believe I'm innocent."

Remembering himself, Ramsay pulled his hand from hers. He believed she didn't procure those missing girls.

Beyond that, he believed that she could quite easily make him a fool. Or a fiend. One of those empty-eyed addicts haunting the opium dens begging for their poison. He believed they were embroiled in the same dangerous conspiracy and that he needed the information in Henrietta's book every bit as much as she did.

"I believe I need to get ye to safety," he finally said, thrusting the book back into her grasp. "I will take ye somewhere they are not likely to find ye. I'll buy ye the time ye need. Now get dressed and pack."

All hope collapsed away from her features. "But my employees. The school. I have to make arrangements—"

"We will make them on our way out of the city." Her silk-clad body blocked his way toward the door, so he backed away from her and took the route around the chair he'd napped in to avoid any dangerous physical contact.

He'd made it to the door latch before she stopped him with the simple weight of her hand on his wrist. Something about her touch shackled him, reminded him that not all restraints were iron.

Some of them could be velvet.

"What about Jean-Yves and Phoebe?" she fretted.

"We'll take them, of course." He flexed his hand on the latch.

"Take them? Take them where?"

Ramsay could stand it no longer. Not her scent, nor the outline of her body in that damned wrapper. He had arrangements to make and fortifications to construct if this was going to work.

He shook off her hand and wrenched to door open, managing to slide past her without allowing their bodies to touch.

"To Scotland," he threw over his retreating shoulder. "Where else?"

CHAPTER ELEVEN

Cecelia winced as her fidgeting produced a loud protestation from the stool she occupied next to the bed where Jean-Yves snored softly.

To her utter relief, he remained asleep.

The poor man had been grim but enduring for the entire train journey from London to Dalkeith, a lovely Midlothian town south of Edinburgh. The bumpy carriage ride across the moors to the cottage had been a decidedly different story, and she'd had to double his dose of the opiate in order make the entire ordeal tolerable for everyone involved.

When Cecelia had quizzed Ramsay about their destination, he'd been disturbingly obtuse in his answer. "I'm taking ye to Elphinstone Croft."

"What's Elphinstone Croft?" she'd asked.

"A place no one will think to look for ye." An odd note in his voice twisted something bleak inside of her, and Cecelia hadn't pressed further.

And when they'd crested the gentle hill, she'd gasped with elation.

Elphinstone Croft had reminded her of a lost paradise. Or perhaps just a neglected one. The white cottage hid in a cluster of trees entirely too narrow to claim the title of forest along the bank of the River Esk. Overgrown ivy and a riot of thorny roses, berries, and wildflowers clung to the decrepit fence and crept up the walls, as though the garden had been trying to devour the edifice at its middle and was halfway finished with the meal.

Ramsay had to rip vines and such from the entry and pit his considerable weight against the oak door before it gave way.

At her questioning look, he explained. "I've not had the occasion to visit for a handful of years."

Jean-Yves had gratefully landed in the first bed Ramsay had been able to provide. Subsequently, it was decided Cecelia could both sit sentinel at the tiny desk by Jean-Yves's bedside and work on the codex in the remaining daylight.

Ramsay offered to keep Phoebe busy with him as they unloaded the food and supplies from the carriage they'd rented in Dalkeith. They would then set about airing the few rooms and uncovering the Spartan furniture.

The deep rumble of Ramsay's voice contrasted with the high exuberance of Phoebe's and became a pleasant distant cacophony by which she worked.

Cecelia was glad the girl hadn't seemed to mind the damp dereliction of the simple croft. Phoebe had taken to the expedition like Francesca would an adventure, or Alexandra had to any less-than-luxurious archeological locales. She had her dolls, Frances Bacon and Fanny de Beaufort, and couldn't be happier to venture beyond the tiny corner of the city that had been her entire world thus far.

As much as Cecelia was charmed by the fairy-tale allure of the croft, she had to admit it wasn't at all what she'd pictured when Ramsay had informed them that their destination was his childhood home in the Scottish Lowlands.

She felt a certain sense of shame to have assumed the elder brother of a powerful duke had loftier origins than herself. It couldn't be more to the contrary.

Even the Reverend Teague's humble vicarage boasted two bedrooms in addition to the cellar, and they'd enjoyed the patronage of wealthy parishioners to keep them fed and clothed.

As far as she could tell, she and Jean-Yves currently occupied the lone bedroom of Elphinstone Croft, above which was a tiny loft Phoebe had immediately claimed as her own.

Cecelia had spread out her volumes of ciphers and references beneath the open window, and had quickly succumbed to her curiosity, dragged into the world of Grecian and Etruscan cryptology.

Before she knew it, her pen dropped from fingers suddenly stiff with abiding cold. She applied the icy hand to the back of her aching neck, kneading at the knotted muscles there as she blinked around the bedroom.

When had night fallen? Had Ramsay left that candle on her desk?

Oh dear, she'd done it again. Alexandra had teased her endlessly about her predilection at university. *Mesmerism by maths*, she'd called it.

The entire world would drop away, cease to exist, for hours upon hours until she was able to solve a particularly perplexing problem.

Except . . . this time, she'd solved nothing. Her only notable progress was the alarmingly long list of codes and ciphers she knew *were not* applicable to the codex.

Cecelia drew in an exhausted breath and was suddenly aware of a miracle.

Or rather, a miraculous aroma. The distinct mélange of garlic, onion, and rendered succulent meat underscored with—she sniffed once again. Was that thyme?

Her stomach made a rude and rather insistent noise that drove Cecelia to venture out of the cupboard-sized bedroom. She turned to close the door behind her as quietly as she could, though it would probably have taken an entire symphony of off-key bagpipers to wake Jean-Yves at this point.

Once she turned to the main room, Cecelia had to swipe off her spectacles, shine them with her handkerchief, and replace them on her nose in order to process the mighty transformation the cottage had undergone.

When she'd arrived, it'd been a graveyard of ghostly furniture covers and grimy windows. With the application of the supplies Ramsay had sent ahead for in town, the tiny windows now sparkled. The one rough, wooden table—which she'd previously feared would leave anyone who approached it speared by several splinters—had been covered by a clean blue cloth.

A rocking chair hunkered in the corner, as though being punished for a slight, and an old but sturdy couch faced the modest fireplace. Tools and sundries were piled neatly next to the door, while a few scattered around the corner that seemed to function as a kitchen complete with an antique water pump that must draw from an old well.

Cecelia found herself utterly charmed by the entire room. One could believe that fairy-tale gnomes had once lived there. Or perhaps witches.

A cauldron even simmered over a cookfire in the stone hearth, and she couldn't imagine a better-smelling brew.

A large and surly Scot perched on said hearth and whittled at a long thin stick with a knife long enough to rival that of the kukris Alexandra had brought back from subcontinental India.

Cecelia caught her breath and pinned her feet to the floor. The firelight gilded his hair with every conceivable fine metallic hue. Copper and bronze sifted like sands beneath the desert sun on the shorter strands near his neck and above his ears. A forelock of gold fell over a brow pinched with concentration, and even threads of silver dusted the thick hair at his temples.

Resting his elbows on knees thrust high by the low hearth, Ramsay appeared to be almost squatting rather than sitting as he worked intently, and Cecelia found the pose both indecent and intriguing.

He'd shucked all but his shirtsleeves and a pair of fawn trousers stretched over thighs tensed to hold his weight and spread so he could hold his work between them. His sleeves had been rolled up to the elbows, revealing muscled forearms dusted with a down of gold hair.

Cecelia watched his large hands make deft and quick work of shaping the stick and stripping it of all bark.

His jaw, generally set into a stubborn square, relaxed with the absorption of his attention to his work enough to soften his lips. It was easy to forget that his hard mouth could be full, as he so often kept it tightly drawn into a frown.

The only other time she'd witnessed that mouth relaxed like this was the night he'd kissed her. That night seemed so long ago, and yet she remembered it with the fresh detail of yesterday.

Because she thought of that kiss every time she lay down to sleep.

Did he?

Next to him, a pile of firewood that appeared to be a decade old hunkered in the corner waiting to be immolated.

She could suddenly relate. She tugged at the high collar of her slate-gray traveling kit as heat licked over her skin.

"Where's Phoebe?" she asked by way of greeting.

Avid eyes found hers, and she offered him what she hoped was a nonchalant smile.

Ramsay jutted his chin toward the ladder leading to the closed loft hatch above the front door. "She collapsed into bed hours ago."

"Oh." Cecelia followed her many appetites farther into the room. She locked her hands behind her as she glanced about her surroundings, letting her gaze alight on anything but the man currently wreaking havoc on her senses.

"Did ye find anything in the book?" he asked.

"No." She'd found her own mouth locked in a disgruntled frown. "At this rate it could take me days. A week. Perhaps more. But I do find myself getting closer . . . I think." Her list of what the code *wasn't* certainly grew by the moment, and she decided to optimistically consider that progress by process of elimination.

He stood, abandoning the stick but not the knife, and retrieved a rough-hewn bowl from the shelf. "Ye take what time ye need," he said without looking at her as he ladled the fragrant stew simmering on the fireplace into the bowl. "I'll take care of ye until then."

I'll take care of ye. Cecelia tried to think of the last time anyone had said that to her.

"You're very kind. Very generous."

"We both ken that's not true." Ramsay carried the bowl to the table and pointed to the rickety chair with his knife. "Sit. Eat."

She sat and picked up the spoon, dipping it into the peasant stew with a delicate motion as Ramsay retreated to the other side of the couch to reclaim his perch on the hearth.

"There'd be more, but yer girl foraged her own portion, most of Jean-Yves's, and half of mine." He shook his head in disbelief. "She's such a wee thing, I doona ken where she put all that food."

Cecelia smiled with a growing fondness. "We share a hearty appetite, I suppose."

He gave a gruff chuckle and retrieved a long feather from a basket of many at his side. "I used to eat like that at her age, and I stayed scrawny until . . ." He let the sentence die away, then seemed about to say something before he changed his mind. "Until I was older." He took the knife to the feather, shaping it in delicate strokes.

Awareness of a strange and civil awkwardness that had bloomed between them ate at Cecelia. He'd avoided all but the barest of contact with her on the train, instead providing Phoebe most excellent and patient company while Cecelia looked after Jean-Yves.

She'd fretted at first that Phoebe's newfound hero worship of the giant Scot would be irritating to him. But he'd suffered her endless barrage of questions with not only patience, but a good humor Cecelia hadn't known Ramsay possessed.

She almost wished that he'd been an ogre. She really didn't need any more reasons to want—er—like him right now. Not while everything was so chaotic. So awful.

Because around him she found herself less self-reliant than she ever had been.

There was a magnetism about a man so large and strong, she decided. That had to be the whole of her problem. He simply radiated some sort of gravitational or magnetic pull, unwittingly drawing her into his orbit. The urge to cast her burdens onto his wide shoulders had become overwhelming. If she wasn't careful, she'd end up relying upon him. She'd give in to the impulse to play the damsel to his knight in shining armor.

I'll take care of ye.

Generally, it was her job to do the caring, a vocation she devoted herself to wholeheartedly. Of course, the Red Rogues and Jean-Yves were dedicated to her in the absolute. She'd never wanted for love.

But there was a difference between being *cared about* and being *taken care of.* She'd never even considered that difference before now.

Lost in such thoughts, she blew puffs of air over the fragrant stew waiting for the steam to cool.

"You cooked this yourself?" she marveled.

Ramsay lifted one shoulder without looking up at her.

"Where did you learn to cook?" she queried.

"Here." He split the feather down the middle with a masterful stroke and then picked up the stick.

Having exhausted the scope of her conversation, she took a tentative bite.

Dark, rich duck meat so tender she barely had to chew melted into a savory broth with the perfect mélange of vegetables and barley.

Cecelia closed her eyes to lend her groan of appreciation adequate dramatics.

When she opened them, Ramsay had frozen mid-motion, his knuckles white on the handle of the knife as he stared at her, unblinking.

"Whoever taught you your culinary skills should be

heartily commended." She loaded the spoon with her next bite with relish. "My compliments to the chef."

He grunted some sort of sound that might have been either appreciative or dismissive before returning to his work.

Cecelia studied him as she ate with as much vigor as her manners would allow. He'd never seemed quite so preoccupied before. Had never stayed silent for so long, at least not in her presence.

Granted, this was the first time they'd ever been alone together when he wasn't either cursing her . . . or kissing her.

For some reason, she ardently wished he'd do one or the other now. Anything but this dour, distant silence.

She couldn't seem to tear her eyes from him as he worked. The cords and muscles of his forearms flexed and shifted with his intricate motions. The movements swift and sure, as though he'd done this thousands upon thousands of times.

Arrows, Cecelia realized around a particularly delicious mouthful. He was crafting arrows. What an odd hobby. Odd and . . . handsome in a rather masculine sort of way.

Cecelia had often caught herself wondering what it was Ramsay did with his free time, being a man without vices and all.

Now she knew.

Captivated, she hungered to learn more. To learn everything. Was this where he'd built a body such as his, tromping about the Scottish countryside? Had he brought her here simply to ignore her? Were they still at odds in his estimation?

She chewed on her thoughts through the entire bowl of stew. Once her hunger had been sated, she could stand his silence—his indifference—no longer.

"You have a lovely home here," she ventured.

He snorted out something that would have resembled a laugh if it hadn't contained such derision. "Ye doona have to be kind," he told the arrow.

His answer troubled her. "I'm not being kind. I'm partial to simple quietude and much prefer cozy houses to grand ones. I find I'm eager to explore the countryside."

That brought him to look up sharply. "Doona go into the woods or venture onto on the moors without me. It's mainly bogs interrupted by patches of swamp and I'd not have ye get lost. Or worse."

"I won't," she promised. She didn't say that the terrain hadn't seemed particularly swampy. Nor did she mention that she'd noticed more agriculture and grazing land than bogs.

She supposed it was best she remain indoors. It made his keeping her safe and hidden a great deal easier. However, if she were locked in here with his current attitude, she might well go mad.

Perhaps they could at least take Phoebe out of doors and allow her to wade by the little dam she'd seen in the river.

Had Ramsay swum in the pond as a boy? she wondered. What had his childhood been like? Certainly not carefree and happy, or he'd be some other sort of man.

He gained his feet abruptly, startling her out of her reverie. "Are ye finished?" he asked, gesturing to her empty bowl.

"Oh. Yes." She made to rise, but he retrieved the bowl from in front of her and took it to the bucket beneath the water pump.

"It was wonderful, thank you. Let me help you clean," she offered. "It's the very least I can do."

"Nay." He abandoned the dirty dishes and went to the

neat stack of trunks and supply boxes by the doorway. "Not until after dessert."

She perked up instantly. "Dessert, you say?"

Cecelia did her best not to admire the very taut view of his backside as Ramsay bent to riffle through one of the smaller crates. He extracted a little flat box wrapped with a ribbon, and an unmistakably sized bottle.

Cecelia clamped her teeth over her bottom lip nearly humming with anticipation.

He didn't.

The box landed before her with an unceremonious thunk. "I believe ye once said ye couldna go without truffles and wine."

A smile broke over her that seemed to spread through her entire body. Were she a spaniel, she'd have wagged her tail until it fell off.

Ramsay's expression stalled for a moment, going carefully blank.

Cecelia did her best not to do something inappropriate to express the depth of her gratitude because the impulse to leap up and kiss him was almost overwhelming. "And here I thought you condemned my affinity for such indulgences."

He gave her a droll look she ignored as she tore into the box.

"I shouldna want yer exile here to be entirely contemptible," he said by way of flippant explanation.

"Chocolate and wine could make a heaven of hell," Cecelia claimed before she sank her teeth into the dark, delectable dessert and moaned her approval, massaging the truffle against her palate with her tongue. "You *must* try one, or perhaps five. They're delicious."

The cork came free of the bottle with a louder pop than usual, causing her to jump a little.

Abashed, she held her fingers up to her lips as she laughed at her own startle, in case her teeth were stained with chocolate.

Instead of returning her smile, he frowned, his grip tight on the neck as he stared at her. "I just realized I doona have wineglasses, not even ale tankards." He gestured to the meager shelves, empty now that they'd used the few bowls and the one plate for supper, apparently. "Ye'll have to drink from the bottle."

"How scandalous of me. How will you ever abide?" She swiped the proffered wine from him and inhaled deeply at the vintage. Sweet berries and cassis. Perhaps a bit young, and not aerated, but what did she care?

"Tonight we will drink like the common folk we were born to be," she said, adopting an admittedly horrific lowbrow accent. She saluted Ramsay, and then sealed her lips over the bottle and tipped it back.

Smooth liquid poured into her mouth, sharp at first, before thickening to sweet, mingling with the chocolate until a dry velvet finish left her wanting more. She corked the rim with her tongue to enjoy the flavor of the first swallow before allowing a second flood of the lovely vintage.

Her appetite whetted, she unsealed her mouth. The bottle made a hollow audible sound, and she pressed her knuckles to the corner of her lip where a small rivulet of wine escaped with a vampiric drip down her chin.

Unsure of what to do next, she extended the bottle to Ramsay.

He made no move to take it. In fact, he stood before her, his gaze affixed to where the drop of wine had disappeared behind her knuckle. His features frozen into an expression she might have recognized as hunger.

"Would you like a taste?" she asked.

"Ye tempt me, woman." His growl held a note of accusation.

Did she? Could she? A thrill lanced through her at the thought. Why ever did temptation have to be negative? Eve tempted Adam first, and women forever paid for it. But, according to the canonical texts, if she hadn't have tempted Adam with the forbidden fruit, then mankind wouldn't exist. And so, might Mother Eve have done Adam, and therefore mankind, a favor?

"I had to eat alone," she prodded. "Must I drink alone as well?"

Two distinct wrinkles of consternation appeared on his forehead. "I've already told ye—"

"I know, I know. *Ye doona indulge.*" She imitated him terribly, but was pleased to see his forehead smooth a little as his consternation relaxed into amusement. "But I ask you, who is here to judge you? Who must you be perfect for now?" She turned in her seat, making a show of checking the empty room for interlopers before lifting a challenging brow.

"Certainly *I*, the Scarlet Lady, queen of iniquity, and so forth, am so far beneath your lofty lordship that a few swills of wine won't sink you to my lowly, contemptible state." She grinned and rocked the bottle from side to side before his nose. "Come now. It's been a long day."

She'd meant to disarm him. However, her tease seemed to do more than that. He looked not disarmed, but defeated.

He took the bottle and sank to the chair across from her, releasing a weighty breath. "Ye might not believe this, but I wasna always such a bore." He sealed his mouth to the same lip of the bottle and drank long and deep.

Unable to form a reply, Cecelia found herself captivated by the crest and sinew of his neck as he swallowed.

How did one build such prodigious strength to even apply to the muscles in one's throat?

His lips lingered on the rim longer than they ought, as though he wasn't finished savoring the taste he found there.

Finally, he returned the bottle to her.

She was more judicious with her subsequent sips of wine. They seemed spiced with a richer, more complex flavor.

Was she tasting the wine? Or the man who'd only just sampled it?

She set the bottle on the table in between them, thinking things she should not. Wanting what could not be. Wondering what might have been had she met Lord Ramsay before she'd known to which family she belonged.

"Lass, I've treated ye unfairly," he rumbled.

Cecelia tried to swallow. Failed. And tried again. She stared at the amber bottle between them, bringing the width and breath of him out of focus.

His statement seemed more than fortuitous considering the direction of her thoughts. Momentous, perhaps. She was ill prepared to meet his eyes. For him to see the earnest pleasure his words brought her.

"Is this another of your non-apologies?" She'd meant to sound lighthearted but feared she failed, utterly.

"Nay," he replied with unmistakable gravitas. "It's an apology in earnest. I am sorry, Cecelia."

The fine hairs on her body vibrated at the sound of her name, and her next breath felt tight and short.

He leaned back in his chair, regarding her with a solemn intensity. "I had reason to hate yer aunt, before all of this," he confessed. "Personal reasons, just as strong as any moral objections, and I let them blind me."

This surprised her enough to take three more drinks

before returning the bottle to the table. "I might have reason to hate her, too, if she had aught to do with whatever happened to poor Katerina Milovic and those missing girls." Cecelia bit her lip to keep it from shaking with emotion. "Tell me, what did Henrietta do to you?"

Did she truly want to know?

Ramsay leaned forward and rested his forearms on the table, and Cecelia carefully listened to him, doing her best not to be distracted by a man in such a state of undress.

It was only his forearms, after all. What the devil was the matter with her? Why could she not stop staring? Why did the fine hairs and toned sinew make her fingers twitch with the urge to touch him?

"Years ago, I think Henrietta realized my political ambitions. She coveted my secrets, my soul, for her collection. And when they were not readily found, she sent a professional, one of her employees, to seduce them out of me." His jaw worked to the side in a fit of gall.

"Did it work?" Cecelia asked anxiously.

He shifted and tilted his head swiftly enough to crack his neck. "I . . . availed myself of the woman she sent me."

"You what?" The question escaped her before she could call it back. She hated the feeling in her stomach that accompanied it. A pang—no, pain. Actual physical discomfort at the thought of him with a lover. Was she angry at his hypocrisy?

Or jealous?

"I didna know Matilda was employed by her, not at first," he explained, misinterpreting her discomfiture. "I courted her for months. I proposed to her."

If he thought that fact made the situation better, he was sorely mistaken.

"Did she accept?" Cecelia hoped she didn't reveal her dismay on her expression.

"Aye." He inhaled sharply, shaking his head. "But the whole affair was short-lived. I came home once to find her rifling through my possessions and personal papers. I confronted her and she confessed her true aim. Begged for my forgiveness."

"Did she love you?" Cecelia queried.

He snorted and took a swig. "She claimed to."

"Did . . . you love her?" She wished she didn't want to hear the answer so desperately. That she didn't fear it so much.

"I desired her." His eyes flicked to hers. "But I can honestly claim I've never loved anyone."

He'd proposed marriage, she wanted to argue. She remembered what he'd said in the Redmayne gardens in regard to love. So why *this* woman, Matilda? What made him desire her enough to do something like that? What sort of beauty had she possessed? What made Cassius Gerard Ramsay fill with enough desire to take a woman to wife?

And . . . why had Henrietta exploited him thus?

Cecelia blew out a disgusted breath, disturbing her ringlets before burying her face in her hands and wiping at the tired eyes beneath her spectacles. "I'm starting to wonder if I've any relations of whom I can be proud." Were they all gamblers, blackmailers, and zealots? Or worse?

"'Tis a thing we have in common," he murmured. "My brother and I have a tainted legacy as well."

She peeked at him through her fingers, curiosity igniting beneath the dismay. "You said your mother broke both of your fathers . . ." She trailed off, as if picking her way carefully through a patch made of emotional thorns, unsure of where the path led next.

"Aye and a good many other men." His tone was singed with bitterness.

"Are you one of those men?"

"Do I appear to be broken to ye?" He held his hands out for her inspection. Of course, he was admittedly impressive, all heavy muscle fortified with Scottish bones and iron will.

But what of his heart?

"I'd hate to meet whatever was capable of breaking a man such as you," she admitted.

"The things ye say . . ." He shook his head once again, gritting his jaw against what appeared to be some powerful words welling behind his lips. Finally, he said, "I believe people allow themselves to be broken, and I refuse to give those who've tried the satisfaction. If I'm knocked down, I rise. Always. I get back up. And I fight. I excel. I win. There's no other option."

"How very . . . Scottish of you." A keen understanding lit within her. A commiserative appreciation. "Your strength is commendable, extraordinary even, but it's impossible to be . . ." She paused a moment, her eyes shifting, as she searched her vocabulary. "Unaffected by your past. It's intolerable to see someone you love broken and to not suffer a few wounds of your own."

"What do ye know of it?" he scowled.

"Plenty," she whispered.

It was his turn to contemplate her. "How many men have ye broken, Cecelia Teague?"

"None," she answered honestly.

"That's very hard to believe." He gestured to the loft. "What about Phoebe's father?"

Cecelia bit her lip. She'd almost forgotten he'd assumed Phoebe was her daughter. Should she tell him the truth? What would it accomplish? Better that he think her a whore and a mother, than a bumbling virgin who was terribly lost and utterly alone.

"Ah." He made a bitter noise. "I forget. Ye donna remember who he is."

"Why does that bother you so?" she asked.

His lips pressed into a thin line, his jaw working over thick emotion before he gritted out, "I canna say."

Cecelia broke contact with his gaze once more under the guise of investigating their quaint surroundings. "It's difficult to picture the previous Duchess of Redmayne as the mistress of this house. How did she come to know the duke?"

"They met at a gala in Edinburgh when I was about four. She was hired as a housemaid for the event and set about finding a lover. A keeper, I think, to make herself a mistress. That she became a duchess was nothing less than a miracle."

"Where was your father?" Cecelia wondered aloud.

"He worked on merchant vessels and was at sea the entire time it took for her to seduce the duke into financing a divorce. So ye see, when people look at me, they doona see the son of a duchess. They find the unwanted get of a devious social climber and Scottish nobody."

She studied him for the emotion this evoked and found nothing. He was utterly calm, closed, and collected. He recited the story as if it belonged to someone else.

"Surely your father was not a nobody," she argued. "Just because he wasn't someone extraordinary in the eyes of the ton. He lived in this house. He loved here, even though that love was a tragic one."

An ancient disgust spread a hard mask across his brutal features, turning them stony yet brittle. As though someone would have to take a chisel to his skin in order for him to move again. "The duke paid my father three thousand pounds for my mother. And he took it, readily. She was naught but an expensive whore until the day she died. And he was a greedy drunk with no sense of integrity."

"Three thousand pounds." Cecelia gaped. Holy God, that was a staggering amount.

If Ramsay's features were stone, then his eyes were now frosted with ice. "It only took him a handful of years to eat, drink, whore, and gamble it away. Did Redmayne or Alexandra ever tell ye how *my* father died?"

His expression indicated that the tale was heartbreaking, but Cecelia couldn't stop herself from asking. Ramsay had begun to paint the portrait of his origins, and she desperately needed him to finish it. "How?"

"He was found facedown in a gutter where he'd choked to death on his own sick, not to mention the other filth that flows to the sewers."

Unable to contemplate the indignity of it, to process the sorrow she felt for Ramsay, Cecelia stood to pace around the room a bit, taking a chocolate with her. "You and your father lived here alone, until you were nine?"

"Aye."

A memory of a previous conversation with him puzzled her. "But you mentioned you didn't attend school with Redmayne until you were fifteen?"

"Aye."

"So . . . Where were you between nine and fifteen?"

"Here."

"Here?" She stopped pacing to look at him. "Here with whom?"

He didn't answer. Didn't look up from where he contemplated his own hands spread on the cloth like the scarred relics of another time.

Cecelia had always felt as though those hands belonged to a different man. One with an altogether more difficult life.

She looked around, absorbed the sparseness of the place. The one bed, the lone couch. The single set of dishes.

His bow and arrow.

A place no one will look for ye.

His father had died, and no one had looked for him. He'd raised himself on this property from a lad of nine years old to one of fifteen. Alone.

The duchess had left her firstborn here to rot for years.

"My God," Cecelia whispered, a hollow pain lancing her breast. "You were here all by yourself, all but forgotten. And you survived on your own?"

"Doona be impressed." He swatted at the air in front of him, waving her veneration away. "The well is good, the river full of fish, and a herd of deer live in the vicinity."

Cecelia shook her head, seeing her surroundings as if for the first time. To her, this cottage was a refuge. To him, it'd been a place of exile. Her heart swelled with emotion for him. "I never realized what it must have cost you to bring us here. What horrible memories it must hold for you."

He snorted, searching the beams as if they might collapse at any time. "It's no great feat, I return here from time to time."

"To escape the city?" she guessed.

His eyes speared through her, alight with a vibrant fire. "To remind myself how far I've come. To remember what I once was."

Cecelia nodded, envying his fortitude. She'd never allowed herself to return to the Vicar Teague's. Not even to the city from whence she came. "It's difficult not to cling to memories," she murmured. "I suppose our recollections define us all in some way."

He shook his head with enough vehemence to expel a demon. "I'm proof they do not."

She was taken aback. "You're proof they *do*. This place, it means something to you. It holds the ghosts of a different life. Of a lonely past and a future that could have been."

"There was never any future for me here."

"I don't know." She tried to picture a peasant couple here, young and happy. "You might have had parents that loved each other. Who shared this home, this life, in poverty, but happiness. This might have been land you worked and a simple legacy you could have been proud of. Instead you were abandoned here. And that has quite obviously made an impression upon you. I daresay it painted every relationship you've ever had."

He made a disgusted sound in his throat and drank before wagging the neck of the bottle at her like a gavel. "Doona look at me and see some lonely child to be pitied. I am so far from that. From *him*. I lifted myself from nothing, into a situation where I want for nothing, and for that I am proud. I am wealthy, educated, respected, and feared. I am powerful in every conceivable way—"

"Yes, but are you happy?"

He looked at her askance. "What does happiness have to do with anything?"

She shook her head, truly pitying him for the first time. "It has to do with everything."

"Man is not meant to please only himself," he stated rather piously. "Do ye ken why Matilda could find no skeletons, no secrets?"

Cecelia shook her head.

"Because I have none. I've done nothing of which I am

ashamed other than allowing myself to hope the one time that she could provide me an honest, contented life." His jaw hardened and he set the wine down, pushing it away from himself as if it were as offensive as the memory of the woman who'd betrayed his one chance at trust. "She proved the one thing I've always known. That women are born with a weapon between their legs, and are willing to deploy it with as much collateral damage as any explosive."

Cecelia shook her head, understanding his anger and also despairing at the abject wrongness of it. "Did you ever stop to consider that your offer of marriage might not have been what she wanted from life? You desired her companionship, her love, her body, and her fidelity, but did you ever stop to think that marriage to a Lord Chief Justice, or a Lord Chancellor, might be too much for Matilda?"

Her words took the wind from his sails. "I didna have to ask, she made it clear enough. She told me she'd rather suck a thousand cocks than shackle herself to a rigid, self-important arse like me. Is that what ye wanted to hear?"

"No. Because that was a terrible thing for her to say." She lifted her chin, adopting a pose of matronly disappointment. "And so was what you said about women and . . . weapons."

He looked both mulish and ashamed, but didn't cede the point.

"Do you not think men use their sex as a weapon?" she pressed. "Most often a violent one? Men have claimed all rights to strength and money and power. What are we women left with? The responsibility of brood mares, to make more men, or to make life comfortable for them? If there must be a war between sexes, what weapons have you left us? What are we but objects to you? A collection of pretty orifices for your pleasure?"

Wintry eyes glittered at her. Not with censure but with wonder, admiration, and—dare she hope—respect. After a breathless moment, he leaned forward, capturing her uncertain gaze with his unblinking one. "I shouldna have said that." One step closer to an apology. Two in one night, did wonders never cease? "I doona feel that way . . . about ye."

Cecelia tried to think of another time she'd been so pleased by a compliment, and simply couldn't. What rubbish. That Lord Ramsay's confession that he finally didn't consider her a lying bitch would mean more than scores of poetry from other men.

Lord, but she was in trouble.

He stood so abruptly he had to save his chair from falling over backward. "It's late," he clipped. "I should turn in."

Cecelia nodded, not wanting to poke at any more wounds. Not when her own were so raw. So ready to be reopened. Her heart ached for him. Bled for the lonely boy who spent silent years struggling for his own survival. For the man who'd fortified that lost child behind barbs of ice encased by a body of such capable strength that he could never be vanquished by vice nor villainy.

She understood the lunacy that accompanied forced solitude, and she'd only ever experienced it for several days at the maximum.

What would several years do to a person?

She swallowed pity and humility and a surge of desperate affection that threatened to escape from her in a bout of tears. "I suppose—" She cleared a husky lump of emotion from her throat. "I'll sleep in the loft with Phoebe." She went to her trunk in front of the supply crates by the door, intent upon finding her nightclothes.

"There's barely enough room for a cat to curl up in the loft," he said. "Nay. Ye'll sleep down here on the couch. I've set it up for ye with clean linen and such."

She blinked over at the worn but overstuffed furniture. It might be comfortable. "But where will you—?"

"Doona worry about that." He went to the door, seeming to drag the weight of his past along with him, though he'd shuttered his every expression behind a fan of bronze lashes.

"Of course I worry." She found her wrapper and fished deeper into her trunk for her nightgown. "You can't simply sleep in a bed of raspberry thorns."

He chuffed. "I've a hunting shed round the back."

She straightened, clutching the silk to her bosom. "But—you're the Lord Chief Justice of the High Court of England. A man such as you does not simply sleep in a shed by the river."

He slid her a level look. "I never took ye for a snob, Miss Teague."

"Well. I . . . I just . . ." She swallowed. How could she make him stay?

"Ye just . . . what?" He stood close to the door, close to her, as large as a titan and cold as a northern loch, gazing down with an odd illumination behind his pupils.

"I'd feel awfully guilty if your hospitality meant that we squeezed you out of your own home. Surely at your age you're not about to sleep on the cold earth. Imagine the aches."

The light behind his gaze dulled and his hand hit the latch. "Doona worry about me. I'm not yet so old and venerable, I canna yet sleep on the ground."

Desperately, Cecelia threw herself in front of the door. "But . . . but . . . wouldn't you be more comfortable if you had a pallet of some sort by the fire?"

He shook his head stubbornly. "It's summer, it's too hot for that."

"Hot? This is Scotland."

His jaw clenched, and when he next spoke it was through his teeth. "I ken that, lass. But I tend to run hot in the night."

Cecelia swallowed. Hard. He didn't run hot at all. He was cool and taciturn. So contained. Was that because beneath his surly surface some sort of volcanic heat flowed like lava through him, just looking for a vent through which to be released?

Bereft of any response, she stood between the door and his body, silently beseeching him to stay.

He released the latch and took a retreating step, putting space between them. "Christ, woman, ye canna have that much of an aversion to the out of doors."

"It isn't that." She hesitated. Her entire torso quivered against the strength of her heart hurling itself against her ribs. "What . . . what if Jean-Yves needs help in the night?"

He glanced over his shoulder at the door to the bedroom. "Ye gave him enough of that damned tincture to tranquilize a horse. I'll be surprised if he wakes in a week. That being said, if he does, ye can call for my help."

Emotion clogged Cecelia's throat once again, this time the tide accompanied by a strange well of anger.

"Aye, I shouldna stay in with ye," he said with undue resolution, as if he were trying to convince himself. "Ye doona need me."

Cecelia had no idea where the emotion came from, but it was powerful enough to sweep her away. A part of her realized it stemmed from something completely unreasonable, and yet she couldn't seem to suppress it in the least.

"How do you know I don't need you?" In an astounding fit of temper, she flung her wrapper back into the crate. "Because I am not constructed with delicate femininity, I am not allowed to be fragile?" She lifted her jaw and glared at him with all the mutiny she could summon. "Because I am intelligent, I am thereby not in need of assistance? Because I am capable, I have no need of protection, is that it?"

Ramsay blinked down at her, his head cocked in a very doglike gesture of confusion. "I never said—"

Cecelia put her hand to her forehead, feeling feverish and strange. Breathless and a bit drunk. "Everyone always thinks I know what to do. But I don't! I *don't* know what to do." She didn't inhale so much as she sobbed breaths into lungs that seemed to refuse to inflate. "I'm so. Lost. So weary." She hated admitting it. Hated herself for her weakness. Hated that he'd see her as weak. "Absolutely everything is a disaster." Blood rushed in her ears, and her vision swam. Her knees didn't seem capable of supporting her weight anymore, and she reached out rather blindly, fearing collapse.

He caught her before she buckled, supporting her weight.

"Don't leave," she pleaded, surging forward against him. Burrowing into his chest and clutching at his arms. "Don't leave me alone. What if someone comes for us in the night?" She did her best to keep her voice down, to make certain Phoebe wouldn't wake to hear the hysteria bubbling within her. "What if you don't hear me scream in time?"

His hand landed on the back of her hair and cupped her head to his chest. "Och, lass. I didna ken ye were so frightened." He whispered this as though the discovery humbled him, then drew her close against his body. Curling over her, around her, he allowed the storm of her tears to break upon him as he sheltered her.

Somehow her spectacles disappeared, and he set them aside before his palm returned to glide up and down her spine in a slow dance as she gave in to her grief.

She cried for her mother. For Henrietta. Phoebe. For the souls who'd been lost in the explosion. For little Katerina Milovic and any girl who was missing, victimized, afraid, or unloved.

She cried for Ramsay. For the boy who survived alone in this cabin, who'd been mistreated. Forgotten. Abandoned.

She wept because people were so unkind. Because they preyed upon one another in ways she couldn't begin to imagine, and that fact made her feel helpless and afraid. She wanted to reach out and heal the entire world, and yet she couldn't even keep those in her household safe from faceless enemies.

"Breathe," Ramsay murmured. "I have ye. Ye're safe."

"I know I am," she gasped through humiliating hiccups. "Because you're here. Because you saved Phoebe and me, even though you hated me. How can I ever begin to thank you for that? I cannot repay you for bringing us to a place that causes you pain by forcing you to sleep in the dirt! It's unthinkable. Unconscionable."

He expelled a long breath full of so many things left unsaid. She heard it leave his lungs through the ear she'd pressed against the warm muscle of his chest.

"I didna mean to sleep, all told. I was going to keep watch," he muttered. "Although, after what I put ye through, perhaps the dirt is what I deserve."

"But don't you see?" She pulled back, craving the sight

of him. Wanting him to witness the depth of her gratitude as well as hear it. "I don't even care that you were cruel. Every time I've needed you, you've been there, quite literally lifting the burden from my shoulders. You can't know what that means to me."

The glaciers that had once been his irises melted into dark pools of azure before he hid them beneath his lowered lids, turning his face away.

"You've barely glanced at me all day." She reached up to cup his cheek, tugging gently at his stubborn jaw.

"Cecelia." He resisted her pull, the bristle of his evening stubble sharp against the soft flesh of her palm. "Doona make me. Not now."

"Do I still disgust you?" she challenged. "Because I cannot tell. Sometimes you look at me like you did that night you kissed me. As though I am extraordinary, or perhaps worthy. And sometimes . . . I see storms in your eyes. Hatred. Wrath and—"

"Nay. God, woman, ye canna think that." He lifted a hand as if to silence her, but the knuckles that brushed the bruise on her cheek were infinitely tender. "I canna look at ye without wanting to bring the man to life who did this, just so I can have the pleasure of killing him again. Slower this time. *That* is the wrath ye read in me. A bruise on yer skin is like an open wound on my soul. It hurts me to look."

Cecelia was so startled by the fervency of his words, contrasted with the reverence of his touch, that she could summon no reply. She stood beneath his gaze, the curves of her body still pressed to the planes of his, and gloried in the sensation his touches provoked within her.

Her hand still shaped to his jaw as his fingers ventured up her cheek to her temple and then threaded in her hair.

Without meaning to, she leaned into his palm, seeking his touch like a cat hungry for affection.

"Christ," he breathed, turning his head to press his lips against the thin and tender skin on the inside of her wrist. "What are ye doing to me?"

CHAPTER TWELVE

Cecelia hadn't the first idea what she was doing, but her body certainly seemed to. It responded so intuitively to his proximity. Blossomed and ached where he touched her.

Ramsay exerted a gentle pressure against her scalp, drawing her closer.

His head lowered incrementally toward her, eyes glazed with intent.

At first, the kiss was a ghost haunting the space between them. A specter of what might have bloomed before all of the chaos ripped their worlds asunder.

Her eyes affixed on his lips, finding a hint of the divine where malice had once been. A glimpse of the eternal. An echo of forever.

Perhaps he could learn how to forgive.

Her heartbeats stumbled, colliding into one another and bouncing off her ribs. Her nerves still clamored. Anxiety throbbed through her veins with every elevated beat of her heart. She closed her eyes and held her breath, unable to watch.

What if he came to his senses before he kissed her?

She needn't have worried.

Ramsay's lips were hot and dry, full and utterly sensual when he pressed them to hers. Tentative and deferential, he brushed light swaths of desire against her mouth, soothing away the fear and replacing it with an equally powerful emotion.

One that would not be ignored.

He skimmed the seam of her lips with his tongue in a warm caress as his hand covered hers on his jaw. He laced their fingers in a motion that sent shivers rocketing through her entire frame like the waves of a sea gale. One crashing over the other with no sign of a break.

She finally released the breath she'd been holding.

He inhaled it, taking it deep into himself.

Was this temptation? Was this the seductive sin the Vicar Teague had warned her about, this inescapable, unrelenting ache? This drive that went deeper than logic or reason ever could. That welled from a part of her so instinctive, so primal, that even language didn't exist within. From a place that only understood what was unspoken.

The vibration of his moan against her lips demanded entry.

Entry she granted with a sibilant sigh.

Apparently, this was a language she spoke too well. Because at her first sign of submission, she found herself against the door, held captive by a mountain of muscle.

He caught both her hands above her head. His tongue delved into her mouth, not just gaining a taste, but claiming territory in hot, silken slides. He tasted of wine and wickedness, a flavor so incredibly intoxicating it threatened to rob her of what little reason she had left.

Cecelia tried to move her hands from where he'd imprisoned them. She wanted to push him away. To pull him closer. To thread her fingers in the silk at the nape of his neck.

And to tug at it with claws.

She wanted him to consume her as his eyes had done so often. With his mouth. His teeth.

His tongue.

She wanted him to lose control with her. To dive into that place where reality fell away. Where no conversation was needed, and no analysis of morality belonged. Where they might only communicate in grunts and groans and cries and screams.

Ramsay didn't allow her to move. He maintained control of the kiss, driving her mad as he licked at the tears that had settled into the corners of her mouth before laving into the depth of her. Leaving the flavor of salt and sadness behind before replacing it with seduction and sin.

A taste she never wanted to be rid of.

His body surged against her. Big and hard and lethally strong. His spine rolled as if a wave poured down his back, ending with a curl of his hips, thrusting the evidence of his desire against her belly.

Long and hot, his sex branded through the layers of their clothing.

A warm rush released at her core, and her intimate muscles swelled and flexed, clamping almost painfully around emptiness.

Her body undulated in a sinuous, unbidden arch, enjoying the feel of him against her sensitive nipples, even through their clothing. She became one long pulse of need, craving his touch everywhere. Longing to explore the masculine mounds of his topography uninhibited.

His imprisonment of her hands was a delicious frustration as he devoured her lips, bruising them with the force of desire so long denied. Of passion left unspent.

Suddenly she felt very much like the cauldron heated over the cookfire. Simmering with a sensual, aromatic potion of ingredients.

Helpless against this craft, urges she'd struggled to keep dormant bubbled to the surface. An intrinsic female sensuality burst forth, luxuriating in the feel of such a ferocious male laying siege to her senses. Claiming her body as his. She felt as she imagined one did in antiquity, when people lived in huts and were swathed in furs and skins. When the rules of civility did not apply, and the greatest of warriors claimed his chosen maiden by right of might.

Ramsay was just such a man. She understood that as she submitted to the delicious demands made by his mouth.

In his soul he was a Scot. Barbaric and tribal. Fierce, independent, and ruthless.

His blood was closer to the beast's than most. His ancestors fought off Romans, Vikings, and a plethora of would-be invaders. That savagery lived inside of him, and he caged it. Fought it. Starved and smothered it beneath propriety and determination.

Yet it endured to pace behind the iron bars of his will like a hungry lion.

God, but she yearned to set it free. To offer herself as his next meal.

Driven by an exceedingly powerful primitive need, Cecelia tangled her tongue with his. Meeting his passion with a claim of her own. Her legs parted over his knee, driving their hips closer. She rubbed against his sex, allowing him to feel the tremors of pleasure rippling down her body.

She purred in triumph when his hips ground against her.

Ramsay broke contact. His breaths, harsh and ragged, landed against her cheek in hot, wine-scented bursts. "Tell me to stop," he panted.

Cecelia stared at him mutely, her breasts heaving against him. She knew what he was asking. He needed her practicality as he battled his lust. He wanted her to tell him that they were still enemies. That they would regret each other. He was asking for the reminder that this heat between them was wrong, somehow.

She could give him none of that, because her reason had been replaced by nature. By desire. She was more aware than ever before that tomorrows were not guaranteed, and yesterdays didn't matter as much as everyone seemed to think.

"Cecelia." Her name on his lips was both invocation and benediction. This moment between them either a beginning, or an ending. Either way, they stood at a cataclysmic divide searching for the bridge across.

She could bring herself to say nothing. They'd talked and talked and that had gotten them almost nowhere. It was time to allow their bodies to do the communicating, to soothe the singular pain of children born of loneliness and the lifelong shame of being one of the unwanted.

That was their common ground. The place where their souls might meet and merge.

She stared up into his savage, brutal beauty, aching to say so many things, yet unable to make herself vulnerable to his rejection.

Pleasure me, she wanted to plead. *Take your pleasure from me. Fill this emptiness and enmity between us with something we both want. Lend me your strength and I'll give you my softness.*

The dirtiest demand leapt to her tongue. She even curled her bottom lip between her teeth but bit down hard, unable to bring herself to say it.

Fuck me.

A whimper of need escaped her, and that was all it took to break down his last defense. A dark mask covered his features, this one dangerous and unrestrained. Cecelia gasped out as a pang of delicious fear pierced her before he dove for her mouth. His fingers plunged into her hair, all sense of gentility replaced with feral lust.

Their kiss became a battle, each of them driving against the other, shoving closer, demanding heat and friction.

He devoured her with strong plunges of his slick, velvet tongue, his hands dragging down her rib cage to mold to her bottom. With one swift flex, he lifted her from where she'd risen on her tiptoes to reach his mouth with hers and curled her legs around his waist.

He pinned her to the door with his hips, his erection trapped against her sex, pulsing with insistent demand through the many layers of her skirts and his trousers.

For her part, Cecelia attacked his shirt, ripping the buttons from their bindings until she could peel it away from his wide shoulders, smoothing her appreciative hands down the rippling cords of his long, beautiful arms.

He was built like an Olympian, his flesh smooth as marble poured over mounds of iron. Blood pumped through thick ropes of veins beneath his skin, warming all the earth and clay of him, animating his every impulse with strength and life.

Her greedy hands danced over him, taking advantage of their position. She raked her fingers through a soft wealth of golden hair over his chest, finding the flat, masculine nipples that pebbled beneath her touch.

He made a noise that wasn't entirely human and allowed her to slide down his body until she stood again so he could gather her hands in his own.

No, she thought, pulling her hands from his grasp. *No, you don't get to control this.*

She wanted him like he was now. Free and wild, uninhibited and mindless. She wanted the man to give way to the animal beneath. If almost every one of their interactions had been a battle, this one would be different in a very unmistakable way.

This was a battle she'd win.

She'd bring the Lord Chief Justice to his knees by what she could do on hers. Her intention caused her both anticipation and anxiety. She'd seen the act and read about it in the volume in Henrietta's library. The one that'd fallen open to her the day they'd met as enemies.

This was a man's ultimate pleasure. The questions remained, was it the giver of pleasure, or the one who received who maintained control?

She'd just have to find out in the practical application.

Cecelia lowered herself until she was no longer on her tiptoes, and then bent her knees slowly, dragging her lips from his mouth to his stubbled jaw and down the thick column of his neck. She was certain to leave a slight trail of moisture, so her intent could be unmistakable.

She stopped to kiss his clavicles and run her cheek along the fine fleece of his chest hair.

Breath sawed in and out of his massive chest as though he'd run a league. He said nothing. Made no move to encourage or deny her.

His rough hand stroked her hair with absent fascination.

Ramsay reminded her of both predator and prey. A hare frozen in the presence of a red fox, too stunned with uncertainty to leap away. A lion hunkering in the bushes, shoulders tense and ready to strike.

Cecelia proceeded with her marvelous discovery of his body as she sank to her knees. She counted his ribs on the way down, dragging curious fingers over the corrugated ripples of his abdomen.

Ramsay caught at her arm, his eyes burning down at her with a blue fire.

Blue flames burned the brightest, the hottest.

"My protection doesna come at a price," he hissed out. The skin of his features stretched taut over his raw bones.

Cecelia settled into the wide cloud her skirts made around her knees and stared up at him with all the anticipatory resolution she felt. "I want this. I want you."

Her fingers fell to the placket of his trousers, trembling but sure. A light-headed anticipation swamped her as she undid each button, brushing at the swollen length concealed beneath.

She reached inside, her cool fingers unable to completely encircle the scorching circumference of him.

Ramsay gasped. His hand hit the door and he leaned on it heavily, as though it were the only thing keeping him from buckling.

Cecelia paid him no mind, mesmerized by this part of him. Drawing the engorged member out of the vee of his trousers, she weighed the heft and length of him in her hand. He was thick. Large. The thin skin of the shaft—darker than the rest of him—pulsed with veins, and the hardness beneath was astonishing. Unyielding and inflexible as bone or steel.

She made a husky sound in her throat as her mouth watered, and he stopped breathing entirely. His free hand wound into her hair once again and this time his fingers curled into a fist, tugging the strands to the edge of pain and forcing her to look up at him.

His shirt gaped open, trapped at his elbows, revealing the stone-smooth pallor of his Scottish complexion.

She gazed up over the cords of his stomach and the mounds of his chest into gilded lightning glinting down at her from eyes that no longer held a hint of winter. His skin was flushed with arousal. His lids at half-mast.

He bared his teeth in a show of dominance, though his hand was gentle as it urged her mouth toward the column of his sex.

He thought he was still in control.

How adorable.

Cecelia tentatively wrapped lips moistened by his kisses around the rimmed crest of his cock.

His hips jerked forward, doing mesmerizing things to the hard ridges of muscle and sinew leading down to his shaft.

A very feminine triumph welled within her at the illicit nature of the act she now performed upon the so-called Vicar of Vice.

He tasted of salt and sin.

She felt no shame, but a hesitant pang thrilled through her that caused her eyelids to fall. She couldn't watch any longer. She couldn't see his eyes, or she might faint from the heady giddiness of power and lust.

Her own loins throbbed with the preponderance of her blood, as she was sure none reached her extremities any longer.

No, she could not watch. She simply needed to feel and

taste. To experience this dance of desire and gorge like a glutton on his sex.

His fingers flexed in her hair, guiding her down further, thrusting the head of his cock past her teeth, seeking her tongue.

Yes, she thought. *Show me what you want. Tell me what to do.*

She explored him with her tongue, licking at the rim before finding a vulnerable vein on the underside of his shaft. Following a rhythmic, throbbing instinct, her hand stroked the length of him that wouldn't fit past her lips, gliding up and down in moist parody of lovemaking.

She experimented with pressure and speed, allowing the hitches of his breath and the hand on the back of her head to guide her.

She rested her other hand on his thigh. His legs, long and thick and corded with strength, had always enticed her, and she loved the feel of them twitching and straining beneath her palm.

His intrusion into her mouth caused it to ceaselessly water as she feasted on his hard flesh. Sensuous liquid sounds permeated the night as she tended to him. They each fought to stay as silent as they could, aware that others slept in different parts of the house.

Cecelia found a curious saline drop of slippery liquid at his tip. She laved at the slit, seeking more.

A raw groan escaped him.

Her answering sigh of appreciation vibrated against his cock, causing him to buck and swell inside her mouth.

Gasping, he curled his hips back, seeking to withdraw. But Cecelia didn't let him. She, too, could be relentless, and was determined to see this through to the end.

She employed the strength of her jaw, sucking him in,

taking him as deep against her throat as she could. Her tongue flattened to make room for him, rubbing at the underside of his rod as she pumped faster.

"Nay," he gritted out. "Ye canna."

Yes, she thought. *I can. You're mine. This is mine.* This wicked intimacy they would always share regardless of the outcome of their current nightmare. At least she'd owned him with her mouth. And he was the man whose lips she would never forget.

A sound the cross between a snarl and a whimper forced its way out of him as he swelled inside her lips impossibly larger, releasing a slippery warm pulse of moisture. The illicit substance tasted both musky and sweet as it slid down her throat.

Cecelia finally opened her eyes, glorying in the sight of him locked within his own skin and strength. Helpless and vulnerable inside her mouth. Arching with a pleasure that looked very much like pain.

This was the beast. This untethered, unselfconscious thing.

This beast was hers. This beast wanted to lay claim to her, as well.

No matter what the man might have to say about it.

Ramsay was lost. Lost in her generous mouth. In the miasma of pleasure she liberally gave.

His humanity retreated behind this creature of carnality she'd tempted out of his past, and all sense of civility was locked away behind throbbing muscles and veins pulsing with explosive delight.

Never had he experienced such bliss. Never had he hungered so drastically that he feared it would take a lifetime to sate him.

The bone-shattering pulses of his climax finally dimmed

enough to lend him back his reflexes. He'd thought he'd be drained. Exhausted by the sheer unparalleled heights he'd experienced in the depths of her mouth.

However, his body recovered splendidly, the animal lust still rippled beneath his flesh, a hunger of his own clawing through him.

She wasn't the only one who needed a taste. There was so much left to do. To discover.

And the night was young.

A growl of delight rumbled through him as he bent to drag her to her feet.

She gasped, "Wha—?"

His mouth hungrily captured hers, cutting off her protest. Plunging his tongue within her mouth, his essence mingled with her singular flavor tasted of ambrosia.

Of course it did. She was a goddess, after all.

He lifted her from her feet without breaking the contact of their lips and again split her legs to encircle his hips. The delicious weight of her was a delight. Her ass in his hands, her thighs soft and strong around him.

He crossed the room in a few long strides and lowered her to the rocking chair. Dragging the generous mounds of her bottom to the very edge with a smooth motion, he hooked her knees over the arms of the chair, imprisoning them open with the width of his torso.

All this he did while distracting her with his tongue swirling inside her mouth.

Suddenly it mattered not how many men had tasted her before. He didn't care.

She'd just claimed him with her mouth. He'd felt it with every instinct he'd honed in this cold, feral, inhospitable place.

And he was about to stake a claim of his own.

She'd learned him quickly, her face a mask of dreamlike

discovery. She'd made him feel like he was the only man she'd ever wanted. Had ever known.

He was about to repay in kind.

He never broke the kiss as he tossed her skirt over her knees and ripped her undergarments asunder.

She made a startled little sound and he captured her wrist, gently but firmly replacing his mouth with her own fingers against her lips.

"I'm going to make ye scream, lass," he vowed against her ear. "So bite down to keep quiet."

Her answer was a delicate flare of her nostrils over a shuddering breath as he pulled away to look at her.

The firelight snapped and sputtered over a particularly dry log, sending showers of sparks into the air behind him.

The light gleamed off where she splayed open for him. Vulnerable. Exposed.

So utterly edible.

Lust threatened to knock him over. Had he not already been on his knees, the sheer force of it would have driven him there.

Her sex glistened with ready moisture. The ruffles of flesh pink and pretty, the little nubbin at their aperture visibly throbbing. Engorged. A soft tuft of dark russet hair protected the secret cove, beckoning to his fingers.

A part of him yearned to see all of her, but there would be time for that. Time to unwrap her as she did those damned truffles. With relish. With delight. With anticipation and impatience.

But now. He must dine. Feast upon her flesh. Sup on her desire and drink of the flood of pleasure he was about to provoke from the warm, intimate depths of her before he staked his final claim.

Christ but she was crafted for sin. Plump and perfect,

her long, thick white thighs encircled by garters of green created a flawless cradle for his shoulders.

He glanced up into her beautiful, heart-shaped countenance, and whatever she read in his eyes caused her to tremble. A ripple of diffidence creased her forehead. Her eyes were peeled wide and gleamed with threatening moisture, and her hand was white and bloodless where she clamped it over her mouth.

She reached for him, but he needed no prompting.

He kissed her. There. Luxuriating in her feminine musk. Never had a woman so seduced his every olfactory sense.

She gave an adorable squeak and lifted her free hand to clutch at the back of the chair behind her.

A dark chuckle escaped him, vibrating against her sex as he settled between her thighs. He was just getting started.

Christ, she was soft. And slick.

His hands splayed on the tender skin of her inner thighs before caressing up to where they met. He played in her intimate curls for a moment before spreading her sex wider. Granting him devious, unrestricted access.

She inhaled sharply, and a tremor overtook her, racking through the strong muscles of her legs.

Someday she would ride him with those long legs. Ride his mouth. His cock.

He couldn't fucking wait.

Nipping and laving at the crests and ridges of her pliant flesh, he glowed with a masculine satisfaction at her every hitching breath and the astonishment in the mewls she couldn't allow to escape from her throat.

He circled the little pearl with a wicked tongue, leaving it untouched. Lowering his attentions, he dipped into the well of moisture, flattening his tongue to spread it higher.

Her breaths were naught but ragged little puffs. The sinew of her legs flexed and trembled, her hips curling and arching toward his mouth in blind demands.

And still he didn't relent.

She strained and twisted until Ramsay had to use his strength to hold her in place. The tiny sounds behind her hand turned to pathetic little pleas.

He'd wanted to take longer, to dine until he had his fill, but, it seemed, he was not impervious to her sweet, husky entreaties for release.

Finally, he feathered his tongue over her crest, applying the very lightest of pressure.

She came apart beneath his mouth, smothering a hoarse cry as her legs struggled to close, but were impeded by the sturdy arms of the chair. Ramsay held her down, pleasuring her relentlessly, flicking his tongue just below her nub.

His vision swam and clouded as she came in long, rolling waves. Her sex rolled against his face, hips bucking, flooding his mouth with the slippery moisture he craved. He stayed with her, pressing her thighs wider with his hands, pinning her down. Spilling pleasure from his lips and tongue, not intending to cease until she could take no more.

He had to be certain he'd launched her to the same place she'd sent him only moments before. That place where time and space ceased to exist. Where names were forgotten and consequences were damned.

He'd never forget the sight of her like this. Open and writhing. Tears rolling into her mussed curls as she convulsed beneath his hungry mouth. She bit at the flesh of her palm, and he found that so decadently sensual, he swelled almost to bursting.

The feral part she'd awakened in him wanted to bite

her thigh. To mark her as his. But she reached down between them, her fingers plunging into his hair. She yanked and pulled, peeling his mouth away from her sex with a loud, wet sound.

"I can't . . ." she panted.

"I know, lass," he growled wickedly, prowling up her splayed body, allowing her to tug him against her.

"I need you close." The confession sounded so small. So young and vulnerable as she grasped at him, burying her face in his neck. "That. That was so . . ." Her breath hit his chest in little puffs as she nuzzled into him, lifting her knees away from the arms of the chair and locking them around his waist.

He swiped at his mouth with the back of his hand before burying his face against her curls. "Ye're the most delicious woman," he crooned. "I'll forever crave yer taste."

"Truly?" She sounded both pleased and astonished. If a voice could blush, hers would have done it.

Had no one ever told her that before?

His sex, already hard and hot, slid against her slick flesh, seeking a home in her welcoming warmth.

He could feel the little pulses of her feminine muscles in the aftermath of her orgasm. When he would have thrust forward, she pulled her head back, looking up at him, her gaze searching and uncertain.

"Ramsay?"

He paused, staring down into eyes as deep blue as the Adriatic Sea, and just as mysterious. "Aye?"

"Will you hate me after?"

He only hated himself for ever causing her to fear that.

Tucking a wild curl behind her ear, he welled with such a deep tenderness it soothed the wild beast he'd become. "I never hated ye, Cecelia," he confided. "Not even when I believed ye deserved it."

She closed her eyes and sought his mouth for a kiss, which he gave her. Her body rolled against his, her hips arching upward in eager invitation.

He found her opening without using his hand to guide him, and wet the crown of his cock with her abundant moisture before driving forward.

Or . . . attempting to.

Her muscles clamped down so tightly he couldn't gain more than an inch. Readjusting her in the chair, he bore forward once more.

This time her cry of distress stopped him before her unyielding muscles had the chance to.

Ramsay's heart surged. Then stopped. His veins turned to ice.

Holy. Fucking. Hell.

He pulled back to look down at her features, which were distorted with plaintive discomfort.

He disentangled himself from her, rocked back on his heels, and looked down.

Blood.

He made his own sound of distress, meeting her glistening eyes with his astonished ones. "Ye're . . . ye're a . . ." He couldn't say it. He stood and turned away from her, stuffing himself back into his trousers and tucking his shirt in as well.

A virgin. His mind screamed the word he couldn't bring himself to say.

When he whirled to face her, she'd closed her legs and righted her skirts, her hands folded primly in her lap though his face had feasted there only seconds ago.

"But . . ." He gestured toward the high walls of the loft. "But Phoebe . . ."

"Is my ward," she explained, still unperturbed. "Though

I have every intention of raising her as my daughter. She deserves that much."

"But ye just . . ." Panic seemed to have stolen his ability to finish sentences, so he just jammed his finger toward the door in front of which he'd thrust his cock into her welcoming lips. "I just made ye . . ." Oh holy Christ, he was headed straight to hell.

"No, no you didn't." She stood, holding placating hands out to him. "I wanted to—to do what we did. To bring you pleasure. I needed to show you—"

"If ye say gratitude, I'll fucking shoot myself." He jammed his fingers through his hair, tugging in frustration.

"Why?"

He felt like he was drowning. Drowning in guilt as the alignment of reality shifted beneath his feet, causing the earth to become unstable on its very axis. "Ye canna tell me ye never did that before."

She glanced at the door, the peach in her cheeks already flushed with pleasure deepening in a most fetching, sensual manner. "All right, I won't tell you that," she said agreeably. "I mean, I *hadn't* done anything we just did before, but we needn't discuss it just now."

"Bloody Christ," he bit out, pacing a room that was becoming tinier by the moment as his mouth filled with every curse in every language he knew. "How did you know what to do?"

"I read it in that book your constable found in Henrietta's study." She moved to block his path. "Why are you angry?"

"I just stole yer virginity." Since he couldn't roar that to the child who slept in the attic loft above them or the dear old broken butler in his bed, he kept his voice to a minimum, and made up for it with large, exaggerated gestures.

She held up her hands, pressing them against his pounding chest. "No you didn't. I gave it to you . . . I mean, I think I did, anyway. I'm not altogether certain I'm rid of it, all told." She patted his chest in a manner that might have been condescending if it had come from anyone else in the world. "If it makes you feel better, no other man has ever really showed my virginity much interest, and I can't say it's ever done me any good. So please, don't feel guilty on my account. I'm old enough to be rid of it, aren't I?" She flashed him a winsome, rather tentative smile.

Had the world gone fucking mad?

Had he?

Had every man who *hadn't* tried to get up her skirts in the past decade? Surely there had been someone at university who'd been drawn to her pillowy curves and delightful dimples.

Not that he should think about that now.

Or ever, *ever* again.

He was such a fucking hypocrite.

"You don't look so well," she fretted. "Should we . . . would you like to sit down?"

"I have to go." Ramsay retreated to the door, swiping his coat from the hook.

"But—"

He whirled on her, his lips pulled back in a snarl. "Ye'll be safe tonight. Ye have my word. But so help me, ye'll stay in this house and doona ye dare follow me, is that understood?"

Her expression darkened, her jaw flexing forward in a stubborn motion for a moment, before she deflated with a heavy shaken breath.

He wished he could at least take the pleasure of slamming out of the cottage, but he simply couldn't bring himself to wake Phoebe or Jean-Yves. And so he closed the door behind him on a very audibly ominous click.

She didn't follow him.

But her flavor lingered in his mouth, and the pleasure she'd given sang through his veins.

Her virginity stained his body. His soul.

And her silent pain was inescapable, becoming his shadow in the dark.

CHAPTER THIRTEEN

Cecelia's head throbbed in sync to the sound of Ramsay's ax splitting wood outside her window.

She'd woken early, having tossed and turned into the wee hours of the morning. Everything ached. Her hips, her back, her head . . .

Her sex.

Restless and emotional, she'd decided to work on the codex, intent upon distracting herself from last night's disastrous ending. And from the scorching memories of what had preceded it.

In the hours between dawn and now, she'd gotten exactly nowhere.

Jean-Yves and Phoebe had both woken and needed tending to, and Cecelia found herself eager for a distraction.

To his credit, Ramsay had seen to Jean-Yves's needs and even hauled and heated water in which the invalid could take a proper hip bath. After, the Lord Chief Justice had prepared a breakfast of hearty bread, fruit, and cheeses in which he didn't partake with the trio of guests.

Ramsay had barely glanced at Cecelia the entire morning, and in order to contain her smarting emotions, she forced a false brightness into her interactions with the others.

Phoebe was content and chatty, eager to romp about the yard and pick wildflowers with her dolls.

Jean-Yves, who'd known and cared about Cecelia for so long, was not so easily fooled.

Exhausted after bathing, eating, and dressing, he allowed her to help him back to bed and tuck him beneath the covers.

"Did something happen?" he asked alertly. "Your heart, it is bleeding, I think. Is it over this giant, grumpy Scot?" His nose wrinkled with distaste as he eyed the Scot through the open window.

Damn his observant nature.

"Don't worry yourself." Cecelia smoothed the blankets over him and lifted the opium tincture from the desk. "My heart is more bruised than bleeding."

His eyes narrowed beneath a web of fine wrinkles. "Do I need to make room for his corpse in the garden?"

She smiled down at him fondly. Had there ever been a man so dear? "No. I do not think he's done anything wrong."

"Tell me what he has done, and I'll tell you if it's wrong," Jean-Yves offered as passionately as one in his condition was able.

Cecelia fought the pink creeping up from beneath her collar and shook her head.

Jean-Yves made a face. "On second thought, I find I do not want to know."

She offered him a contrite little smile that went no further than her mouth, and handed him the laudanum with water at the ready.

Jean-Yves refused the medicine. "The pain is bearable this morning," he said. "I do not want to develop a taste for oblivion." He sucked at his teeth, lifting one bushy caterpillar brow up his creased forehead. "Besides, I think this Scot will finish breaking your heart while I am sleeping, no?"

"No," Cecelia said glumly, slumping into the desk chair. "He's being logical. In order for any sort of life together to work, I'd have to be other than I am."

His mouth twisted. "What do you mean?"

"He's the Lord Chief Justice. I'm a bastard and the owner of a notorious gambling hell."

She sighed and dropped her chin into her palm, resting her elbow on the desk. "Ramsay would not take my heart if I offered it and so he cannot break it. I do not think it's worth anything to him." The thought tore at her raw emotions, stinging her eyes with unwanted tears. She'd been nothing but an open wound since the moment he left, and she hated her own weakness.

"Then he is a fool, an idiot, an incomparable ass." Jean-Yves's dudgeon caused his breath to speed, and he clutched at his ribs.

Cecelia leaned forward, her hands hovering over him, finding no place to land. "Please, do not worry about my heart. We're safe for now, and if Lord Ramsay is anything, he's a man of his word. He'll take good care of us."

"I always worry about your heart, *bonbon*, it is the softest heart in the whole world." Jean-Yves leaned back, closing his eyes and breathing slowly. "I just don't understand," he murmured as though talking to himself. "A man does not hold a woman like he held you the night of the attack unless she is precious to him. I thought—perhaps—you'd finally found someone who would try to be worthy of you."

Cecelia shook her head, unable to lend voice to the suspicion that she might never be deemed worthy in his eyes. "He thinks he is not broken," she murmured, turning her face to the window. "But I know different. And he'll have to admit it before he can be put back together."

"I am glad you are intelligent enough to see that," Jean-Yves praised her. "So many women try to fix a man that is broken, and he ruins her, instead."

Cecelia dropped her head into both hands for a moment, fighting the tears back instead of giving in to them. She had work to do, a family to care for. She hadn't time to nurse a broken—no, bruised—heart. "God, I'm such a child. Why do I cry so often?"

"Because you feel so much, it easily spills over."

"I just . . ." A hot tear tracked down her cheek, and she dashed it away. "I just wish I were not so difficult to love."

"Your love is a treasure, Cecelia," Jean-Yves said. "I do not know this Lord Ramsay well, but I think perhaps he does not question *your* worth to *him*, but deep down he knows he is not worthy of you."

She very much doubted that, but didn't want to give Jean-Yves more ammunition against the man upon whom their survival relied at the moment.

"Why do affairs of the heart have to be about worthiness at all?" she lamented. "Why can't people simply accept themselves and each other for the lovely, flawed beings we are? If one is doing one's best, can that not be enough?"

He sent her a fond smile. "You are always enough, *mon bijou*. Just remember that."

Cecelia took his hand and kissed it before turning to her work.

Or trying to, anyhow.

Yesterday, the waters of the River Esk could be heard through the open window, meandering somewhere out of sight of the main structure. But today all Cecelia could focus on was the tireless sounds of Ramsay's ax splitting through wood.

Agitated and distracted, she had let the cool summer breeze ruffle the pages of her books and lift tendrils of her hair to tickle her cheek. She wished the surly Scot would cease to dominate her ponderings. That he wouldn't pose yet another problem to solve.

They were searching for her would-be murderer. For evidence relating to the mysterious Crimson Council. Why couldn't she focus on that rather than her would-be lover?

One may not have a lover if one is dead, and so one must concentrate, she admonished herself.

She gave it her most valiant effort, squirming in her chair for the time it took for Jean-Yves to fall back asleep. Eventually, his snores coincided with the sounds of cracking wood to completely drive her bonkers. The numerals and symbols, dots and dashes coalesced into nonsense, and it was all she could do not to go cross-eyed.

Heaving a sigh, she pushed herself away from the desk and swept out of the bedroom. She'd never been one to let a thing fester. She needed this fixed between them before she could work.

Opening the door, she blinked against the sun and let the sounds of summer filter over her.

Phoebe waved at her from over by the fence, where she constructed something like a woven hammock of blooming hollyhocks for Frances Bacon and Fanny de Beaufort. A newly woven butterfly net rested next to her, unused.

Had Ramsay made it for her?

Cecelia waved back, affixing a smile for the girl before turning toward an overgrown trail that led behind the house.

Branches and bushes snagged at her, and she had to pick a thistle out of the eyelet lace at the cuff of her sleeve. So apropos for a path leading her to Ramsay. To get through to the man, she'd have to reach past the over-grown brambles and thorny vines protecting his unused heart.

When she sighted him, she reached a hand out to catch herself against the wall of the house.

Naked to the waist, Ramsay lifted an ax over his head like Odin's own woodsman. The early-morning sun glinted off the razor-sharp edge of the tool as he brought it down with a brutal swing, shearing through a thick stump of wood as though it were made of paper.

Cecelia lurked in the shadows of the west side of the house like a voyeur, doing her best to regain her composure.

His marble skin glistened with a light sheen of sweat as he sank the ax into the stump he used as a chopping block. He tossed both halves of split wood onto a growing mountain against a ramshackle shed that was little more than a lean-to.

He'd chopped enough firewood to heat a small village in the dead of winter.

Cecelia took the moment to appreciate the sheer height and breadth of him. He was built like a conqueror put on this earth to shame and dominate lesser men. He might have been a warlord in days past. A marauder or pillager, perhaps.

Come to think of it, that he'd become a good man was nothing short of miraculous. He could have quite easily used all that impressive strength for evil. Indeed, he might have used his tragic past as an excuse for cruelty.

It took a singular kind of man to commit such consummate drive, intellect, and sheer power to strive for excellence. To succeed. To become an unstoppable force for justice rather than tyranny.

Cecelia studied him as he split log after log with one mighty blow like an executioner. There was a rhythm to his work, so much so that she timed it out in seconds.

Split. Gather. Toss. Take up ax. Lift. Swing. Split. Repeat. It was mesmerizing, hypnotizing even. She might lose time here, and reason, watching the ridges of his ribs and abdomen gather strength and collapse with every swing. Tracing the unfamiliar angle of his arms as he lifted them over his head, showcasing the power of his arms.

That tremendous body had been at her mercy last night. Had belonged to her hungry gaze and hungrier mouth. She'd locked every bit of his astonishing strength into a seizure of bliss.

And then he'd returned the favor with a supreme skill that had both humbled and terrified her.

She was becoming increasingly attached to the churlish Scot. There was no dancing around it. The sight of him stimulated her in every conceivable way. The scent of him enticed her.

And the taste of him intoxicated her beyond all reasoning.

What had Jean-Yves said only this morning? *I don't want to develop at taste for oblivion.*

Ramsay had taught her last night the oblivion sex could offer. And it appeared she'd developed the taste for it in a single dose. She felt craven, as though he'd woken a new hunger in her body just as vital as that for food.

She had very few innate talents, but the rhythm and

structure of sexual relations apparently came as easily to her as maths.

What was it about the discovery of her virginity that vexed him so? Did he blame himself for taking what she gave? Or was she at fault once again for a lie of omission?

There was only one way to find out.

Breaking away from the shadow of the house, Cecelia smoothed down the soft cotton of her robin's-egg-blue day dress and drifted through an overgrown graveyard of what might have been a vegetable garden once.

Ramsay brought the ax down with a particularly brutal swing, embedding the blade a good two inches into the platform of the ancient trunk.

"Lovely day for it," Cecelia called, her cheeks bunching around the rims of her spectacles as she squinted against the sun.

Wasn't Scotland supposed to be gloomy and gray?

Ramsay's nostrils flared on a grunt, though he didn't look at her as he bent to retrieve the split wood and toss it on the woodpile. Instead of settling into the grooves created by the other logs, they crashed against the lean-to and clattered to the earth.

She'd thrown off his rhythm, it seemed.

Inside the lean-to, a coarse pallet was spread over straw and grass, two heavy patchwork quilts folded neatly at the edge.

Had this been the "structure" in which he'd slept? Lord, she felt awful.

"Speaking of lovely days," she said, forging ahead. "I might remind you that it's July, and you've split enough firewood to keep us here through Christmas. I don't know about you, but I'm not planning on staying that long."

She'd meant the teasing observation to perhaps create

a crack in the wall of ice he'd constructed between them, but his frown only deepened as he snatched his shirt from where it hung on a peg of the lean-to and punched his fists into the sleeves.

"Did ye make any progress on the codex?" he asked without ceremony.

Cecelia's smile faltered.

"Not as such," she answered honestly, mourning the lost sight of his chest as he did up the buttons.

He barely flicked a glance her way. At least not one long enough to notice that she'd taken extra time with her coiffeur and unwrinkled her most comely summer frock that brought out the blue in her eyes and the darker shades of crimson in her copper hair.

"Did ye require something?" he asked as he did up his cuffs.

Her shoulders slumped as even the pretense of optimism abandoned her. "I feel like we should discuss . . . last night."

He astonished her by shaking his head. "There is no need."

She blinked after his broad back as he grabbed his vest and pulled it across his wide shoulders while stalking toward the house.

She willed her feet to move, jogging after him. "*I* have need. I want to explain—"

"Ye owe me no explanation," he replied shortly.

Now, there was a fine turn of events for you. Cecelia puffed a little, forced to trot behind him on the brambly path. All this time he'd demanded nothing but endless explanations, and now when she was dying to give one, he'd have none of it.

They each waved to Phoebe on their way inside, pretending all was well for the darling little girl.

Cecelia's smile died the moment she crossed the threshold. "But things have changed between us, have they not?"

"Aye." He ran his fingers through his hair, darkened to the color of sand by sweat and dirt as he searched the small room for something, still refusing to look at her. "They've changed irrevocably."

"Shouldn't we—explore that? Perhaps come to some sort of comfortable understanding?" *Please*, she wanted to beg. *I can't stand the silence.*

"We will." He finally looked at her, or rather, looked through her. "Just not now."

"Why?" she asked, trailing him still as he turned and tromped across the kitchen floor.

"There isna time."

"Why not?"

Stopping before the fireplace, he took up his bow, quiver, and several of the arrows he'd been making the night before. "I have to hunt."

"To hunt?" She echoed, looking back at their pile of food and sundries, both dried and fresh. It would keep them for a great while. "Hunt what?"

"Deer," he answered gruffly. Clomping back toward the door.

"Deer?" She was beginning to sound like an annoying, monosyllabic parrot, even to herself. But he was acting strange, and her nerves were so shot she could hardly string a thought together, let alone absorb and analyze his strident behavior. "Where . . . where will you go to hunt deer?"

He turned around in the doorway and thrust a hand toward the forest. "In the direction of deer." His obtuse answer combined with his impatient intonation smothered her fear with frustration.

"Why are you angry?" she demanded, doing her best to keep her voice reasonable. "What did I do?"

"I'm not angry, Miss Teague." The harsh note in his voice belied the claim, but his features gentled from barbaric to merely austere. "Not at ye, anyway."

Miss Teague? Why did his respectful moniker sound like a punishment? Cecelia stepped forward, reaching out to him. "Then talk to me."

He flinched away from her touch, putting a hand out to stop her. "I am not myself today," he offered by way of explanation. "I canna be trusted with discussions or decisions. Not now." He looked up at her, his eyes both beseeching and bleak. "Just . . . do what ye can to figure out the codex so we can go back to our lives, aye?"

Cecelia pressed her lips together, biting her cheek hard enough to draw blood.

She managed a nod, and he turned away and tromped toward the tree line.

Go back to their lives. Their separate lives. Was he in that much of a hurry to be rid of them? Of course he was. He hated this place, almost as much as he detested her company in it. He might desire her, but he didn't want her. There was a difference. He'd made no compunctions about that.

She didn't fit into his life. Not in Scotland, and surely not in London.

However, as a man so vehemently against any moral turpitude, he must be panicking. Because he'd absconded with her, performed sexual acts with her, and if anyone were to find out about it, society would dictate they marry with all due immediacy.

They neither of them desired a spouse.

Was he so upset because he, as a self-proclaimed honorable man, was now obligated to propose?

She'd turn him down, of course she would. She was no one's obligation. Furthermore, her family belonged nowhere near the office of the Lord Chancellor. She'd be his ruination; they both knew it.

Cecelia made certain his broad back disappeared into the forest before she sank to the table over which they'd shared wine the previous night.

Burying her face in her arms, she finally succumbed to her tears.

Chapter Fourteen

If idle hands were the devil's workshop, then this precarious situation made Ramsay the devil.

Because his thoughts, urges, and desires were endlessly wicked, and it wasn't only his hands Cecelia Teague need worry about.

Nay, it was better he remain outside and give in to other masculine urges.

Such as bashing things. And killing things.

Ramsay didn't stray far from the cottage, not when his only directive was to protect those within. Rather, he took up a perch he'd erected years ago in a tall oak directly above a path where the deer meandered down to graze and drink at the river's edge. From this vantage, he could see for miles. The cottage, the road, the river, and anyone who might be coming or going.

Deer were not his only prey.

It seemed he'd learned an affinity for perching above the world at a young age, from this very spot.

Deciding what lived or died.

If his peers could see him now. Trading the white wig and dark robes of his station for a sodden shirt and the trappings of a huntsman.

It'd prove them right. Everyone who'd whispered that a savage Scottish nobody with a grasping, devious legacy didn't deserve the station to which he aspired.

Theirs were the voices that had haunted his dark hours, that drove his every decision for so long. He achieved not despite them, but *to* spite them. He studied harder, worked longer, and did better than them all so that when he entered a room, the naysayers dare not breathe in his direction. In fact, they all had to bow and address him as *my lord*.

And he knew the title tasted like ashes in their mouths.

He used to live for it. Dine on it. The power, the prestige, and the prescience awarded to those within the circles he'd forced his way into. Because it didn't matter what title they were born with, or what privilege they enjoyed; they still couldn't keep him beneath their boots.

No one would again. Because *his* word was law now. And his judgment final.

Except a new voice rose in the night. A soft, husky alto that sounded of smoke and sex.

Cecelia Teague.

He whispered the two words to the wind in reverent tones. It felt as though her name should always be spoken thus.

There were gods whose names were never allowed to be uttered, whose depictions were forbidden.

Ramsay had never understood such worship.

Until now.

A part of him had known the moment his lips had touched hers that the cosmos had shifted.

Nay, before then.

Perhaps in the gardens at Redmayne Place when they'd spoken of the numerous reasons a union would be disastrous for them both. Or even at Redmayne's wedding almost a year ago, when he'd spied her across the ballroom in a peacock mask, lingering at the refreshment table.

He'd been mesmerized by her even then, so much so that he'd gone out of his way to *not* be introduced, because something fierce and ferocious he'd thought he'd buried decades ago stirred at the very sight of her.

He'd thanked God the moment he'd found out she was innocent of Henrietta's crimes.

And cursed that same divinity the moment he'd discovered she was innocent in every sense of the word.

By taking that innocence from her.

A branch broke in the distance, and Ramsay froze at the sound of footsteps approaching.

He held his breath, and gripped his bow. He'd a rifle at his side, as well, but he avoided using it whenever possible. Gunshots tended to advertise one's position.

A doe stepped from the brush, her long downy ears twitching this way and that, her nostrils testing the wind.

Ramsay nocked an arrow, pulling it taut as she stopped and looked behind her.

A little fawn, no larger than a hound, toddled out from the safety of the thicket. It glued its little speckled body to its mother's haunches, scampering to keep up with her careful strides toward the river.

They hadn't spotted him above them, but they sensed danger was nearby.

Ramsay dropped his arm, resting the arrow at his side.

No matter how hungry he'd been in his life, he'd never killed mothers. Didn't even set snares at rabbit burrows. Once, a fox had stolen some smoking fish, and he'd hurled rocks at it, stopping only once he'd realized *she* was quite obviously nursing kits.

Mothers should live to protect their young.

He thought of Cecelia. He always thought of Cecelia. His every stream of consciousness seemed to lead back to her. In this memory, she was desperately fighting to save her little ward. She'd been struck down in the alley, threatened, and witness to bloodshed, and still her first thought had been for Phoebe.

When she'd found the girl unharmed, her relief and tender joy had humbled him.

Cecelia. The girl had called her Cecelia that night. Not Mother, or Mama.

He generally had such an eye for detail. He certainly should have suspected then. But murder had been flowing through him at the time. He'd grappled wrath and fury back into the darkness in order to safely conduct the ladies home.

Another reason the woman was extraordinary. She mothered a child that wasn't even her own. According to her, she'd been fancy-free before the death of Henrietta Thistledown. She'd traveled and gallivanted as one third of a trio of redheaded Rogues, had enjoyed an education and a small but comfortable fortune. But when a bevy of students and dependents and a motherless child had landed in her lap, she'd taken the responsibility for their employ and well-being upon her shoulders without a second thought. She became their champion against the likes of him.

And worse.

Ramsay shut his eyes and listened to the deer saunter beneath him as he contemplated the tight fist curling around his heart.

Cecelia Teague made him question everything.

Everything.

His stance on women, family, morality, integrity, the past . . .

The future. *Their* future?

For so long he'd wanted nothing like a family. He'd striven only to attain the height of power that the common people were seizing every day from the old monarchy and hierarchical structures. Certainly, the aristocracy was giving way to men like him: men of industry, intellect, education, economy, and the means to shape an empire though the force of the rising democratic structures of government.

And now he was wrapping his fingers around Excalibur, as it were, poised and ready to pull the sword from stone and claim what was his due.

But at what cost? His soul?

His heart?

Are you happy? Her simple question bounced between his temples, taunting him like a ball thrown down a hill, forever rolling away.

Happiness had never been an expectation of his. His childhood had been a nightmare of drunken beatings, shouting matches between his parents, and an empty belly. When his mother left and his father died, survival had been his only goal. He worked day and night for heat, clean water, and food. Who had time to contemplate happiness when you had to fight the scourge of starvation, silence, and isolation? When every adult you came into contact with tried to either take advantage or take what was yours by right?

He'd perched up here some days shooting at anyone who dared approach. Not knowing if they were looters or neighbors.

Once in a while, they'd been both.

He forgot how to act or eat properly first. Then how to speak. In the years he'd lived in this cottage alone, an empty hole had opened up in his chest. This cold, silent void where a family ought to have been. Where mercy might have lived.

Where vagaries like happiness and love could have been nurtured.

He'd never succumbed to the silence or the emptiness, but he'd always carried it with him, even after he'd been taken to Redmayne Keep.

He couldn't believe it. More than twenty years had passed since he'd been dragged from this place, feral and filthy. A bestial, inhuman creature driven by nothing but instinct.

And the process of civilizing him had been both painful and humiliating.

He'd pledged never to become that creature again.

Which was what made Cecelia Teague such a danger to him.

Because she spoke to everything that had once made him little better than an animal. Despite her innate gentility, her intelligence, and her impeccable manners, she drew from him a carnal—nay—carnivorous instinct he found impossible to ignore, let alone control.

As evidenced by the prior night.

Ramsay's body responded, tightening at the memory. Hardening with need.

The first time he'd met her as the Scarlet Lady, he'd been so angry, so self-righteous. Partly because he'd wanted to know what it would feel like to have that generous mouth wrapped around his cock.

He might have guessed it would be a singular experience.

But he'd never expected to lose himself in unparalleled bliss. He'd never have thought she'd surpass his every previous encounter, exceed his most salacious fantasies. That her body would be the vehicle to a rapture most men were not fortunate enough to attain.

He'd lain awake all night with the taste of her coating his mouth, the pleasure she'd wrought in him still thrumming through every sinew and cord of his body. He'd been so grateful for the chill of the evening, and yet he'd yearned for her warmth. Even after the heat had cooled, something else became insistent. Some other organ than his sex.

He didn't simply want to fuck her, but to hold her. To comfort her. To *find* comfort with her.

The thought of making her laugh held more innate appeal than receiving a knighthood. He'd rather spend an afternoon indulging her appetites for chocolate than dining with royals and Continental contacts.

Even after he'd cleaned his teeth this morning and washed all traces of her away, her essence clung to him like it was now a part of him.

And therein lay the crux of the problem.

She threatened to topple all he built. To leach his ambition from him and replace it with contentment—nay, complacency.

That, he could not abide.

He could not simply melt into her comfort. Couldn't allow her softness to smooth away his sharp edges and temper what had made him hard, angry, and unrepentantly ruthless. He could not indulge, not without facing dastardly consequences.

But there was still honor to consider. His. Hers. And a mutual desire that was undeniable.

Only one thing to be done about it.

Claim her in every absolute way.

Marry her.

She was now Cecelia Teague and the Scarlet Lady. But . . . what if she could become someone else?

Cecelia Ramsay.

With her considerable skills, soft heart, and unparalleled intellect, she could be such a force in his world. Even though they both were cursed with tainted legacies, there was a chance to build a dynasty together that future generations would be proud of.

He could protect her, pleasure her, grant her and Phoebe opportunities they'd never have otherwise. Both freedom and respectability.

And perhaps, she could teach him something about happiness. And the odd indulgence.

Every time she smiled at him, with every kiss or intimacy they shared, a little light had ignited within that dark void inside him. He felt less empty.

What would a lifetime of her smiles do?

Ramsay shook his head, pushing the longing away and replacing it with resolve.

There would be time for that. But today, he had to stay sharp. Dangerous. Especially if he was about to take on the fortress built around the current Lord Chancellor and steal his dubious throne. All the while, he had to keep Cecelia safe. And to do that, he mustn't allow distractions.

Something else stalked along the game trail, confidently picking its way through the thicket.

Ramsay took in a deep breath, drew a bead, and let his arrow loose.

CHAPTER FIFTEEN

The afternoon sun had been uncharacteristically relentless. Ramsay swiped at his forehead and squinted at the sky. He had time for a dip in the loch before the shadows became long, and he could think of nothing better.

Even though it was bloody and disgusting work gutting, skinning, and stringing up a buck to treat the meat properly, Ramsay didn't mind; it kept him occupied and away from temptation.

Wiping his hands, he snuck into the house to retrieve a clean change of clothing, hoping to slip away unnoticed.

No such luck.

Phoebe sat at the table, swinging her feet off the ground as Jean-Yves allowed her to cheat at whist.

Ramsay glanced around for Cecelia and couldn't decide if he was relieved or disappointed not to find her. She'd be working at the desk on that dratted codex.

Phoebe beamed at him, the divot in her chin deepening. "There you are. Why are you stained?"

Cecelia's butler eyed him with rank misgiving, but

nodded in a respectful manner. Well, respectful for a Frenchman, anyhow.

"I skinned a buck just now, lass," he explained, extracting a fresh shirt and trousers from his trunk.

"Seems a waste to shoot a buck if we are only here but a few days," Jean-Yves harrumphed from behind the fan of cards he held up with his uninjured arm.

Ramsay frowned, but he didn't rise to the occasion.

"There are several large families hereabouts who would be glad of what meat we doona use." He wasn't in the habit of explaining himself, especially not in his own home. But he'd long since understood that the Frenchman was more a father figure than employee of Cecelia's, which disposed him to dislike and distrust a man who had designs on her.

Designs so undeniable, any fool could decipher his intent. His desire.

Jean-Yves was no fool.

Ramsay couldn't say he minded the older man's protective nature. Were he a father, he'd not approve of their current situation for his daughter, that was for certain.

Phoebe scooted off her chair and landed on the scuffed boots she'd taken to wearing daily to romp out of doors. "I don't believe I've tasted buck," she said, drifting closer to watch him curiously. "Is it delicious?"

"It can be." He stepped around her, refusing to be charmed by her tiny voice and perfect little proper accent. He fetched a towel for drying along with a bar of soap and opened the door. "I'll be back to prepare supper."

He shut the door behind him, but it didn't remain closed for long.

"Where are you going?" Phoebe chirped, chasing him down the path.

"To the loch shore, wee one. I willna be far."

She scampered around to block his path. "I'll go with you, so you won't be alone."

A little copy of Cecelia, this one, sweet-natured and forever championing the lonely. Except she didn't look like her at all. She was little for her age with eyes the color of a murky sea. He'd thought her hair a light brown the color of wet sand, but little gold strands glistened from unruly ringlets. Her features were strong and square for a lass, but striking. She might be handsome when she grew, and if not, she'd at least be imposing.

"Ye canna go with me," he answered. "I need to bathe."

Her little nose wrinkled in a feminine gesture of displeasure identical to the one his mother used to wear. "Is the bath behind the lock?"

He paused. "What?"

"Locks are not for bathing, they're for—for locking, obviously."

A chuff of mirth escaped him, and he almost gave in to the urge to tousle her fair little ringlets. "Not a lock, Phoebe, a loch."

She shifted her eyes, blinking rapidly in confusion.

"What ye Brits call a lake, we Scots call a loch," he clarified.

Her eyes widened. "Why?"

"Because that is our language."

She made a sound of wonderment. "You have your own language?"

"Aye."

"Will you teach it to me?"

"Nay."

"Why?" She pouted.

"Because I'm stained with blood and offal and I need to go bathe."

"That's all right, you can teach me along the way, and

I'll play in the shallow pool by the rocks whilst you bathe in the deep end."

He began to shake his head. "I doona think—"

"What do you call that rock?" She pointed to what was once a stepping-stone.

"*Clach*," he answered absently. "But ye should stay here—"

"And this?" She pulled the dilapidated fence open, sweeping her hand most gallantly for him to pass.

"*Tha thu nad pian ann an asail*," he muttered.

Her forehead wrinkled. "All that for a gate?"

"Nay, it means . . ." *You are a pain in my ass*, he didn't say. "It means . . . go tell Jean-Yves ye're going to the loch."

She sprinted inside with an exuberance Ramsay, even as a vital man, couldn't remember ever possessing.

He chuckled, waiting on the outside of the hip-high gate.

Ramsay often lost patience quickly with children, but oddly enough he found Phoebe's precocious curiosity easier to bear. He could identify with her relentless need to understand things. To bend the world to her will. And her constant well-meaning nature was endlessly lovely.

When she emerged only three breaths later, she'd already shucked her pinafore and nabbed a towel of her own.

"I decided you can teach me how to swim, too," she panted, grabbing his hand and tugging him toward the forest. "Do let's hurry. How do you say tree in Scottish? Scots?"

"Gaelic," he corrected, sauntering after her. "And it's *craobh*. Also, English lasses canna swim in Scottish lochs, you'll freeze yer wee noggin off."

She pitted her entire strength against his arm, urging

him to hurry. If he let her go, she'd fall flat on her little nose. "If you can do it, I can," she declared.

"Is that so, now?"

"I'm not afraid of the cold." She stopped tugging and changed tactics, turning to face him. "Please, Lord Ramsay. *Please?*" Her eyes must have taken up half of her face as she laced her fingers and pleaded as though she were at church praying for relief. "When will I ever again be allowed to swim in the wilds of Scotland?"

"With Cecelia as yer guardian, I imagine ye'll have the chance to do all sorts of things," he said, wondering if she realized how lucky she was.

A little anxiety peeked through her pluck. "I'll have to go back to London when this is over. And Cecelia said I must be educated, that she'll tutor me, or send me to school if I like."

He nodded approvingly as he struck out again through the meadow at a much more meandering pace. Earth crunched beneath their boots, and a summer breeze ruffled their hair with the sweet smell of blossoms and loamy earth. The moment was a gentle one, a simple one, and Ramsay found himself enjoying the company of the tiny chatterbox. "Ye should go to school," he urged. "Ye must learn to be a lady, I suppose."

She screwed up her face, another uncannily familiar expression. "I think I'd rather be a doctor than a lady."

"A doctor, ye say? Have ye been talking to Alexandra?" His sister-in-law was an archeologist first and a duchess second, at least in her own estimation.

"A lady doctor," she announced. "One who takes care of women who are having babies."

"Ye mean a midwife?"

"No," she stated vehemently. "My mother, she died

giving birth to me. A midwife didn't know what to do, but a doctor might have done."

"I see," he murmured, incalculably glad for the umpteenth time to have been born a man.

Phoebe prattled ceaselessly as she walked, and Ramsay did his best to follow along. She spoke of Frances Bacon and Fanny de Beaufort. Who, apparently, didn't accompany them on their outing as they preferred not to get wet.

The loch was little more than a grotto dammed by a rock wall that might have been a bridge in centuries past, collapsed by any number of marauding armies or clannish skirmishes or nothing more violent than the forages of time.

Ramsay settled Phoebe on the other edge of the wall where the river slowed to a trickle allowed by a break in the dam. He threatened to truss and blindfold her if she peeked over the wall as he bathed, only half joking.

He washed in record time, chuckling quietly as he listened to the girl sing with astonishing lack of intonation as she played. Donning his trousers, he climbed the rocks and peeked over to find her wrapping a ribbon around a bouquet of wildflowers.

"Are those for Miss Teague?" he asked, teetering over the dam and making his way down the rocks toward her.

"Yes." She presented the bouquet to him with pride. "I think *you* should give them to her."

He quirked an eyebrow at her. "Do ye, now?"

She nodded ardently. "Aren't dashing men supposed to give ladies flowers?"

Rubbing his chin, he eyed the bouquet with consternation. "Aye, but I'm not dashing."

She brought the flowers back to her chest, studying him

intently, measuring his amount of dashingness. "Well . . . not as dashing as some of the men who would visit Miss Henrietta and Genny," she admitted with no small amount of sincerity. "But I think Miss Cecelia likes you in spite of that. Besides, you're big and brave and have better hair then most men your age."

"A distinguished commendation, indeed," he said wryly.

"And you saved her just like d'Artagnan," she said dreamily. "If she's any sort of proper damsel, she's supposed to love you after that, so . . ." She reoffered the bunch of flowers to him.

Ramsay hesitated to take them, because Cecelia Teague was no sort of proper damsel.

Phoebe pressed them upward, standing on her tiptoes. "I brought a purple ribbon, as that's Cecelia's favorite color."

"I'd noticed she wears violet often." He gingerly took the flowers, hoping they'd not disintegrate in his big, unwieldy hands.

"Don't you think she's rather fetching in violet?" The girl's countenance glowed with shy mischief. "In most colors, really. And I know some women look plain with spectacles, but not Cecelia. She's lovely all the time."

"She is lovely all the time," he agreed before adopting a stern look. "Ye're playing matchmaker, are ye?"

Phoebe shrugged, climbing up the bank to skirt the dam. "Do you think you'll marry her?" she queried, disastrously portending nonchalance.

"Would ye mind?" he asked.

She plopped down on the line of grass that skirted the black pebbled sand of the loch and began to unlace her boots. "Will you let me go to university if she marries you?"

Ramsay couldn't contain a smile. "If ye want to be a doctor, I'll not stop ye."

She paused for a moment, chewing on a troubling thought. "Do you think . . . you'll kiss her?"

"I already did once," he confided with a waggle of his brows.

She giggled and relieved her little foot of her second boot.

"But . . ." Her face was serious as she stood, brushing the sand from her skirts. "You won't make babies, will you?"

Ramsay's heart stopped, and he wanted to squirm out of his skin. "What do ye ken about the making of babies?" he hedged. She was raised in a gambling hell, after all, and he wouldn't think of even approaching such a grown-up subject with a girl of seven.

She blushed and he wanted to gag. "I know that a man and a woman make babies when they're sleeping."

"Sleeping?" he cringed, wishing he'd left her at home.

She nodded sagely. "That's what Henrietta said. A man and woman must sleep together to make babies."

"Sleeping," he echoed carefully. "That's all Henrietta told ye? Nothing else?" He was afraid to be relieved.

She pressed a hand to her little belly. "I shouldn't like to wake up with a baby," she decided, and then pierced his heart with the fear in her eyes. "Moreover, I shouldn't want one to take Cecelia like I did my mother. Perhaps you shouldn't sleep with her until after I'm a doctor."

A fond tenderness wriggled in between Ramsay's ribs at the little girl's distress.

He could neither lie to her nor tell her the truth.

What he would do with Cecelia had little to do with sleeping.

Instead, he held out his hand. "Let's see if I can get her to marry me first, and then we'll chat more about babies, aye?"

Tiny fingers wrapped around his palm and simultaneously he felt them clutch at his heart, as well. "All right." They walked to the water's edge and watched it sparkle in the late-afternoon sun for a moment. Tentatively, she touched her toe to the water and then pulled her foot back as though a viper had bit her. "Oh no!" she squealed dancing from foot to foot. "It's too cold, I don't think I can."

Ramsay smiled a smile that reached all the way down to his chest. "Ye canna just dip in yer toe, ye have to plunge in with everything ye have."

She looked up at him, her eyes sparkling with trust as she prepared herself for the deed.

Once Cecelia deciphered the code and provided him with evidence, he'd have to decide what to do.

To set them both free.

Or to jump in with everything he had.

CHAPTER SIXTEEN

A breakthrough dumped Cecelia out of her spell, and she leapt from her desk chair with a victorious sound of glee.

Out the window, forest shadows crept toward the house threatening evening, and she idly wondered why no candle had magically appeared on desk as it was wont to do.

Noise filtered through the door, a great deal of noise, in fact. Masculine voices, rich and animated. Phoebe's contralto breaking through the rumble like sunshine through thunderclouds.

Drawn by the jolly din, Cecelia burst out of the bedroom, impatient to share her discovery.

"Excellent news!" she announced to the room at large.

"Did you solve your riddle book?" Phoebe's head turned owlishly over her shoulder from where she stood by the roaring fire holding a large towel open like a highwayman's cloak to catch its warmth. Her hair was plastered to her head and hung in wet gathers down her back.

Cecelia's mouth twisted wryly. "Well, I haven't solved it, no—"

"Did ye at least identify the code?" Ramsay queried from where hunched at the table, rubbing at his thick glossy hair with another towel.

"Not precisely," Cecelia stalled, blinking back and forth from the handsome Scot to her ward. Why were they soaked through? Had it rained today? Surely, she'd have noticed.

Her eyes lingered upon Ramsay for inordinately longer than they ought. His cream shirt, only half dry, clung to the generous swells of his chest and shoulders, his nipples beaded against the chill of damp clothing. He appeared alert but relaxed, his skin rosy from the sun and his eyes gleaming in a way she'd never seen them before. A pleasant, loamy scent drifted about the room, like sun-warmed rocks and wildflowers, and Cecelia had to blink a few times, wondering if she'd fallen asleep at the desk and walked out into a dream.

When she'd last encountered Ramsay, he'd refused to look at her and spoken in monosyllabic grunts. He'd left as if he couldn't escape her presence fast enough.

And now his gaze swallowed her whole as he intently scanned her from head to toe in a manner she considered most unsuitable with a child present. He caressed the curves of her with his eyes, as if she stood before him naked, rather than in a rich summer gown.

Her brain threatened to melt out of her ear into a puddle of simpering, preening female absurdity.

What had been his question?

Frazzled, Cecelia looked to Jean-Yves for help, and he set down the knife on the counter where he arranged sandwiches on a plate. The old man took pity on her, though he didn't spare her from his look of droll disappointment. "If you did not decipher the codex, nor identify the code, what possible news could be excellent, *mon bijou*?"

Determined not to allow herself to be distracted by the previously petulant Lowlander, she brandished the book like an American preacher on the Sabbath.

"I've been looking at this all wrong." She hurried to the table and flipped open the book to where the bevy of numbers made an odd-looking list. "I'd assumed Henrietta had used a Pollux code, which is usually dots and dashes, but I thought she might have replaced them with numbers. It was the only explanation for these repetitions." She pointed to the numbers she referenced. "But no matter what I tried, the code remained indecipherable. So then I simplified it to a Caesarean code, which helped not at all, but somehow also seemed to make sense. Which could mean only one thing . . ."

She looked up expectantly, and met three identical blank looks.

Jean-Yves now stood over her, his arm slung to his body in an odd parody of a maître d' as he held his tray aloft, waiting impatiently for her to finish.

"Don't you see?" she prompted excitedly. "It's bacon."

"Bacon?" Ramsay looked at her as if he feared she'd lost her mind.

"Like Frances Bacon!" Phoebe held up her doll triumphantly, doing her level best to make some sort of connection.

Cecelia smiled fondly at the girl. "Just like," she praised. "Baconian ciphers are tedious but ingenious because the meaning isn't in the numbers or letters themselves, but how they are assembled, most often in clusters of five representing one letter."

Jean-Yves motioned for her to pick up the book, which

she did, and he replaced it on the table with his plate of sandwiches. "I suddenly regret not putting bacon on these," he muttered.

"Me too," Phoebe emphatically agreed. "Bacon is delicious."

"So—" Ramsay reached for the book, and Cecelia handed it over the platter. He opened it, his brows bunching together as he scanned the formulae as if he might now understand. "If ye employ this Baconian cipher, ye'll decode the message?"

"I've done it already." She beamed.

"Aye?" Ramsay straightened and then turned his head sideways as if he could see the code more clearly. "But ye said ye didna solve the riddle," he reminded her slowly.

"My problem was that I assumed Henrietta only used one code. However, upon employing the Baconian cipher, I uncovered a second set of coded information, but this one is much shorter. So all I have to do is figure out this code." She tapped her finger to her chin. "That is, unless there is a third layer, but that isn't very likely."

"Have you gotten to the good news part yet?" Jean-Yves asked impatiently, taking the seat next to her. "I'd like to eat my supper."

"I'm that much closer, likely halfway. Tomorrow I get to work on turning numbers into letters!" She shook her fists in front of her in a gesture of celebratory victory as the room at large blinked at her for another moment before collectively deflating.

"Halfway?" Ramsay repeated the word as if he'd never heard it before, frowning his obvious discontent. "What do ye have to do in order to finish?"

Jean-Yves held up a staying hand. "You'll regret that question, my lord. I suggest we eat before another lengthy cryptography lesson puts us early to sleep." He winked over at Cecelia, who falsified a smile.

She didn't mind the teasing, really she didn't. However, she suddenly wanted to slump back into the room and hide from them all. From *him*.

Was Ramsay's desire to be free of her so consuming that the thought of another three days in her presence caused him such obvious chagrin?

Reaching for a sandwich, she put one on Jean-Yves's plate, and called Phoebe over while dishing her meal in silence.

It would forever be impossible to get a room excited about maths. Such was her life. If she'd been in the room with another mathematician, he'd have realized that she'd concluded what might have taken most ingenious code breakers the better part of several days in only three.

She mentally congratulated herself and bit into a delectable ham and olive sandwich. "If this is supper, what's in the cauldron over the fire?" she asked.

"Water for yer bath."

A silken undertone in Ramsay's voice caused Cecelia to swallow prematurely, and a chunk of sandwich made a slow and painful descent of her chest.

She reached for a drink of Jean-Yves's ale to wash it down, ignoring the Frenchman's protestations.

When she glanced back up at Ramsay, a glimmer in his eye made her certain he was picturing her taking said bath. How she knew, she couldn't say, but the wicked gleam remained, brushing her in places she'd rather not consider in a crowded room.

Confused and increasingly distraught, she searched his features for answers. Did he want to be free of her because of temptation, or in spite of it? Why insinuate his displeasure with her one moment, and then scorch her clothing from her body with his gaze the next?

Phoebe approached the table, hiding something behind her back.

"I see you and Lord Ramsay already had your baths," Cecelia noted, smiling across at the dear girl.

"Lord Ramsay had to wash the blood of his deer from him in the loch," Phoebe explained, affixing a rapturous look up as she took her place beside him. "Then he taught me how to swim."

"Did he, indeed?" Cecelia also cast a level gaze toward the Scot in question. "I imagine that's why your lips are blue."

"I'm almost warm." Phoebe rushed to cut off any objection by complimenting her. "And I think it's wonderful that you found the bacon code. You're ever so clever, Cecelia."

"Thank you, darling." She was glad someone thought so. "Aren't you hungry after swimming?"

"Don't you think she's clever, Lord Ramsay?" Phoebe gave him a meaningful look, nudging him with her elbow.

Ramsay paused with a sandwich halfway to his mouth before looking down at the girl rather than across at her. "Aye, she's both clever and wise, little one. Now eat yer supper."

"And beautiful," Phoebe added. "You can't forget beautiful, because you mentioned how lovely she was by the loch."

Jean-Yves's ill-muffled chortle drowned out Cecelia's drastic intake of breath.

Phoebe slid a bouquet of heather with little sprigs of gypsophila from behind her back as two cheeky dimples appeared next to her mouth.

"Are those for me?" Cecelia asked, flushing with maternal pleasure.

Phoebe didn't answer. Instead, she nudged the Highlander in his biceps, her finger giving before his muscle did. "Here. Lord Ramsay, here."

"What's going on?" Jean-Yves asked. "You picked flowers for Lord Ramsay, *petite*?"

"No," Phoebe said from the side of her mouth toward Jean-Yves. "He's supposed to give it to *her*." She thrust the bouquet beneath Ramsay's nose, forcing him to drop his sandwich. "Go on," she urged. "Don't be shy."

Ramsay curled every finger slowly around the base of the bouquet as if it might be the little girl's neck. "Impeccable timing, lass," he muttered.

Phoebe beamed, oblivious—or perhaps immune—to the sarcasm oozing from Ramsay's comment. He thrust the flowers at her over the table, and Cecelia had to wipe her fingers on a linen before she reached for them.

"No," Phoebe crowed. "Not like that. You must stand and present it to her properly."

"Gallantly, I daresay," Jean-Yves chimed in, earning him a soft elbow jab from Cecelia.

"Gallant, exactly," Phoebe agreed with an emphatic nod as she sat and gathered her sandwich into both hands. "A moment like this demands gallantry. A hero cannot simply hand his lady a flower."

"I'm no hero," Ramsay said at the same moment Cecelia thought it prudent to point out, "I'm not his lady."

Phoebe ignored all of this. "There must be a gesture of some sort, wouldn't you agree?"

"A grand gesture," Jean-Yves agreed.

Cecelia had a few choice gestures for her butler, but she couldn't bring herself to make them in front of a child.

She watched half in hope and half in agony as Ramsay set his jaw and stood.

Following his lead, she faced him, her heart pounding out of her chest. She very studiously avoided looking in the direction of the rocking chair, keeping her eyes focused on the flowers.

Ramsay reached in and plucked the largest, most vibrant blossom from the bouquet and extended it toward her. He stepped closer in order to tuck the flower into her hair.

Rough-skinned fingers skimmed the shell of her ear, causing shivers of delight to erupt over her entire body.

Along with pulses of need in a few secret places.

Overwhelmed, Cecelia closed her eyes and breathed him in. His scent was a masculine undercurrent to the fragrant flowers, soap and earth and water and sky. A scent as delicious to her as a room full of books and leather furniture. Or the most sumptuous truffles.

"Scottish heather," he murmured. "For an English rose."

His voice vibrated through her, a now-familiar sensation. It lifted the fine hairs on her body and brought forward an awareness she found both exhilarating and alarming.

When she opened her eyes, he had thrust the bouquet to her, watching her with veiled expectation.

"Thank you," she breathed.

He nodded, then moved away from the table.

"Where are you going?" Phoebe asked.

"To prepare the bath," Ramsay said. "Jean-Yves and I will take the chairs onto the porch and share a port whilst ye ladies bathe."

"Leave some port for me, if you please," Cecelia called, claiming her seat at the dinner table.

"Aren't you going to eat?" Phoebe pressed of Ramsay,

holding up her own sandwich interrupted by one perfect crescent indentation of her teeth.

Ramsay may have hesitated, but then he continued toward the fire to retrieve the full cauldron of boiling water. "I'll eat outside."

Cecelia did her best not to stare as Ramsay hauled, heated, and prepared her bath with volumes of water no mortal man should have been able to carry at one time.

Jean-Yves caught her distraction at once and leaned over. "You've been chewing the same bite for ten minutes," he whispered.

Cecelia swallowed, her denials all dying on her lips as she met the older man's knowing gaze and blushed at the smile that told her he was vastly entertained.

Finally gathering the thoughts Ramsay had scattered like marbles, she said, "I'd regard anyone in the exact same manner were he to perform such an impossible feat."

Jean-Yves grunted, but in French, the sound landing somewhere between disgust and amusement. "You've never in your life looked at anyone the way you look at him."

To save herself from having to reply, she bit into her sandwich with a little too much gusto and avoided further conversation with Jean-Yves until he shuffled out with Ramsay to leave her to her bath.

She'd never been able to lie to him. And she was increasingly less able to lie to herself.

She didn't just look at Ramsay, she *saw* him. She noticed him with her entire being. Her senses were so attuned to his presence, she wondered if he hadn't some strange electrical current other creatures just simply didn't possess. Some magnetism charged only to her, drawing her forward until she was unable to resist pressing against him.

Cecelia didn't linger in the bath for long, as she couldn't stand the idea of Jean-Yves's discomfort out of doors. He'd been quite mobile today, but broken ribs did tend to wear on one. She shivered into her nightgown and wrapper and traded favors of brushing and braiding hair with Phoebe while Ramsay hauled away the bathwater.

She resolutely faced the fire, unwilling to be caught watching him a second time.

Jean-Yves settled into the couch next to her as she sat plaiting Phoebe's hair, who in turn braided that of Frances Bacon and Fanny de Beaufort.

"Are you going to arrange my hair next, *bonbon*?" Jean-Yves teased Phoebe, rubbing at the fine gray fluff he usually kept beneath a hat.

Phoebe giggled. "Will you tuck me in tonight, Jean-Yves?"

The man tapped her on the tip of her button nose fondly. "If you think I'm climbing that ladder to the loft, you're about to be sorely disappointed, *mon petite coeur*."

"You can read to me here," she offered. "Join us, Lord Ramsay?"

The Scotsman had finished hauling away the bath and had occupied himself by stomping about in the kitchen, setting it to rights. At her question, he hesitated, his gaze colliding with Cecelia's.

He said nothing as three sets of eyes speared him, each with different sorts of expectations.

What was he thinking, Cecelia wondered, to cause his harsh, rawboned features to appear so cautious? Tentative, even. He blinked at those hunkered on his spare furniture as one might regard an unfinished puzzle if one held the wrong piece. She might have identified the look in his eyes as longing, were it less hollow and bleak. Or perhaps she read his expression completely wrong. Maybe his diffidence had nothing to do with longing, but aversion instead.

It was impossible to tell.

"You can sit next to Cecelia," Phoebe offered magnanimously. "And we'll all watch Jean-Yves make the most hilarious faces."

At the mention of her name, all expression was carefully schooled from Ramsay's face. "I've things to see to outside," he said, taking a lantern and striding out of the room.

Cecelia pretended to laugh when Phoebe did at Jean-Yves's antics, and couldn't remember at all what they'd read. She kissed the girl's forehead and tucked her into bed before seeing to Jean-Yves.

"You don't have to tuck me in," he groused. "I'm no child."

"I don't mind."

"Go to him, Cecelia," Jean-Yves said gravely.

"What?" she gasped.

"He is of two minds about you, and it is tearing him apart." The wizened Frenchman grabbed her hand and stayed her with a gentle tug. "Snatch him up or shoot him down, *mon bijou*, but either way put the poor man out of his misery, *oui*?"

"*His* misery?" Cecelia huffed, wondering just how much Jean-Yves had guessed about what had transpired between her and Ramsay. "I've tried to talk to him. He won't have any of it. He is so infuriatingly confusing, I want to rip my hair out, or his."

"I think that is the most wrathful I've seen you in our lives." Jean-Yves's caterpillar brows climbed up his forehead as he sank deeper into his patchwork quilts.

Cecelia fluffed the man's pillow and checked his sling. "He makes me doubt who I am and what I want," she admitted. "I think he would love me if I were other than who I am."

"Why do you say this?"

"I'm a chubby bespectacled spinster bastard who inherited an infamous gaming hell in which both my aunt and my grandmother have at one time or another worked as a prostitute. A connection with me would shame a man like Ramsay," she lamented.

"And he is the unwanted elder son of a Scottish drunk who lost his wife to a duke and drowned to death in his own sick." Jean-Yves shrugged and then gasped with pain as his shoulder protested. "Also," he continued with a bit more strain, "it's widely acknowledged his mother was nothing more than an expensive whore."

"Jean-Yves!" Cecelia reproached without any true heat.

"I'm only saying, *mon bijou*, that this man, Ramsay, brought you here not only to keep you protected, but to show you his own shame," Jean-Yves said with a sage nod. "He might not even know that he's done it."

"You truly think so?" Cecelia pondered the implications of this.

"There are many safe places in this world he could have taken us." He grimaced as he readjusted his position as he muttered, "And so many more comfortable."

"I promise we can go home soon," Cecelia said. "I do believe I'll finish in a few days."

"Finish your business with the Lord Chief Justice before you decipher that codex," the old man advised. "Because you know you have enemies, but you'll need to know where this man fits in your life before we leave here."

Cecelia chewed on the inside of her cheek, appreciating the advice. "Should he—should we—would you be upset if I loved him? If he were to share his life with us?"

Jean-Yves's expression softened, deepening the grooves around his features and aging him starkly. "I share my life with you, Cecelia, what's left of it. Which means I share my life with the man you choose."

"But what do you think of Ramsay? What if I were your daughter? What would you tell her to do?"

A faint glimmer of emotion entered his eyes as he reached up with his good hand to touch her face. "You know influenza took my girl when she was small. I've been blessed with more years with you than with her. I consider you as much my daughter as my employer and my friend. You have to know that."

"Don't make me cry," she begged. "I've been nothing but a waterfall for days."

"This Ramsay. He is a man of means and position, and that is desirable. Beyond that, he is a man who would protect you with his life, and any father would want that for you." He hesitated. "Just . . . do not choose anyone who makes you consider yourself anything other than the treasure you are."

Welling with tenderness, Cecelia smoothed the man's brow as though he were a child. "I love you. I wish I could have called you Papa."

He shooed her hand away, turning a bright color of pink beneath his olive-tinged skin. "*Je t'aime*," he muttered. "Now let an old man sleep."

Cecelia crept out the door. She crossed the little cottage on silent slippered feet and snatched the candle from the tabletop. The bouquet caught her eye, and she picked up the flower he'd tucked behind her ear and put it back into her hair. She liked heather, she decided; it smelled of Scotland.

She turned a tankard into a vase for the wildflowers and drifted out the door in search of a gruff Scot.

Cecelia found him not in the shack but next to it, fully clothed and stretched out over his blankets beneath the stars. His hands locked behind his head, he glared up at the sky like it had done him an injustice.

Perhaps he cursed whichever star he'd been born beneath. The one that fated his life to be a battle against a fickle current, forever swimming upstream.

In the moonlight, his harsh features were smoothed and muted to a savage but golden beauty. He was brutality in repose. Distant. Remote.

A lion at rest.

The only acknowledgment of her presence was the tilt of his stern chin as he noted her approach.

He said nothing, his gaze remaining affixed to the sky.

She read a tension building in his body, however. Though he'd retreated from her in every way, she had no doubt he felt the same pull as she did. The same magnetic awareness. It electrified the night between them until she was certain it might be powerful enough to cause them both to glow like the streetlights on the Strand.

If only she could find him, wherever he went. Indeed, if eyes were the window to the soul, then his were walls of ice, opaque and unapproachable.

Blowing out her candle, Cecelia relied solely on the waxing moonlight as she sat next to his long, recumbent body, her wrapper creating a lake of crimson silk around her.

Tension began to creep into her own bones as the silence stretched as taut as a fiddle string between them.

Could he not have mercy on her? Receive her or reprimand her? Could he not make anything between them easy?

No, of course he couldn't. He told her he was a man without mercy, and she should have listened.

She puffed out a breath and looked to the sky, wondering if they found the same constellations. If they perceived the darkness in a similar fashion.

The firmament wasn't a pure black, not this soon after the summer solstice and with such a bright moon. A thin midnight-blue mist cast a fairylike glow upon the forest, and if Cecelia were a more fanciful woman, she could truly believe she'd been transported to some island of the Fae, out of time and space. Enchanted and mesmerized by the beauty of her surroundings, and yet tormented by a disdainful silence.

"Look!" she gasped, pointing just past Gemini and Orion. "A falling star. It's supposed to be good luck."

He twitched, but made no move toward or away from her. "The stars doona fall for men," he muttered.

Cecelia chewed the inside of her cheek, wondering what to say next. Perhaps she shouldn't have come out here . . . Maybe Jean-Yves didn't know as much about Ramsay as he thought he did.

She felt tentative—no, *nervous*—and she had to swallow around a dry tongue as she fought for conversation. "Did you find what you were hunting for in the woods earlier today?"

"Aye," he answered.

She waited for him to expound.

He didn't.

"You promised you wouldn't hate me," she whispered, drawing her knees in close.

At this, he finally sat up. "What?"

"When I—when we—" She couldn't bring herself to say it as the memory of their shared pleasure plagued her into a painful blush. "I asked you if you would hate me after, and you promised you wouldn't. And yet . . . here we are."

His face softened. "Cecelia—"

"I didn't ask for this, you know," she burst out, turning on her hip to face him. A foreign fury built within her, welling past frustration and beyond aggravation into a new form of anger she didn't understand. She flushed hot and cold, her limbs trembled with it, and she felt as though she needed to release it into the night. To do something uncharacteristically barbaric like throw or hit something.

"I'm trying so hard to keep up," she lamented with helpless tugs at her hair. "To keep everyone happy. And alive. To understand this new world that's been dumped into my lap and to make sense of enemies I never made and did nothing to deserve. Like you, for example!"

He reached out for her carefully, as one might attempt to soothe a madwoman.

She slapped his hand away. Unable to sit still any longer, she pushed to her feet, obliging him to do the same. "Half of me doesn't even want to decipher that damnable codex, and do you know why?"

He appeared astonished. Lost. "I canna—"

"Because I'm terrified to find out what kind of woman Henrietta might have been. What kind of woman I might have to become to survive this world." She could stand it no longer. She *had* made a mistake coming out here. He distracted her. Spun her about. Perhaps she should have gone to Redmayne instead to keep her safe, to someone who didn't hold of piece of her heart in his big, brutal hand.

"Did you know I'm afraid all the time?" she asked. "Not just for me, but for Phoebe. For everyone I care about. For *you*." She was nigh to panting now, pacing in front of him like a banshee, her red train trailing over the soft Scottish grasses.

"I don't want to keep secrets anymore. I don't want to know anything else about anyone's sins. And do you know what's the most ridiculous thing about it all, Lord high-and-mighty Chief Justice? I fear that you'll hate me even more than you do now, once I find something in that codex to condemn those you venerate. I fear that worse than I fear the information that might cost me my life. Because I *like* you, Cassius Gerard Ramsay, Lord even knows why. You're critical, grumpy, terrifying, and all sorts of wrong for me, but damned if I don't think you're the most beautiful human to walk the face of this earth—"

Ramsay surged forward and shackled his hands around her arms. *Her* arms, which were thick and soft and not even a bit dainty. And yet he might be the only man alive who could span their circumference.

And damned if she didn't love that, too.

"Doona ye ken ye're the only thing that matters to me?" he snarled, his eyes glinting with wrath that might have driven her to flee if her knees hadn't melted on the spot.

Cecelia blinked up at him, her jaw unhinging.

She hadn't kenned that. She hadn't kenned that in the least. He'd never given her the foggiest notion.

"I could never hate ye, Cecelia, but ye're changing every truth I've ever believed in. Ye're making me wonder if I can actually trust a woman for the first time in my life." He held her fast, his fingers tightening and yielding on her arms, as if he couldn't decide whether to pull her close or set her away from him. "Before I met ye in

Redmayne's parlor I had no room for a wife or a child, but damned if it's not what *I* want, now."

Cecelia's heart stopped. Had he said . . . wife?

"Ye're soft where I am hard," Ramsay continued with a vehemence that belonged to the same fury simmering in her own blood. "Ye're kind when I am cruel. Ye remind me that there's mercy along with justice and that the world is not just black and white but shades of gray.

"Elphinstone Croft has been my personal hell for years. But *ye*." He shook her a little, then turned her away from him to face the dilapidated cottage glowing white and in the moonlight. "I could stay here with ye, with Phoebe, with that fucking Frenchman who doesna like me, and I'd be content. Here. The one place I thought I'd forever detest. For the first time in my entire hopeless life I'm . . . I'm at peace, Cecelia. I am content. I doona care about anything that awaits us back in London. And the fault is yers."

He didn't at all seem like a man at peace. He was a wall of muscle and wrath behind her. His body hard and unyielding and endlessly warm. "But—" she said, puzzling. "But you've been so . . . distant. So callous. How can I believe—?"

"Doona ye think I'm plagued by the same fear?" he thundered. "Someone out there wants to take *this* from me. To take ye from me. It is more important than ever that I not be distracted by temptation, do ye ken? I canna allow myself a moment's peace, because though no one yet knows about this place, someone might find out. And there's a chance they'll come for us. I *have* to be on my guard. I have to keep *ye* alive."

He turned her back around to face him, and she could

feel the restraint quelling his strength. Stretching his muscles to the breaking point.

That fact sparked an answering heat within her.

Yes, this was what she yearned to hear, what she wanted to know. A reason for his cruelty.

Kindness.

At least, the fear of it.

Ramsay devoured her with his gaze, but he finally mustered the strength to set her firmly away. "So help me, woman, it matters not to me what is in that fucking book. Not anymore. Not when it comes to ye. All I want to do is throw ye over my shoulder, take ye to the village, and make ye my wife. I'd not let ye leave my bedchamber for an entire week until I've worshiped every brilliant beautiful inch of ye." This was hissed out between teeth that refused to separate. "But because of where we are and who we're with, I've vowed not to touch ye again, and I swear to Christ it's been the hardest thing I've ever had to do. So pardon me if I've been a bit distant, but it's taken every drop of willpower I possessed not to finish what we started on that fucking chair. And once I begin, the world might burn to the ground before I'm through and I'd not even notice."

He threw his hands up and whirled away, stalking over to his pallet, obviously intent upon putting distance between them.

"So if ye'd hie yerself inside and stop tormenting me, I'd consider it a kindness."

Suddenly Cecelia couldn't stop smiling. In fact, the smile spread all the way through her, thrilling her to her very toes with happiness.

He wanted her. He'd wanted her all along. He thought she was beautiful *and* brilliant. *She*, pudgy, bespectacled

Cecelia Teague, tempted the Vicar of Vice to the brink of his iron will.

A heady knowledge, that.

Instead of going inside, she went to him. Pressing her hand against his back, she felt the column of muscle bracketing his spine tense and twitch beneath the thin fabric of his shirt.

Stimulated, encouraged, and intensely curious, she slid both hands to the front of him, encircling his torso. The fingers of one hand splayed on the corrugated mounds of his abs and the other on the place where his heart hurled itself against his ribs.

"Cecelia." Her name was half a groan and half a plea. "Please. I canna bear—"

"You could guard me here, you know, in the garden," she invited in a timid voice.

He placed his hands over hers, the rough fingers trembling as he peeled her away before turning to face her. His mouth opened as though to admonish her, but no words escaped.

His eyes were no longer shards of ice. They'd kindled into something else entirely. A flame hot enough to burn through her clothing and scorch the flesh beneath.

Cecelia allowed her wrapper to slip off her shoulder, and watched his control disappear with every increment of skin unveiled to the moonlight. "You could *thoroughly* guard every inch of me beneath the stars."

"Ye're killing me, woman," he said through increasingly harsh breaths.

She sidled closer, her face to the sky. "I'd rather be kissing you."

He stood still. His nose flaring, his every muscle locked as though he violently grappled with invisible shackles. "Ye should run, Cecelia." His voice became impossibly lower. More growl than groan.

More animal than human.

Her loins bloomed at the sound, a delicious thrill of excitement mingling with her arousal. "I'm not afraid of you."

"Ye would be if ye understood what I wanted to do to ye."

A bizarre instinct overtook her, much like that of conquered prey about to be devoured. She felt both powerful and passive. Like a lioness surrendering to her mate. She wanted him to unleash the beast growling through him and devour her. She yearned to be his prize, his temptation.

His indulgence.

Instead of reaching for him, she watched him through lids half closed as she lifted her hand to the collar of her wrapper, drawing her fingertips down to separate the folds in a move both bold and bashful. As she undid the garment, she unbound the man, and as soon as it pooled into a puddle of silk at her feet, she knew the last shreds of his control joined it.

Before she could breathe, his arms clamped like steel around her, his hands bunching in the thin lace of her nightgown. His hips and mouth crashed against her at precisely the same moment in an ardent, almost violent claiming.

His tongue burrowed past her lips in an erotic intrusion as he fused their mouths and their bodies. The ridge of his sex ground against her belly. The heat and girth and taste of it a scorching memory she yearned to reacquaint herself with.

His restless hands splayed on her back, creating a gentle

counterpoint to the ardent kiss as they slid down her spine, dipping into the dramatic curve of her waist and shaping over her hip. He stopped there, toying at the curve as though searching for something.

"Yer drawers," he whispered against her mouth.

"I don't wear them to bed," she admitted shyly.

He said a few things in a language she'd never before encountered and fisted her shift in his hand. "If ye keep surprising me like this, woman, tonight willna last long."

"I'm sorry," Cecelia said contritely, deciding she loved when he called her woman.

His woman.

"Doona ye dare apologize," he commanded before swooping to claim her lips once more. He distracted her with drugging kisses as he attacked the ribbon keeping the wispy sleeves of her garment around her shoulders. Once he'd untied it, the cotton and lace slid away from her curves to join her robe.

The chill of the night air caressed her everywhere, and she burrowed against him, suddenly shy and anxious. Though this man had already turned her most private places into a banquet, Cecelia had underestimated what being naked in front of him would feel like.

She thought of her breasts, a pendulous burden two times the size of Alexandra's. She thought of all the places she was round and soft and large, now unshaped by a corset.

What if Ramsay saw her true shape and was repulsed?

He made to step back and look at her, but Cecelia clung to him like a burr, pressing their mouths so firmly together their teeth met.

His fingers ventured where his eyes could not, gliding down her shoulders and stroking across her chest until he angled away enough to fit his palms to the weight of her breasts.

They shared a gasp that broke the kiss, and Cecelia stared in unblinking awe as he palmed her bosoms with the appreciative sound of a man finally given reprieve. "I've dreamed of these in the night," he confessed as his thumbs moved to caress the hard and sensitive points of her nipples.

"You did?" she squeaked. "You have?" A start of pleasure trilled from her breasts down her belly and landed in her sex.

"Och, aye," he groaned. "Mythical breasts, these."

He gave her a look so hot, so full of erotic promise, Cecelia swayed, clutching at him as her legs trembled and melted.

Then Ramsay did something no man had ever done before.

He bent to hook his hands beneath her knees, then swept her up in his arms.

Cecelia wasn't given warning, or time to protest, so she kept her hands locked about his neck and buried her face into his shoulder.

He knelt with her in his arms, only breaking the kiss to settle her onto the makeshift pallet of blankets.

A self-conscious wave threatened to douse her ardor, and she instinctively lifted her arms to cover her body, curling in upon herself. Strange explanations bombarded her tongue, apologies for the roundness of her stomach, the length and girth of her thighs, and the unsightly dimples at her knees. She couldn't seem to lend any of them voice, as they threatened to choke her.

To make matters worse, Ramsay didn't join her on the blankets. Instead, he sat back on his haunches and gazed down at her with those features carved from stone.

She reached for him, feeling suddenly needy and unsettled. "You don't have to look," she said. "Just come here."

"How can I not look?" he asked her as though she'd gone mad. His growl had deepened another impossible degree, to that of a Gregorian monk at prayer. "I didna know such perfection existed."

In that moment Cecelia didn't care if anything subsequent proved to be folly, she merely realized she was falling for this strong giant brute, with all the subtle grace of a landslide. Plunging artlessly into love with him even though every logical thought told her she should not.

Logic didn't belong in this mysterious Scottish forest. Only this. Only them.

"Christ," he panted. "Ye are a goddess, Cecelia. Ye should be wooed in a gilded bed, not on this pile of blankets."

She rose and locked her arms around the back of his neck, stopping his mouth with a desperate kiss. She opened her lips, this time not in submission or invitation, but for the purpose of her own exploration.

His blankets and furs on the ground were more than comfortable, but now that she was without her wrapper the evening summer air chilled her to her core.

She shivered and pulled him closer.

And then he was upon her, covering her with his body like a blanket of sensual need. He pressed her into the earth, kissing her with fervent urgency. His restless hands upon her. Touching her everywhere. Discovering her with rough and masculine delight.

Cecelia's legs parted of their own accord to make room for his bulk. His loins pressed against her sex, separated only by his trousers. The intimate pressure turned her hot all over and he ground against her with a wicked roll of his hips, all the while trading deep velvet licks into each other's mouths.

Her hands found the buttons of his shirt and released them one by one.

Ramsay ripped his mouth from hers and stared down at her with intent eyes, darker than she'd ever seen them. Dark as midnight and magic and the depths of the sea.

"God," he said with a halting breath, trembling as though the weight of his own body might prove too much. "If this be a dream . . . I swear to Christ . . ."

"This is no dream," she promised, tentatively reaching into his shirt to brush the mounds of his shoulders with hesitant hands. "Though I'm not excited for morning to come." Her fingers drifted lower, sweeping through fine gold hair to find the hard disks of his chest. Lord but he was solid. Heavy and hewn from some other clay than most men.

He crouched over her like a giant cat intending to spring at his next meal.

But she was already caught. Already imprisoned beneath him and ready to be devoured.

A fingertip traced at the waist of his trousers and he pulled away, capturing her hands in his own. "Let me taste ye first," he crooned. "Once ye release me, I willna be able to stop myself."

"You?" she teased, pushing sparkle into her eyes. "The paragon of willpower?"

"Not anymore," he grieved. "Not when it comes to ye."

His full mouth began a maddeningly slow journey down her body, stopping in the strangest places to brush hot kisses and sample her skin with his curious tongue. He nuzzled into the hollow between her jaw and her ear. Nipped at her clavicles. Lingered over the downy trail between her breasts.

He did stop there to cup the orbs once again, tracing

his tongue over the white skin to circle the pink ridge of an areola before opening his lips over the peak of her nipple. He stroked and laved in a hot spiral, until Cecelia arched her back off the ground with a hungry moan.

Her hips rose of their own accord, begging for his attentions.

Taking a moment to pay equal courtesies to her opposite breast, he charted her curves with impatient hands.

Her belly quivered as he stroked it, and she squeezed her eyes shut. For a man to whom she'd attributed so much coldness, he certainly could evoke trails of fire on her skin with his skillful fingers.

She'd heard tell of substances so cold they would burn. She wondered if Ramsay's passion was thus. Invoked from a place so bleak and lonely it sought her warmth, but would only leave her singed and wounded in the end.

When his fingers trailed through the soft hair at the apex of her thighs, all worries vanished into the vaporous mist, replaced by carnal instinct and indescribable need.

Cecelia whimpered when coarse male skin met her slick intimate flesh. Not because it was uncomfortable; quite the opposite. The tip of his finger cleaved through the petals of her sex, gliding through the abundant moisture he found there.

Her mouth fell open in astonishment as he synchronized the motions of his tongue on her pebbled nipple and his finger on the tinier pebble protected by folds of pliant flesh. He worked in wet circles around the swollen places, teasing them with tender little flicks before darting away. Then he would linger in lazy strokes, leaving trails of slick wetness.

Her hips lifted off the ground as a flood of liquid fire drenched her loins. Pressure built low in her belly and he groaned against her breast, succumbing to a tide of his own lust.

He dragged his mouth away from her nipple and lowered himself further down her body.

Cecelia instantly missed his heat. She reached for his shoulder to draw him back up, but her fingers made no indent in the bunched muscle there. "You don't have to—"

"Aye," he said, splaying his big hands on her thighs, pressing them open and down to expose her utterly. "I get to."

She shivered before a bloom of sweat beaded on her as a sensual heat turned her blood to molten honey.

He stopped to gaze at her for a moment, harsh features tightening with a look she would recognize anywhere.

Hunger.

His head lowered beneath his shoulders as he delved into her with one long voluptuous lick up the center. His inhale was deep and slow, as though he savored a fine vintage of wine.

Cecelia might have been embarrassed if he hadn't scandalized her further by teasing the snug little ring of flesh at her opening with his fingertip. The muscles there immediately seized, pulsing and clenching around emptiness.

Her fingers likewise clenched at his shoulders, his neck, and then laced in his hair with rhythmic, desperate little claws as he kissed her sex before chasing the little nub of her pleasure this way and that. She gasped in delight or disappointment depending on whether he caught it or not.

His hot breath against her moist folds devastated her beyond all ability to speak, to reason, to think beyond the next motion of his tongue.

And then he sank his finger inside of her.

Cecelia separated from herself. Perhaps she floated above their bodies in the mist watching someone else perform this incredible act.

She threw her head back for a moment as bliss threatened to overcome her, but she didn't give in to it. Not yet.

Who knew how long she'd get to have the forbidding, wintry-eyed Scotsman dining at the very core of her? As much at her mercy as she was at his.

Looking down her body, she watched him with that detached part of herself. Her hips bucked and twitched with pleasure. Her loins rushing with heat and demand. Tendrils teased at her as he gave her a few barely there licks.

Ramsay's eyes were closed. His eyelids fluttered with a singular delight. His tongue rolled and dipped, slipped and slid around her like a truffle.

Dear God, she realized, a stab of ultimate pleasure lancing through her, as she was able to hold it off no longer. He might be a man endlessly able to deny himself. But in this moment, *she* was his chocolate and champagne.

She was his indulgence, and she very much hoped he might develop a craving.

"Give over to it, Cecelia mine." The words landed warm against her core. "Doona fight this, there is more to be had. I'll pleasure ye until ye beg me to stop."

"Don't stop." The plea came out more plaintively than she'd liked. "Never stop."

He didn't.

He feasted as she writhed. He groaned when she sighed, the vibration against her sex bringing all the stars in the firmament that much closer.

One finger was replaced by two inside her as his tongue centered just below the little pearl and Cecelia detonated.

She came apart in sparks and shards and quiet screams. Shattered into euphoric spasms of pleasure that replaced her body with incandescent light and the heat of the cosmos.

Cecelia, mine.

Her heart beat the words. They pulsed through her, riding waves of pleasure augmented by hope, lifting, lifting, *lifting* her higher until she might have flown beyond their little glade had a large and rather weighty Scot not ruthlessly held her thighs to the earth.

When the immolation passed, she collapsed back onto the blankets, unaware that her shoulders had left them. She struggled to regain her breath, trembling and shuddering with the aftermath of ecstasy.

She waited for Ramsay to climb up her body and take his pleasure, but he didn't get higher than her belly.

Wiping his mouth, he rested his head just below her ribs, the scruff of his cheek abrading the tender skin there. His arms plunged beneath her and he found a perfect place to release his weight and lounge upon her as she suspected they each fought to regain their senses.

Cecelia stroked through hair gilded by moonlight with soothing fingers, unable to form words as of yet.

And truly, there was nothing to say.

His lashes skimmed her skin with languid blinks, though his heart pounded somewhere in the vicinity of her nether regions.

How could she have thought him cold? Or empty? When the silence between them was so full?

He was a man who didn't comprehend the complexities

of the human emotion with his mind, but his body did with interest. How had she not seen it before? He was a creature of instinct. Of primal, primordial blood that belonged to this feral land. And he'd locked that part of him away for so long, he no longer knew how to connect with it in his conscious mind.

Because it could control him.

Poor Ramsay. Cecelia gave a flushed and pleasured sigh, patting him on his shoulder before tracing the shell of his ear with fondness. He had so much to learn about connection, and communication, but wasn't this an oh-so-excellent place to start?

"Never lose yer soft places, woman," he commanded tersely.

"I shan't," she promised with a yawn, thinking it would be the easiest vow she'd ever made. "Ramsay?"

"Aye?"

"Don't you want to . . ." She swallowed, suddenly shy. "I mean, shouldn't we possibly . . ." She lifted her hips, unable to say it.

He rose to his elbow, his eyes two azure beams of fire that stripped her lungs of breath. Though when he shook his head, he befouled the moment. "I canna tonight," he bit out. "I will ravage ye, Cecelia. Ye've siphoned my control and reduced me to a rutting beast and it's best if I doona come anywhere near ye with my—"

"Oh for the love of my giddy aunt!" she laughed. "Stop treating me like I'm some sort of virginal damsel who will break beneath your attentions!"

He reared back even further, frowning down at her. "But . . . ye are—*were* a virgin. I took that from ye."

"I survived," she shrugged, the movement of her breasts snagging both their notice.

His because . . . well, breasts.

And hers because she realized she was dressing down a man while completely naked and spread beneath his torso.

"I hurt ye," he rasped, though it was *his* gaze that contained a wound. "Ye should have heard the sound ye made."

Cecelia shrugged again, this time distracting him in purpose. "Oh tosh, I've made more distressed sounds getting dressed in the morning."

He tilted his head to the side in that way he was wont to do when befuddled.

Cecelia took pity upon him. "My corset hurts me, my boots hurt me. Riding sidesaddle hurts me. Every time someone offers me a more judicious portion of food, it hurts me. I am a woman, Ramsay, I am used to pain. The loss of one's virginity only happens once and I'm certain it's worth the cost. I'm even more certain I'll bear it better than most. Now." She wriggled beneath him. "If you please."

His golden brow rose over eyes alight with myriad things, most chiefly a mystified sort of surprise warring with a boyish mischief. "If I please . . . what?"

"Oh, don't make me say it," she pleaded.

A dark chuckle overtook him as he lowered his great body to nuzzle into her hair. "Ye confound me, woman," he purred into her ear. "Tell me what ye want, and I'll give it to ye."

"I want you." Cecelia turned her head, sifting her fingers through his hair as she returned her breath against his ear. "And you can have me, Ramsay," she offered gently, reaching in between their bodies to stroke his hard length over his trousers. "In whatever way you want me. I can take it. I can take you. All of you."

Her words were like a spell, summoning forth something dark and demonic he'd kept chained in the deep place he hid from the world. He grew impossibly larger beneath her fingers, stretching to an intimidating size.

A sound reverberated from low in his chest, and all sense of control drained away in an almost tangible rush.

He captured her lips with his in a violent kiss as he grappled with the fastenings of his trousers.

Cecelia's hands landed on each side of his massive jaw, but it truly was too late for all that. She'd reap her just deserts, and something inside her told her it would be the most delicious experience yet.

Once the final barrier between them had been stripped away, he wrenched her beneath him, a creature of frenzy and lust, pushed her thighs wide, and angled his hips between them.

There was a moment of fright. A single, breathless knowledge that once he'd claimed her this night, neither of them be the same. His weight was both a comfort and a burden, and she did the only thing she could think of to release a sudden rush of anxiety.

She bit the muscle between his neck and his shoulder.

He snarled and drove forward, pressing inside.

She cried out and, heedless of her claim, her body bore down against his intrusion, but to no avail. He sank deep into the tight heat of her, nearly spearing her in two.

The stinging of tears in her eyes was more pervasive than the stinging pain in her core.

He stilled. Froze. Staring down at her with eyes both inhuman and alarmed.

"Christ," he hissed between a jaw locked completely shut. "Christ. Fuck. Christ." He was quaking. Sweating. And his eyes threatened to burn a hole into hers.

But he didn't move.

Cecelia closed her eyes and pulled him against her, breathing deeply, needing his strength flush against hers.

He scooped her close to his body, enfolding her in his warmth and strength. Crooning a lyrical language in harsh, throaty groans.

She splayed her fingers down the brackets of his spine, tracing the flexing muscles as her own finally accommodated his intrusion.

The moment her body accepted him fully, his hips moved. They rocked slowly for a few tender moments, before everything accelerated. His breath, his heart, the wet glide of his shaft inside of her.

Lord, it was lovely. An aching sort of delight coiled within her. Lighter and less intense than what she experienced beneath his tongue. There was something unparalleled about this act. The rhythm of it. The wild impatience. The fierce gleam of possession in his gaze as he took her again and again, pushing deeper each time.

She was undone. Unraveled. Completely thrown open and bared to the world.

Who'd have suspected that all this time, she'd been a lock and he was her key?

She shaped to him as though they were made for each other. Not just sex to sex, but their bodies as well. Her curves and swells gave way for his cords and planes as they fused to each other in a singular motion.

Cecelia kneaded his flexing back, glorying in his strength and bulk, in the sheer magnificence that was this man.

"Christ," he blasphemed in time to his intensifying thrusts. "Sweet. Sweet. Too sweet."

He swiped his thumb against his tongue before reaching down between them and thrumming at her little bead once. Twice.

On the third time, Cecelia lost herself to the night.

CHAPTER SEVENTEEN

Cecelia's mewls of pleasure ripped him apart.

Ramsay had always paid homage to religion, because he was supposed to and all that, but he'd never truly believed heaven existed. Not until he found it.

Between Cecelia Teague's thighs.

It was there he lost his soul, his heart, nay, every part of himself. He poured the very essence of life into her in long, paralyzing pulses. Throwing his head back, he realized if there were gods, they were the pagan, bacchanalian kind who would only be appeased by blood and sex.

Deep down, he longed to pay homage to both.

Locked in the most intense bliss he never could have conceived of, Ramsay began to fear the loss before it had even begun to fade.

And thereby couldn't wait to do it again.

Seven. Fucking. Years. He'd wait another seven for this. For her.

He'd wait a lifetime.

Once his bones unlocked and his limbs began to work

again, Ramsay still couldn't bring himself to let her go. He attended to her, cleaning them both with his discarded shirt before gathering her close and rolling to his back.

He draped her over him, thighs parted and her delicious weight settled across his chest and hips. She seemed apprehensive at first, but her legs trembled too greatly to protest for long, and so she splayed in a lazy heap of luscious woman as her hair spilled across his shoulder.

He stroked the spun-copper silk, brushing her locks gently with his fingers, massaging little points of tension on her scalp and her neck idly as they each listened to the other breathe.

Her breath disturbed some of the hair on his chest, tickling it pleasantly, and he scratched at it.

Cecelia took the opportunity to grasp his fingers and press a kiss to each one.

The little gesture nearly melted him into a puddle of tenderness.

"I felt guilty that you'd been exiled out here," she said between her ministrations to his knuckles. "But now I see the benefits of sleeping beneath the Scottish stars."

A languorous yawn overtook her, and she stretched over him like a sated cat who'd had her fill of cream.

"If ye insist upon moving like that, woman, ye'll not have time to recover before I'm inside ye again."

She gave a little whuff of exhausted laughter before lifting her head to peer down at him curiously. "I understand now why people pay such lofty prices if sex is like that."

Ramsay was so struck by her tousled beauty, he had trouble processing her words for a good half a minute. "It's rarely ever like that," he said with a pleasured sigh.

Her lashes fanned down over her cheeks as she traced

an invisible design on his shoulder with her fingertip. "So . . . you consider me a satisfactory lover, then?"

"Satisfactory?" He snorted, letting his head land on the ground with a thump. "If ye were any better, ye'd have killed me."

"You're having me on," she accused.

"Do ye not see what ye've done to me, woman?" He swatted at her backside, a motion that turned into a grope. "How can ye question my word?"

"Because I did little better than lie there and enjoy your skill, all told."

"Skilled, am I?" He flashed her a grin full of masculine arrogance.

It had the opposite effect than he'd imagined. Her own features froze, and then fell, as she stared at him in astonished silence.

"Did something trouble ye?" he asked with concern.

"I do believe that's the first time I've ever witnessed a smile on your face," she said in a hushed tone. "It's quite . . . brilliant." Her fingers reached out and traced his mouth before she settled her soft lips against his.

At this, Ramsay made a silent vow to smile more.

"Artifice has never come easy to me," he said, trying to ease his sober statement with a wry sort of half smile. "I think most people smile when they doona feel it. And I've mastered many skills and etiquette, but that is not one of them."

"I like that about you," she said brightly. "Then your smiles are genuine. Rare. Something to be treasured. Like diamonds."

"The things ye say," he murmured, wondering if the blush creeping up his skin was visible in the moonlight.

She nuzzled him, and the affectionate gesture touched him deeply.

"Can I ask you something?"

He chuckled. "Ye could ask me to skewer the moon with my bow and arrow at this moment and I'd give it my best effort."

Her eyes crinkled at him with pleasure. "Cassius isn't exactly a Scottish name, is it? It's unique enough I've often wondered why your parents might have given it to you."

His smile died a slow death on his face as some of the warmth leached from him. She'd poked at a wound she couldn't have known he had. He measured his words carefully, unwilling to break the perfection of the aftermath with meaningless trifles.

"I doona ken if they taught ye Latin at yer school."

"*Et non est, sed in ea didici mea*," she answered. They did not, but I learned it on my own.

Of course she did. God, she would never cease to impress him.

"Then"—he hesitated—"ye ken the history of the word?"

She looked up as though to retrieve a memory. "Well, it was the name of the man who killed Caesar. One of them, anyway."

"Not the name, lass. The word."

Her forehead wrinkled as it was wont to do while she puzzled something out. "Cassius could be a derivative of the word *cassus* but . . . that cannot be right."

Her eyes brimmed with confusion, then concern.

Ramsay turned his head away, unwilling to see the pity that would follow.

"Surely your mother didn't name you . . ." She stalled, no doubt searching for a synonym.

"*Empty*. Or *nothing*. Whichever ye prefer." He finished the sentence she could not. "My mother was also a clever woman, and she had ways of being hateful that were just such as this. Almost deniable, but certainly on purpose."

Cecelia scooted up his body, which responded despite the ache in his soul. She laid her cheek against his and held him. "I just can't imagine a mother doing that to an infant. You'd done nothing wrong."

Ramsay let out a long sigh, knowing he'd puzzled over it his own self more than a few times. "Emptiness is what she felt in this place, I think. Her marriage was empty, as was her life here. Her heart, certainly. I was a product of all that emptiness. She hated me before I even arrived here, I suspect."

"Do you think that is why she left you here for so long?" She pulled away to face him again, and couldn't seem to stop herself from pressing butterfly light kisses over his cheek and jaw.

He nodded, thinking her kisses were like a balm to him that he'd never had as a child. Or ever, really. "It would have been easier for her if I'd died. She had her duke to marry, and Piers, her heir, along with a bevy of lovers and secrets. What need did she have of me? I reminded her she was common. That she was an imposter in their world."

"She was wrong about you." Cecelia's vehement words were spoken in a voice harder than he'd imagined she could conjure, and he studied her features intently as she continued. "You became a credit not only to her, but to the entire empire. Despite her malicious name, and everything that came after. I'm glad she lived long enough to watch you rise. To prove her wrong. You should be proud of that."

He smoothed his fingers across her face, hoping to wipe away the wrath that didn't set well on features as lovely as hers. That she felt such an emotion on his behalf was both wonderful and humbling. "I was proud when we met, but I'm not certain I should be now."

"And why not?" she asked anxiously. "Because of me? Because of what we've just done?"

"Nay," he soothed. "Because of the Lord Chancellor."

"But you had nothing to do with his crimes," she said, and her defense of him caused his shard of a heart to double in size.

"I've been shaken, to be honest. I rose to where I am because I had a keen instinct about the nature of people. If they were lying to me, or not. Which they most often are," he added wryly. "I'd be able to tell what they wanted from me. What precipitated their actions, and how far they were willing to go to get what they wanted."

He studied her for a long time, wondering why he was about to reveal this. "I thought ye were among the first people I'd ever met who'd truly muddled that instinct. Who'd been able to distract me long enough to fool me."

"I didn't set out to fool you," she said. "I hope you believe that."

He shaped his hand to her jaw. "I ken, lass, I ken. But to suspect I might have been working for the worst kind of criminal for so long. That I've been aspiring to become like him. Allowing him to influence my prejudices . . . It makes me question everything I ever believed about which side is good and which is not."

"Your heart has always been good, that's what matters." She quirked a smile down at him, this one full of sadness and softness, but no true sense of pity. "I am sorry for what you have suffered," she said. And he knew she meant it. "But I am also glad you've questioned your instincts about me."

"Ye're not the only one," he muttered.

"How so?"

"Count Armediano. The first time I met him, I thought he was a trustworthy sort. I sensed something of a kinship there."

She frowned. "But then you found out he was at Miss Henrietta's right before the explosion."

"I hated him before that, darling." He filled his palms with her rump, enjoying the pliant curves of abundant flesh. "I hated him the moment he touched ye."

She turned her head so he wouldn't see her shy but pleased smile, but there was no hiding from him. "I'm glad you're no longer my enemy. I wanted very much for you to like me from the start."

"I do like ye." He touched his nose to hers, learning the language of affection. "It's impossible not to. Ye have a way that captures everyone's heart."

"Not everyone," she grieved, burying her face in his neck.

Ramsay rubbed his hands across the impossibly smooth skin of her back and locked his arms around her, wondering if he'd ever bring himself to let go.

"You know," she sighed, "when I was little . . . I used to dream about this."

"About what?" he murmured, thinking he might be lulled off to sleep by a goddess.

"I confess I was a lonely little girl before the Rogues came into my life. And I would sometimes think about how lovely it would be for someone to hold me like this. To shelter me. To accept me and care for me. Care *about* me."

Ramsay ached for that lonely little girl. If only they'd always been able to keep each other's loneliness at bay. "I meant what I said. I would care for ye for the rest of our lives." He held his breath as she stilled, and considered not letting her up when she struggled onto her hands to look down at him again.

"You're not proposing, Lord Chief Justice?" Her eyes sparkled at him as she regarded him with mock distress. "After everything we've said against it?"

He remained stone-cold sober, staring up at her with all the earnestness in the world. "Aye, I'd make ye my wife, Cecelia. I'd not have taken ye to bed otherwise."

"I know that about you," she said ruefully. "You're nothing if not honorable. Though . . ." She made a great show of looking about their surroundings. "I wouldn't say you've taken me to bed, exactly. More . . . to nest." She let out a little laugh, stretching and arching up in a way that lifted her breasts.

Ramsay would have buried his face between them if one thing didn't trouble him mightily. "Ye havena answered," he prodded. "Would ye consider being my wife?"

She sobered as well. Leaning back, she dismounted him in a fashion that gave him the most erotic view of his life. Sitting next to him, she dragged a blanket to cover her more diverting bits.

"I worry for our future, don't you?" She caught her cheek in her teeth in that way she did when she was puzzling over a conundrum. Lord, he wondered how she had any cheek left.

"Ye needn't worry," he reassured her. "I ken I've been insufferable, but we've proven we make better allies than enemies. That we can trust each other. Everything is different now."

"Is it?" she fretted. "How will you explain taking the Scarlet Lady as your consort? Won't that make things indescribably difficult for you? Are you willing to give up all you've achieved to tie your tidy life to my chaotic one?"

Touched by her concern, he reached out and tucked a

silken ringlet behind her ear before lifting her chin with the crook of his finger. "Ye needn't worry," he soothed. "It's no widely known ye're the Scarlet Lady. Once we indict the criminals responsible for yer troubles, we'll marry and I'll adopt Phoebe right away. We'll dismantle Miss Henrietta's and sell the property under any number of business holdings I own. No one need trace it back to ye—"

She pulled out of his reach, her face a mask of denial. "I don't want to sell Miss Henrietta's."

"Why wouldn't ye?" He shook his head at her.

"Because it's necessary. So many women depend on it," she insisted gently. "I intend to rebuild Miss Henrietta's as soon as possible with the help and patronage of Alexandra and others like her. I want Genny and whichever girls still work there to remain, and I intend to expand the school."

He sat up, his heart pounding. "Ye canna be serious."

"I'm perfectly serious," she said earnestly. "I've been looking for my path for so long, Ramsay, and I believe I've found it. These women, they rely upon me for their incomes. Alexander, Frank, and I have been all over the world, and the one thing I've noticed is that when women are educated and able to work, not only are their lives made better but so are those of their children and their communities. I want to be part of that in my home country. I feel very passionate about this."

"And that is commendable," Ramsay said carefully, meaning it with every part of himself. "But surely ye can do it in some other way then a gambling hell."

"Perhaps, but I'm very good with numbers. I could make a go of it." She thrust her chin forward in a stubborn fashion. "Ever since Henrietta's was attacked, I've become more determined than ever to see it rise from the ashes for the betterment of all."

"Where does that leave us, then?" he demanded. "Because ye were right to worry, I canna remain Lord Chief Justice and marry an infamous game maker. Do ye have any idea what people get up to in yer establishment? Ye've not even opened yet." His blood began to rise in concert with his fear. Was this falling apart before it had a chance to be knitted together?

"I have some idea, I'm not an idiot. And I'm not asking you to marry me," she replied with determined patience. "Perhaps we could make a less . . . conventional arrangement?"

His frown darkened. "I'd not turn ye into my whore."

"Mistress, then," she offered with a teasing waggle of her eyebrows.

"Semantics," he growled.

"Not semantics. You wouldn't pay me, obviously. We've each our own fortunes. We could just . . . be together."

"Nay," he said. "It's impossible." He had to have her. To possess and protect her. How could she not understand that?

A sober frown wrinkled her forehead. "But only moments ago, you said you would shoot the moon if I asked it of you. That you could stay here with me forever."

"Aye, then let us stay here." He seized her shoulders, desperately needing her to understand. "Let us work the earth if we must. Or do nothing at all. I'm wealthy enough to retire. Let us do anything where we are not considered lower than the sewer rats in the eyes of London society."

Cecelia put her hands over his and brought one to her lips. "I love it here. But I cannot stay. I am resolved. I would share my life with you, if you are brave enough to share my chosen future with me." She gestured to the air between them. The space that seemed to be growing into a chasm by the second.

"Ye have to understand what ye're asking," Ramsay said. "Ye're expecting me to give up not only my hard-won position, but my reputation. My very reason for *existence*."

"No," she rushed. "No, I do not intend for you to give up your life. But that certainly seems to be your expectation of me. To give up what I have, what I want, so that we might be together. Do you expect me to conform to the societal expectation of what a woman should be so that I'll fit neatly into the world?"

"Well . . ." He blinked rapidly, wondering why her question suddenly sounded like he wasn't being at all logical. "Yes."

She gasped in as if someone had punctured her lungs with a knife, and then breathed out a shaky sigh. "If there's one thing you'd have learned in a lifetime with me, it's that I don't fit neatly anywhere." She regarded him with infinite sadness, but he could tell he'd not surprised her in the least.

Ramsay fought desperation at the retreat he read in her eyes, and on its heels a fury surged.

"I'm not the one being unreasonable here!" He slapped the ground in frustration. "I simply doona want a mistress or an exile. Ye've seen how dangerous this life is."

"If you want me as a wife, you'll get everything I am." She stood, dropping the blanket and snatching up her wrapper. "If we were to marry, I'd take you despite your pride and your perfectionism, not because of it." She donned the robe in a graceful motion and belted it firmly.

Ramsay didn't even get the proper chance to mourn the loss of her skin as she continued to set fire to the hopes he'd planted for them, leaving them in ashes. "I'm *not* perfect, Ramsay. I *do* indulge in the pleasures life has to offer, and I don't intend to stop. Life is for *living*. To enjoy. I'll not tie my fate to yours if you're only going to smother me with expectations. I'll not have it."

Ramsay stood and stalked forward. He captured her lips with his and kissed her with wild, desperate abandon. He poured all of his need, his will, his desire, and his feeling into her mouth. Hoping it would reach her heart. Wishing she would soften.

When she broke the kiss and turned away, they were both breathing heavily. Her lips were bruised and his felt swollen, along with another part of his anatomy begging for him to give in so he could be inside her again.

"Will ye not yield, Cecelia?" he whispered urgently. "Even for a chance at this?"

She whirled around, all semblance of gentility and kindness wiped away by a stronger emotion than he'd ever seen. Pain, the same pain he'd spied gazing back at him from the mirror.

The kind of pain that eventually turned into rage.

"Why is it *I* who must yield to *your* ambitions?" she demanded, slicing her hand through the air. "Because I am a woman? Do you realize how many men have requested me to yield because of my sex? The vicar who raised me. Who imprisoned me because he believed I was at fault for the indiscretions of others." She paced again, making large, passionate gestures, each word of her refusal a shard of glass embedded in his heart.

"Every professor I ever had asked me to yield my seat, my marks, my chosen passion to a man. Every male student who was forced to sit next to me, or humbled himself to ask me for help in private because my mind was superior to his, only to depose me publicly for being fat, tall, bespectacled, or, worse, unmarried—no, *unmarriable*." She said the word with a disgust that pounded the nail into their coffin.

"Because I wore a dress, my existence as an intellectual has been an insult to everyone. They've all asked me to be other than I am. Men seem to think that because they must give me their seats on the train, I must yield to them my very identity. Or my choices. My body or, in this case, my *entire life*." She marched up to him, looking like Boudicca the warrior queen, proud and angry and determined. "I have not, and I will not, and it is wrong of you to ask," she said with absolute finality. "Can you not love me, even if I do not yield?"

Ramsay felt himself turning hard. Cold. Building walls against the barrage of her words so he didn't have to hear them, to wonder if they made sense.

"We have not yet spoken of love," he said in a voice that would have been inaudible if her nose wasn't almost touching his.

She stumbled backward, clutching her heart.

He'd driven the knife home.

"I see." She bent down, gathered her nightgown and turned to take the path back to the house.

"Cecelia." Ramsay was not a man who chased a woman, but he did it for her. He did his best to explain. That he knew best. That she could not ask him to return to nothing. "I am who I am every bit as much as ye are. Who am I if not the Lord Chief Justice of the High Court? What achievements could ye take pride in? What do I have to offer ye if not my position? My reputation? My principles and my pride?"

Her steps faltered, and her chin touched her shoulder. "Those are excellent questions," she said stiffly. "You'll have to find the answers yourself before we discuss this again."

As she walked away with her back straight Ramsay already knew the answers.

Nothing. He had nothing to give her because he'd been born nothing. Hollow.

Empty.

CHAPTER EIGHTEEN

"Will you not *play* with me, Cecelia?"

Phoebe's voice was generally dear and sweet, but it reached an octave the next afternoon that penetrated Cecelia's tearful headache and tried her apparently finite reserves of patience.

"I'm sorry, darling, but it's imperative that I finish this." Perhaps if she'd slept rather than sobbed, she might feel differently, but alas, she endeavored to solve this situation with ever more haste so she could run away—no, not away, but *back*. Back to London.

To her life.

She could not stay here with Ramsay. Not after last night. Not after how many times she thought about abandoning everything, her ideals, her needs, her responsibilities, and her pride to fall back into his arms.

"But you finished that book *yesterday*," Phoebe said with a plaintive whine. "Why have you started it over?"

Because she had to have missed something. She stared down at the coding text index, scanning the first page for any hint of a clue that might show her where to start so she didn't have to read the whole blasted thing again.

"Can you not rest? Just for a bit?" Phoebe pressed, laying her doll over the open page. "I'll let you be Fanny de Beaufort, even though she's more beautiful than Frances Bacon."

All the cogs and wheels of Cecelia's thoughts ground to a halt as the girl's compassionate offer plucked something out of her brain. She leafed through the index back to A through D.

B. Bacon. The Baconian cipher.

And not too far beneath . . . Beaufort!

Cecelia flipped to the corresponding chapter. The Beaufort cipher was a polyalphabetic grid where one must have the key word to unencrypt language.

Holy God. The hint had been the *dolls'* names all along.

Cecelia slid off her chair and knelt in front of Phoebe, caressing the doll. "Darling, did Henrietta ever tell you why she named Frances and Fanny?" she asked. "Did she ever mention a key?"

Phoebe shook her head.

No, she wouldn't, would she? Henrietta had been too canny and careful to leave anything so important to the memory of a child.

"Please give me a little while longer," she begged Phoebe. "And then I shall be finished, and we can play."

"All right," the girl said agreeably. "Might I stay here on the bed if I'm quiet?"

"Of course."

The girl was not quiet in the least, but Cecelia focused the best she could, tapping her pen against her lip, trying to think of a word. Of *any* word Henrietta might have used as the key.

The key is in the color we both hold dear.

She bolted straight, remembering the letter. Of course! Henrietta was the Scarlet Lady, and Cecelia was a Red Rogue. Hortense, Henrietta, and Cecelia were natural redheads. Not to mention Francesca and, to a lesser extent, Alexandra. That had to be it!

She attempted to use the letters *red* first, but it was too short. And *scarlet* didn't work, either; nor did *ruby*, *vermillion*, or *burgundy*.

However, as soon as she established the word *crimson* into the Beaufort grid and used it against the integers, entire words began to form.

Elated, Cecelia sat back and stared at the first completed sentence.

The Crimson Council.

Beneath the bold letters was a list of names she carefully uncovered, and a few were so incredibly familiar, she gaped down for a lost expanse of time.

Sir Hubert, the Lord Chancellor, obviously.

The Duke of Redmayne? Though a line had been slashed through his name, and Cecelia presumed that was done once the previous Redmayne had hung himself. This she surmised because she recognized a few other notable names crossed out who were also deceased.

And then, Luther Kenway, Earl of Devlin.

Hadn't Kenway's garden been the one in which the young girl, Katerina Milovic, had been found?

"Oh dear," she breathed, realizing she was on the precipice of several truths she didn't want to know.

"What's wrong?" Phoebe inquired.

"Nothing's wrong," she said. "But would you go and fetch Lord Ramsay and Jean-Yves for me? I've learned something they'll want to know about."

"Did you solve the puzzle?" She jumped up and down,

and her enthusiasm restored all of Cecelia's goodwill toward her.

"I think I have."

"Oh wonderful, I'll tell everyone!" She scampered out into the main house, which was empty as Ramsay and Jean-Yves were both out of doors.

Cecelia turned page after page, realizing that Henrietta had devoted entire sections to a certain person. To pass the time, she quickly decoded each name at the top of a page, gasping at the contents. Everyone was in here.

Everyone. The royal family. The upper crust of aristocracy. Titans of industry and politics.

Cecelia was still writing things down when Ramsay burst into the room. Even though their hearts were at an impasse, her body didn't seem to understand.

Once their eyes met and held, little electrified sensations danced across her flesh and quivered in her belly. Her sex bloomed and released a soft rush of readiness even as her heart plummeted.

His eyes had regained their glacial frost. She could no longer decipher their depths.

He'd effectively shut her out.

"What did ye find?" he asked, striding to tower behind her and peer down at the notepaper she used to scribe the messages from the codex.

"The Crimson Council." she said. "I've found what Henrietta knew about them."

He scowled down at the paper, seeing Redmayne's name on it. "I've heard of it spoken in whispers, but everyone considers it tripe. A conspiracy conjured by madmen and rabble-rousers. I'd never lent credence to the rumors."

"What rumors?" Jean-Yves had shuffled in behind him and he joined Ramsay at the elbow, peeking down at her notes.

"It's been said a society of men who consider themselves loyal to Britannia beyond her monarchy, her Parliament, and her politics conspire in secret to puppet-master the empire's rise." Ramsay crossed his arms. "A week ago, I'd have said it was bollocks. Now . . ." He eyed the codex. "How fast can ye unencrypt this book?"

"I could teach you how," Cecelia said. "With the two of you helping, it shouldn't be but a day."

"Right, let us move this to the kitchen, then."

Cecelia, Ramsay, and Jean-Yves worked tirelessly on the papers. They wrote down things they never wanted to know. Not just scandalous secrets and hefty debts, but discoveries of every crime from theft to murder to, in a few cases, high treason.

The Crimson Council, according to Henrietta's findings, had been established some several centuries past to manipulate the outcome of the War of the Roses. It had since groomed many a man to join, but seemed to be less active in politics by modern standards, and more a fraternal order dedicated to money, prestige, and power. The members had done despicable things . . . including hiring a procurer of young foreign girls for the pleasure of sick, wealthy men.

Henrietta kept a blackmail tally in the codex, but it seemed that she'd often avoided the members of the Crimson Council. She never mentioned being part of these procurements of young girls, but it seemed she believed she was being framed for these crimes.

But by whom? Cecelia wondered, doing her best not to be distracted by Ramsay's scent. By his nearness and his distance.

Anyone in this codex could have murdered her aunt and made her death seem like natural causes.

Cecelia turned the page and began to work on a new

page . . . With each letter she spelled out, another boulder of dread weighted her stomach, until she felt as though she might be sick.

CASSIUS GERARD RAMSAY?

The question mark had been traced many times, as though Henrietta had reason to puzzle over him.

"You're pale, *mon bijou*," Jean-Yves noted from across the table. "Should we stop to eat?"

Ramsay leaned in from next to her, the hair on his arm almost touching her.

Cecelia stared at the name, attuned to the sound of his breath, to the warmth of his body close, but not touching. She didn't want to decipher any more. She didn't want to uncover his secrets.

She didn't want to hate him.

"What does it say?" His voice was low. Terse and harsh.

"There's not much here," she said, pointing to a total of three lines of script. "Perhaps you were telling the truth when you said you had no secrets."

"What did she write about me, Cecelia?"

Cecelia swallowed, unable to look up. Clenching her pen tightly enough to turn her fingers white, she began the process of using the key. He verbally read each word she revealed.

NO ENTRY TO OFFICE OR DOCUMENTS.
NO EVIDENCE OF CLANDESTINE MEETINGS
WITH LC OR OTHER CC MEMBERS.

"We can assume LC means Lord Chancellor, and CC is Crimson Council, yes?" Cecelia babbled.

"Aye, what else?" he asked impatiently.

Cecelia returned to the cipher.

NO LONGER TRUSTS MATILDA.

"Matilda?" Cecelia echoed. "That is the woman Henrietta sent to—"

"Matilda was my mother's name," Phoebe joined the conversation from over by the fireplace where she'd been whispering to Frances and Fanny.

They all might have been a tableau of statues frozen in stark astonishment. Even the motes of dust seemed to hang still in the air, afraid to move.

To make it real.

Nigh on eight years, Ramsay had said, since he'd had a woman.

The woman Henrietta sent to spy on him.

Matilda. Phoebe's mother who died in childbirth.

Phoebe had barely turned seven years old.

Cecelia wanted it to be true, and then she didn't. She watched the little girl with new eyes. Phoebe wasn't the right color to belong to the golden giant beside her. Her hair was honey, not flaxen gold. Her eyes hazel rather than blue. She was so little for her age.

And yet. She'd a dimple in her chin that might claim to match Ramsay's. And strong, broad, handsome features.

"*Mon Dieu*," Jean Yves whispered.

Cecelia glanced over to Ramsay who'd yet to move. To speak.

To even breathe.

He stared at the girl, who had risen to her feet and rubbed at a tiny stain on her pink pinafore.

Phoebe blushed, self-consciously aware she was the subject of rather intent conjecture.

Though his features didn't so much as twitch, his eyes glittered with myriad things.

"Ramsay?" Cecelia ventured.

His hand lifted to silence her. "When is yer birthday, lass?" He whispered the question to Phoebe, but it carried through the house like a cannon blast.

"The fourteenth of June," she answered brightly. "Next year, I'm going to ask Cecelia for a parasol, that is if I don't get one for Christmas."

Ramsay's chest deflated drastically, as if he'd been kicked in the ribs by a rather powerful ghost.

Cecelia looked down at the codex, blinking a well of tears away as they blurred the last coded sentence. She needn't bother with it. It didn't take a genius or even a mathematician to figure out his secret.

Ramsay had fathered a bastard.

The Scot said nothing. He stood so quickly his chair toppled over, strode to the door, and slammed it shut behind him.

CHAPTER NINETEEN

It was a blessed, *blessed* thing that Ramsay had something to butcher.

Every time he cleaved into the deer as he dressed and prepared it, he had to wonder whose bones he'd rather be breaking. Who most deserved the crux of his rage? The Lord Chancellor? Matilda? Henrietta?

Himself?

Once the meat was prepared, Ramsay bathed and swam alone, knowing no one would come looking for him.

A father.

His rage had no place to land. All his tormentors were not ghosts.

And if he was honest, he'd no one to blame but himself.

Ramsay remembered back to the day he'd found Matilda's dark head bent over his desk after she had picked the lock to his home office. He'd railed at the beauty like a harbinger of wrath and righteousness. Had condemned her for all manner of things.

Even after she confessed that Henrietta had sent her. She'd asked him for his mercy, his forgiveness. But he'd allowed his pain at her betrayal to flare into fury. He'd looked at his lover, the woman he'd considered marriage for, and he'd thrown her out into the gutter. He'd told her she belonged there. Had vowed to her the next time he saw her, it would be in shackles. That he'd love nothing so much as to see her rot in a prison for a treacherous slag.

And, in the end, she'd reaped the greatest revenge. She'd given birth to his daughter, and let his enemy raise her.

This was his nightmare.

Every time he'd kicked the door to Henrietta's establishment in, he'd put little Phoebe at risk. He'd been too blinded by his own self-importance, his distrust of women, and the vendetta he excused with ambitious ideals, to much care how his actions might affect those in his warpath.

If he'd have taken Henrietta down earlier, he'd have impoverished his own daughter.

And Cecelia.

Not to mention the employees of the gambling hell and the students beneath.

So why didn't the old hag tell him? Why didn't she come to him with this secret and do her level best to blackmail him out of his vast fortunes as was her wont?

Instead, she raised up *his* daughter.

Ramsay stood in the lake and heaved great swaths of water with his arms in a very uncharacteristic fit of temper. He roared to the sky and created waves of his ire.

He'd have to tell Phoebe who he was.

A pang of anxiety paralyzed him as the last of the sun

dipped below the trees. In the silence, he could hear Cecelia's and Phoebe's voices filtering through the thin forest as they ventured near to pick berries from the overgrown forest. Even at this distance, the false brightness in Cecelia's interaction plucked at him.

His daughter adored Cecelia already because she'd taken the girl in and shown her the love any motherless child would yearn for. She'd have made certain Phoebe's dream of being a doctor was realized.

Cecelia. Who'd shown him to the gates of heaven, and then, with a few words, plunged him back into the cold depths of his own desolate hell.

After he bathed, Ramsay climbed to his hunting perch. From his vantage in the old oak, he watched as Cecelia took Phoebe inside. He followed their candlelight through the windows as the stars came out, knowing their routine by now. They ate their collected berries with clotted cream for dessert, then washed, cleaned teeth, braided hair, told stories.

And he sat outside as he always did. Apart.

Alone.

This time by choice, because life had taught him many things about conquering and survival but blessed little about connection.

Longing stole his breath as it banded around his chest. It fought with another emotion welling from within. He wished he wasn't possessed of the acumen to identify it for what it was.

Fear.

What he feared most he could not say. Love? Loss? Humiliation and abandonment?

How sentiment might weaken him. Might render him vulnerable.

Eventually the night drove him from his watchtower,

and he strode toward the woodshed. It was too late to reveal anything to Phoebe now, and he was too weary in every possible way.

She'd seemed ready enough to accept him as a father figure when he'd spoken to her earlier, but only inasmuch as he would make Cecelia happy.

And now that he couldn't, would she be disappointed to call him Papa?

As he passed the house, Ramsay smelled the sweet pipe tobacco Jean-Yves was fond of smoking on the porch. He quickened his pace, hoping the old man would let him pass in peace.

No such luck.

"Fancy a smoke, my lord?" Jean-Yves held up a long pipe in greeting and offering.

"I doona smoke," he answered shortly, nodding his head in respect for the elder.

"If anyone should ask, neither do I," the Frenchman said with a shrug. "Cecelia doesn't like it. She worries for my lungs. But she is putting young Phoebe to bed, and what she does not know, she cannot worry about." Bushy brows waggled in the flaring light of a match as he lit a coal in his pipe.

Ramsay couldn't say why he drifted to the dilapidated porch when all he wanted to do was retreat.

"Here." Jean-Yves handed him a bottle of caramel liquid. "The whiskey is shit, but it does the trick."

"The whiskey was meant to be used medicinally, not recreationally," Ramsay muttered, taking the glass. "I didna buy it for the label."

"If ever there was a medicinal use, this would be it," Jean-Yves chuffed. "When I found out I was going to be a father, I drank an entire bottle of wine in one hour. But my liver was younger then."

Ramsay couldn't say the idea didn't appeal to him, but he didn't want to dull his senses, not when he had two precious women to protect. To be respectful, he brought the bottle to his lips and took a judicious sip, wincing as the liquid hit the back of his throat like fire and acid.

The Frenchman was right. It was shit.

Still, he took a second drink.

He and Jean-Yves watched the nearly full moon crawl across the night sky for a long, silent moment before the elder man spoke in soft tones. "I remember when my daughter was your Phoebe's age. It is a time of questions and patience and many, many different colors of ribbons."

"My Phoebe," Ramsay murmured, his heart doing an extra thump. He loved her already. He'd fallen for her brilliant crooked smile and dimpled charm before he'd even known of their relation. He wanted to teach her more than how to swim; he wanted to teach her how to fight, how to learn, how to be Scottish.

He would protect her. Raise her. Spoil and scold her. He would love her more than a child had ever been loved. She would *belong*, and live every day knowing she was wanted. She would not only be a doctor, but the *best* doctor. He would fight any school that wouldn't take her. He would buck any system that wouldn't allow her to achieve the dreams of keeping mothers alive. He'd help her break down the walls erected by men around institutions and businesses and women, themselves.

He'd make it so she'd never have to yield.

Christ, he'd been such an ass. So incredibly blind.

After all of the grief he'd heaped upon Cecelia's head since they'd met, *he* was the one with a hidden scandal.

He'd been so blinded by anger, by his own inflexible biases, he may have forever lost the one woman he truly wanted. Because he lacked courage.

While he grappled with his thoughts, his shame, Jean-Yves continued, "I lost my beloved daughter to influenza when she was but a couple of years older than Phoebe. My wife seemed to be fighting off the disease at first, but the grief stole her, too, and I was left alone so young. Younger than you."

"I—I'm sorry." It was what one said, and yet it felt insufficient. Ramsay's chest hollowed out at the thought, and he'd only known of his progeny for a matter of hours. He couldn't imagine the loss after raising a beloved daughter from infancy.

Jean-Yves leaned forward, staring at him intently. "I need to ask you if you plan to take her from us."

"What?" Ramsay stared into the stark expression of the wizened man. Not for the first time, he wondered just what exactly was the relationship between Cecelia and the Frenchman. What had forged such a strong bond?

Jean-Yves glanced out into the night, adjusted his shoulder sling, and suddenly looked very, very tired as he answered the question Ramsay never asked.

"Just as petite Phoebe is your responsibility now, so is Cecelia mine. She gave me this gift of her little broken heart when she was a girl at Lake Geneva, and I have done my best to guard it as her father should have for many years." He blinked back to Ramsay, his eyes hard and serious. "You have hurt her, but she will recover from your loss," the man said bluntly. "But if you plan to rip that child from her arms, I must prepare myself for her grief."

"I'm not a monster, of course I wouldna deny them their attachment to each other." Ramsay took a sip, retreating from the man behind the bottle before he confessed, "The ludicrous irony of this situation is—if Cecelia would have consented to be my wife—I would have ended up raising Phoebe, regardless of what the codex revealed. My own daughter." He looked into his terrible whiskey and saw only bleak darkness. "I've buggered everything."

"Yes, Cecelia told me she refused you." Jean-Yves gave a rather caustic harrumph and took a long drag from his pipe. "She soaked my good shoulder with her tears."

She'd wept over him? Ramsay hated that he'd caused her tears.

"Ye are a good father to her, Monsieur Renault."

The man's teeth clicked on his pipe as his jaw tightened. "Someone needed to be."

"Aye," Ramsay said carefully. "I've heard the Vicar Teague was an uncompromising man."

"You don't know the half of it."

Ramsay waited for the man to elucidate, but he didn't. Unwilling to pry, he put his hand over his chest, rubbing at the ache that landed there at the very thought of her loss.

It was where she belonged. In his heart . . . She was lodged there among the mire of things that caused him pain.

And joy.

"Ye approve of her refusal, no doubt." He leaned over to accept a little more whiskey.

"*Au contraire*," Jean-Yves said vehemently. "I was hoping you'd tame her a little bit. Or at least take over the responsibility of her protection from me. I worry for her when I am gone. Alexandra has her duke, and Francesca her revenge. Cecelia has always been a bit lost, I think. A bit lonely and aimless. Now she has this venture and with it comes danger. I wondered if you might be the answer . . ." He sighed, letting his sentence trail away. "Anyway, I am getting too old to keep up with these Red Rogues anymore.

And they refuse to slow down." He put his hands to an aching back, though his complaint was softened by a fondness so tender it might have been called love.

"I tried," Ramsay murmured. "She will not be tamed."

"You failed." A meaningful nod of Jean-Yves's head precipitated a puff of smoke in his direction. "You failed because you do not like women."

When Ramsay would have spoken, Jean-Yves put up a hand and made a very Frankian noise of disgust and condescension. "I'm certain you think you have many good reasons, but none of them apply to Cecelia. She has more honor than any soldier. More compassion than any saint. And she is the perfect balance of softness and strength. You are not worthy of her, and I mean that as no slight because none of us are. I know she is not without flaws, but you made her feel unworthy of you, and that is where you lost my support, *mon ami*."

It'd been years, perhaps decades, since anyone dared to give Ramsay such a dressing-down. He felt a defensive ire well within him, but he fed it no heat.

Because the old man was absolutely correct. It was he who was unworthy of Cecelia's fathomless well of love. Granted, he couldn't think of a man alive who would deserve it.

"I like women just fine. I just . . . doona trust them," Ramsay admitted. "I doona trust anyone."

"With good reason, I imagine," Jean-Yves relented.

"I wanted to trust Cecelia. I like and respect everything about her. I always have, even when I didna want to."

"Then why don't you go in there and tell her so?" Jean-Yves pressed, gesturing expansively toward the door. "Tell her you care not for her plans, but you will bear the brunt of the world for her so she can do what she wants.

God knows your shoulders are wide enough to carry some of her burdens, no?"

"Aye, but *I'm* not strong enough," Ramsay said in a voice so low it was nearly carried off by the breeze.

"To allow her to be herself? To put aside your lofty prejudices to—"

"I am not strong enough to watch the world despise her." He cut the old man off as the passionate truth tore out of him.

"It tears me up inside that someone made attempts on her life. It's all I can do not to lock her and Phoebe in a tower so no one can hurt them. I doona want to be the husband of a game maker, nay, but more than that, I doona want to live with the fear that every day she spends in that den of vice, she puts herself at risk!"

He'd expected the proclamation to make him feel weak and vulnerable, but something inside him warmed at the approval he read in the old man's expression.

Jean-Yves tipped his glass at Ramsay. "Do you not put yourself at risk on that bench of yours, Lord Chief Justice?"

"That's different," he grunted.

"Because you are a man?"

"Aye, goddammit. Because I am a man." He paced, railing against the unfairness of it all. "Because I have fought for my country and my life, because I can survive what she cannot—I have conquered hells on this earth she couldna even conceive of. And because it is my duty, nay, my *privilege* to protect those I love."

Jean-Yves sat back and regarded him through squinted eyes. "Yes, Lord Ramsay, I believe you have done some very manly things. You have come a long way from here." He gestured to Elphinstone Croft and the surrounding glade. "I heard some of your troubles and I commend you for your accomplishments. But now you must listen to me." He struggled to his feet with an ornery grunt, waving off the helping hand Ramsay offered before reaching for the whiskey.

"For all you've revealed to Cecelia, you know very little about her," Jean-Yves said. "Locking her in a tower would be her personal hell, because she spent so much of her youth locked in a vicar's cellar."

An ache in Ramsay's belly turned into a stab of pain for her, followed by a whip-burn of anger prickling across his flesh. "What?"

"When the man she called Father wanted to punish the world, which was often, he punished her, instead. He would lock her in the cellar for days. He would starve her. Beat her. Humiliate her. He would make her feel both small and fat. She would have the indignity and anger of a bitter, impotent man heaped upon her young shoulders. She bore the shame of every woman and every sin starting at Eve and ending with her.

"So perhaps you were abandoned here, but at least you had water to drink and the sky to look at. You could have run to the city, and you chose not to because you had the will to survive and the means to do so. She had nothing but the darkness and the hatred of a pious man with a dead prick."

A wall of emotion pushed Ramsay against the porch post, and it creaked dangerously beneath his weight. "Nay," he whispered.

She'd mentioned knowing a bit about loneliness.

About being unwanted.

He had no idea she'd such a deep, devastating understanding of it. His fingers curled; he could already feel the throat of the Vicar Teague snapping beneath their strength. "But she was rescued . . . and sent to Lake Geneva . . . to you."

"Yes. Rescued by Henrietta, apparently, and sent to school at de Chardonne. But do you think her troubles ended there?" Jean-Yves scoffed. "When I met her, she was a plump and friendless little girl alone in the garden I tended. No one would eat with her, because she was nobody to them. They laughed at her for being clever. They laughed because she was round and quiet and shy. And when it is in the nature of many bullied children to become cruel, she cultivated kindness and empathy."

The man's eyes warmed with veneration. "I was nothing but a peasant, yet she took an active interest in my life and my passion for the garden. She befriended me, hungry not just for the food we shared but for any kind word. Any companion, even an ornery, lonely old widower. She dug in the dirt beside me, heedless of her pretty dresses. She made diagrams of my gardens and memorized all the names of my favorite flowers."

A tender smile touched Ramsay's mouth, even as his heart broke for her. Cecelia as a little girl had faced very similar cruelty to what he'd known from other children. A child with no title, no name, but endless expectations to live up to in an institution full of people who thought they were better. She understood him perhaps more than anyone else.

And he never tried to return the favor.

Jean-Yves was right. He didn't deserve her love. No man alive did. And yet she would give it. Endlessly. Because that's who she was.

"Did you know that your brother's duchess killed her rapist?"

Stunned, Ramsay gaped at the Frenchman, who lifted his hand to smooth back wisps of disappearing hair.

He and Redmayne had become close. Why hadn't Piers confided this in him?

Possibly because of his status as a justice.

Possibly . . . because his family didn't trust him to put them above his principles.

A new wave of shame threatened to pull him out into the cold.

"Our Cecelia helped me carry the dead body without hesitation," Jean-Yves continued. "She put the duchess's monster in the ground and she toiled next to me with a shovel to bury him."

The old man's eyes glittered a little in the silvery shafts of moonlight, suspicious moisture gathering at the corners. "And then Cecelia took responsibility for that traumatized girl. She bathed her, cared for her, slept beside her, loved her through the aftermath of her terror.

"Did you know she hired me, and barely allows me to work? Because of her my tragic life has become full of adventure and contentment. She sacrifices everything she is, everything she has, and asks for so little in return. She is kindness personified, even though very few have shown her a modicum of what she is willing to give. And *you* . . ."

The man leaned forward, thrusting an accusing finger toward Ramsay. "You would ask her to forfeit her new-found legacy? To choose between her passion for life and her passion for the man she loves? This world is cruel to women, *mon ami*, and I thought if anyone had the fortitude to be different, it might be you."

"The man she . . ." *Loves?* Unable to say the word, Ramsay looked down at his hands trying to process all he'd learned in the space of a few breaths. He'd known her to be extraordinary but . . . "I didna ken," he breathed. "I didna know any of this about her. I thought her sunny disposition and optimistic idealism came from a life of mostly privilege and contentment."

"Her brightness has always come from within. She looks into the darkness, and smiles," Jean-Yves said poetically, his features arranging into an expression of adoration. "She was—she is—like a flower forever starved for rain. If you show her one drop of kindness, of love, she will bloom for you. But what you cannot do, Lord Ramsay, is ask an exotic orchid to be an English rose. Because that woman in there would love you. Would accept you. She would raise your child beside you and lay her life down for you both. But what she will not do is allow you to mold her into something she is not just so you are comfortable. If that is the kind of woman you seek, then you must let her go and find that elsewhere."

The truth of it slammed into Ramsay with all the weight of a steam engine.

Of course. How could he claim the woman only to change what made her captivating? Would he love the parody of herself she would become if she capitulated to his supercilious demands?

He stalled. That was the second time the word *love* had snuck into his thoughts.

Did he . . . love Cecelia?

He loved her inability to only eat one truffle or have only one glass of champagne. He loved her voice, her laugh, her wicked wit. He adored every curve and handful of her plump and perfect body, and he even treasured the way she challenged him. Gently, with humor. With a sparkling eye and generous wells of patience and forgiveness.

Had he reached the bottom of those wells? Had he been too insufferable? Too intolerant? He'd hid loneliness behind rage and cowardice behind hypocrisy.

He'd have to do so much better. To be better.

She had principles of her own. Just because they didn't mirror his, did it mean they were wrong?

What if she could teach him how to be like her? How to relax and enjoy moments. How to walk the earth as though the devil may care, and how to reclaim regard for others. A regard he'd thought forever lost.

The question might not be if he loved her but, rather, if there was anything he *didn't* love about her.

And the answer to that was no.

Even her reasons for keeping the gambling hell were noble.

In fact, the only thing he resented about her was her ability to live without him. Because she would carve out a happy life whether he was a part of it or not.

And he . . . well, he couldn't rightly fathom going back to a world without her in it.

He might not love what she'd picked as her profession, but he could live with it.

Because he had to live with her. He wanted her to be the mother of his child. Children. He wanted her to teach them to be as kind and generous and moral as she was. As independent and adventurous.

He wanted her to teach them how to love.

And perhaps he could learn alongside them.

"Ye're right," he whispered. "Ye're right, about everything. Do ye think I've lost her?"

"I think you should go and—"

Ramsay held up his fist for silence as a shadow caught his eye.

Something—someone—lurked in the glade beyond the gate.

As he squinted into the night, he thought he caught the outline of a man's head and torso ducking behind the fence lined with overgrown berry bushes plagued with thorns.

All thoughts of the past dissipated as his military training snapped into the fibers of his muscles, readying them for violence.

He scanned the moonlit night, looking for others. No one else out in the open, but anyone could have been waiting in the trees.

"Get inside, take the rifle, and give Cecelia the pistol," he commanded in a voice too low to carry. "Someone is out there, so I need ye to hole up in the bedroom and cover the window and the door. Shoot anyone who isn't me. Now pretend to retire for the night."

"I'm going to bed," the Frenchman said without missing a beat. He sounded glib enough to be convincing. "I'll leave you to your thoughts." Sotto voce, he asked, "What about a weapon for you, my lord?"

"Kick my bow and arrows to me."

Jean-Yves opened the door and sauntered into the cabin. Once he was inside the doorway, something fell on the floor.

"How clumsy of me." Jean-Yves bent down and kicked the bow and arrows that had been resting next to the doorframe to Ramsay.

Wily old man, Ramsay approved, understanding why the Scottish and French had made such excellent allies over the centuries.

Still, he would have preferred a firearm to his bow, but if he went inside to do it, he'd lose his prey. A man—a warrior—made do.

Ramsay remained still for a moment, listening for the sounds of movement. A preternatural silence had overtaken the night, a certain proof that he was not alone.

The shadow had been lost between the fence and the tree line.

He dropped low, snatched his bow and arrow, and crouched behind his side of the blackberry bushes as he crept along the edge until he reached the gate. He knew the old hinges would creak if he were to open it, so the only option he had was to vault over.

This would leave him exposed to anyone with a gun.

Taking a bracing breath, he leapt up and dove over the hip-high gate, ducking to roll onto the other side, returning to the shadows.

Had it been a different moon on a different night, Ramsay wouldn't have been able to see the shadow streak for the woods. He wouldn't have been able to nock his arrow and let it fly.

The shadow stumbled as the arrow found purchase in his leg, but he limped forward, diving into the trees.

Ramsay hesitated; if this was a ploy to draw him away from the house, he shouldn't take it. However, he had the upper hand on the interloper, because he could navigate these woods in the dark. He knew every tree by memory. He had no doubt he could cut the man off at the river if he ran now.

He scanned the night, searching for more shadows. The night was still, too still, but he could see nothing moving in the moonlight.

Ramsay launched toward the forest with his bow, staying low until he hit the tree line. He then angled west toward the bridge, knowing that it would be cleverest to make a tactical retreat that way if one wasn't familiar with the territory.

He quickly neared the river and flattened himself to an ancient ash tree, pausing to listen.

Not a handful of rapid heartbeats later, he heard a branch snap in the distance. Then a soft muffled curse.

He waited, every muscle tense. Every breath even.

The other man's approach was impressively quiet, but Ramsay was attuned to these woods. He knew the easiest path to take, had guessed correctly and hidden behind the right tree, which afforded him the chance to spring forward and chop at the man's legs with his bow.

His opponent fell hard. Harder than he'd expected him to, as the man was quite a bit larger than he'd guessed judging by the sounds he'd made while approaching.

Ramsay fell upon him, his fist flying like the hammer of an ancient god.

His fist landed in the dirt as the other man rolled to the side fast enough to avoid the punch and returned a punishing elbow to Ramsay's ribs.

Ramsay absorbed the blow with a sharp curse. This time, his jab caught the man in the mouth with a satisfying crunch.

His satisfaction was short-lived, however, as blood was spit right into his eyes, momentarily blinding him.

Fucking insufferable move.

Ramsay's next punch was more to keep the blighter busy while he swiped his other sleeve across his eyes just in time to see the glint of a knife.

Ramsay leapt off the assailant in time to avoid a slash.

They circled each other. Two shadows in the dark, the full moon filtering through leaves in strange and eerie shafts of silver.

The blade made a lightning-fast slash and Ramsay stepped in rather than away, imprisoning his attacker's wrist. He drove the man backward; the man's few attempts at breaking his hold proved futile against his superior strength.

Then, through some feat of impossible acrobatics, his opponent tossed the knife from his captured hand into the air. He twisted his body to catch it with his free hand before Ramsay drove him back against a tree trunk with his elbow lodged in his throat.

"One more move and I'll slice your artery and let you fertilize the forest with your corpse," threatened a voice as smooth as the blade now lodged against his upper thigh.

"Not before I snap yer neck," Ramsay vowed, leaning his elbow in, demonstrating the leverage he had against the other man's spine.

An impasse, it seemed.

"My lord Ramsay?" the man asked in disbelief.

He froze.

Dark eyes glinted at him from an all-too-familiar, far-too-handsome face.

"Count Armediano?" Ramsay tried to reconcile the insufferable Italian with his flawless accent with the voice that *now* hied from somewhere south of the Scottish border, but north of Hadrian's Wall. Newcastle or Northumberland, perhaps.

Finally, their enemy had a face. Homegrown British.

"How did ye find us?" Ramsay leaned his superior weight against the man.

"I followed the past," he answered cryptically.

"If ye're an Italian count then I'm an English debutante," Ramsay growled. "So who the fuck are ye?"

"If you were an English debutante, I'd be shoving something else between your thighs." The insolent fool made a lewd motion with his hips.

"Now is not the time to be glib," he warned.

"All right, all right, my name is Chandler, and I'm . . . well, let us say that I am employed by the Home Office."

"Ye're telling me ye're a spy?" Ramsay dug his elbow deeper into the man's neck. "Horseshit."

"Your brother will vouch for me," the man gasped, his knife inching higher on Ramsay's thigh.

"That's hardly a recommendation," Ramsay retorted, though he quickly alleviated some of the pressure so Chandler could speak.

The agent laughed as if they might be at a garden party, his teeth flashing white in his swarthy face. "I could be Italian," he claimed blithely. "My parentage has yet to be specified."

"I care not where ye're from, I only want to know what ye're doing on my land and how my brother is caught up in all of this."

"He's not that I can tell," Chandler answered. "However, I requested an invitation to the Redmayne dinner party because two of my open investigations happened to intersect, and the duke was all too happy to oblige."

"Which investigations?" Ramsay demanded. "And how do they involve Cecelia Teague? Is that why ye wanted to get her alone? To interrogate her? To implicate her? Do ye work for the Crimson Council?"

His opponent stilled, his lithe muscle still strung tight enough to strike. "What do you know of the Crimson Council?"

"Ye first."

The man grimaced as Ramsay ground his back against the tree. "All right! I've been digging into the background of Lady Francesca Cavendish, the Countess of Mont Claire, who as you know was a school chum of your lovely Miss Teague's and Lady Redmayne's. I'm told they are part of a society they call the Red Rogues, and I wondered if the Red Rogues had aught to do with the Crimson Council, as all of the women are shrouded in mystery and have led very odd and fascinatingly singular lives."

"To say the least," Ramsay muttered.

"Furthermore, Her Majesty has heard increasingly alarming accounts regarding this Crimson Council, and she requested that I, personally, investigate the matter. My findings have led me to none other than the Lord Chancellor, which was why you and I had the misfortune of meeting each other at Redmayne's soiree." He shrugged, as though giving himself over to the vagaries of fate.

"What accounts?" Ramsay asked.

Chandler's eyes darkened further. "We at the Home Office think someone is stealing young immigrant girls and using them for sport. I'd received intelligence that Henrietta Thistledown was their procuress, but upon further investigation, I was unable to verify."

Ramsay wavered, taken aback. He'd received the exact same intelligence.

"Who gave ye this information?" he asked, afraid he already knew the answer.

"A nameless source of someone employed by Miss Thistledown, herself. I was sent a letter."

Ramsay had received just such a letter. He'd like to further compare notes with the man, but time was of the essence, especially tonight.

He needed to return to Cecelia.

"What about Henrietta's?" Ramsay shook him once, hard enough to rattle his teeth. "Ye were there the day the explosive went off."

"Pure coincidence, I assure you," Chandler claimed with a quick, disarming smile. "I had been assigned to follow a certain member of the royal family and was side-tracked by a pretty pair of . . ." He paused, making a big gesture in front of his chest. ". . . eyes." Despite his being seconds from certain death, he winked and flashed a cocksure grin.

Ramsay made a face but released the man, all the while remaining on his guard.

He knew better than to take anyone at his word.

"Now." Chandler slicked a hand through his ebony hair and sheathed his dagger in his boot. "I've told you what I can. Care to share what you know of the Crimson Council?"

"I ken next to nothing about it," Ramsay said, which was not altogether a lie.

"I have it on good authority that Cecelia Teague might, but she disappeared right about the same time you did," Chandler said with a sly look toward him. "You wouldn't know anything about that, would you?"

Ramsay didn't answer. "If Cecelia is in possession of any information regarding the Crimson Council, that makes her important to ye and to the Crown. Important enough to warrant protection."

"Categorically," Chandler agreed. "She's in no danger from us, but I have it upon good authority that Henrietta was Miss Teague's maternal aunt, and that she was also in possession of a number of secrets that may not have died with her . . . some of which could be dangerous to the Home Office and even Buckingham Palace. Did she ever mention anything about such things?"

"Do ye think I'd tell ye if she did?" Ramsay challenged.

"Yes." Chandler stood straight and met his glare with frank assessment. "Because I know you are a good man, Lord Chief Justice, an honest one."

"How do ye ken that?"

The emissary adopted a sly look. "I have my ways."

"I doona ken what sort of man ye are," Ramsay challenged.

To his surprise, Chandler laughed. "Fair point. Fair point." He scratched his head and slapped at the earth and leaves on his pants. "Though one didn't have to be a spy to notice your protective instincts toward the voluptuous Miss Teague."

"Use more respectful descriptors, or I'll take that knife from ye and slice yer bollocks off," Ramsay warned.

"My case in point." Chandler only grinned again, rubbing at a dark evening stubble and wiping blood from a split in his lip. "May I ask you what brought you both all the way to the edge of Blighty?"

"Two attempts were made upon Cecelia's life," he decided to admit to the man.

Interest arrested Chandler's expression. "The explosion and . . ."

"And a contingent of the Lord Chancellor's personal staff who accosted her near her house in Chelsea."

Chandler's dark winged brows rose. "You mean, the ones they found dead in the street? Did you have anything to do with that, Lord Chief Justice?"

"I can neither confirm nor deny . . ." Ramsay picked up his ruined bow and rose, eyeing the man skeptically. "If ye're after the Crimson Council, why are ye all the way out here?"

"I followed one of the Lord Chancellor's men."

Ramsay was stabbed by a jolt of alarm. "Where are they now?"

"Lost them a few miles back," Chandler said, abashed. "Fucking bog almost claimed my horse."

"I have to get back and warn Cecelia." Ramsay claimed

his bow. "Can ye make yer way back to Elphinstone Croft even on yer leg?"

"You didn't crack me that hard," Chandler said defensively. "More surprised me, is all. Well done, by the way, it's not often I'm taken down."

"I meant when I shot ye with my arrow back in the glen."

"What glen?" Chandler's forehead furrowed. "I've never been shot by an arrow in my life."

The stab of alarm turned into a knife of terror twisting in Ramsay's guts. He had been a fool to leave her. The hope he hung his entire soul on was that he'd not yet heard a gunshot.

"Run," he said as he bolted for home, desperation turning his feet into agents of Icarus. "They've already found us."

CHAPTER TWENTY

Cecelia swam in a soupy fog, weightless and boneless. She might have been a blob of jelly for all she could tell. Was she awake? Locked in a dream?

Or a nightmare.

Every now and again, an image would be summoned from the miasma of darkness, adding to the primal scream locked wherever her chest belonged.

Were these images memories? Or were any of these strange things happening right now?

Glacial eyes melted into a lake of lust. Brutal hands caressed her gently as they made love beneath the stars.

We have not yet spoken of love.

Pain pierced where her heart should be. Tears leaked where her eyes should be. Her vision refused to clear.

Blood also leaked from a man's leg as someone stitched it closed. Voices were harsh. Male. Excitable.

Fire. She remembered fire. She'd thrown pages into said fire and it had burned them all up. Pages with her handwriting. But the book? Had she burned the codex? Surely not.

Phoebe hid in the loft and locked the hatch as she'd bade her to.

Did they find her? The enemies she'd let in the house?

Why had she done such a stupid thing? *Who* had she let in the house? Why could she not remember?

Jean-Yves was on the floor at Elphinstone Croft. Still. So still. Had they killed him this time? Oh God!

The pain in Cecelia's chest became a torturous flame. It singed her with shame. Her face hurt, too, this wound sharp and throbbing.

She'd been hit. Again.

Where was Ramsay?

Had she shot someone?

Is that who bled from the leg?

Awareness returned to her body incrementally, and she realized that the blood in her veins did not reach the arms tightly tied behind her. The ground below rocked softly, clack-clack-clacking in her ears.

A train. How had she gotten on a train?

Where was Ramsay?

"I do believe she's awake."

Cecelia knew that voice. She'd thought it belonged to a friend once. But who? *Who?* What was wrong with her?

"Should I give her another dose?"

Winston! Henrietta's butler . . . Had *he* been an enemy this entire time?

"Better not. The Lord Chancellor said we needed her alive," answered an unfamiliar man.

"Can't have her waking up and screaming, though," Winston said dispassionately.

"I'm more likely to scream if my bloody leg festers,"

whined the stranger with a waspish voice. "We could gag her, I suppose."

Winston made a heartless noise. "Just a small dose. If it's too much and she doesn't wake again, I don't think it'll be that much of a tragedy for anyone."

Cecelia was screaming already, she just couldn't seem to get her throat to work. She desperately wanted to struggle but hadn't the strength. The needle pricked her arm and she could feel the liquid oblivion course through her. She struggled against it like a swimmer in a riptide. Quickly, as she was overtaken by the darkness, her last thought was of Ramsay. Could he be counted among those who would mourn her?

Or had the way she'd left things truly turned his heart back to stone?

When Cecelia next woke, she knew exactly where she was, in a manner of speaking.

The smell was unmistakable. Loamy and musty, but . . . this time mixed with an acrid char.

She was underground.

An acid wash of panic crawled down her flesh, biting like a thousand tiny insects. The fear anchored her in the moment, sent her heart pumping hard enough to wash out the vestiges of whatever venom swam within her blood.

If she didn't give over to the terror and allow it to sweep her away, she could use the fear. Hone it to help her escape.

Testing her limbs, she found her feet free, but her hands were not. She swallowed another surge of panic, this one threatening to overwhelm her.

What she needed was information. Knowledge helped to combat fear.

What could she glean right away?

She lay on her side on the floor in a dim room. The only light filtered from somewhere behind her. The floor against her cheek was gritty with dirt or sand, but smooth and hard beneath. Her hands remained tied behind her back.

What did she remember?

She'd been reading by the fire at Elphinstone Croft.

Jean-Yves had rushed in, kicked something out the door, and slammed it shut.

"Someone is outside." He'd pressed a pistol into her hand and then went to the bedroom where the rifle was kept. They'd sent Phoebe into the loft, gotten rid of the loft ladder, and then crouched in the bedroom with their guns.

"Who is out there?" Cecelia had whispered around the terror in her throat.

"I do not know. Lord Ramsay has gone after them."

She'd felt safer, then. Surely Ramsay could take on the world. He was a mountain of a man with tireless reserves of fortitude. He was a soldier, a Scot, and a war hero.

She'd been so certain they were safe.

So how had she been captured? How did she end up beneath the earth?

Finding the ground untenable, Cecelia squirmed and maneuvered until she could roll to her knees. From there, she stood.

Oh God. This couldn't be happening. She was underground. Beneath the earth. Trapped. Locked.

Again.

She fought a flare of breath-stealing panic, looking around for any clue that might help her. She found a source of light, a tiny window in the door of her prison. A tiny, lovely window.

The etched glass she recognized immediately. She

wasn't just beneath the ground; she was beneath *her* ground. Henrietta's School for Cultured Young Ladies.

A sinister face appeared in the glass, and she jumped, letting out a cry of shock.

"She's awake," Winston called from the other side of the door.

"Thank you, Winston."

With a cold wash of ice, Cecelia's memory returned, flushing over her with absolute heart-rending betrayal.

She'd put her gun down at Elphinstone Croft. She'd let her enemy through the door. She'd been the architect of her own demise.

Because she'd trusted Genevieve Leveaux.

"Genny?" she whispered, unable to believe her own memories, even as they slammed back into her with bone-jarring force.

The woman had pounded on the door, begging to be let in. She'd cried out that she'd come to Scotland to warn Cecelia. That Lilly and the girls were in danger.

She'd sounded so frightened, so incredibly convincing, Cecelia had admitted her immediately.

And she and Jean-Yves had been ambushed.

"Genny." Cecelia rushed to the door. "Genny let me out."

"Hello there, honey." The soft regret in Genny's dark eyes conjured a little flame of hope in Cecelia's middle. Perhaps Genny had been helpless in all this somehow, coerced by the Lord Chancellor to betray her. One couldn't fault her for that.

"Genny? *Please.* Don't keep me underground." Cecelia fought sobs of hysteria threatening to overtake her. "Tell me everyone's all right, that they're alive."

Ramsay would not have allowed her to be taken. Had he been overcome? Killed? Where was Phoebe? Jean-Yves?

She couldn't imagine a world without them in it.

Genny tilted her head to the side, her ringlets flowing flaxen over her bare shoulder. "Honey, there are too many bodies to count now, all because of this." She held up the codex. "I couldn't tell you who survived and who didn't."

Cecelia leaned forward, pressing her forehead to the glass, fighting a dark anguish. "I know," she sobbed. "Burn it. It's brought nothing but pain."

That pain welled within her. Deep and abiding. Was this how she ended? Was everyone she cared about hurt or . . . worse? Were they after Frank and Alexander next? She wanted to ask again, to insist, but was terrified of the answer. If she did not know, there was still hope.

And hope might be all she had left in the end.

"Step back, doll." Keys rattled on the other side of the door as Genny unlocked her prison. "I'm coming in there with you."

The kindle of hope flared to a bright glow, and Cecelia scurried out of the way.

The door opened. Winston and two other men preceded Genny into the room. Two of them carried crystal oil lanterns and set them on what used to be student desks before the explosion and subsequent chaos had decimated what Cecelia could now see had been a classroom.

Something else filtered into the room behind them. Something that extinguished any hope with astonishing immediacy.

The cries of children.

They echoed down the long hall, each of them breaking her heart. The calls and pleas of captive young girls locked beneath the earth as she was. Begging for mercy. To be released. To be fed.

This was her fault, Cecelia realized. Once she'd gone to Scotland, Henrietta's had become the hellish prison

Ramsay had initially suspected it was. The girls hadn't been here when she'd taken custody of the property, but they'd been moved in when she'd fled.

There were no words for the horror of the din. For the memories they evoked in Cecelia. All the blood drained from her extremities and, had her stomach not been empty, she'd have heaved its contents onto the ashes at her feet.

"What have you done?" The demand escaped as a hoarse whisper of dismay. "What sort of nightmare has this place become? Did Henrietta know about this?"

Genny's features arranged themselves into a smug, repulsive mask of disgust.

Cecelia stepped back, shocked at the first time the woman hadn't appeared a stunning beauty.

"Henrietta Thistledown could dress this place in all the lace and silk she wanted, but at the end of the day the girls who worked in the casino were all still nothing but a line of pretty cunts. And she was the queen of us all."

Cecelia flinched. "I'm sorry if she was cruel to you, Genny. But I never would have been. I would have made this place a haven, you have to believe me."

"Oh honey, I believe you. I have nothin' against you, personally," Genny rushed to assure her. "You're an absolute peach, I declare. I wish we could have truly been friends. Business partners, even."

Perplexed, bemused, Cecelia glanced at the men fanned out to Genny's right.

Winston, almost unrecognizable without his Georgian costume, was younger than Cecelia had first assumed.

Next to him stood a big, bald man with no neck to speak of and an extra layer of bulge around his muscles. To his right, a lovely-skinned Indian man with a long, bushy beard clasped his hands in front of him.

"Genny." Cecelia felt a flare of a different sort as she read a sort of sinister anticipation in their eyes. "Genny what are they doing here? What is going on?"

"You should have married, Cecelia, after your tenure at de Chardonne." Genny acted as if she'd never asked a question. "You should have nursed fat babies and settled down, then Henrietta wouldn't have been so goddamned proud of you."

Cecelia shook her head, wishing she understood. "What does my getting married have to do with anything?"

Genny's expression darkened from unkind to truly demonic. "Do you realize I worked for that woman nearly twenty years?" she hissed. "She thought she was above us. That she could outsmart every person in this godforsaken empire, and I'll be damned if she didn't almost do it." Genny crept closer, brandishing the codex. "I licked that woman's boots for twenty. Fucking. *Years*. I was her servant, her handler, her confidante, and her lover. And you know what the scum-sucking bitch left me?"

Cecelia took a step back against the woman's advance. She couldn't help herself; she'd never in her life been regarded with such abject hatred. Not from the Vicar Teague. Not from her fellow male students at university.

Not even from Ramsay when he thought she was responsible for the worst crimes imaginable.

"*Nothing*." Genny tossed the codex to Cecelia's feet, where it landed with an innocuous whump. "That woman left me not one goddamned thing else but a love note with instructions to look after you and that little brat with a promise that *you'd* take care of me." The last part of the sentence she forced between clenched teeth.

"Phoebe?" Cecelia rushed forward. "Tell me you haven't hurt her."

"You are so like that sanctimonious, undeserving cow!" Genny's lips curled into a masculine sort of snarl. "No, no you're worse. You never once had to lie beneath a rutting boar of a man to feed yourself. You never had to fight off drunk men and work on your feet for endless nights just to avoid working on your back."

Her fingers turned to claws as she gestured her hatred. "*You* were educated, spoiled, coddled. I fucked half the ton while you went on holiday with them. And when Henrietta found me, I helped earn the money on the card tables. Money she sent to you. I built this empire with her, and she leaves it to *you*?" She shook her head in abject disbelief. "What makes you think you deserve this?"

"I—I don't!" Cecelia insisted. "I never wanted—"

"I don't give a silken shit what you wanted," Genny said. "I only care what you can do for me now."

"What? What would you have me do?"

Genny pointed to the book at her feet. The dratted codex. The bane of Cecelia's existence. "I know you've deciphered it. I saw the pages burning in the fireplace before I fished them out. There's a fortune worth of information in there, and I need every word, do you understand?"

"Tell me something first." Cecelia was stalling for time, wondering if she could get a message out somehow, her brain churning for anything to cling to that might help her escape this helpless, hopeless place. "Is Lord Ramsay alive? Jean-Yves? What about Phoebe? Is she harmed? Please tell me what happened to them!"

"You'll get information when I get what I want from you," Genny scoffed.

"No." Cecelia shook her head, drawing herself up. "That's not how this works. I will tell you what is in the codex when you assure me those I love are safe."

"Love?" Genny sidled closer, her laugh long and low and unsettling. "What is it about fucking Lord Ramsay that shags a woman's brain right out of her head? You and Matilda both. Spend a few nights with him and suddenly he's wrapped those unwieldy paws around your heart and squeezed all sense out of it."

Cecelia suddenly felt for poor Matilda. She'd been torn between two loyalties. That to her employer, and then to herself. How devastated she must have been when Ramsay had thrown her out of his house and his life.

"Don't tell me you loved that horse-cocked lummox of a Scot," the American spat, tugging at the lace sleeves of her nearly white gown.

Loved. Past tense. Did that mean Ramsay was no more?

Cecelia swallowed around a lump of despair. What if he'd died without knowing how she felt about him? What if she never had the chance to change his mind? She had fully intended to once she was through being peevish. It'd taken everything for her not to prostrate her pride and her principles at his gigantic feet and ask to be carried about like a damsel again.

What if she only ever received the gift of *one* of his smiles in her entire life?

If he was truly gone . . . she would even miss his frowns. The darling way he struggled to remain grumpy in her presence. The way tenderness and lust turned his wintry eyes a darker, warmer blue.

To lose him would be the greatest tragedy in her life. And for his daughter to lose him as a devoted father was the greatest heartbreak she could think of.

Ramsay. She loved him. Every solid, starched, stubborn inch of him.

A ragged sob tore its way out of her throat, closely followed by another. "I'll die before I help you hurt those girls out there," she said with a flinty resolve.

Genny's eyes narrowed, a frightening glint hardening in their depths as she glanced to Winston. "You and Phoebe were given everything, because Henrietta wanted to keep you both innocent. Unspoiled. You're a bit old to be worth much, but if you don't comply, I'm going to let Winston and the boys have their fun with you. Keeps them loyal."

"I don't care," Cecelia claimed, though the threat horrified her down to her very core. "I won't be party to the evil you're perpetrating down here."

"There's nothing to be done for the girls out there, their fates are sealed. . . . But what about Phoebe . . ." Genny adopted a speculative look. "I know how much a man will pay for a girl her age. Hell, I've been selling virgins to disgusting men for some time now."

"*No.*" The truth drove the breath out of Cecelia's lungs and took the starch from her bones. She crumpled, landing hard on her knees and bowing in front of Genny in an age-old posture of supplication. "Please. Do what you want to me. Take everything. The house, the business, the fortune. Just don't hurt Phoebe. Let those girls out there go."

Genny squatted down in a most unladylike manner, pushing the codex against the floor. "I fucking told you already, those girls are bought and paid for, I'm just waiting for their owners to come collect," she said. "The Lord Chancellor will pay me more money than Midas if I decode this before they take the girls to the country house, so you'd better start writing, or I'll make Winston bend you over that desk first before the other two have a go."

Cecelia had to check her courage against the threat, wondering how much she could take before she spilled every secret she knew. For Phoebe? She'd do anything. Endure anything.

"Are you a part of the Crimson Council?" she whispered. "Did they put you up to this?"

"Honey, no one put me up to this." Genny stood, looming over her like the whore of Babylon. "In this world it's eat or be eaten, and I'd rather eat at the table of the Crimson Council than just about anywhere on this earth. Henrietta refused to provide them what they wanted, but I have no such scruples. And I killed her when she began to piece it together."

"The bomb? That was you?" She'd been such a blind, trusting fool. So worried about the wolf at the gate that she hadn't noticed the snake hissing into her ear.

The woman gave a faint smile, as if mildly amused by the memory. "I thought the blast would be smaller, all told, and I was certain it would take care of Phoebe. I pushed that burning log toward you, as well, but how could I have guessed Ramsay has the reflexes of a mongoose?"

"You're evil," Cecelia accused. "To subject girls to such things. To conduct this violence against women? Vulnerable women?"

"You think I wasn't sold to my first man by a woman? You think Henrietta didn't do the devil a few favors before I employed foxglove to send her to hell?" Genny turned back to the door, resting her hand on the latch. "I ain't evil, doll, just angry. Angry and ruthless as any man would be in my position. You understand."

"No. I don't," Cecelia said, fuming now. Genny had taken everything from her. Including the aunt she could have known and loved. The only family she truly had left. "Nothing could cause me to commit such deplorable acts!"

"That's because you're weak. You think your goodness will save you but it's your greatest folly, and that's why you'll never set foot outside this room again." Genny nodded to Winston. "Hand her the papers, and if she stops writing before she's finished with that entire book, then tear her apart from the inside."

"Gladly." The man watched her alertly, his droopy, doglike eyes glimmering with anticipation.

Cecelia gaped at Winston, unable to believe her ears. She'd helped him out of the blast. Made certain his wounds were tended to and offered him a salary even though the house was currently not in business.

How could he repay her kindness with the threat of the ultimate cruelty?

Cecelia reached for the book, wondering if wrongly decoding could buy Phoebe some time, when a masculine scream pierced the air outside the room. It was full of a pain so pure, it sent shivers reverberating up and down Cecelia's spine.

The door burst open, sending Genny crashing to the floor.

Ramsay strode in, bringing with him with his particular brand of frigid, unnatural calm. A sinister expression turned his features from grave to positively reptilian. He moved like a predator. Unconcerned. Unrepentant.

Utterly lethal.

He didn't touch her with his gaze so much as skipped over her to skewer the other inhabitants of the room with shards of ice.

He'd not reverted to the London Lord Ramsay. His hair was still as wild as it'd been in Scotland. His trousers and coat were not fresh, as though he'd slept in them, and the untamed, unkempt kit added to his imposing figure.

This was not a man of stricture. Nor was he shackled by the bonds of the law.

This Ramsay was capable of anything.

Relief flooded Cecelia with such violence, she surged to her feet and might have cheered. He was alive! Ramsay was alive and he would save Phoebe in time!

"Touch her and I'll shatter the tender parts of yer skulls with my bare hands," he said in that soft, terrifying way of his. "I'll leave ye alive long enough for ye to be aware whilst I hollow out yer insides, do ye ken? Ye'll feel pain like none ye've imagined, and in the end, ye'll beg for the mercy of execution."

Cecelia absurdly reminded herself to tell him later that, despite what he'd claimed, he was an excellent wordsmith.

Astonishingly, he allowed the men to recover from their awestruck amazement and fall into fighting stances, producing various weapons.

Winston and his unfortunate neckless companion twitched with sudden agitation, fanning out in a wider arc. The larger man held a cleaver-style knife, and Winston a dagger. The Indian drew a pistol from behind his jacket.

"Shoot him!" Genny screeched.

"Think about what ye do," Ramsay warned. "Ye might not know me, but I'm relentless, patient, and thoroughly unbothered by blood. I will kill ye as slowly as the plague, and discard yer remains on yer doorstep as a message to all who would avenge ye. Do you ken? Are ye ready for the hell I'll unleash upon ye?"

"It's true." None other than the Count Armediano sauntered in with a pistol cocked in front of him aimed right between the Indian's eyes. "I had a recent altercation with Ramsay, and if I'm a surgeon, he's a butcher, and I can't say for certain which one is more dangerous."

Had Cecelia's hands not been bound, she'd have lifted them to rub at her eyes, if only to make sure she'd seen what was happening correctly.

Count Armediano? His ebony hair was slicked to his head, but his gray suit was just as crinkled as Ramsay's. He wore no jacket to speak of, and he'd rolled up the sleeves of his shirt. The taut muscles of his forearms rippled as he toyed with the trigger of his pistol.

"I said kill these bastards." Genny struggled to push herself off the floor, her eyes wild and her expression mutinous. "If you don't, the Crimson Council will have your heads, so either way you're in danger."

Ramsay turned on Genny. "When I'm finished with this rubbish, ye'll wish yerself invisible, madam," he said with barely leashed control.

"You can do nothing to me," Genny said with a laugh, unable to keep a note of hysteria from it. "The Lord Chancellor—"

"Is being arrested as we speak by Scotland Yard's finest," Ramsay said with apparent relish. "But mark me, if ye speak out of turn again, I'll have yer tongue."

A gunshot startled a scream from Cecelia's chest. She ducked, and when the ringing in her ear subsided, it was replaced by an even more terrible sound.

The terrified shrieks of frightened young girls locked in their own cells with no idea of what was going on.

The Indian dropped to the ground in a heap, and Count Armediano dove for his gun, all the while keeping a bead on Winston.

"Chandler," Ramsay seethed at the man now dual-wielding pistols. "Must ye shoot in such close quarters?"

Chandler? Cecelia gaped.

The so-called count's lack of a Continental accent was impressed upon Cecelia as he shrugged well-built shoulders and replied, "I saw him twitch, my lord."

"What . . . what is going *on*?" Cecelia asked rather dazedly, staring at the bloom of blood on the back of the Indian's linen suitcoat.

"Count Armediano is as much a moniker as Hortense Thistledown," Ramsay supplied shortly. "His real name is Chandler."

Chandler. Why did that name sound familiar?

"I changed my mind about this place." Genny inched to the desk upon which sat the fine crystal lanterns next to the inkwell and codex. "It can burn to the ground." She seized the lamps and hurled them.

Cecelia dove, but she knew she wouldn't get out of the radius of the flames in time. Not with such a powerful accelerant. She landed painfully on her shoulder, rolling out of the way as the lamp arced toward her.

Unable to get to her in time, Ramsay shoved Winston into the path of the lantern. It shattered against him, engulfing him in inescapable flames. They flared a spectacular light against the cracked walls of the classroom as he danced about in unimaginable pain.

Genny tossed the other at Chandler, though he was able to get a shot off before he was forced to dive out of the way or suffer Winston's fate.

The lantern broke against the door, spilling fire over their only escape.

When Ramsay leapt toward Cecelia, scooping her out of Winston's careening conflagration, Genny lifted her skirts and leapt across the threshold, but not before her the fabric caught.

She screeched and ran out of sight, trailing flames behind her train.

Chandler leapt after her, his own trousers barely avoiding the fire as he ran out of sight.

Ramsay ripped his shirt down his arms and began to beat at the flames in the doorway to very little effect.

"Behind you!" Cecelia jumped out of the way as the no-necked man advanced with his knife.

Ramsay whipped his shirt, now smoldering with flames, and caught the man around the wrist. He leapt closer, disarmed the fellow, caught the cleaver, and with a mighty swing of his arm sank the blade into the man's neck from behind.

Cecelia would never again have to wonder why they called the blade a cleaver. Had she been in the vicinity, blood would have drenched her.

She knelt next to where Winston's knife had been abandoned when he'd gone up in flames.

The man in question collapsed against the far wall, having given up the ghost.

She lowered herself, doing her best to grab the knife from the ground with bloodless fingers.

Right then, Cecelia was snatched up from behind, her hands freed, and her body clutched to a familiar wall of muscle that drove her relentlessly forward.

The now almost headless man had been tossed over the flames in the doorway, creating a temporary bridge.

"Jump!" Ramsay boomed from behind her.

She jumped, allowing herself to be swept up and over the corpse and the fire, only to be unceremoniously dumped into the dusty hallway.

Ramsay fell upon her legs the moment they were on the other side, smothering what few of her skirts had ignited. That done, he lunged up her body, his features now a mask of both fury and yearning, and he crushed his mouth to hers for a brief, life-altering kiss.

Tearing himself away he ordered, "Run, dammit. I'll free the girls."

He leapt off her and slammed the door to the classroom shut. It was too late to be much of a help; the flames had crawled into the hallway.

"Ramsay, here!" Cecelia turned to see that Chandler had grappled Genny to the ground. He tossed the ring of keys he'd ripped from the woman's belt over Cecelia's head.

Ramsay caught them and ran for the furthest door.

Cecelia struggled to her feet, lurching after him. She met him just as he was dragging the lock open.

The look he gave her was full of fury. "I told ye to run," he snarled. "Get out of here."

"I'm not leaving you to do this alone!"

"I love ye, ye daft woman, and I canna do this if ye're in danger!"

"If you love me, you know I will not leave these children down here, so hurry up, you stubborn Scot. We don't have time for you to realize I'm right."

His glare should have doused the flames with all its icy wrath, but he dragged open the door, seized the child behind it, and shoved her toward Cecelia before moving on.

Cecelia's arms were full of clutching hands, braided hair, and tearful sobs. Her heart breaking, she pointed toward the stairs, instructing the girl to stay low beneath the billows of smoke gathering in the air.

They freed seven girls in all, the last two rooms proving empty.

As Cecelia opened every closet and searched all nooks and crannies, she was vaguely aware of someone bellowing her name. She ignored it until she was lifted like a flour sack and hauled toward the stairs. "We have to go,"

Ramsay coughed out. "The fire is reaching the next story."

Cecelia's throat and eyes burned, her lungs threatened to seize, but she couldn't leave. "Phoebe!" she sobbed, kicking her legs out. "We haven't found Phoebe!"

Ramsay subdued her with his strong hold, speaking into her ear. "I pulled Phoebe from the loft in Scotland. She's safe at my brother's with Jean-Yves."

Cecelia could have collapsed in relief. Genny had lied to her. Thank God. As it was, she allowed Ramsay to pull her up the stairs and propel her through the smoke-clogged foyer for the second time in as many weeks.

This time, though, Cecelia cared little that the palatial estate might burn to the ground.

Because everyone was alive. Safe.

And Ramsay had said he loved her.

CHAPTER TWENTY-ONE

Ramsay stood on the vast lawn of Henrietta's estate and watched the chaos of the conflagration unfold.

He didn't just hold Cecelia against him, he enfolded her, curling his shoulders over her and pressing his cheek to the crown of her precious head. The flames engulfing the manor tossed incredible colors into her wild hair, and he let the vibrant hues mesmerize him as he did his utmost to compose himself.

His fury at the thought of what might have happened to her tonight had razed his control completely to ashes. That any man could have followed Genny's order before he'd gotten to her set his very soul on fire.

He'd used that fire to kill for her.

How could he have allowed this? How could he have become so attached to her in such a short time that her presence was necessary for his very breath? Her smiles were the meat he fed on and her voice was the sustenance to his soul.

He tugged her closer, feeling every inch of her along

his frame. Her head tucked between the mounds of his chest. Her belly round and soft against his hip. Her thighs pressed to his.

She belonged in his arms, now and always.

He only had to convince her to stay.

Their chaotic heartbeats had synchronized and were now finally beginning to slow. They'd helped the fire brigade contain the blaze, but in the end, there was nothing to be done but to let the manor burn until it was reduced to rubble.

The captive girls they freed had been carted to the hospital where their families would be contacted, and Ramsay knew he and Cecelia would make certain they would be not only compensated, but made entirely comfortable for life.

Chandler had dragged a humbled Genny away with a cheeky salute, and Ramsay was certain he'd not seen the last of the swarthy, stealthy bastard.

But none of that mattered at the moment. There was this woman in his arms, the one who'd stolen his heart, and he had to make her understand somehow that it was a heart worth keeping.

That he would be careful with hers if she would only give it to him.

Should he wait until she'd rested and eaten and had time to process the loss of her property?

Something told him it was the right thing to do.

But letting her go without making certain she understood his intentions also seemed untenable.

Christ, he really was terrible at this.

"What are you thinking?" Cecelia asked, pulling back to look up at him with eyes that were as deep as eternity. "You're very serious." She paused, feathering her audacious, elegant fingers down the muscles of his bare back. "More so than usual, I mean."

Ramsay closed his eyes for a breath, basking in her touch. "I'm feeling an affinity to yer manse," he stated honestly.

Her nose wrinkled adorably. "Aflame?"

"Destroyed." He lifted a hand to rub at a smudge on her cheek, only serving to make it worse.

Instead of pulling away, she turned her cheek into his palm until her lashes fanned against his fingers in little arcs of barely there sensation. "What destroyed you?" she asked.

"Ye did," he murmured. "Ye've ruined me, Cecelia. Ye've dismantled everything I thought I was, everything I've wanted to be. Ye ripped the bits of me that were festering and rotten away from myself, and now I doona ken what I am. Who I am."

"I'm sorry," she whispered, her lashes gathering with little reserves of tears.

"Nay, I doona mind. Not anymore. I just . . . need ye to help put me back together."

Her chest depressed with a hard breath as her eyes glittered up at him with emotion. But she said nothing, and the silence called forth an unprecedented tumble of truth from his lips.

"This world of ours has always been a hollow gray place for me. Empty and meaningless, like my name. But then I met ye, and ye were naught but vivacious color. Ye overwhelmed every sense I possess." He filled his other hand with her cheek, framing her face, holding it like a precious, fragile thing. "Ye fill me to the brink, Cecelia. When we are together, I doona remember what loneliness is. And without you, I doona ken the point of anything."

He pressed his lips to her forehead. Her eyelids. Her nose. The prominent bones of her cheek and the corners of her mouth, all the while pouring his heart out between tiny tastes of her. "I fought it, at first, thinking ye were a weakness. A vulnerability. But nay. Ye make me strong, Cecelia. Ye give me life. Ye provide me a purpose that is greater than my own ambition. Ye taught me what the word *family* might mean. I would have that family with ye."

He caught a wayward tear as it leaked from her eye, smudging it away from her cheek. She gave a delicate sniff, her expression pinched with an anxiety that sent his heart plummeting to his stomach.

"I want that," she said in an earnest, tortured whisper. "More than anything I want that. But, Ramsay, nothing has changed."

A worried frown pinched his brow. "What do ye mean?"

"I know Miss Henrietta's is currently burning to the ground, but I fully intend to rebuild."

"I doona care," he said. "I'll help lay the fucking stones."

She drew back, her eyes wide "But you said—"

"I ken what I said. And I'm telling ye I was wrong. I've spent too many years honoring the wrong ideals. Respecting the wrong men. It all means nothing, Cecelia. Not anymore."

"But your position," she argued.

"I'll be a nameless pauper before I live without ye. I meant what I said at Elphinstone Croft. I was surrounded by the loneliest, most miserable place I'd ever known, and I was happier there than I'd ever been. And I've realized, it was because ye were with me. Cecelia, *ye* are my happiness. If I have ye and Phoebe, I need nothing else. If ye think well of me, then I've achieved the perfection I've striven for for so long."

Cecelia's smile was more brilliant than the flames. Than the sun on the summer solstice. It pressed her cheeks against his hands as she drew her fingers up his arms to his shoulders. "It appears, my lord Chief Justice, that you've changed your mind about love. Or did I hear you incorrectly?"

He shook his head. "Nay, ye heard the right of it. I meant it when I said it. I love ye Cecelia Teague. I love ye and I'm sorry. I'll never stop being sorry for the hurtful things I've said to ye. Ye'll never hear another cruel word from my lips. And I'll rip anyone's tongue out who dares disparage ye."

Cecelia surged to her toes and pressed her lips to his in a tumultuous, ecstatic kiss. It was messy and wet and tasted of salt and ash and desperate happiness.

His body responded immediately, and he had to drag her shoulders away from him lest he debauch her here in front of London's fire brigade and half of Scotland Yard.

"And here I thought your brother was the savage one," she panted, flashing him a mischievous grin.

"He is," Ramsay insisted, clutching at her. Unable to let her out of his grasp, lest she slip away again. "I'm not . . . usually like this. I've never . . ." He forced his fingers to unclench from her, only to thrust them through his hair. "I've never lost such control, Cecelia. I've never felt the kind of fear and rage I did when I returned to the house to find ye'd been taken. Chandler was right, I became a butcher last night, and I'd do it again for ye and Phoebe. I'd burn this entire city to the ground if ye asked me."

Cecelia reached for him, smoothing a hand over his

chest. "That doesn't sound much like the Vicar of Vice to me," she teased gently.

He shook his head, nostrils flaring, his fists clenched at his side. "I am not him," he insisted. "I mean it, I doona even ken who I am anymore, but . . ." He gathered her hands into his, imprisoning them over his heart. The one that beat only for her. "Will ye not answer me, lass?"

She quirked an eyebrow up at him. "Answer you? I've not heard a question."

His lips compressed into a thin line. He was bungling this again. "Will ye just be mine, Cecelia? Will ye share yer life with me, in any capacity ye deem fit? Will ye love me? *Can* ye love me, after all that's happened?"

"Of course I can, you silly Scot." She stepped closer, nuzzling into him. "I already do. I think I have for quite some time."

"Why didna ye tell me?"

"Because I'm so far from perfect," she murmured. "I didn't ever want you to hate me for asking you to accept me despite your principles."

"Nay," he said. "I should have accepted ye always."

He gathered her to him once again, linking his arms about her shoulders and burrowing his face into her hair.

"I love you," she whispered against his heart.

A carriage with his seal pulled up and a man jumped down to the door. "My lord Chief Justice," the driver said diffidently.

"Let us go home," Ramsay suggested.

"Where's that?"

He nudged her nose with his. "Wherever ye are."

Home, as it turned out, was a vast West End estate called Rutherleigh Point.

Cecelia couldn't see the entirety of it from the carriage

window, but the red stone gables and charming floor-to-ceiling windows thrilled her to no end.

Ramsay had told her that Phoebe and Jean-Yves were inside waiting for her, and so she lifted her soiled skirts and dashed up the front steps as quickly as she could.

The door slammed open and she called for the girl.

Phoebe appeared at the top of the grand staircase, clutching at the rather splendid white marble rails.

"Cecelia!" she called, nearly tripping down the steps in her exuberance. She flew off the third from the last step straight into her arms. "I was so frightened for you. So frightened, but I knew that you wouldn't leave. That you'd come back."

Her throat stopped by waves of emotion, Cecelia merely clung to the girl, petting her bouncing curls and doing her best not to cry.

"Why are you so dirty?" the girl asked.

"There was a fire," Cecelia explained. "Miss Henrietta's burned to the ground."

Phoebe sobered. "Is everyone all right?"

"Yes, they'd all moved out after the explosion, remember?"

"Oh." Her little forehead wrinkled. "They could move in here, probably, could they not? There's ever so many empty rooms."

Cecelia glanced back at Ramsay, who'd donned a coat over his bare chest. He ran a hand across his soiled face and spoke a few words in Gaelic that needed no interpretation.

"We'll figure something out," Cecelia placated the girl.

After a while, Phoebe squirmed to be let down, and Cecelia was forced allow the girl her freedom. "Cecelia, Lord Ramsay told me on the train that he's my papa!

That's what you were trying to figure out all along? The riddle in Henrietta's book?"

"Yes," Cecelia said. "Yes, darling, it was. Wasn't it a fantastic riddle? A wonderful find?"

"I always wanted a papa," Phoebe whispered. "But I never thought he'd be so big and handsome and *rich*." She extended her hands to encompass the vast grand hall. It was bigger than Henrietta's by far. Grander, even, than Castle Redmayne, the duke's estate.

"It's like a fairy tale, isn't it?" Phoebe asked.

Cecelia had to admit, it was, indeed.

Ramsay called for a bath and then allowed Phoebe to take Cecelia on an unofficial tour of the place. They weaved through room after room, some gilded in French paper and others in expensive paint.

Almost all of them empty.

He'd turned the library into a comfortable study, she noted, and a few bedrooms were well appointed, but beyond that the space was utterly wasted.

"It's a house," Ramsay said a little bashfully. "A status symbol, really, but I never had much need to make it a home."

"You do now," Phoebe said, clutching at his hand and pulling him toward the kitchen.

"I do now." Ramsay looked back at Cecelia, reaching out to tug her along. His eyes glimmered with a powerful emotion, but beyond that, Cecelia could make out no traces of the arctic coldness she'd found before. All she could see was a blue as deep and clear as the summer sky.

After they'd eaten and settled Phoebe, Ramsay pulled Cecelia into his bedroom and locked the door. It was a simple room, she noted, masculine and spare. Like the man.

The man who was becoming someone else. Someone who smiled. Someone who prowled toward her with every intention of perpetrating both vice and villainy upon her person.

Cecelia allowed herself to be caught. Hoping he'd carry her to the tub in the corner.

"I'm glad you've overcome your mistrust of women," she teased. "Seeing as how you're now outnumbered by them."

"Only by one," he noted before dipping down to root in the hollow of her neck. "Perhaps I can persuade ye to allow me to plant a son inside ye."

Her womb shivered in a very hasty response.

"What if you sired another daughter?" she asked. "I can't really pick, now can I?"

"I'll happily raise a bevy of daughters, if ye consent to mother them on my behalf." His lips caught at her earlobe, nibbling gently.

Her body bloomed, undulating against him.

"You'll have Redmayne, I suppose, and Jean-Yves to help even the odds," she said a bit breathlessly. "But then there'll be Alexander and Frank."

He made a soft noise, exploring her jawline with his full lips. "I'll need to hire a staff now that I've taken on a wife and child," he proposed before kissing the tip of her nose tenderly. "I could leave that to ye when ye're Mrs. Cassius Gerard Ramsay."

"Cassius," She tested his name, remembering what it stood for. Pulling back, she looked up into his dear, handsome features. "Do you still feel you are empty?"

Suddenly, his arms closed around her waist and he pulled her down over him on the bed, rolling until she straddled him. Filling his arms with the weight of her.

"Not anymore," he said seriously, and as he stroked her cheek, she felt a tremor in his powerful hands. "Not ever again."

She sighed happily and he pulled her down to possess her mouth in a kiss that left them both breathless and writhing.

He hastily peeled off her clothing, levering up to peel off his own.

When he had her bared above him, he filled his palms with her buttocks and lowered her against his shaft, letting her rub and writhe against the impressive sex like a kitten begging for attention.

She gave a broken sigh as his fingers toyed and teased her. She arched and danced over him, anchoring her hands on the springy hairs of his unyielding chest.

He was a golden god. A paragon that hardly belonged to this world.

But he belonged to her.

She dragged her palms down the delineations of muscle on his stomach, counting them, until she found the little trail that led her to the velvet silken skin covering the hardness that throbbed for her.

He expelled a guttural moan. "I love ye."

Lost in the enchantment of the moment, she almost forgot to reply as sensation and need robbed her of speech.

But as she lifted her body and sank down slowly in a slide of silk and fire, she whispered the words they'd say every night for the rest of their lives. "I love you."

This time, their passion wasn't a storm. It contained no thunder or urgency. It was a whisper, one the very night stilled to hear. It was warm rather than hot and unhurried rather than frenzied.

This was a moment of discovery between them. Of

intent and trust and utter fulfillment. Ramsay's touch contained awe, and his gaze was full of promises.

This time, when they arched together in a glorious spasm of bliss, Cecelia knew that, though she'd not been his first lover, this was the first time Cassius Gerard Ramsay had ever made love.

ACKNOWLEDGMENTS

As always I couldn't produce these books without a truck-load of help.

I'm especially thankful to the team at St. Martin's Press. Monique, Marissa, Mara, and the bevy of others who guided this book from inception to distribution.

I'm eternally grateful to Christine Witthohn, who is always looking out for my best interests, even when I'm not.

I have to thank Cynthia St. Aubin, Staci Hart, Tanya Crosby, and Kim Loraine, who all touched this book in a unique way and, with their friendship, helped to inspire such fierce female characters.

Read on for a sneak peek at the next scintillating
novel in the Devil You Know series
by **Kerrigan Byrne**

The Devil in Her Bed

Coming in 2021
from
St. Martin's Paperbacks

Before Francesca could close in on her prey, a familiar feeling lifted the fine hairs on her body. A strange dichotomy of warmth and chill. Something like the gaze of a god, or the presence of a ghost. It struck a chord of awe in her, and a bit of fear, if she were honest.

Turning, she used a sip from her champagne glass as an excuse to scan the teeming, glittering, whirling mass of revelers.

There. Across the ballroom. A man stood out by standing still.

He stared at her from the shadows of deep-set eyes.

And just like that, in an overheated room overfilled with people, they were utterly alone. She and the ghost.

Francesca blinked a few times, just to be certain he wasn't, indeed, some figment of her imagination or truly a specter of the dead.

No, he was still there. Staring.

Strangely discomfited, Francesca affected an air of

nonchalance. When others would have retreated, she lifted her glass in a slight toast.

I see you. I see you watching.

Her next thought was to wonder how on earth she'd missed him before?

He had harsh-hewn features that contrasted with his immaculate, elegant attire and a commanding brow. His nose was bold rather than broad, and his mouth defied description. It shouldn't have tempted her. Not as hard as it was. Hard like his gaze.

He was a hard man all over, it appeared, and extraordinarily fit. Not as monstrously big as Ramsay, or as tall and rangy as Redmayne, but a man of medium height, bred to stand in a crowd, not above it.

The pallor of his skin, the perfection of his slick auburn hair, and the sartorial grace of his stance seemed incongruous with the rest of him, somehow. Like he'd once been a wild thing and only recently, if impeccably, tamed. A sportsman, maybe?

The man was, in a word, striking.

In response to her gesture, his lip quirked, and his angular chin dipped in a nod. He drifted forward with such poise, exuding an overabundance of authority and such inadvertent menace that people melted aside before he took a step. Both repelled and entranced, the crowd moved away from the force of his dynamic presence, and then they looked to see what had prompted them to instinctually do so.

Some of them seemed to know him, and he murmured a returned greeting to a few as he passed.

But he didn't stop until he'd reached Francesca.

No, he didn't tower like Ramsay, but he hadn't the need. Everything about him bespoke domination. Power. Unequivocal strength.

Something deep, deep within Francesca trembled. Not with fear, per se. It was more feminine than that. Abruptly, *ridiculously*, she wanted to purr at him. To do all the things she'd done before to attract a man.

To see if she could cast a spell as powerful as his.

Francesca abandoned her glass of champagne so he wouldn't see it quiver.

Here was a man who would smell her weakness, and at the moment that weakness began in her knees and worked its way into all sorts of alarming places.

"Dance with me."

Francesca rarely responded to commands, and this one was no different. The issuer didn't have to know, however, that her lack of response was an involuntary mutism caused by his astoundingly seductive Scottish brogue. His voice was smooth and dangerous and beautiful, like molten ore hardening into lethal steel.

"Dance with me," he said with an air of someone unused to repeating himself.

Francesca adopted a demeanor of disinterest to cover his effect on her. "You're not on my card, sir." She turned toward Murphy, but the ghost stayed with her as if he'd anticipated her move.

"Do ye care about any of those men on yer card?" He reached out and flicked his thumb over the ribbon tied at the wrist of her glove on which the filigreed card dangled.

"Not particularly." Dear lord, had her voice ever sounded that breathy before?

"Then forget them, and dance with me."

He stood so close, too close. Awareness of his proximity threatened to overwhelm her. Instead of retreating, as her instinct bade her to, she stepped in.

"And just who are you, that you're so impertinent?" she demanded. "Surely you're aware it is against protocol to dance with a man to whom I've never been formally introduced. You do us both a dishonor."

The dark and wicked shadows in his eyes jangled her nerves, but an impish charm almost concealed those shadows enough to convince her they hadn't really existed at all. "Since when have ye cared about protocol, Lady Francesca?"

He had her there. Since never, that was when. She did what she liked when she liked, and the devil may care about the consequences.

She was at a disadvantage here. He knew such things about her when she didn't even know his name. In fact, she couldn't decide what unsettled her most, that she had been waylaid from her private mission. That he was asking her to dance in this impolite way . . .

Or that she was tempted to say yes.

More than almost anything she'd been tempted to do in years.

She looked up at him, not too far, but just enough, and found an adventure she hadn't yet enjoyed. A flirtation she'd never allowed herself to have. When one chased a singular goal, all other idle pursuits sort of just disappeared. Her every interaction had been calculated, save for Alexander and Cecil. Her every desire stashed on a shelf deep within herself, deep enough to have gathered dust and been forgotten.

"My lady?" The man held out his hand, and Francesca was suddenly aware of everyone looking.

Cripes. These Scots. They certainly did breed a specific sort of man. Sensual and arrogant. Bold. And this one wielded a smile that would disarm the most protected of hearts.

She'd doubled the guard on hers, throwing in a few ramparts and spikes . . . maybe a moat for good measure.

Tossing the last dash of her champagne, she took his hand and led him to the dance floor.